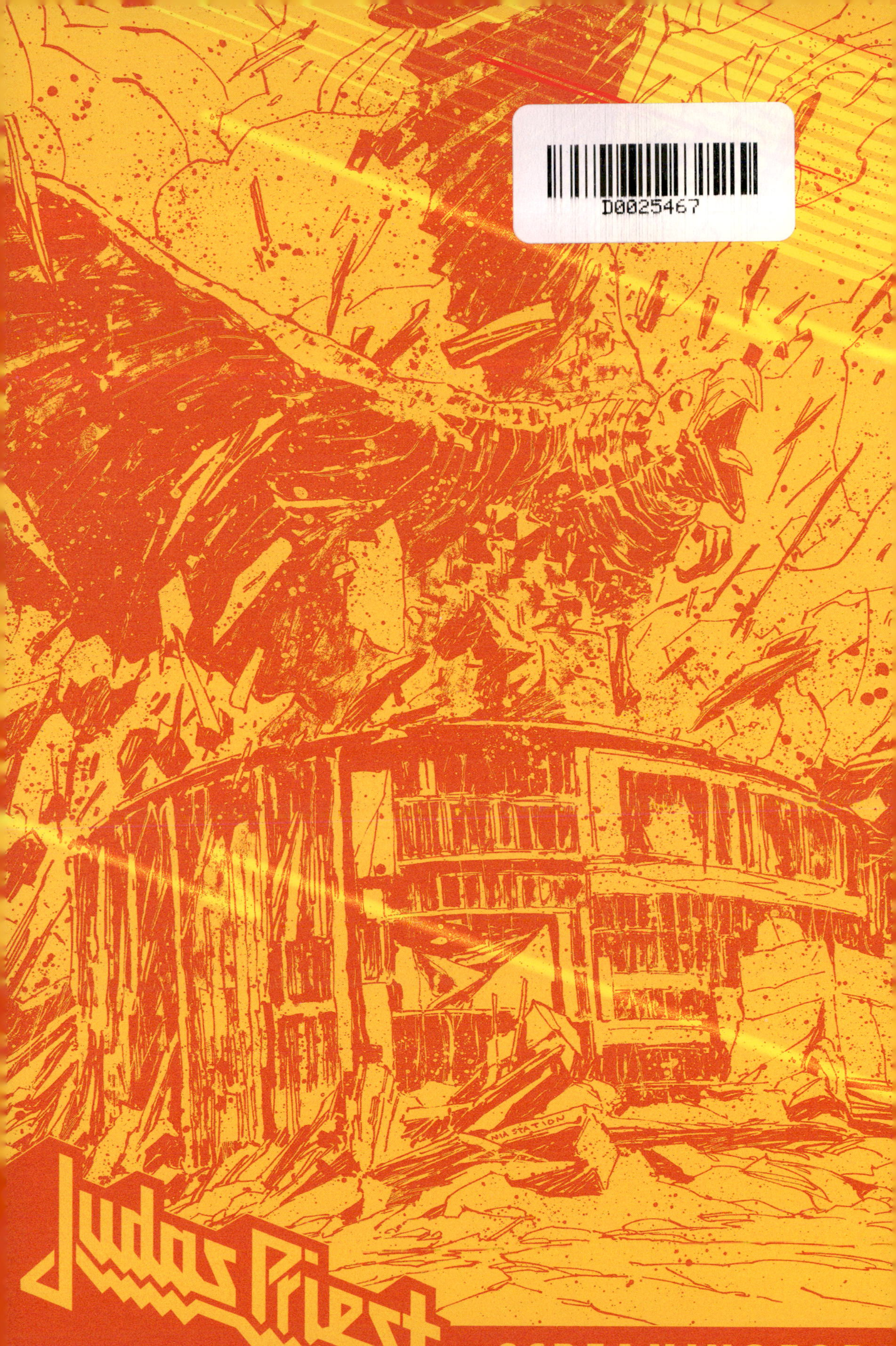

Judas Priest

SCREAMING FOR VENGEANCE

PUBLISHERS	Joshua Frankel & Sridhar Reddy
CFO & GENERAL COUNSEL	Kevin Meek
CHIEF BUSINESS OFFICER	Josh Bernstein
CHIEF TECHNOLOGY OFFICER	Aleksey Zelenberg
SENIOR V.P., STRATEGY	Jim Fynes
V.P., EDITORIAL	Rantz Hoseley
V.P., PRODUCTION	Courtney Menard
V.P., LOGISTICS	Steven Ettinger
V.P.S, MARKETING	Dominique Rosés & Ariella Tigertail
V.P., COLLECTIBLES	Clint Weiler
ARTIST & REPERTOIRE LIAISON	John Domingos
DESIGN DIRECTOR	Lauryn Ipsum
MARKETING DESIGNER	Colleen Tighe
MARKETING COORDINATORS	Griff Conner & Penelope Vargas
ASSISTANT EDITOR	Jasminne Saravia
FULFILLMENT SPECIALISTS	Orlando Black Eyes, Clarence Head, Dominique Kelly, & Isaiah Kelly
CUSTOMER SERVICE	Gabriel Rosés

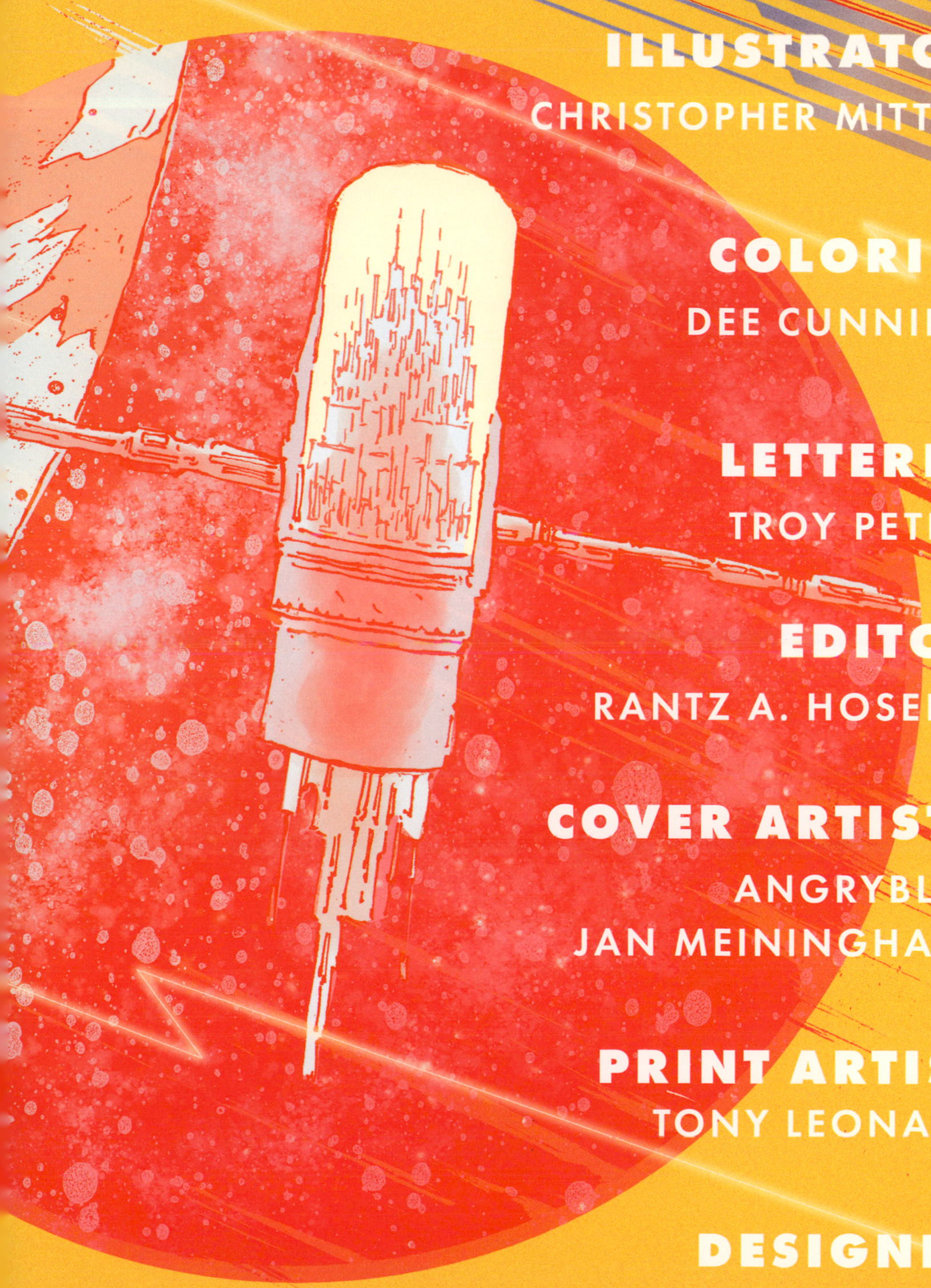

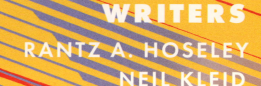

WRITERS
RANTZ A. HOSELEY
NEIL KLEID

ILLUSTRATOR
CHRISTOPHER MITTEN

COLORIST
DEE CUNNIFFE

LETTERER
TROY PETERI

EDITOR
RANTZ A. HOSELEY

COVER ARTISTS
ANGRYBLUE
JAN MEININGHAUS

PRINT ARTIST
TONY LEONARD

DESIGNER
LAURYN IPSUM

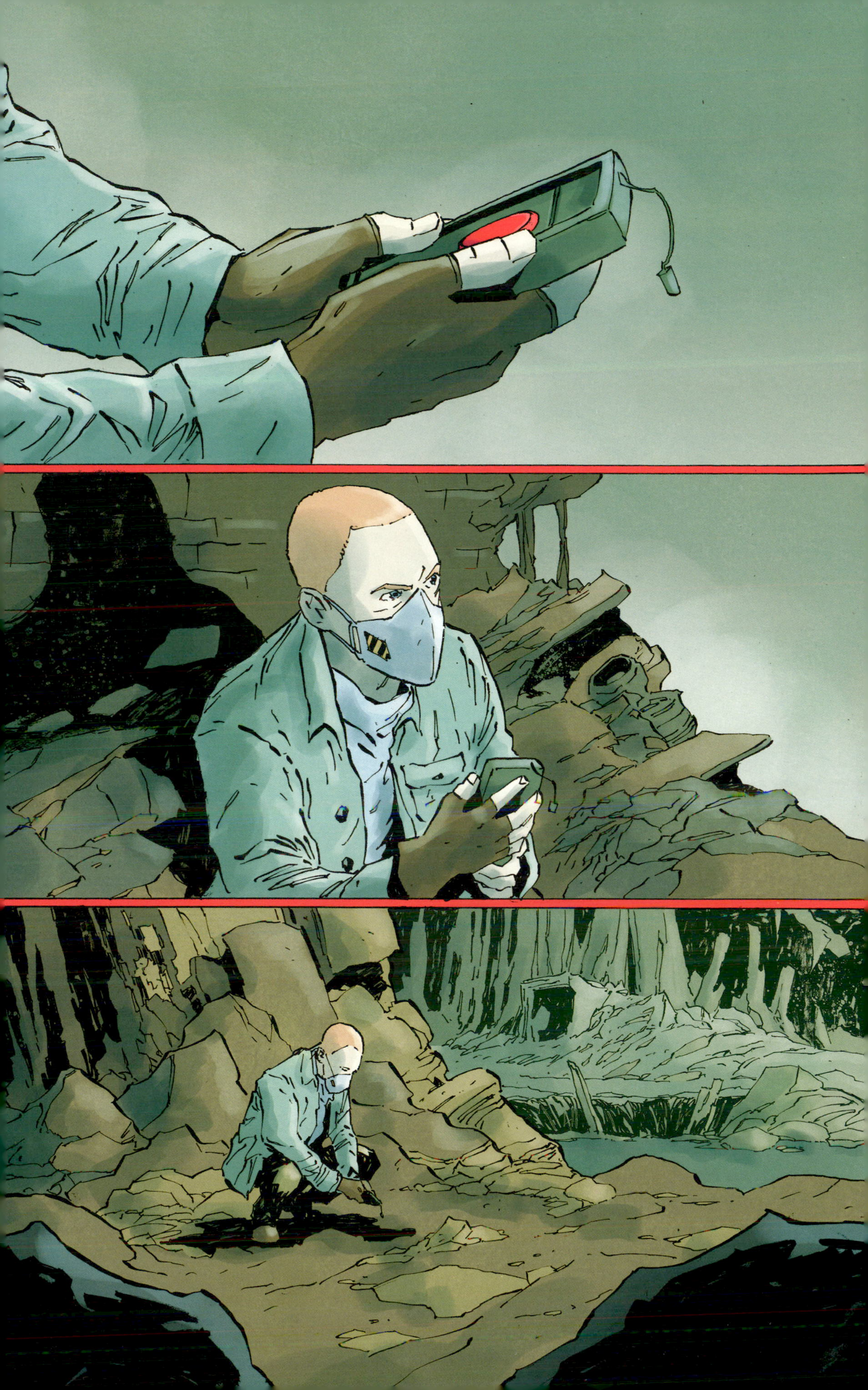

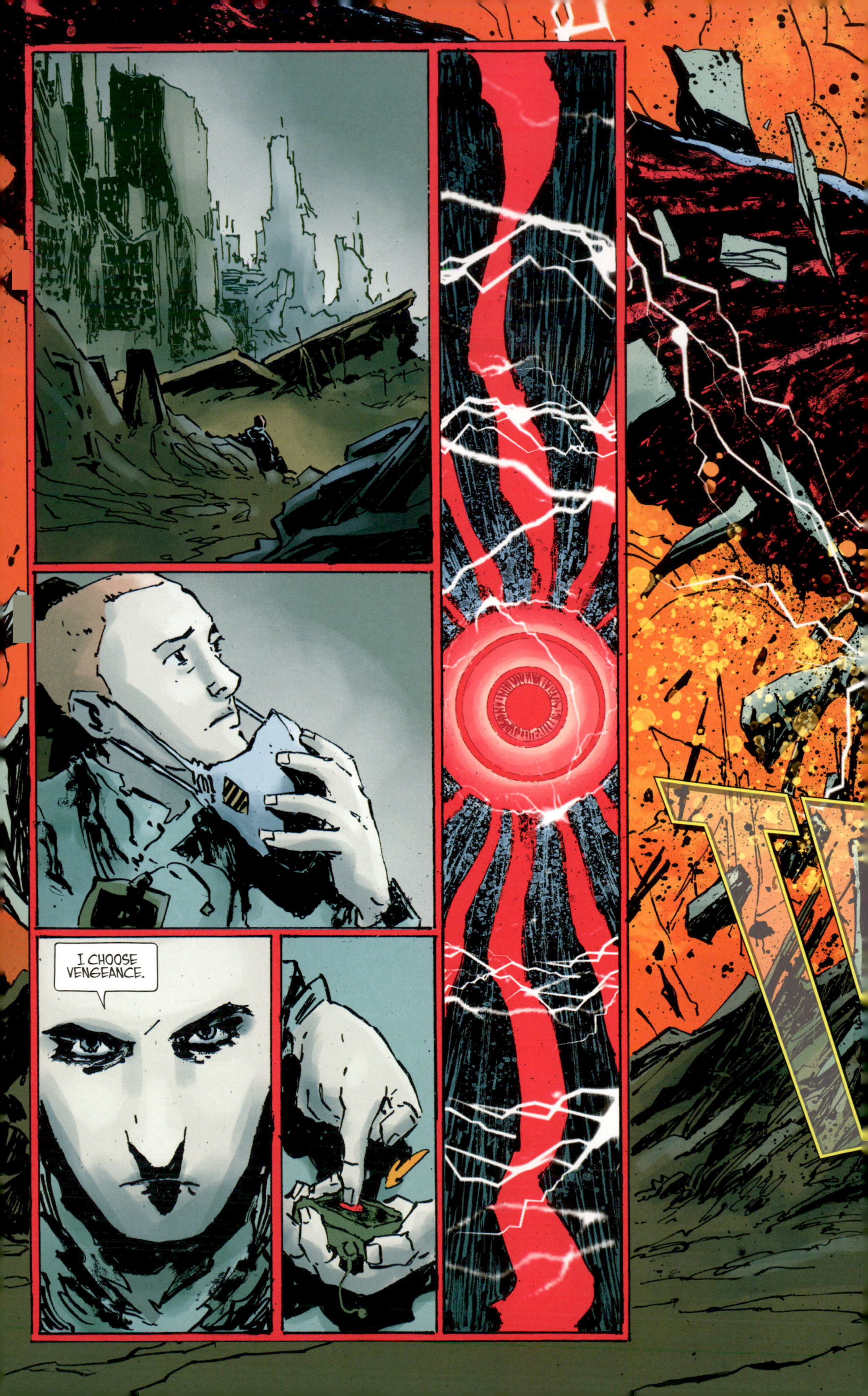
I CHOOSE VENGEANCE.

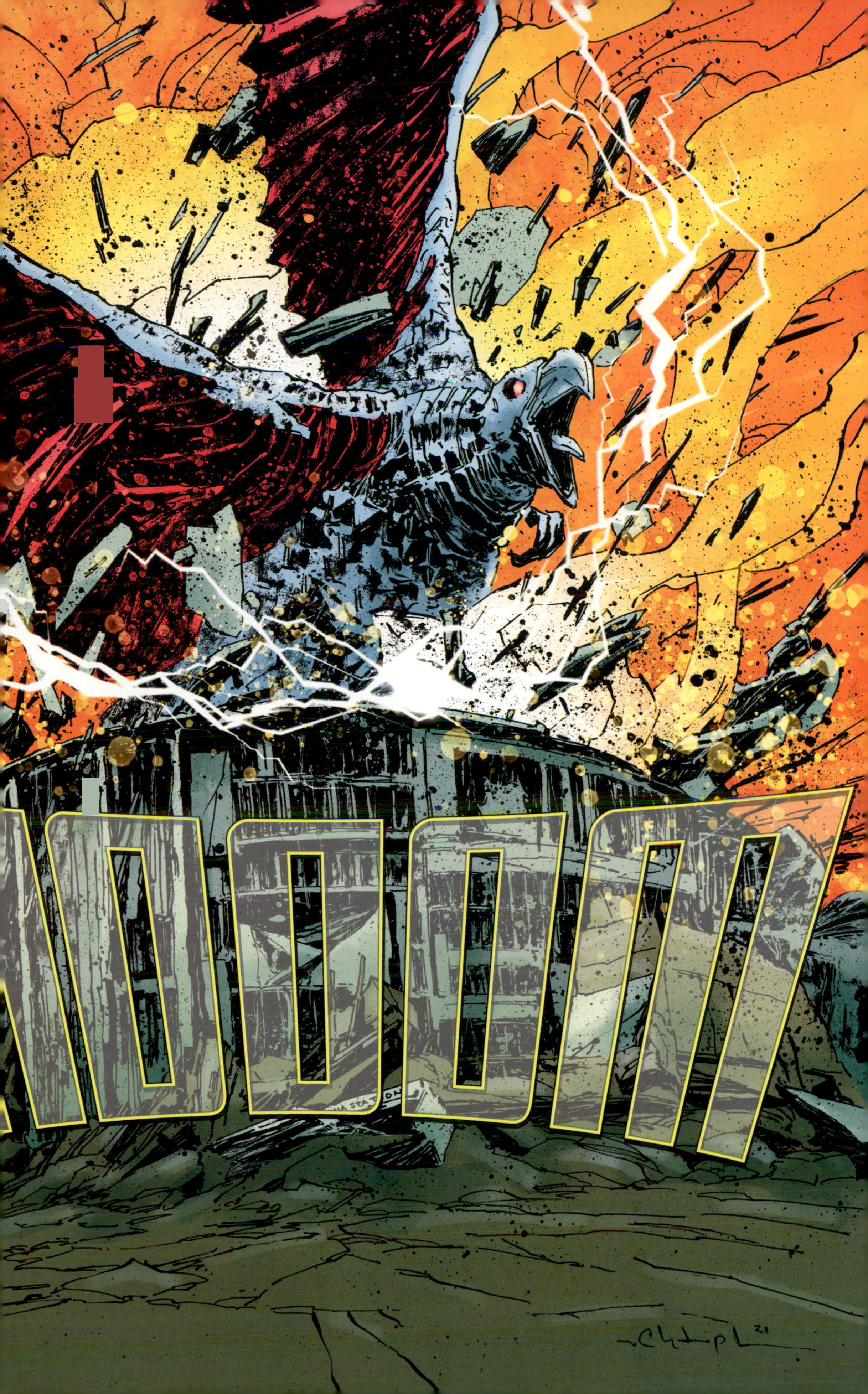
OOOM

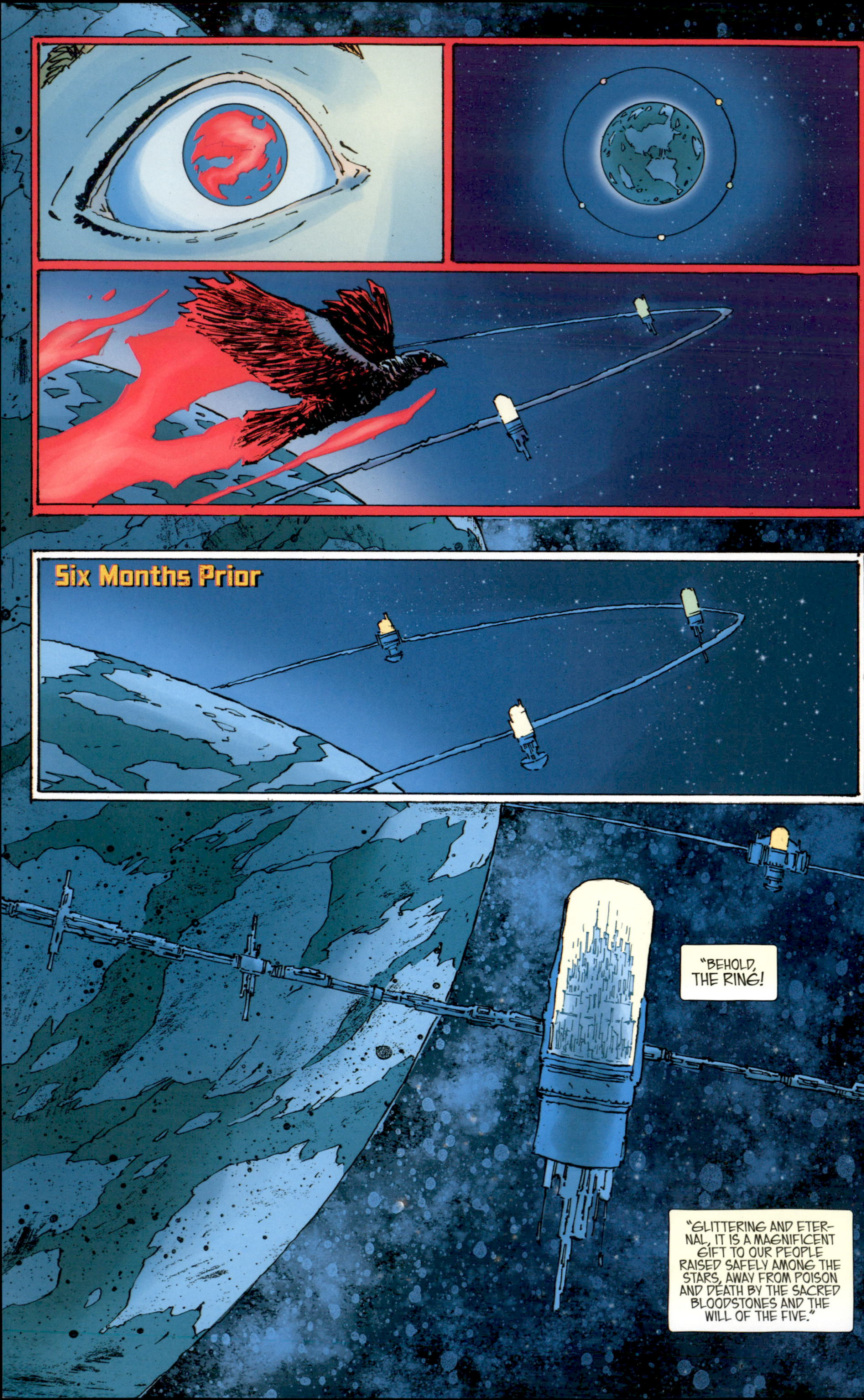
Six Months Prior
"BEHOLD, THE RING!
"GLITTERING AND ETERNAL, IT IS A MAGNIFICENT GIFT TO OUR PEOPLE RAISED SAFELY AMONG THE STARS, AWAY FROM POISON AND DEATH BY THE SACRED BLOODSTONES AND THE WILL OF THE FIVE."

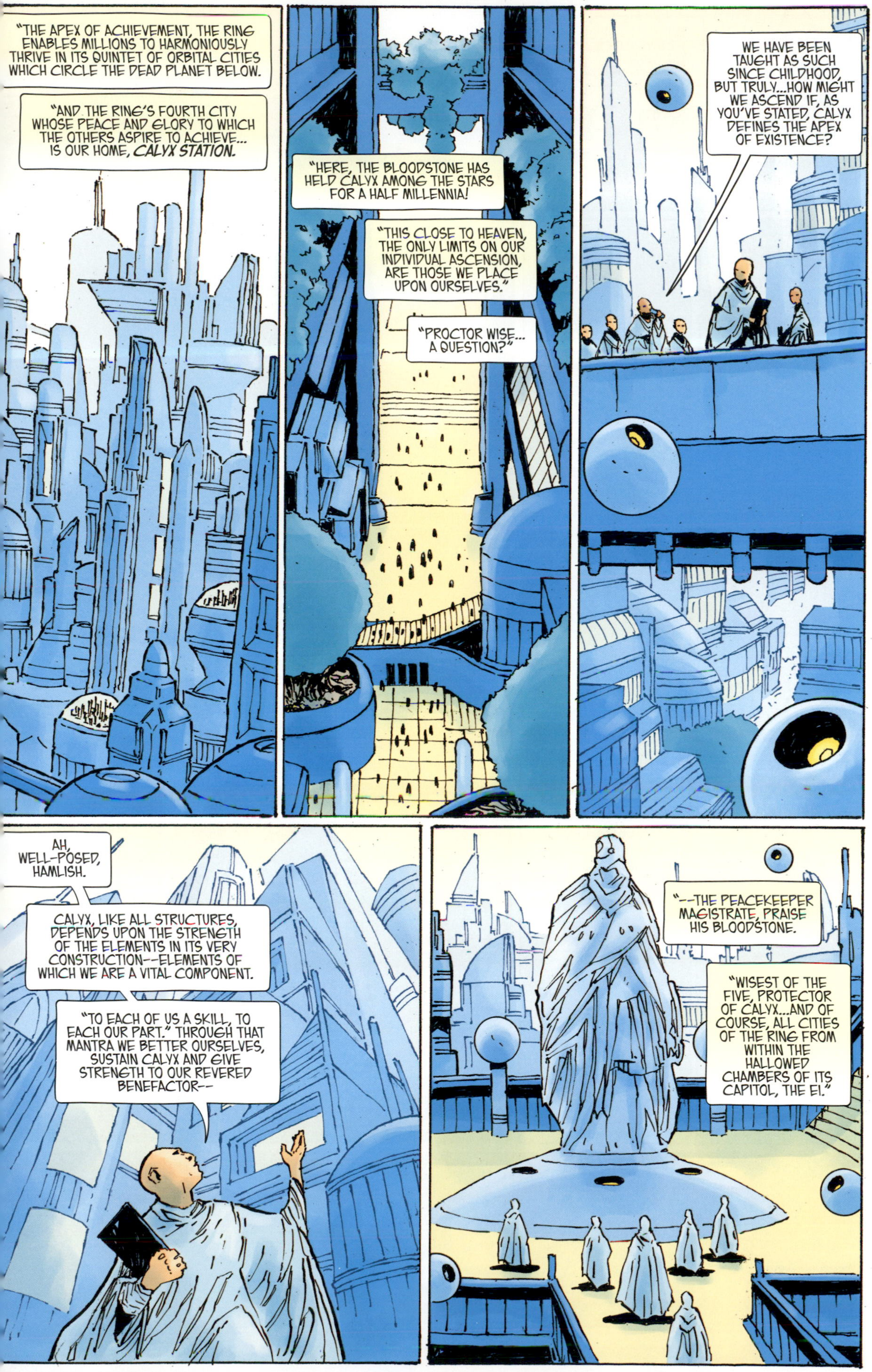
"THE APEX OF ACHIEVEMENT, THE RING ENABLES MILLIONS TO HARMONIOUSLY THRIVE IN ITS QUINTET OF ORBITAL CITIES WHICH CIRCLE THE DEAD PLANET BELOW.
"AND THE RING'S FOURTH CITY WHOSE PEACE AND GLORY TO WHICH THE OTHERS ASPIRE TO ACHIEVE... IS OUR HOME, *CALYX STATION.*
"HERE, THE BLOODSTONE HAS HELD CALYX AMONG THE STARS FOR A HALF MILLENNIA!
"THIS CLOSE TO HEAVEN, THE ONLY LIMITS ON OUR INDIVIDUAL ASCENSION, ARE THOSE WE PLACE UPON OURSELVES."
"PROCTOR WISE... A QUESTION?"
WE HAVE BEEN TAUGHT AS SUCH SINCE CHILDHOOD, BUT TRULY...HOW MIGHT WE ASCEND IF, AS YOU'VE STATED, CALYX DEFINES THE APEX OF EXISTENCE?
AH, WELL-POSED, HAMLISH.
CALYX, LIKE ALL STRUCTURES, DEPENDS UPON THE STRENGTH OF THE ELEMENTS IN ITS VERY CONSTRUCTION--ELEMENTS OF WHICH WE ARE A VITAL COMPONENT.
"TO EACH OF US A SKILL, TO EACH OUR PART." THROUGH THAT MANTRA WE BETTER OURSELVES, SUSTAIN CALYX AND GIVE STRENGTH TO OUR REVERED BENEFACTOR--
"--THE PEACEKEEPER MAGISTRATE, PRAISE HIS BLOODSTONE.
"WISEST OF THE FIVE, PROTECTOR OF CALYX...AND OF COURSE, ALL CITIES OF THE RING FROM WITHIN THE HALLOWED CHAMBERS OF ITS CAPITOL, THE EI."

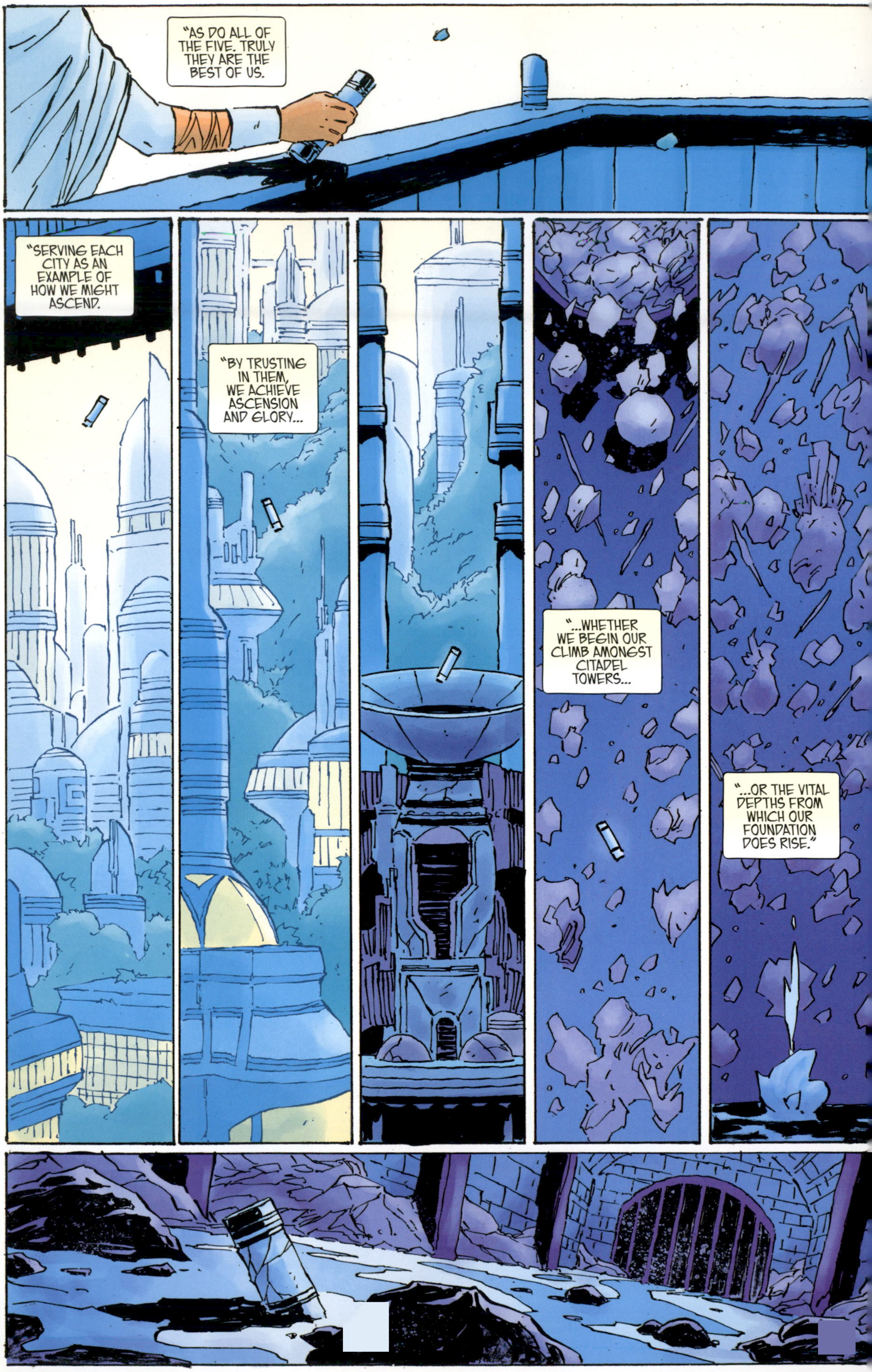
"AS DO ALL OF THE FIVE. TRULY THEY ARE THE BEST OF US.
"SERVING EACH CITY AS AN EXAMPLE OF HOW WE MIGHT ASCEND.
"BY TRUSTING IN THEM, WE ACHIEVE ASCENSION AND GLORY...
"...WHETHER WE BEGIN OUR CLIMB AMONGST CITADEL TOWERS...
"...OR THE VITAL DEPTHS FROM WHICH OUR FOUNDATION DOES RISE."

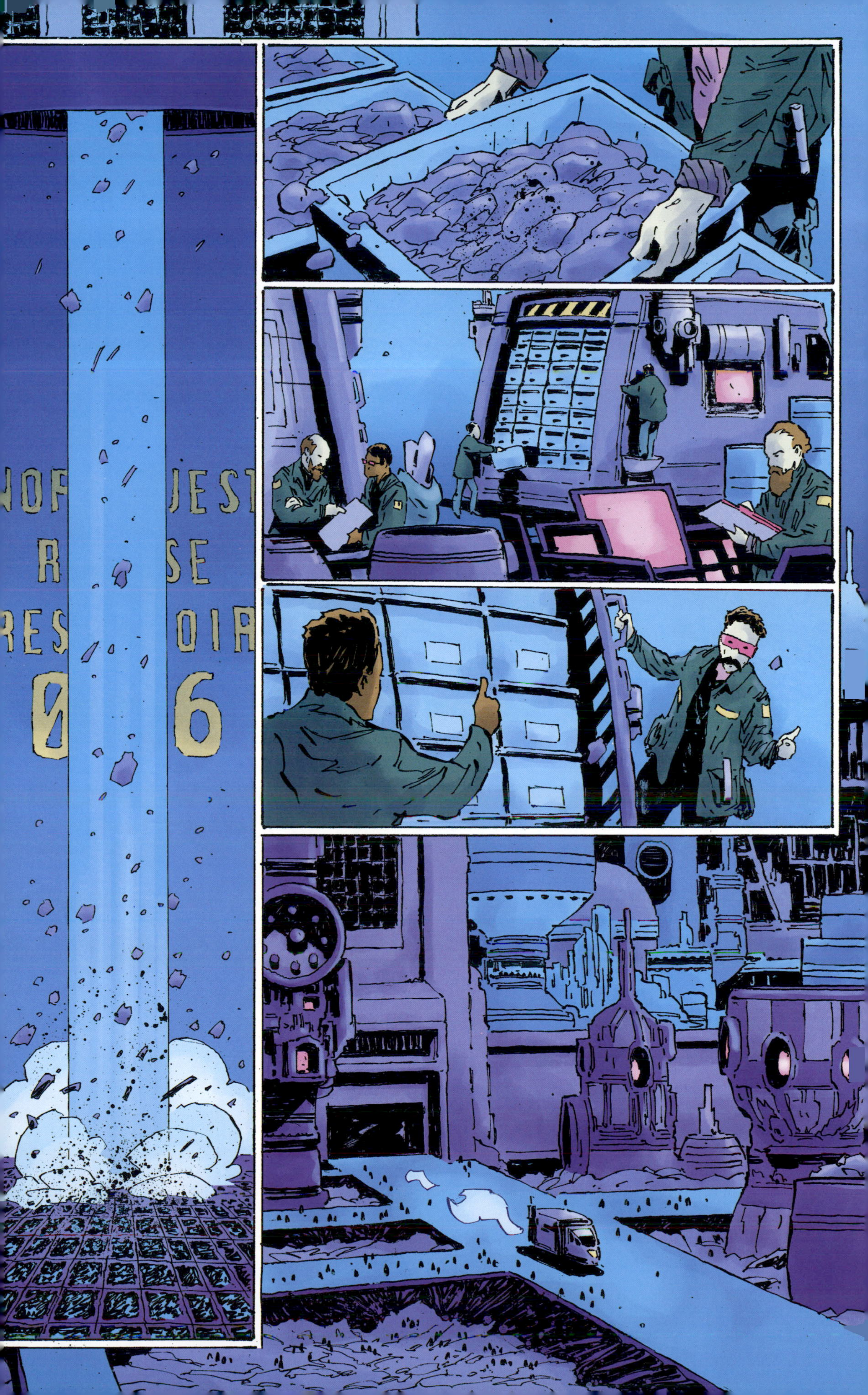
NOF JEST
R SE
RES OIR
Ø 6

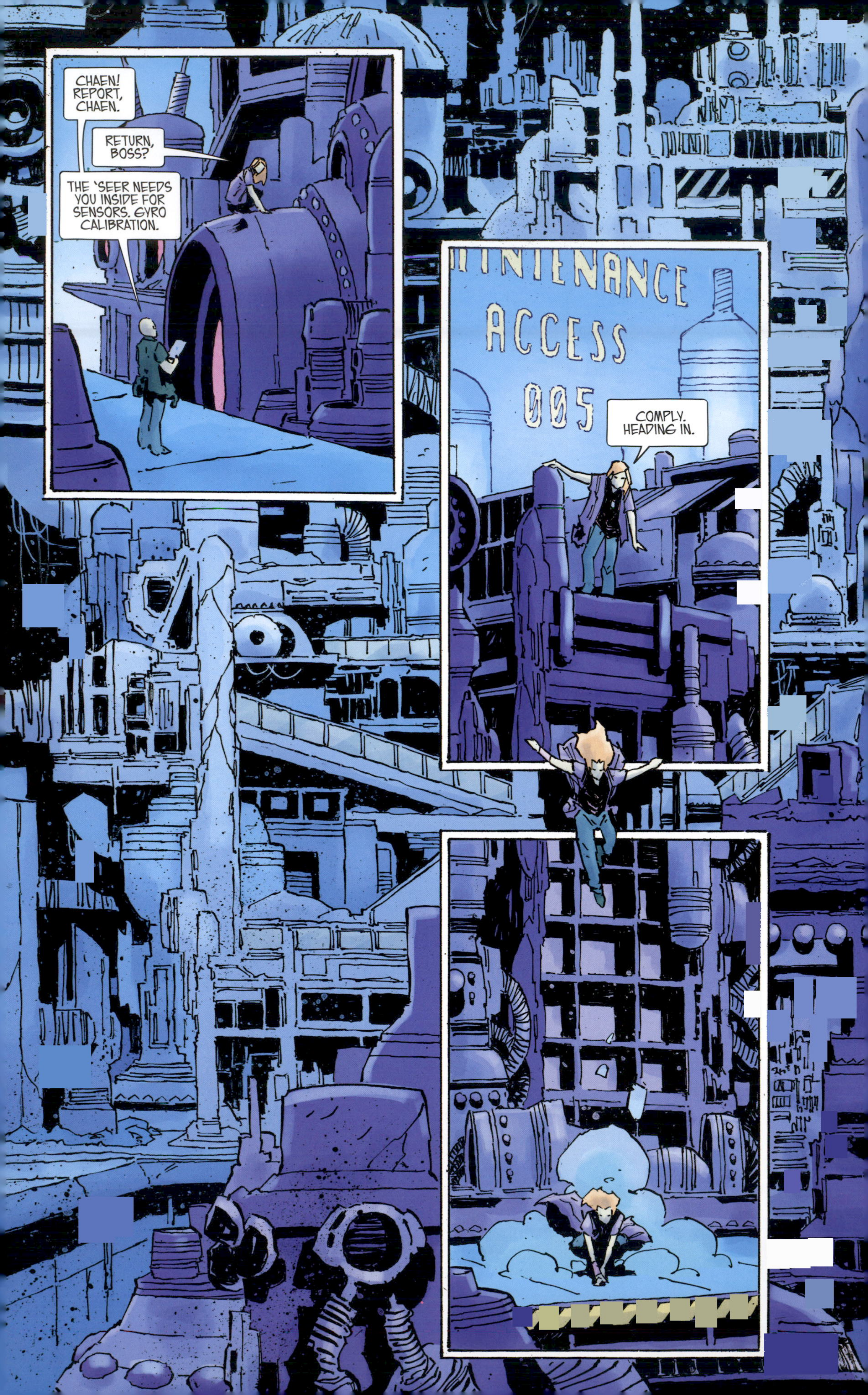

CHAEN! REPORT, CHAEN.
RETURN, BOSS?
THE 'SEER NEEDS YOU INSIDE FOR SENSORS. GYRO CALIBRATION.
NTENANCE ACCESS 005
COMPLY. HEADING IN.

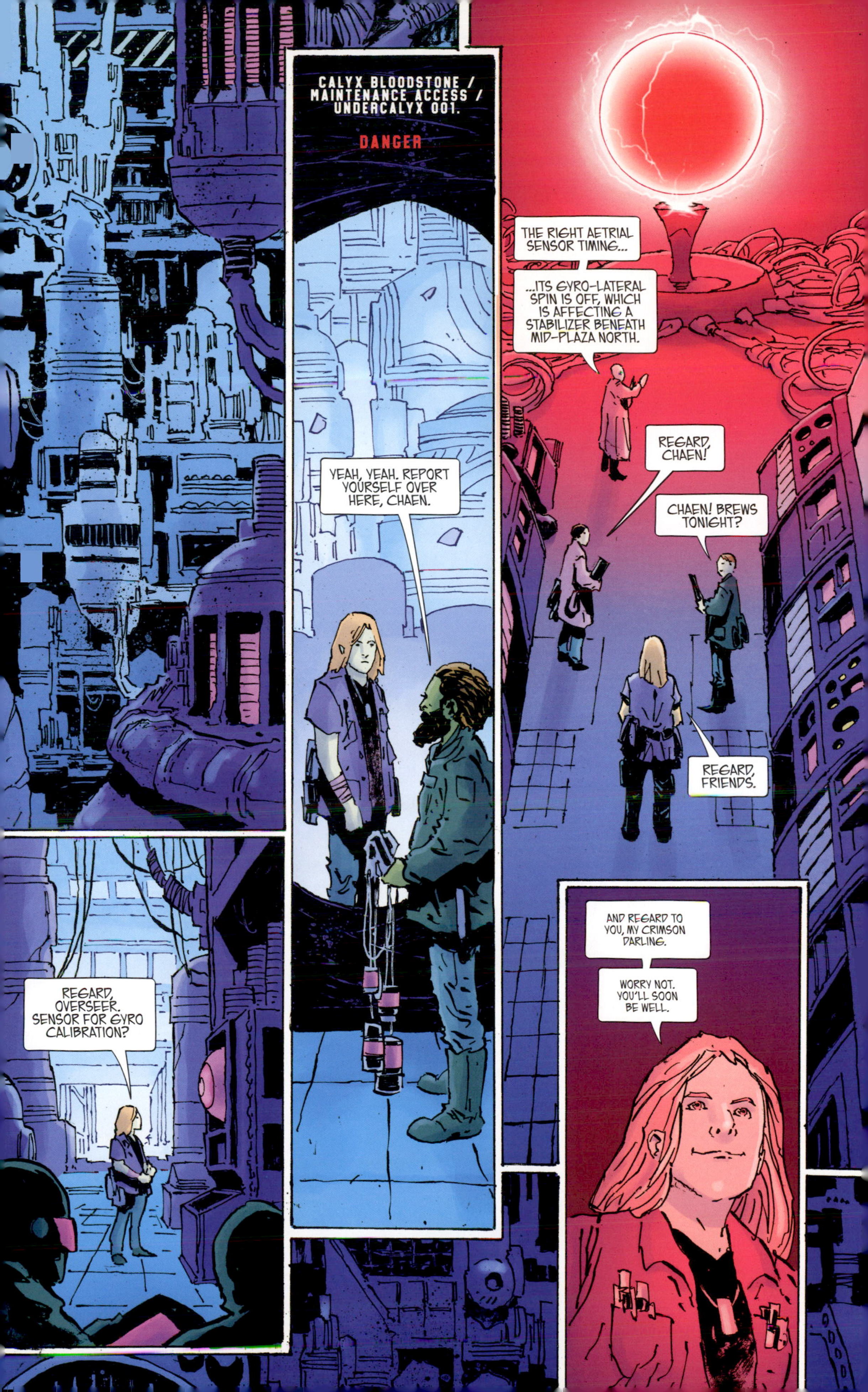
CALYX BLOODSTONE / MAINTENANCE ACCESS / UNDERCALYX 001.
DANGER
YEAH, YEAH. REPORT YOURSELF OVER HERE, CHAEN.
THE RIGHT AETRIAL SENSOR TIMING...
...ITS GYRO-LATERAL SPIN IS OFF, WHICH IS AFFECTING A STABILIZER BENEATH MID-PLAZA NORTH.
REGARD, CHAEN!
CHAEN! BREWS TONIGHT?
REGARD, FRIENDS.
REGARD, OVERSEER. SENSOR FOR GYRO CALIBRATION?
AND REGARD TO YOU, MY CRIMSON DARLING.
WORRY NOT. YOU'LL SOON BE WELL.

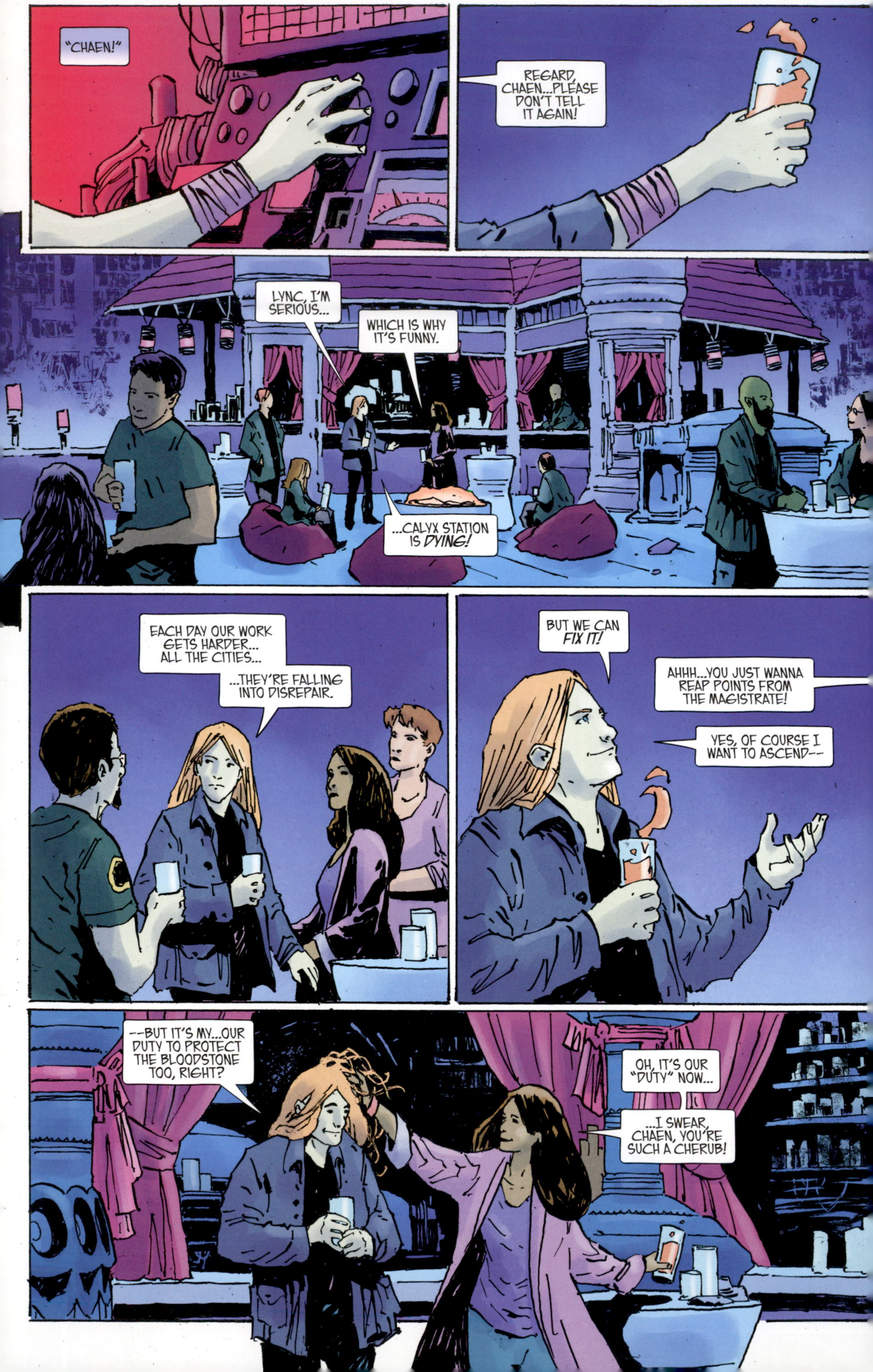
"CHAEN!"
REGARD, CHAEN...PLEASE DON'T TELL IT AGAIN!
LYNC, I'M SERIOUS...
WHICH IS WHY IT'S FUNNY.
...CALYX STATION IS *DYING!*
EACH DAY OUR WORK GETS HARDER... ALL THE CITIES...
...THEY'RE FALLING INTO DISREPAIR.
BUT WE CAN *FIX IT!*
AHHH...YOU JUST WANNA REAP POINTS FROM THE MAGISTRATE!
YES, OF COURSE I WANT TO ASCEND--
--BUT IT'S MY...OUR DUTY TO PROTECT THE BLOODSTONE TOO, RIGHT?
OH, IT'S OUR "DUTY" NOW...
...I SWEAR, CHAEN, YOU'RE SUCH A CHERUB!

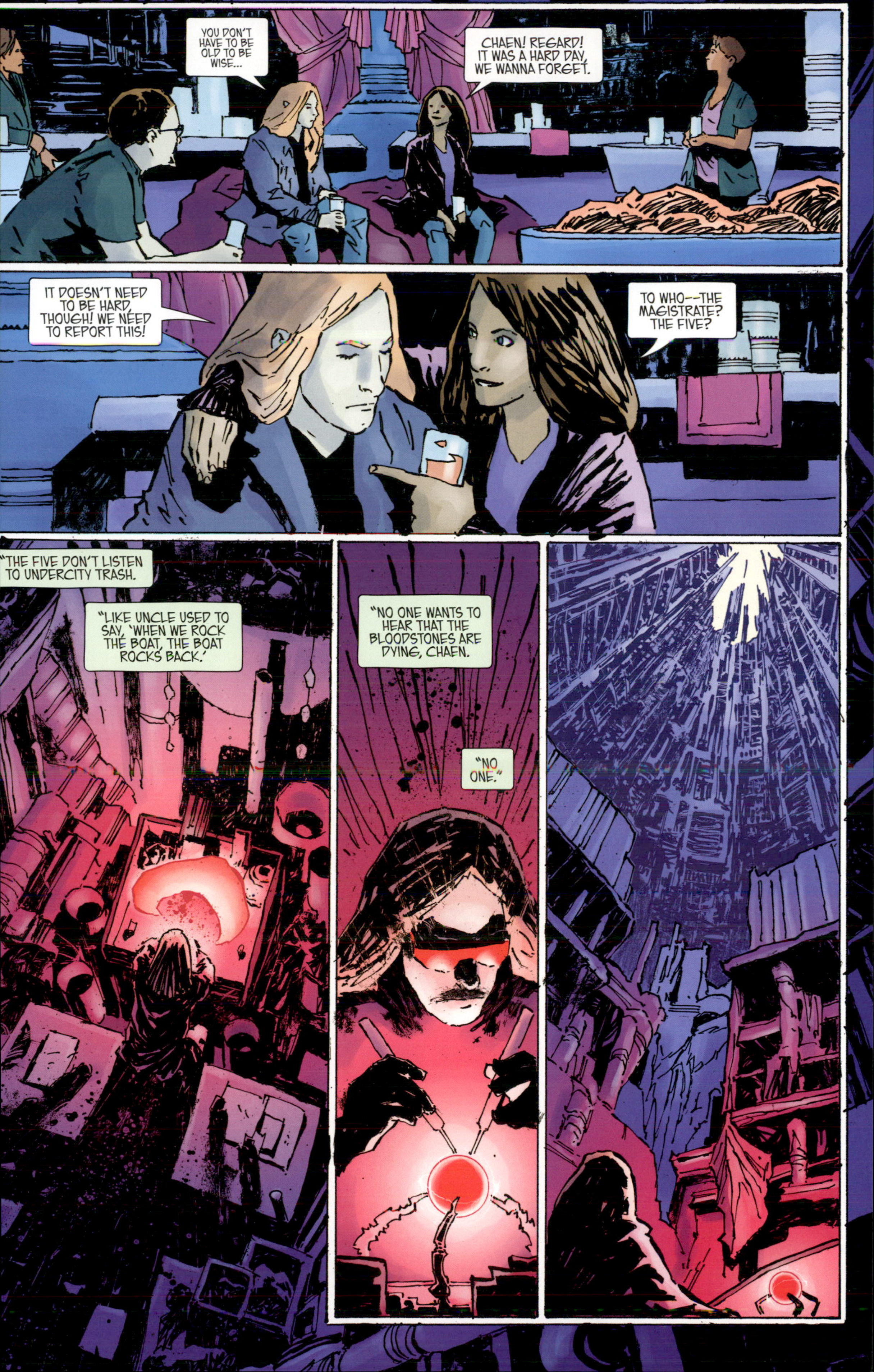

YOU DON'T HAVE TO BE OLD TO BE WISE...
CHAEN! REGARD! IT WAS A HARD DAY, WE WANNA FORGET.
IT DOESN'T NEED TO BE HARD, THOUGH! WE NEED TO REPORT THIS!
TO WHO--THE MAGISTRATE? THE FIVE?
"THE FIVE DON'T LISTEN TO UNDERCITY TRASH.
"LIKE UNCLE USED TO SAY, 'WHEN WE ROCK THE BOAT, THE BOAT ROCKS BACK.'
"NO ONE WANTS TO HEAR THAT THE BLOODSTONES ARE DYING, CHAEN.
"NO ONE."

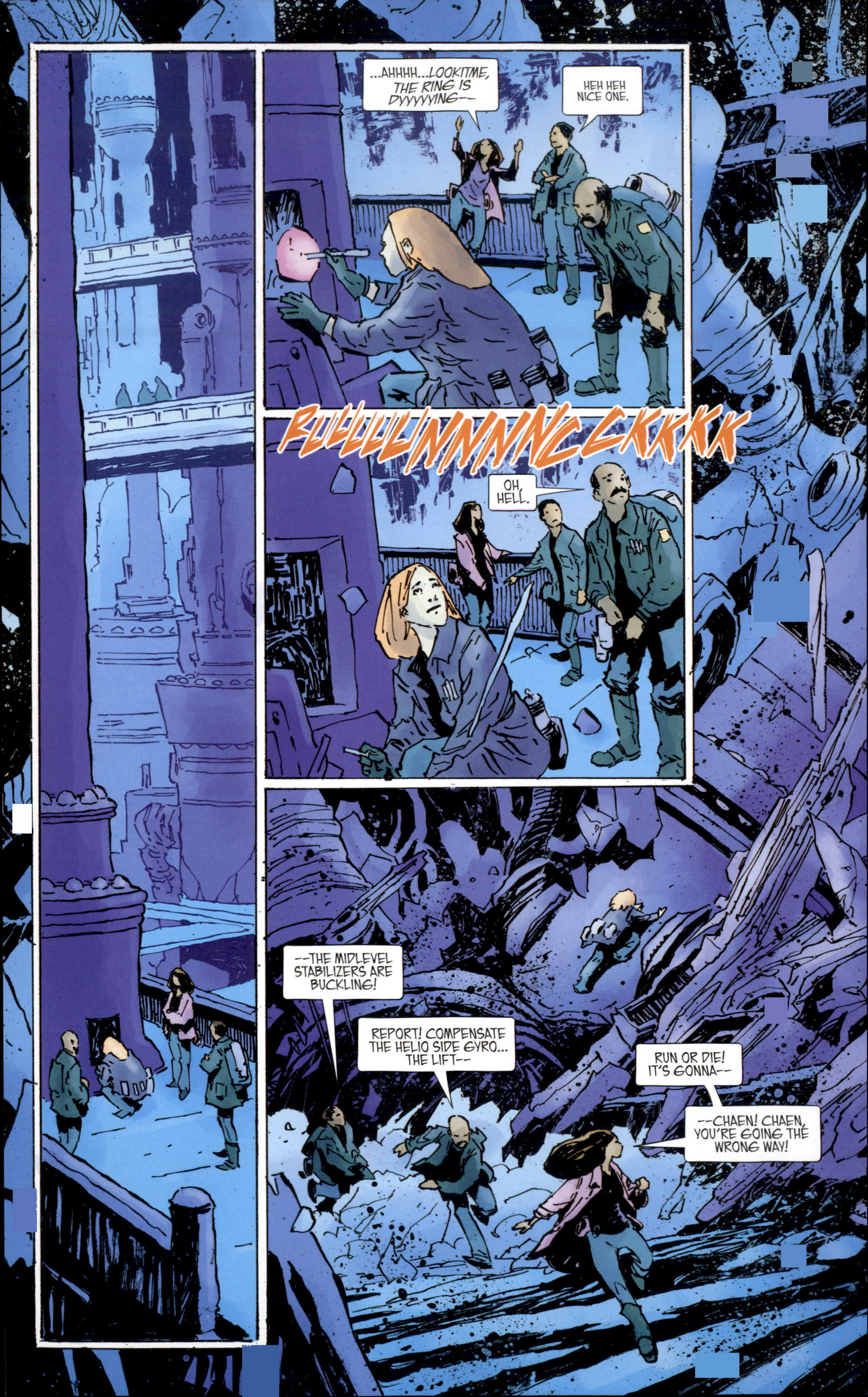
...AHHHH...LOOKITME, THE RING IS DYYYYYING--
HEH HEH NICE ONE.
RULLLLNNNNNCKKKKK
OH, HELL.
--THE MIDLEVEL STABILIZERS ARE BUCKLING!
REPORT! COMPENSATE THE HELIO SIDE GYRO... THE LIFT--
RUN OR DIE! IT'S GONNA--
--CHAEN! CHAEN, YOU'RE GOING THE WRONG WAY!

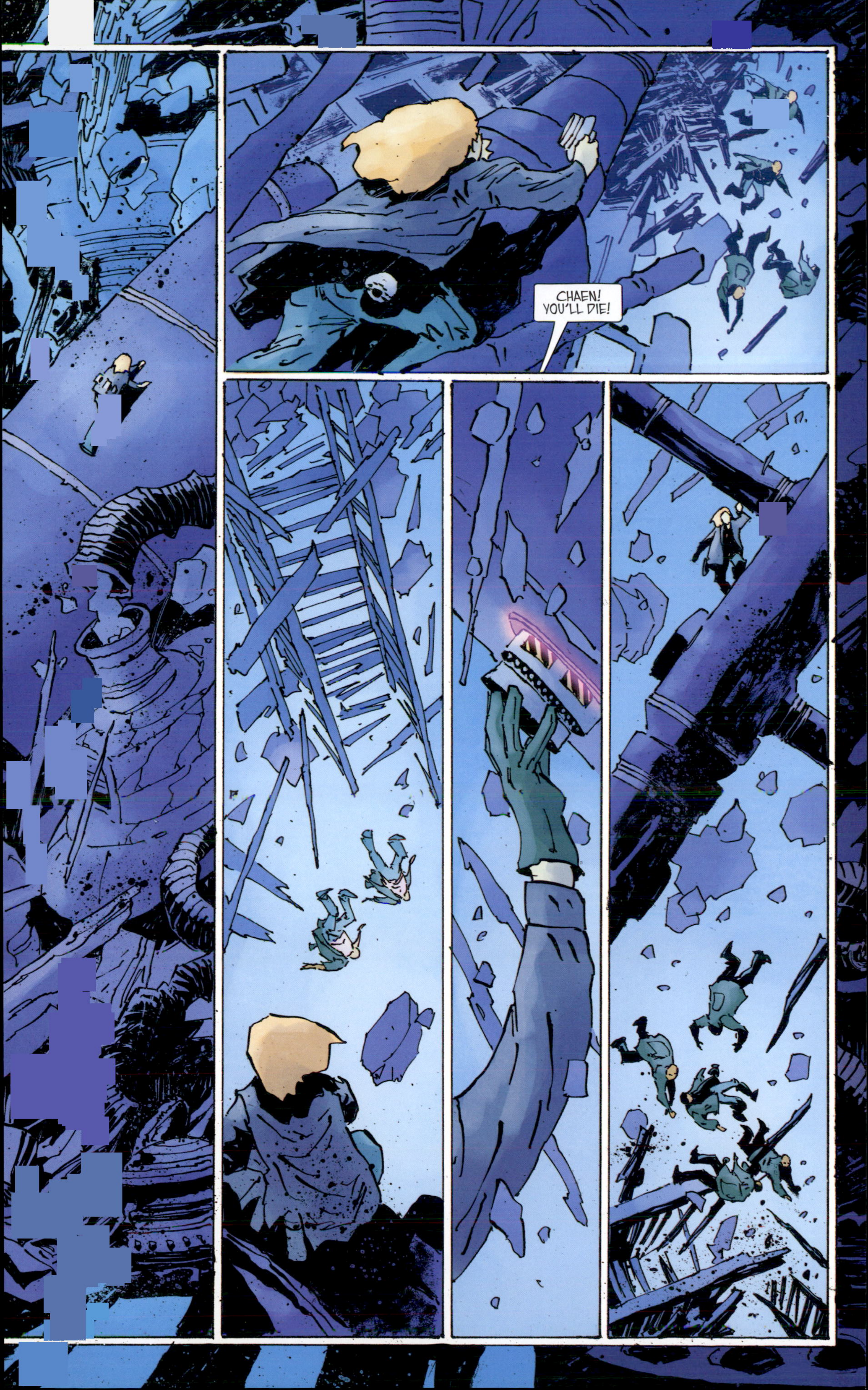
CHAEN! YOU'LL DIE!

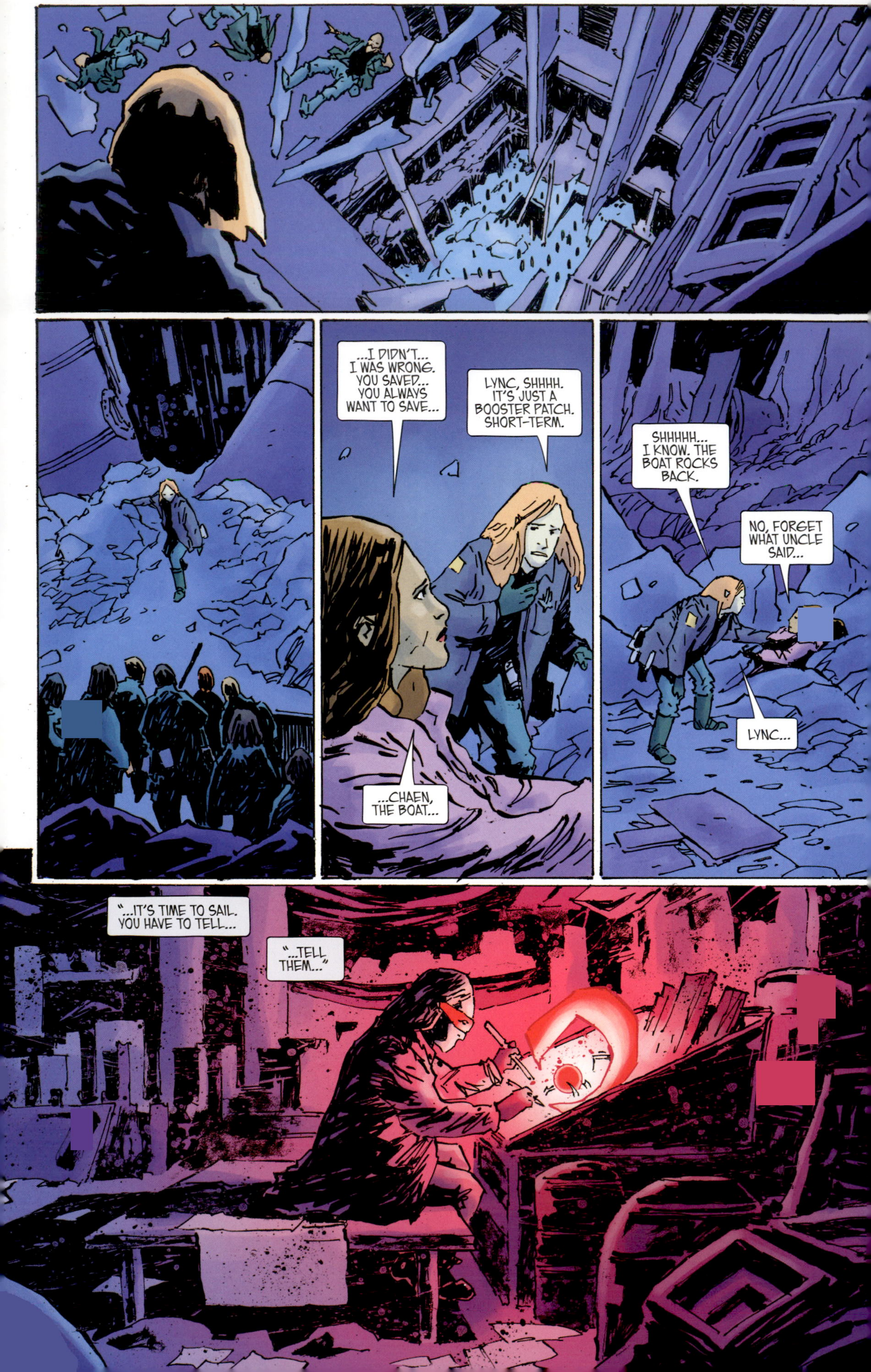
...I DIDN'T... I WAS WRONG. YOU SAVED... YOU ALWAYS WANT TO SAVE...
LYNC, SHHHH. IT'S JUST A BOOSTER PATCH. SHORT-TERM.
...CHAEN, THE BOAT...
SHHHHH... I KNOW. THE BOAT ROCKS BACK.
NO, FORGET WHAT UNCLE SAID...
LYNC...
"...IT'S TIME TO SAIL. YOU HAVE TO TELL...
"...TELL THEM..."

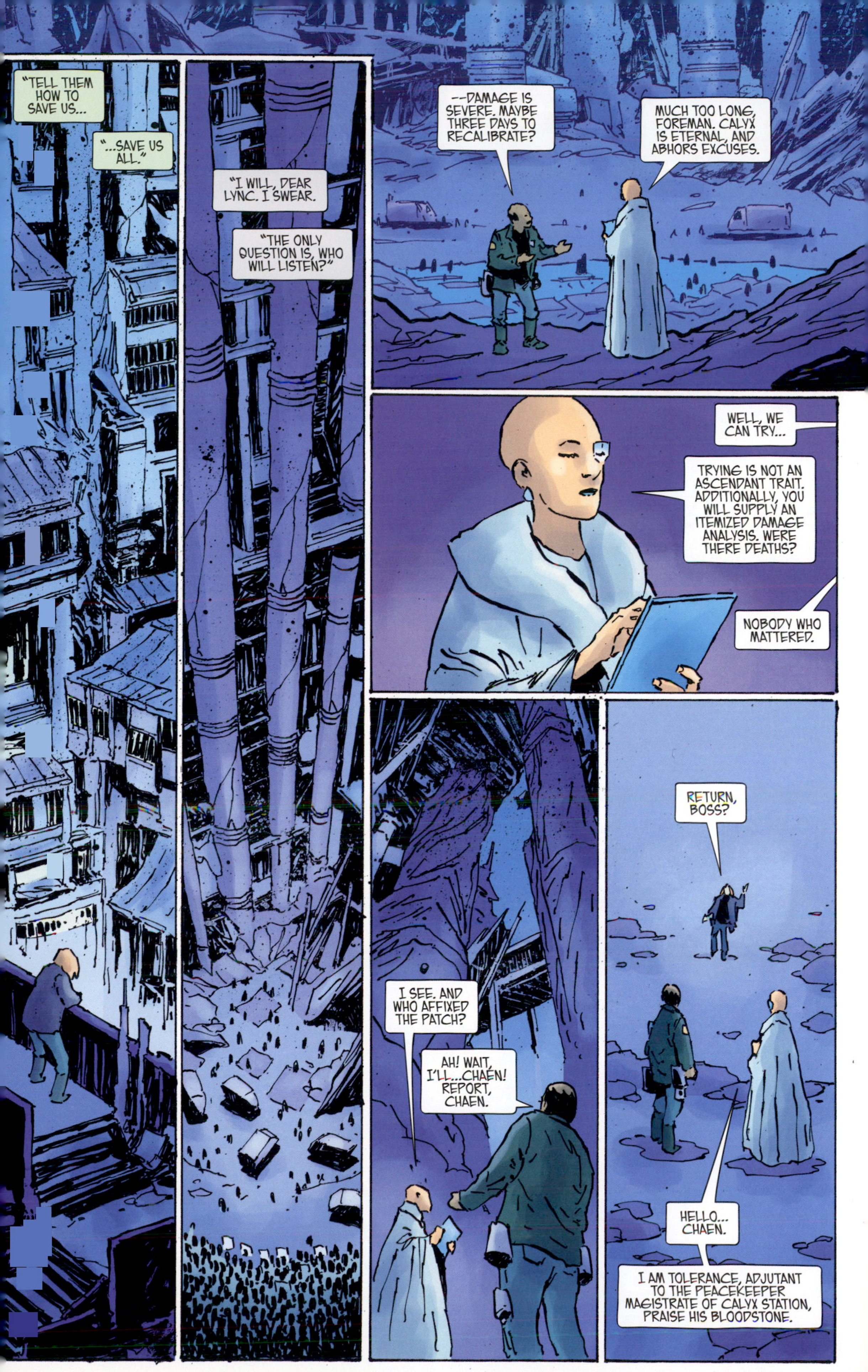
"TELL THEM HOW TO SAVE US...
"...SAVE US ALL."
"I WILL, DEAR LYNC. I SWEAR.
"THE ONLY QUESTION IS, WHO WILL LISTEN?"
--DAMAGE IS SEVERE. MAYBE THREE DAYS TO RECALIBRATE?
MUCH TOO LONG, FOREMAN. CALYX IS ETERNAL, AND ABHORS EXCUSES.
WELL, WE CAN TRY...
TRYING IS NOT AN ASCENDANT TRAIT. ADDITIONALLY, YOU WILL SUPPLY AN ITEMIZED DAMAGE ANALYSIS. WERE THERE DEATHS?
NOBODY WHO MATTERED.
I SEE. AND WHO AFFIXED THE PATCH?
AH! WAIT, I'LL...CHAEN! REPORT, CHAEN.
RETURN, BOSS?
HELLO... CHAEN.
I AM TOLERANCE, ADJUTANT TO THE PEACEKEEPER MAGISTRATE OF CALYX STATION, PRAISE HIS BLOODSTONE.

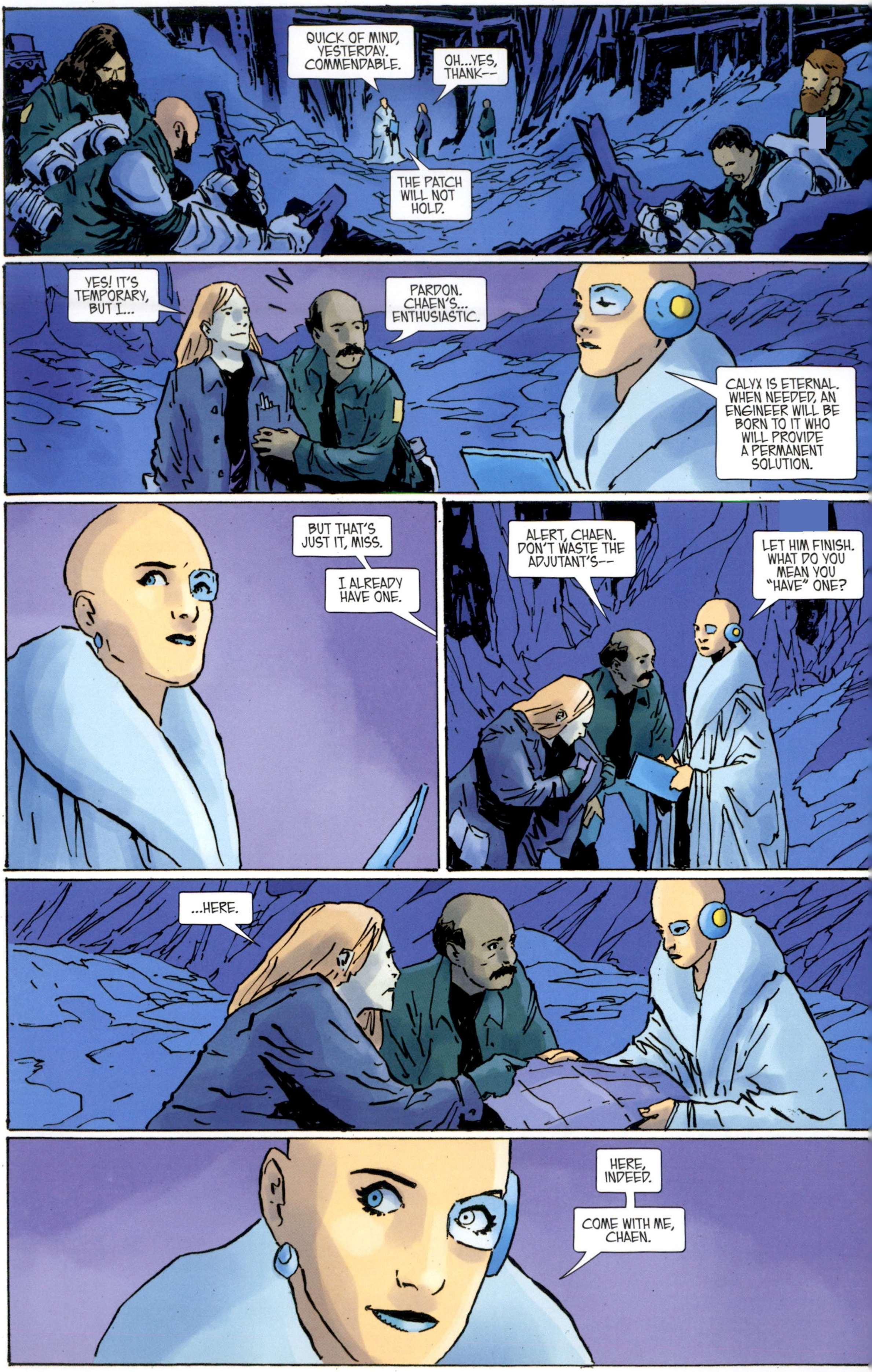
QUICK OF MIND, YESTERDAY. COMMENDABLE.
OH...YES, THANK--
THE PATCH WILL NOT HOLD.
YES! IT'S TEMPORARY, BUT I...
PARDON. CHAEN'S... ENTHUSIASTIC.
CALYX IS ETERNAL. WHEN NEEDED, AN ENGINEER WILL BE BORN TO IT WHO WILL PROVIDE A PERMANENT SOLUTION.
BUT THAT'S JUST IT, MISS.
I ALREADY HAVE ONE.
ALERT, CHAEN. DON'T WASTE THE ADJUTANT'S--
LET HIM FINISH. WHAT DO YOU MEAN YOU "HAVE" ONE?
...HERE.
HERE, INDEED.
COME WITH ME, CHAEN.

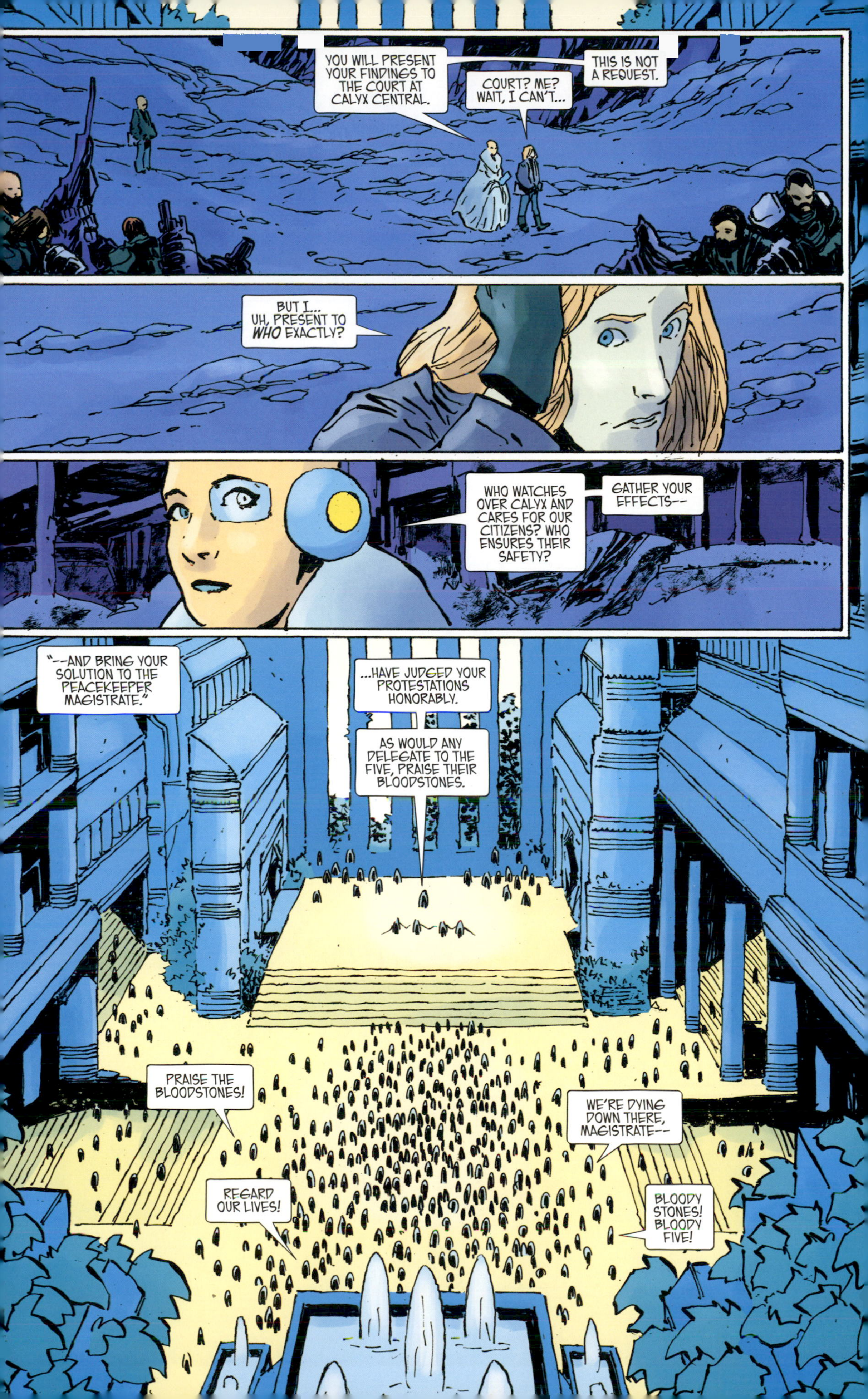

YOU WILL PRESENT YOUR FINDINGS TO THE COURT AT CALYX CENTRAL.
THIS IS NOT A REQUEST.
COURT? ME? WAIT, I CAN'T...
BUT I... UH, PRESENT TO *WHO* EXACTLY?
WHO WATCHES OVER CALYX AND CARES FOR OUR CITIZENS? WHO ENSURES THEIR SAFETY?
GATHER YOUR EFFECTS--
"--AND BRING YOUR SOLUTION TO THE PEACEKEEPER MAGISTRATE."
...HAVE JUDGED YOUR PROTESTATIONS HONORABLY.
AS WOULD ANY DELEGATE TO THE FIVE, PRAISE THEIR BLOODSTONES.
PRAISE THE BLOODSTONES!
WE'RE DYING DOWN THERE, MAGISTRATE--
REGARD OUR LIVES!
BLOODY STONES! BLOODY FIVE!

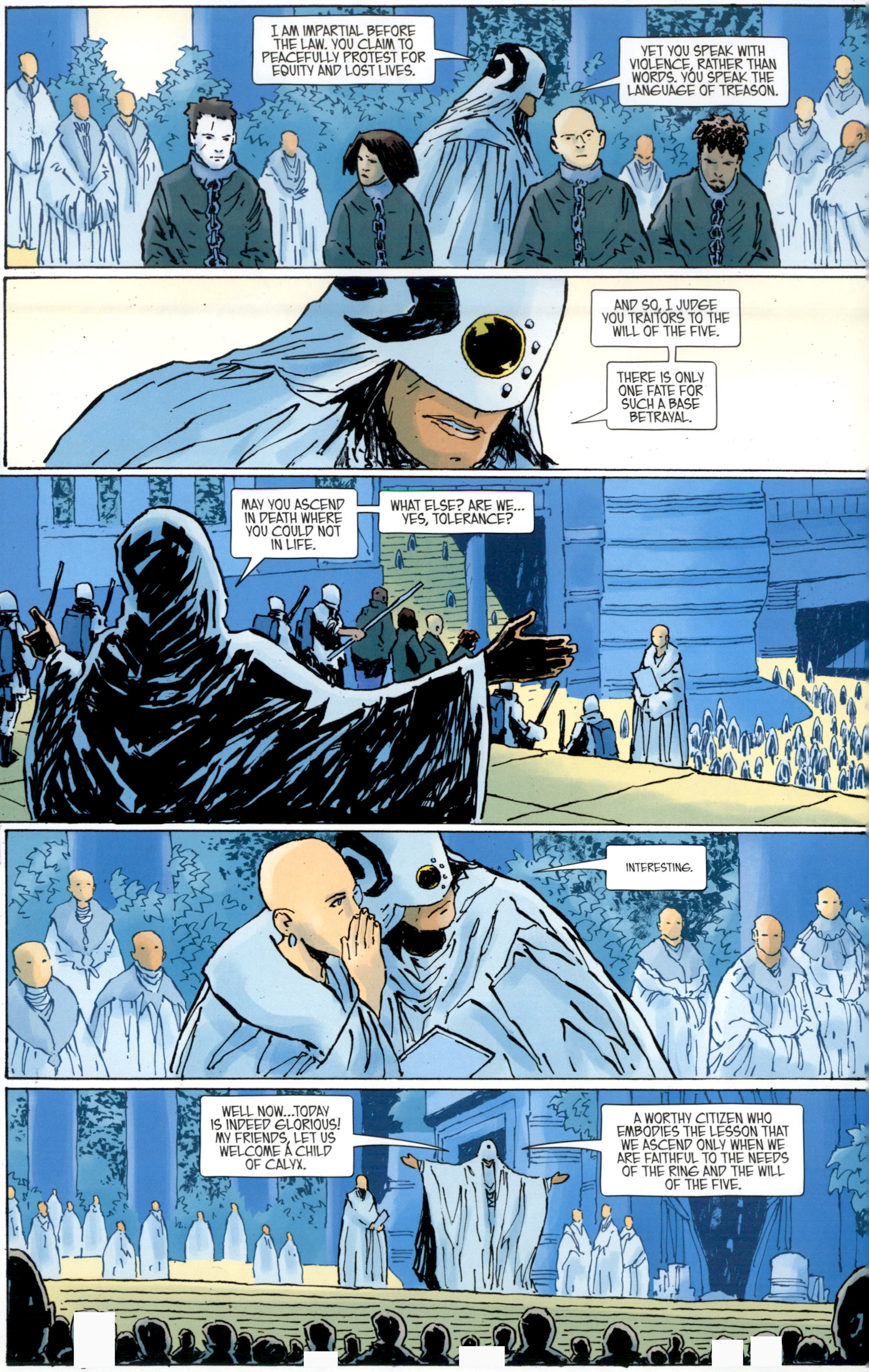
I AM IMPARTIAL BEFORE THE LAW. YOU CLAIM TO PEACEFULLY PROTEST FOR EQUITY AND LOST LIVES.
YET YOU SPEAK WITH VIOLENCE, RATHER THAN WORDS. YOU SPEAK THE LANGUAGE OF TREASON.
AND SO, I JUDGE YOU TRAITORS TO THE WILL OF THE FIVE.
THERE IS ONLY ONE FATE FOR SUCH A BASE BETRAYAL.
MAY YOU ASCEND IN DEATH WHERE YOU COULD NOT IN LIFE.
WHAT ELSE? ARE WE... YES, TOLERANCE?
INTERESTING.
WELL NOW...TODAY IS INDEED GLORIOUS! MY FRIENDS, LET US WELCOME A CHILD OF CALYX.
A WORTHY CITIZEN WHO EMBODIES THE LESSON THAT WE ASCEND ONLY WHEN WE ARE FAITHFUL TO THE NEEDS OF THE RING AND THE WILL OF THE FIVE.

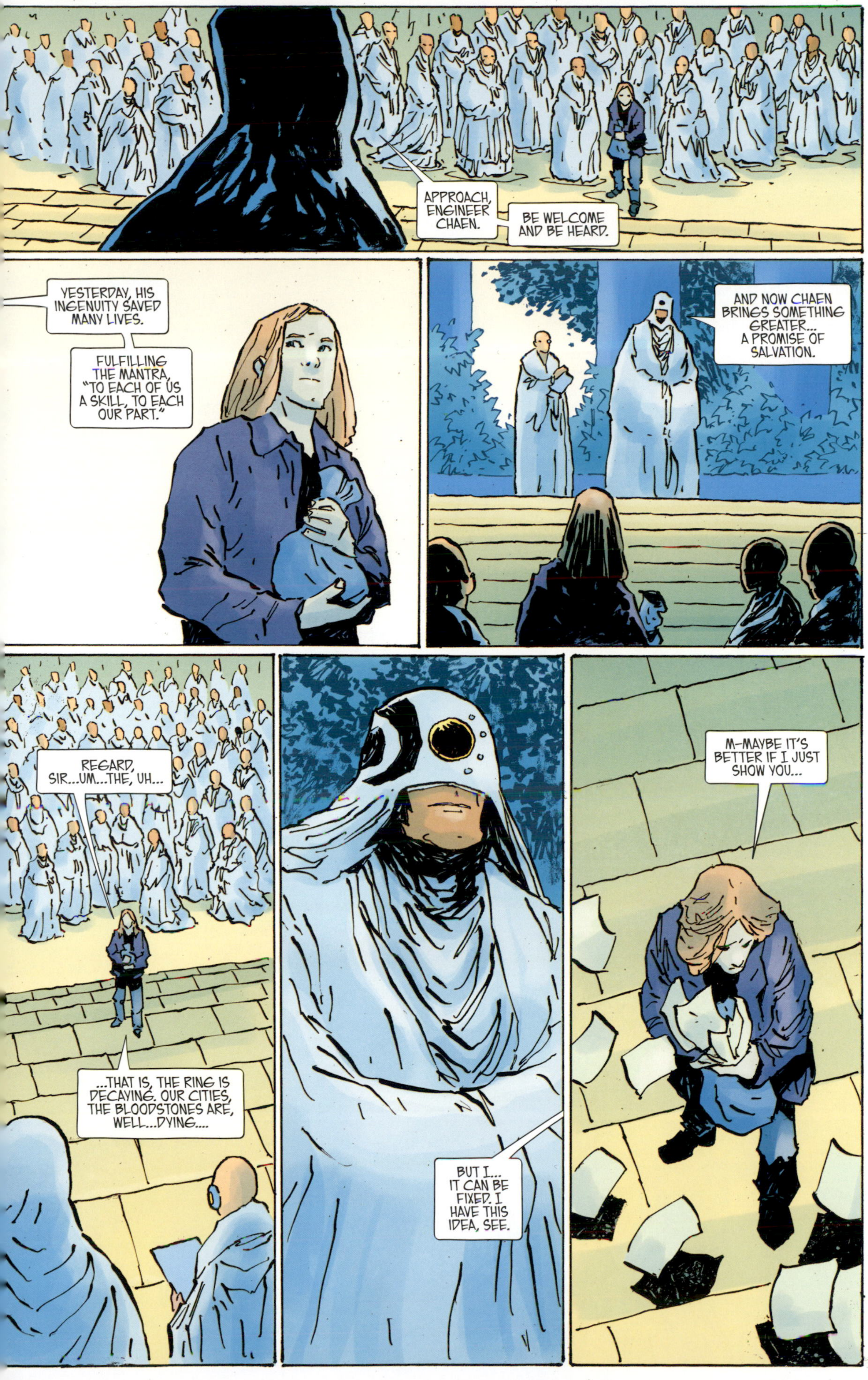
APPROACH, ENGINEER CHAEN.
BE WELCOME AND BE HEARD.
YESTERDAY, HIS INGENUITY SAVED MANY LIVES.
FULFILLING THE MANTRA, "TO EACH OF US A SKILL, TO EACH OUR PART."
AND NOW CHAEN BRINGS SOMETHING GREATER... A PROMISE OF SALVATION.
REGARD, SIR...UM...THE, UH...
...THAT IS, THE RING IS DECAYING. OUR CITIES, THE BLOODSTONES ARE, WELL...DYING....
BUT I... IT CAN BE FIXED. I HAVE THIS IDEA, SEE.
M-MAYBE IT'S BETTER IF I JUST SHOW YOU...

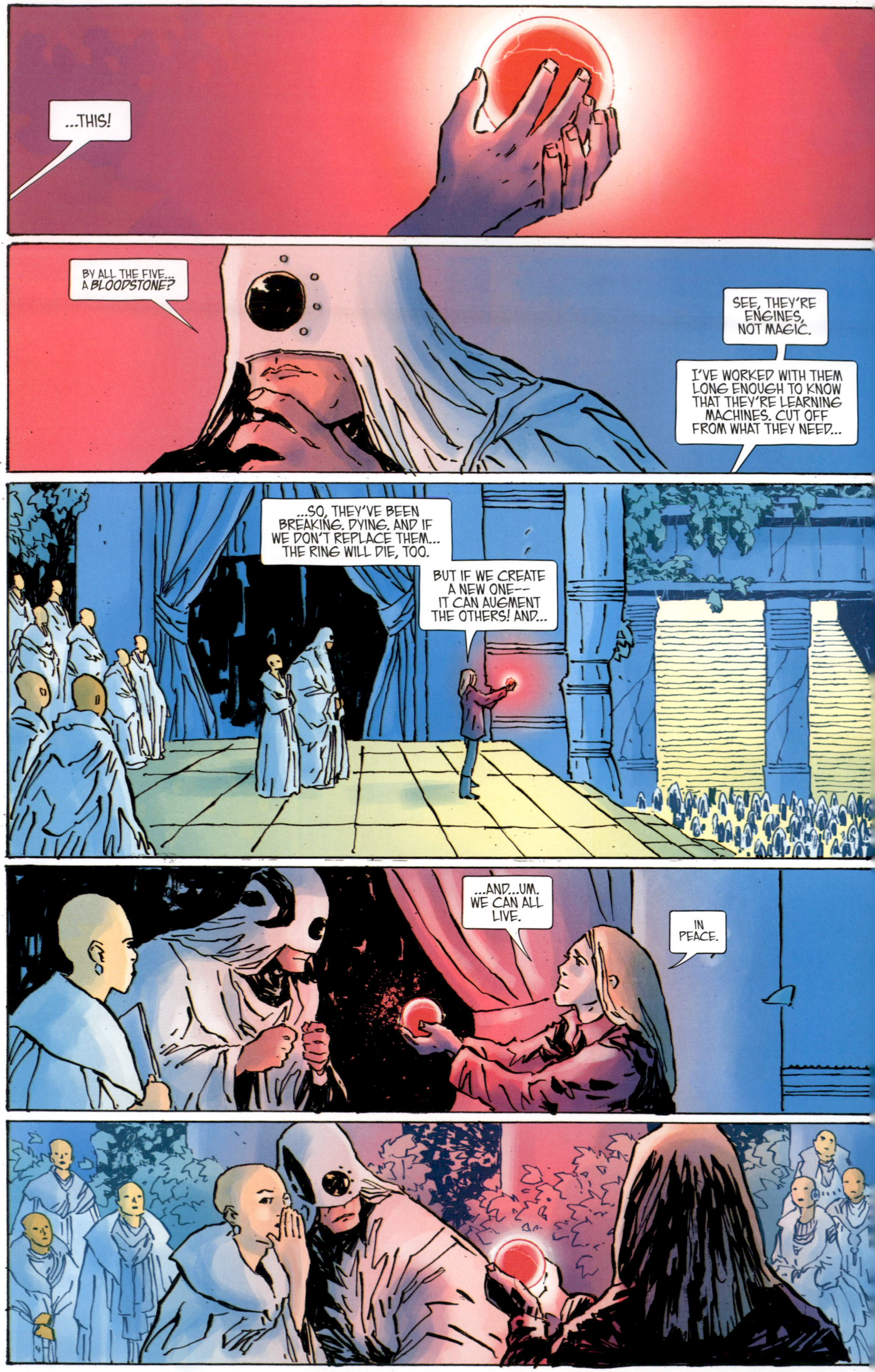
...THIS!
BY ALL THE FIVE... A *BLOODSTONE?*
SEE, THEY'RE ENGINES, NOT MAGIC.
I'VE WORKED WITH THEM LONG ENOUGH TO KNOW THAT THEY'RE LEARNING MACHINES. CUT OFF FROM WHAT THEY NEED...
...SO, THEY'VE BEEN BREAKING. DYING. AND IF WE DON'T REPLACE THEM... THE RING WILL DIE, TOO.
BUT IF WE CREATE A NEW ONE-- IT CAN AUGMENT THE OTHERS! AND...
...AND...UM. WE CAN ALL LIVE.
IN PEACE.

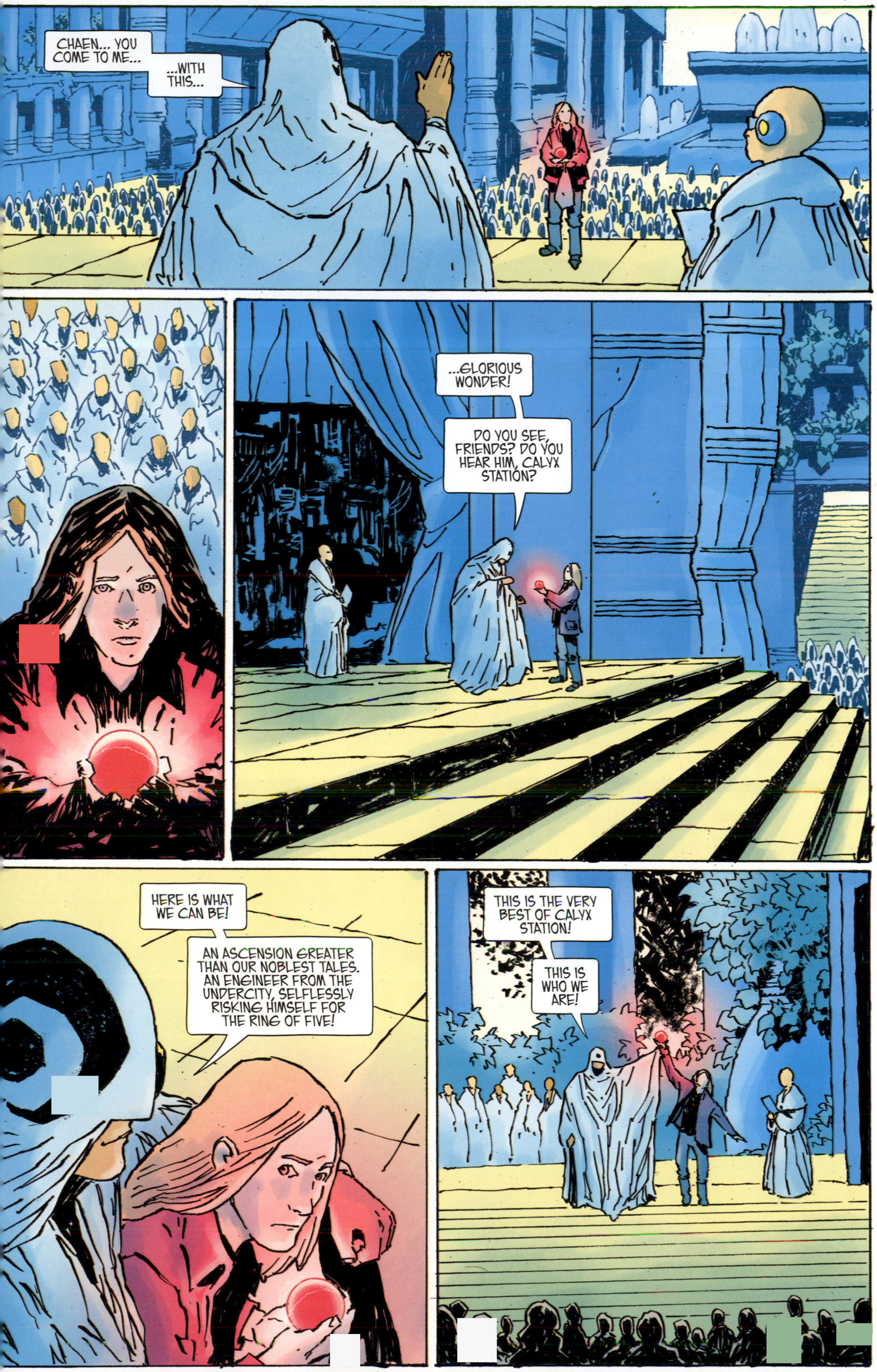
CHAEN... YOU COME TO ME...
...WITH THIS...
...GLORIOUS WONDER!
DO YOU SEE, FRIENDS? DO YOU HEAR HIM, CALYX STATION?
HERE IS WHAT WE CAN BE!
AN ASCENSION GREATER THAN OUR NOBLEST TALES. AN ENGINEER FROM THE UNDERCITY, SELFLESSLY RISKING HIMSELF FOR THE RING OF FIVE!
THIS IS THE VERY BEST OF CALYX STATION!
THIS IS WHO WE ARE!

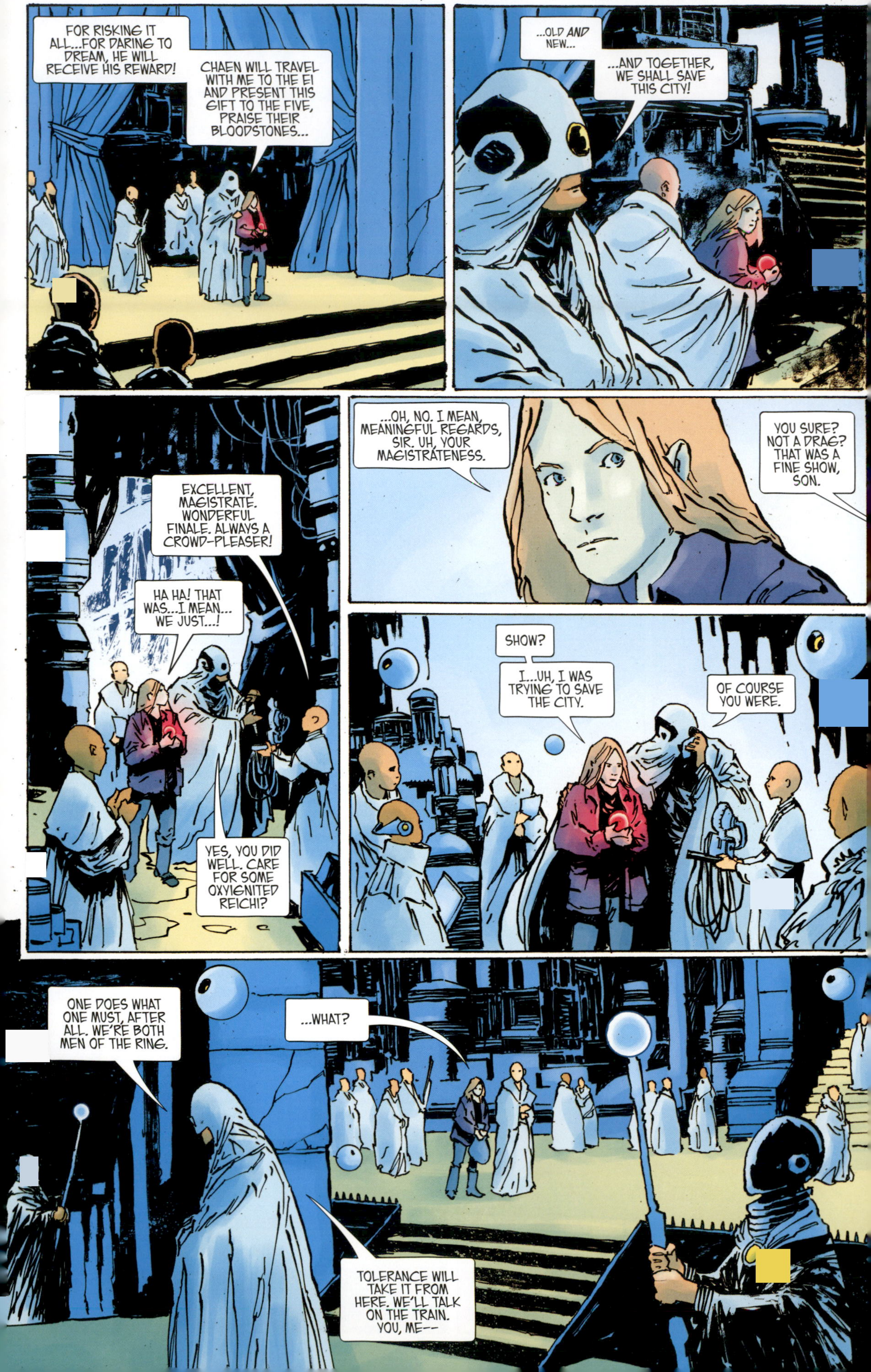
FOR RISKING IT ALL...FOR DARING TO DREAM, HE WILL RECEIVE HIS REWARD!
CHAEN WILL TRAVEL WITH ME TO THE EI AND PRESENT THIS GIFT TO THE FIVE, PRAISE THEIR BLOODSTONES...
...OLD AND NEW...
...AND TOGETHER, WE SHALL SAVE THIS CITY!
EXCELLENT, MAGISTRATE. WONDERFUL FINALE. ALWAYS A CROWD-PLEASER!
HA HA! THAT WAS...I MEAN... WE JUST...!
YES, YOU DID WELL. CARE FOR SOME OXYIGNITED REICHI?
...OH, NO. I MEAN, MEANINGFUL REGARDS, SIR. UH, YOUR MAGISTRATENESS.
YOU SURE? NOT A DRAG? THAT WAS A FINE SHOW, SON.
SHOW?
I...UH, I WAS TRYING TO SAVE THE CITY.
OF COURSE YOU WERE.
ONE DOES WHAT ONE MUST, AFTER ALL. WE'RE BOTH MEN OF THE RING.
...WHAT?
TOLERANCE WILL TAKE IT FROM HERE. WE'LL TALK ON THE TRAIN. YOU, ME--

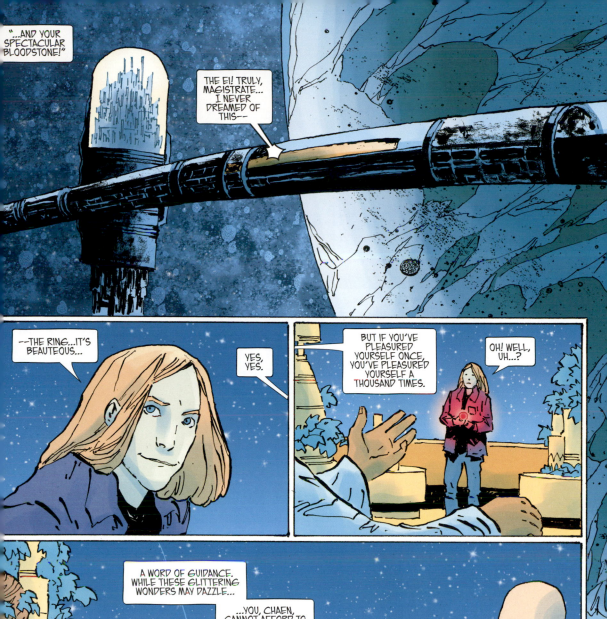

"...AND YOUR SPECTACULAR BLOODSTONE!"

THE E! TRULY, MAGISTRATE... I NEVER DREAMED OF THIS--

--THE RING...IT'S BEAUTEOUS...

YES, YES.

BUT IF YOU'VE PLEASURED YOURSELF ONCE, YOU'VE PLEASURED YOURSELF A THOUSAND TIMES.

OH! WELL, UH...?

A WORD OF GUIDANCE. WHILE THESE GLITTERING WONDERS MAY DAZZLE...

...YOU, CHAEN, CANNOT AFFORD TO BE SPELLBOUND BY THEIR MAGNETIC TRANCE...

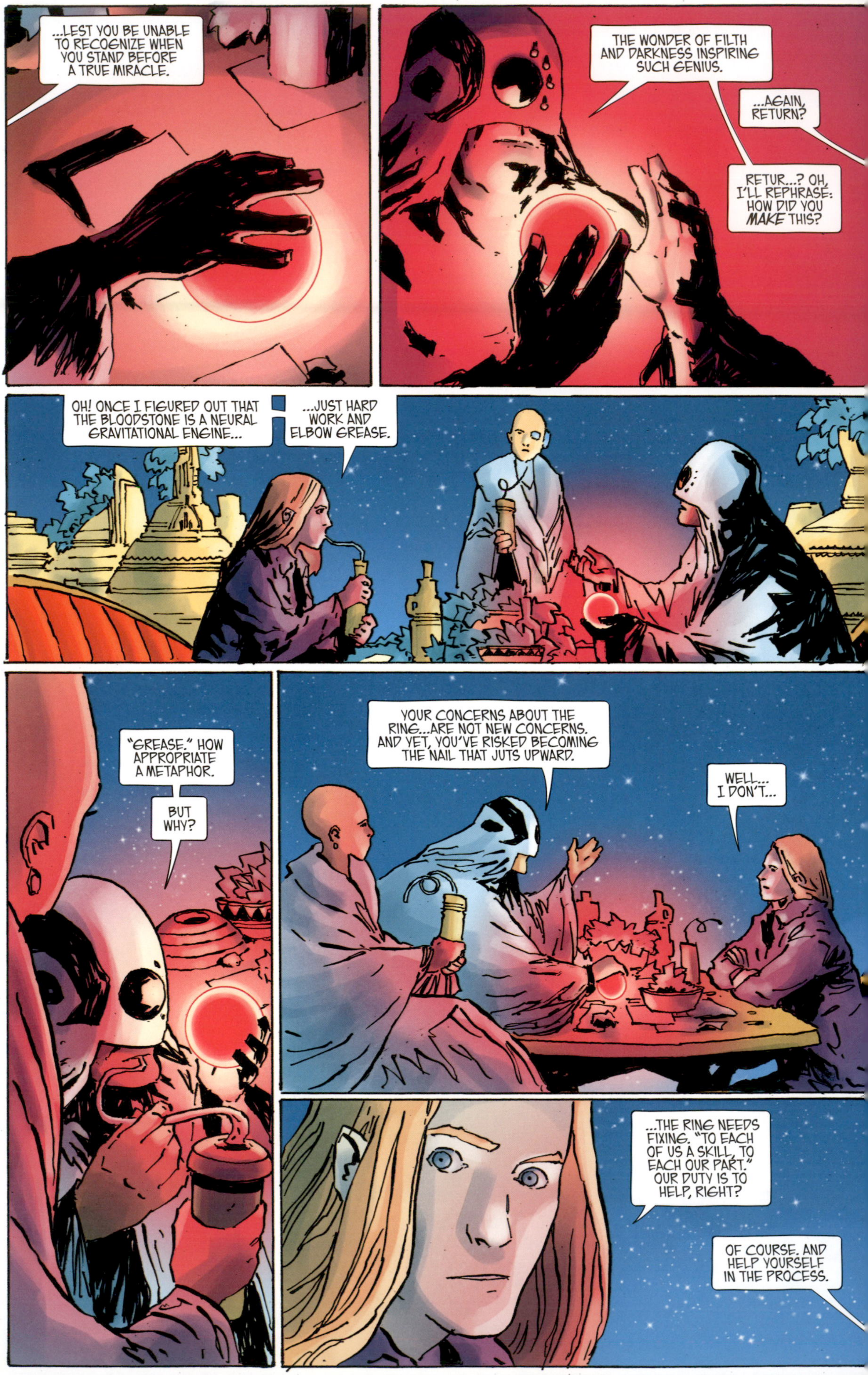
...LEST YOU BE UNABLE TO RECOGNIZE WHEN YOU STAND BEFORE A TRUE MIRACLE.
THE WONDER OF FILTH AND DARKNESS INSPIRING SUCH GENIUS.
...AGAIN, RETURN?
RETUR...? OH, I'LL REPHRASE: HOW DID YOU *MAKE* THIS?
OH! ONCE I FIGURED OUT THAT THE BLOODSTONE IS A NEURAL GRAVITATIONAL ENGINE...
...JUST HARD WORK AND ELBOW GREASE.
"GREASE." HOW APPROPRIATE A METAPHOR.
BUT WHY?
YOUR CONCERNS ABOUT THE RING...ARE NOT NEW CONCERNS. AND YET, YOU'VE RISKED BECOMING THE NAIL THAT JUTS UPWARD.
WELL... I DON'T...
...THE RING NEEDS FIXING. "TO EACH OF US A SKILL, TO EACH OUR PART." OUR DUTY IS TO HELP, RIGHT?
OF COURSE. AND HELP YOURSELF IN THE PROCESS.

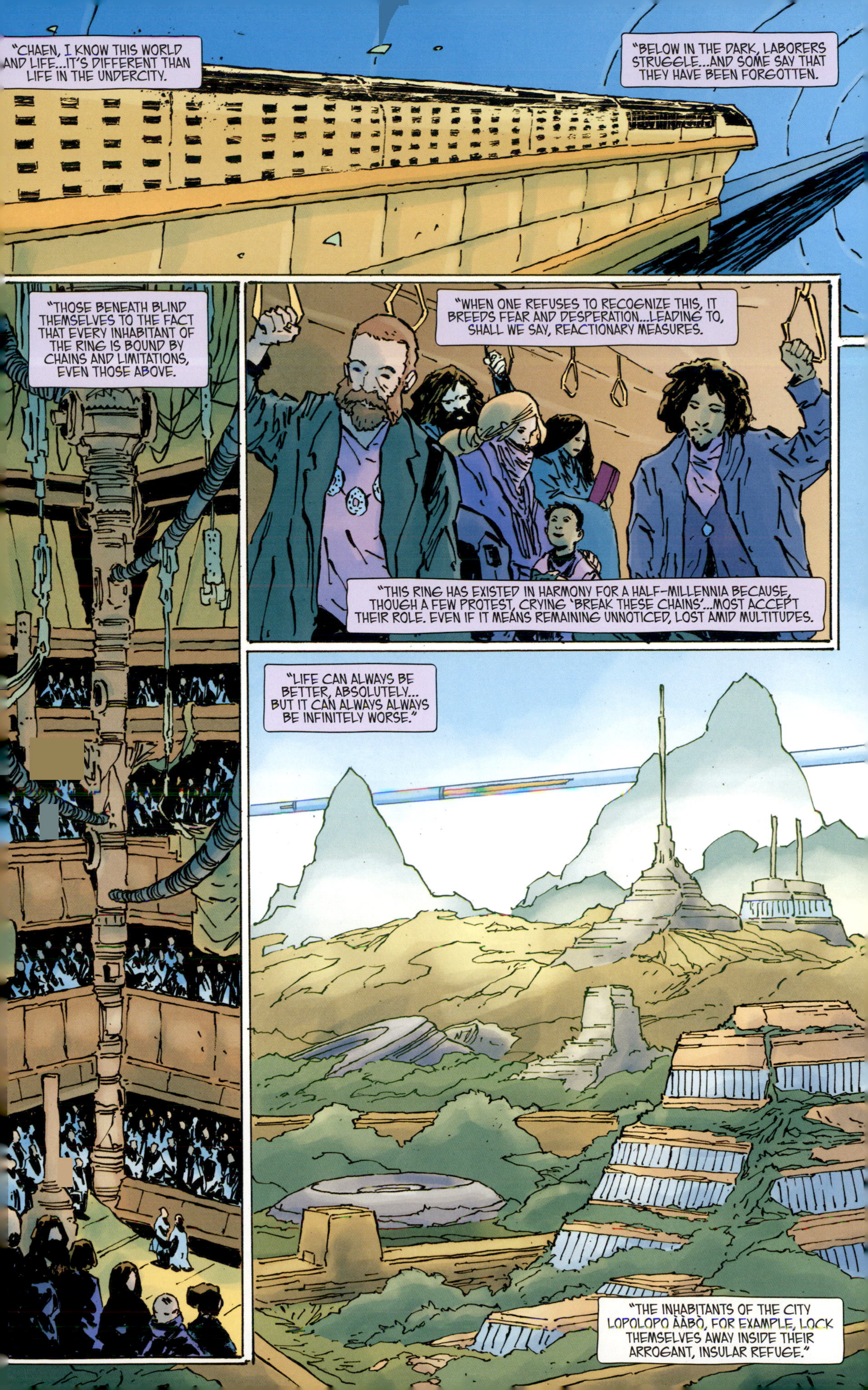
"CHAEN, I KNOW THIS WORLD AND LIFE...IT'S DIFFERENT THAN LIFE IN THE UNDERCITY.
"BELOW IN THE DARK, LABORERS STRUGGLE...AND SOME SAY THAT THEY HAVE BEEN FORGOTTEN.
"THOSE BENEATH BLIND THEMSELVES TO THE FACT THAT EVERY INHABITANT OF THE RING IS BOUND BY CHAINS AND LIMITATIONS, EVEN THOSE ABOVE.
"WHEN ONE REFUSES TO RECOGNIZE THIS, IT BREEDS FEAR AND DESPERATION...LEADING TO, SHALL WE SAY, REACTIONARY MEASURES.
"THIS RING HAS EXISTED IN HARMONY FOR A HALF-MILLENNIA BECAUSE, THOUGH A FEW PROTEST, CRYING 'BREAK THESE CHAINS'...MOST ACCEPT THEIR ROLE. EVEN IF IT MEANS REMAINING UNNOTICED, LOST AMID MULTITUDES.
"LIFE CAN ALWAYS BE BETTER, ABSOLUTELY... BUT IT CAN ALWAYS ALWAYS BE INFINITELY WORSE."
"THE INHABITANTS OF THE CITY LOPOLOPO ÀÀBÒ, FOR EXAMPLE, LOCK THEMSELVES AWAY INSIDE THEIR ARROGANT, INSULAR REFUGE."

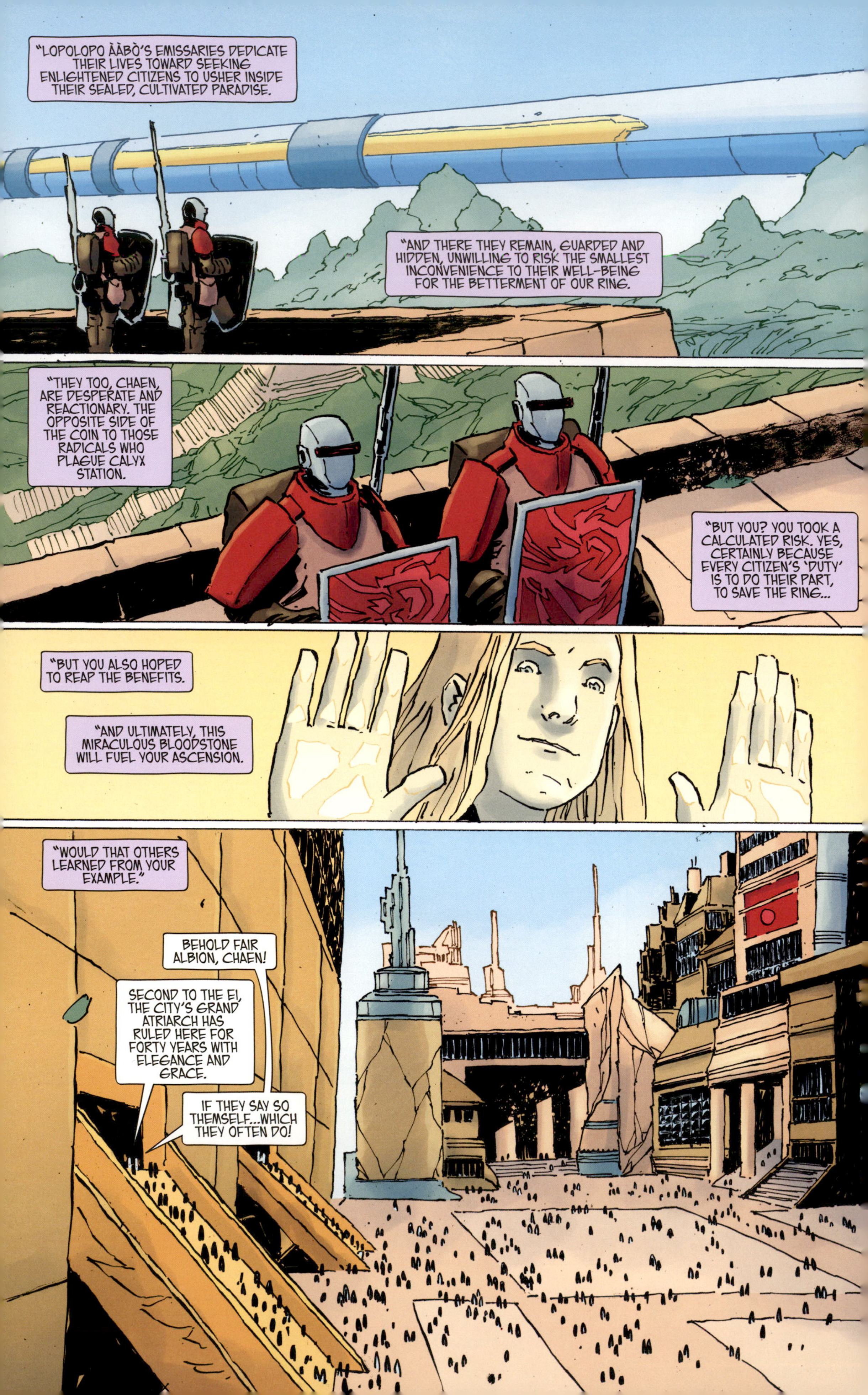
"LOPOLOPO ÀÀBÒ'S EMISSARIES DEDICATE THEIR LIVES TOWARD SEEKING ENLIGHTENED CITIZENS TO USHER INSIDE THEIR SEALED, CULTIVATED PARADISE.
"AND THERE THEY REMAIN, GUARDED AND HIDDEN, UNWILLING TO RISK THE SMALLEST INCONVENIENCE TO THEIR WELL-BEING FOR THE BETTERMENT OF OUR RING.
"THEY TOO, CHAEN, ARE DESPERATE AND REACTIONARY. THE OPPOSITE SIDE OF THE COIN TO THOSE RADICALS WHO PLAGUE CALYX STATION.
"BUT YOU? YOU TOOK A CALCULATED RISK. YES, CERTAINLY BECAUSE EVERY CITIZEN'S 'DUTY' IS TO DO THEIR PART, TO SAVE THE RING...
"BUT YOU ALSO HOPED TO REAP THE BENEFITS.
"AND ULTIMATELY, THIS MIRACULOUS BLOODSTONE WILL FUEL YOUR ASCENSION.
"WOULD THAT OTHERS LEARNED FROM YOUR EXAMPLE."
BEHOLD FAIR ALBION, CHAEN!
SECOND TO THE EI, THE CITY'S GRAND ATRIARCH HAS RULED HERE FOR FORTY YEARS WITH ELEGANCE AND GRACE.
IF THEY SAY SO THEMSELF...WHICH THEY OFTEN DO!

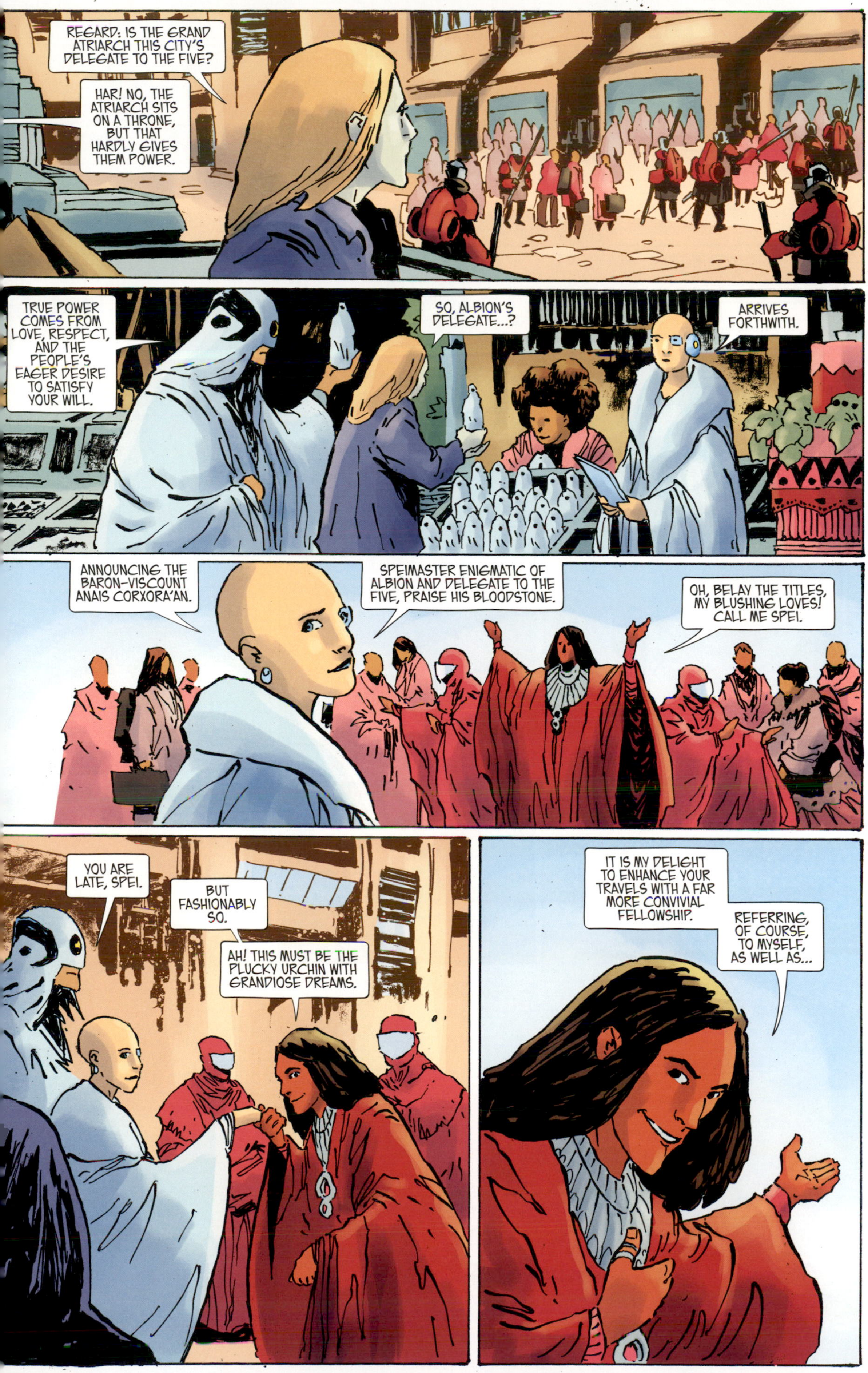
REGARD: IS THE GRAND ATRIARCH THIS CITY'S DELEGATE TO THE FIVE?
HAR! NO, THE ATRIARCH SITS ON A THRONE, BUT THAT HARDLY GIVES THEM POWER.
TRUE POWER COMES FROM LOVE, RESPECT, AND THE PEOPLE'S EAGER DESIRE TO SATISFY YOUR WILL.
SO, ALBION'S DELEGATE...?
ARRIVES FORTHWITH.
ANNOUNCING THE BARON-VISCOUNT ANAIS CORXORA'AN.
SPEIMASTER ENIGMATIC OF ALBION AND DELEGATE TO THE FIVE, PRAISE HIS BLOODSTONE.
OH, BELAY THE TITLES, MY BLUSHING LOVES! CALL ME SPEI.
YOU ARE LATE, SPEI.
BUT FASHIONABLY SO.
AH! THIS MUST BE THE PLUCKY URCHIN WITH GRANDIOSE DREAMS.
IT IS MY DELIGHT TO ENHANCE YOUR TRAVELS WITH A FAR MORE CONVIVIAL FELLOWSHIP.
REFERRING, OF COURSE, TO MYSELF, AS WELL AS...

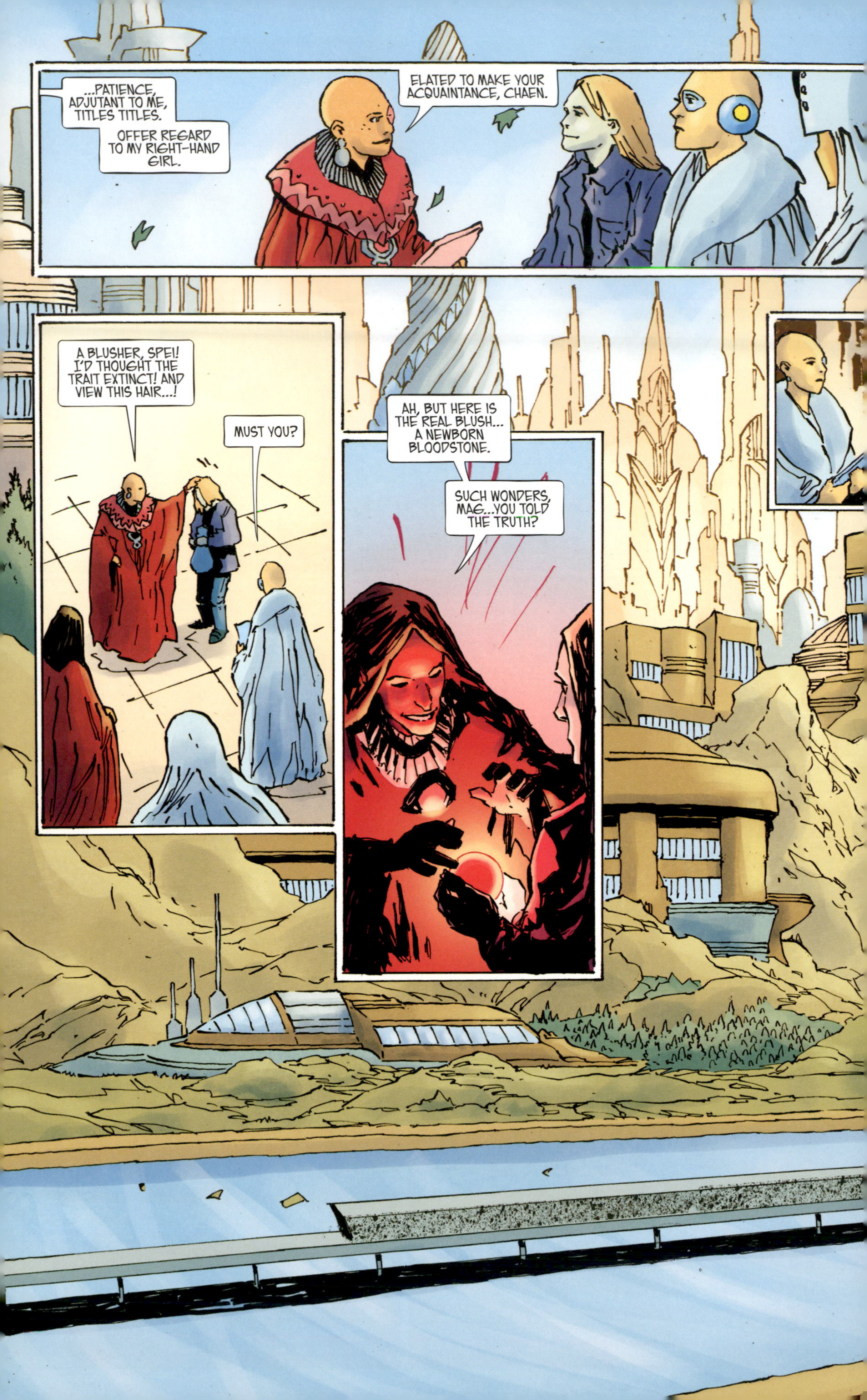
...PATIENCE, ADJUTANT TO ME, TITLES TITLES.
OFFER REGARD TO MY RIGHT-HAND GIRL.
ELATED TO MAKE YOUR ACQUAINTANCE, CHAEN.
A BLUSHER, SPEI! I'D THOUGHT THE TRAIT EXTINCT! AND VIEW THIS HAIR...!
MUST YOU?
AH, BUT HERE IS THE REAL BLUSH... A NEWBORN BLOODSTONE.
SUCH WONDERS, MAG...YOU TOLD THE TRUTH?

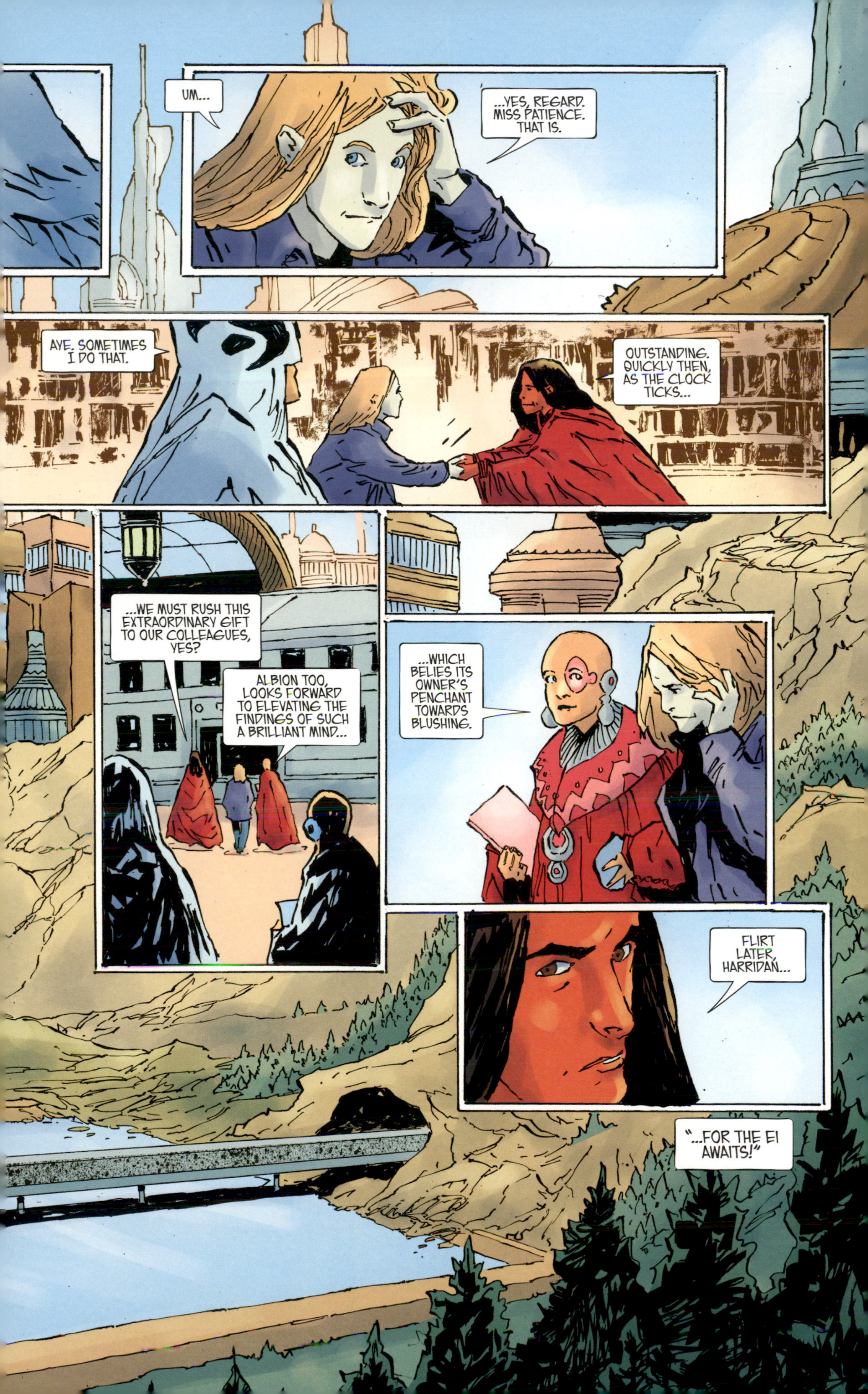
UM...
...YES, REGARD. MISS PATIENCE. THAT IS.
AYE. SOMETIMES I DO THAT.
OUTSTANDING. QUICKLY THEN, AS THE CLOCK TICKS...
...WE MUST RUSH THIS EXTRAORDINARY GIFT TO OUR COLLEAGUES, YES?
ALBION TOO, LOOKS FORWARD TO ELEVATING THE FINDINGS OF SUCH A BRILLIANT MIND...
...WHICH BELIES ITS OWNER'S PENCHANT TOWARDS BLUSHING.
FLIRT LATER, HARRIDAN...
"...FOR THE EI AWAITS!"

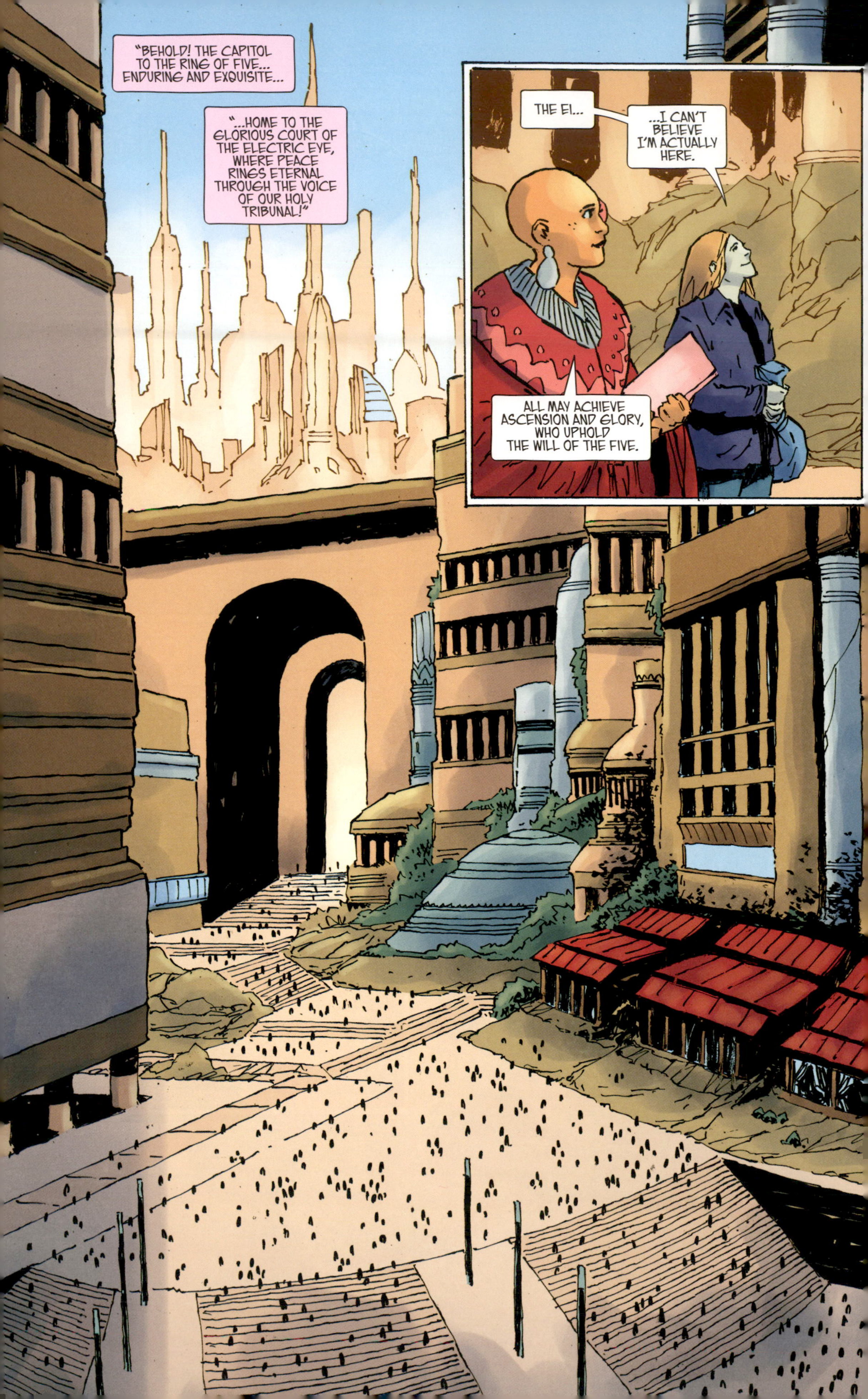
"BEHOLD! THE CAPITOL TO THE RING OF FIVE... ENDURING AND EXQUISITE...
"...HOME TO THE GLORIOUS COURT OF THE ELECTRIC EYE, WHERE PEACE RINGS ETERNAL THROUGH THE VOICE OF OUR HOLY TRIBUNAL!"
THE EI...
...I CAN'T BELIEVE I'M ACTUALLY HERE.
ALL MAY ACHIEVE ASCENSION AND GLORY, WHO UPHOLD THE WILL OF THE FIVE.

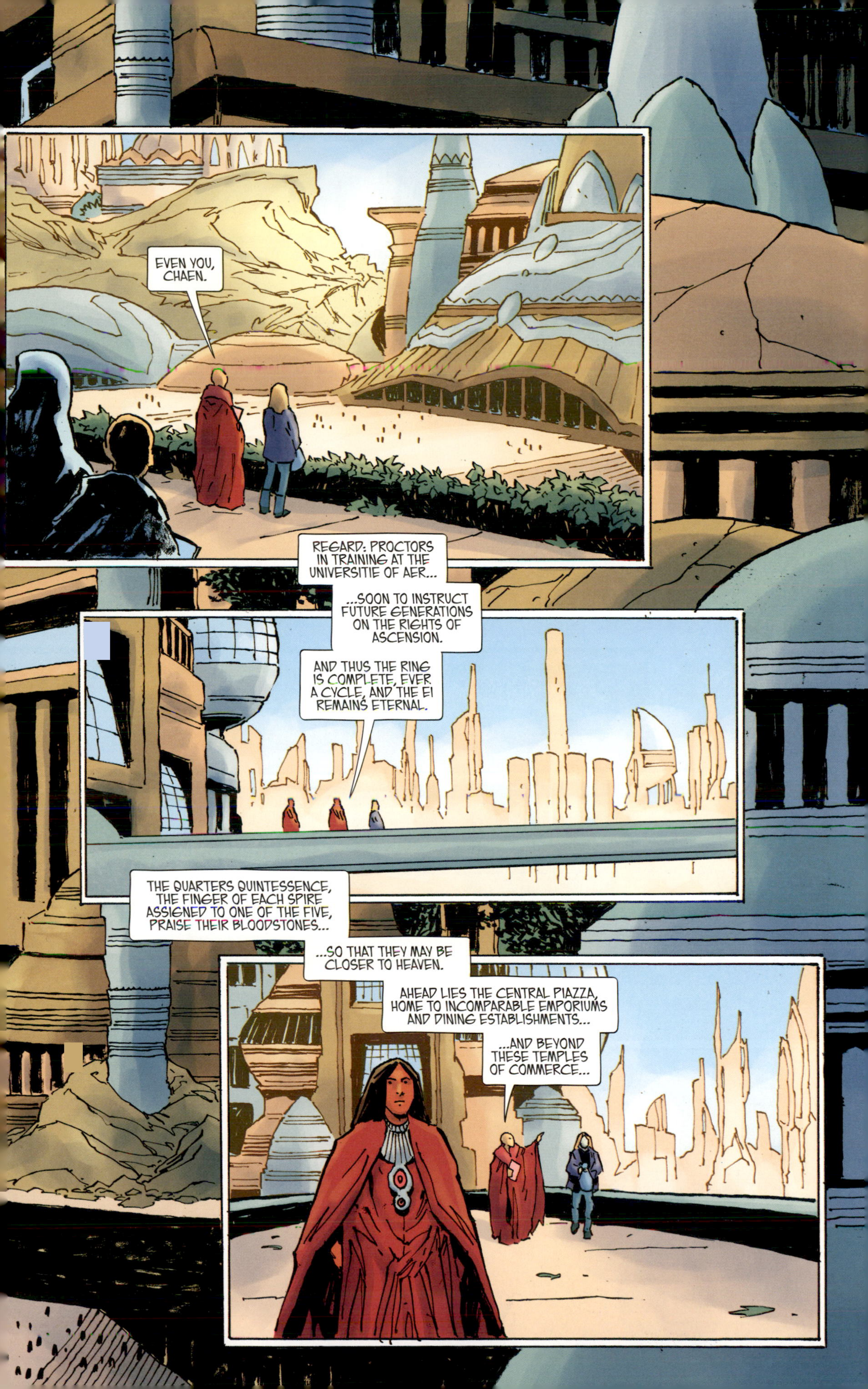
EVEN YOU, CHAEN.
REGARD: PROCTORS IN TRAINING AT THE UNIVERSITIE OF AER...
...SOON TO INSTRUCT FUTURE GENERATIONS ON THE RIGHTS OF ASCENSION.
AND THUS THE RING IS COMPLETE, EVER A CYCLE, AND THE EI REMAINS ETERNAL.
THE QUARTERS QUINTESSENCE, THE FINGER OF EACH SPIRE ASSIGNED TO ONE OF THE FIVE, PRAISE THEIR BLOODSTONES...
...SO THAT THEY MAY BE CLOSER TO HEAVEN.
AHEAD LIES THE CENTRAL PIAZZA, HOME TO INCOMPARABLE EMPORIUMS AND DINING ESTABLISHMENTS...
...AND BEYOND THESE TEMPLES OF COMMERCE...

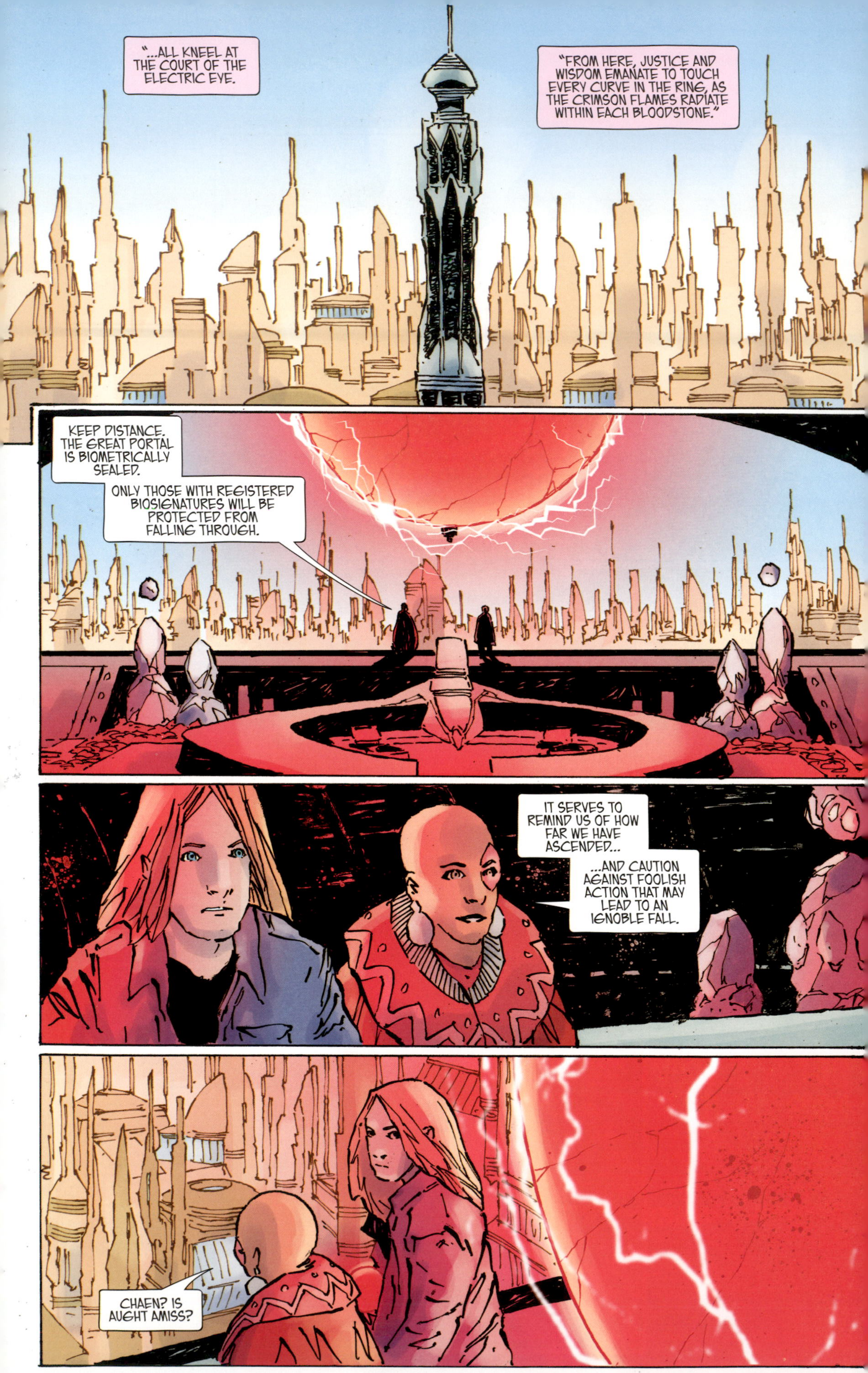
"...ALL KNEEL AT THE COURT OF THE ELECTRIC EYE.
"FROM HERE, JUSTICE AND WISDOM EMANATE TO TOUCH EVERY CURVE IN THE RING, AS THE CRIMSON FLAMES RADIATE WITHIN EACH BLOODSTONE."
KEEP DISTANCE. THE GREAT PORTAL IS BIOMETRICALLY SEALED.
ONLY THOSE WITH REGISTERED BIOSIGNATURES WILL BE PROTECTED FROM FALLING THROUGH.
IT SERVES TO REMIND US OF HOW FAR WE HAVE ASCENDED...
...AND CAUTION AGAINST FOOLISH ACTION THAT MAY LEAD TO AN IGNOBLE FALL.
CHAEN? IS AUGHT AMISS?

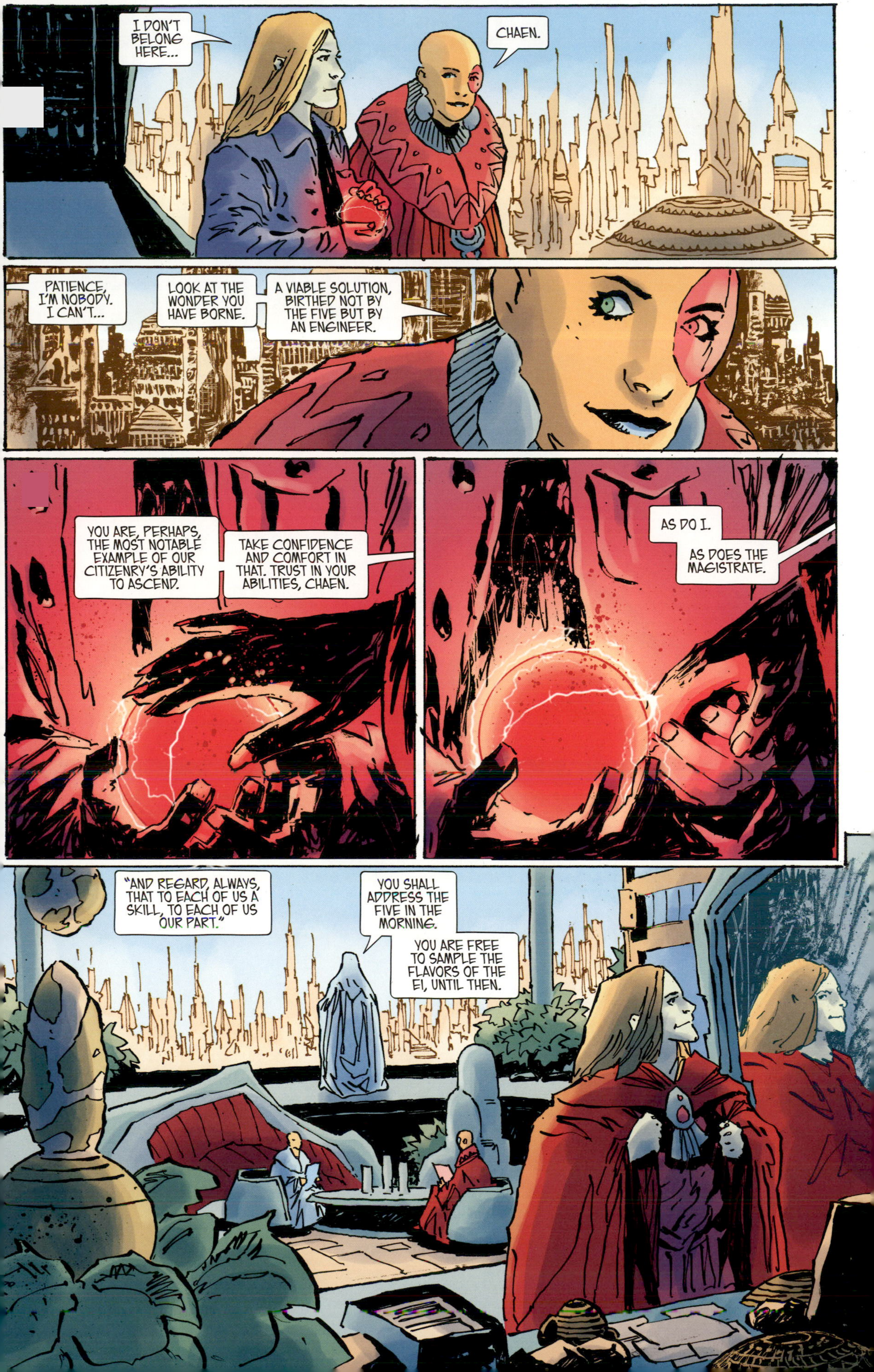
I DON'T BELONG HERE...
CHAEN.
PATIENCE, I'M NOBODY. I CAN'T...
LOOK AT THE WONDER YOU HAVE BORNE.
A VIABLE SOLUTION, BIRTHED NOT BY THE FIVE BUT BY AN ENGINEER.
YOU ARE, PERHAPS, THE MOST NOTABLE EXAMPLE OF OUR CITIZENRY'S ABILITY TO ASCEND.
TAKE CONFIDENCE AND COMFORT IN THAT. TRUST IN YOUR ABILITIES, CHAEN.
AS DO I.
AS DOES THE MAGISTRATE.
"AND REGARD, ALWAYS, THAT TO EACH OF US A SKILL, TO EACH OF US OUR PART."
YOU SHALL ADDRESS THE FIVE IN THE MORNING.
YOU ARE FREE TO SAMPLE THE FLAVORS OF THE EI, UNTIL THEN.

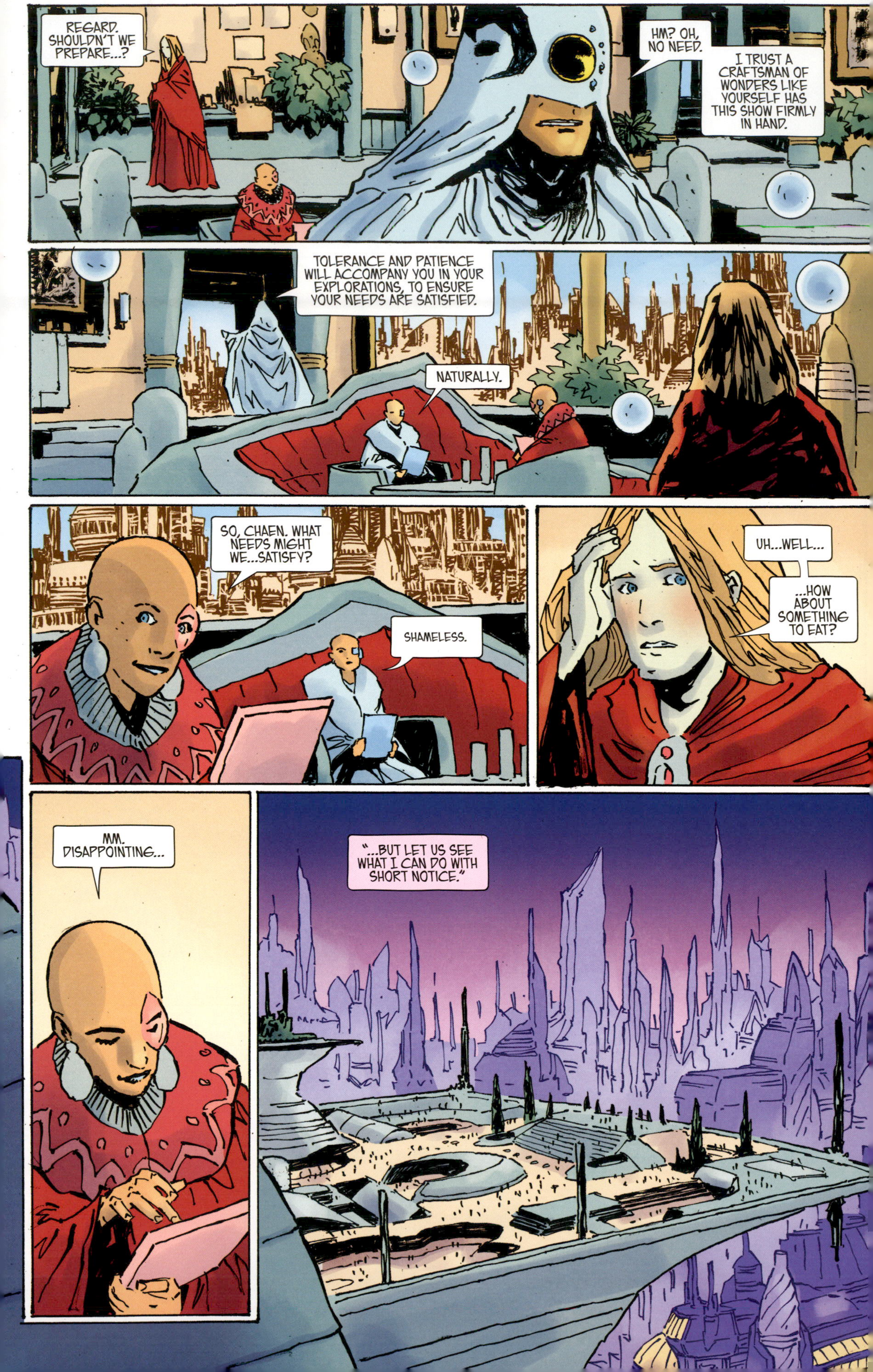
REGARD. SHOULDN'T WE PREPARE...?
HM? OH, NO NEED.
I TRUST A CRAFTSMAN OF WONDERS LIKE YOURSELF HAS THIS SHOW FIRMLY IN HAND.
TOLERANCE AND PATIENCE WILL ACCOMPANY YOU IN YOUR EXPLORATIONS, TO ENSURE YOUR NEEDS ARE SATISFIED.
NATURALLY.
SO, CHAEN. WHAT NEEDS MIGHT WE...SATISFY?
SHAMELESS.
UH...WELL...
...HOW ABOUT SOMETHING TO EAT?
MM. DISAPPOINTING...
"...BUT LET US SEE WHAT I CAN DO WITH SHORT NOTICE."

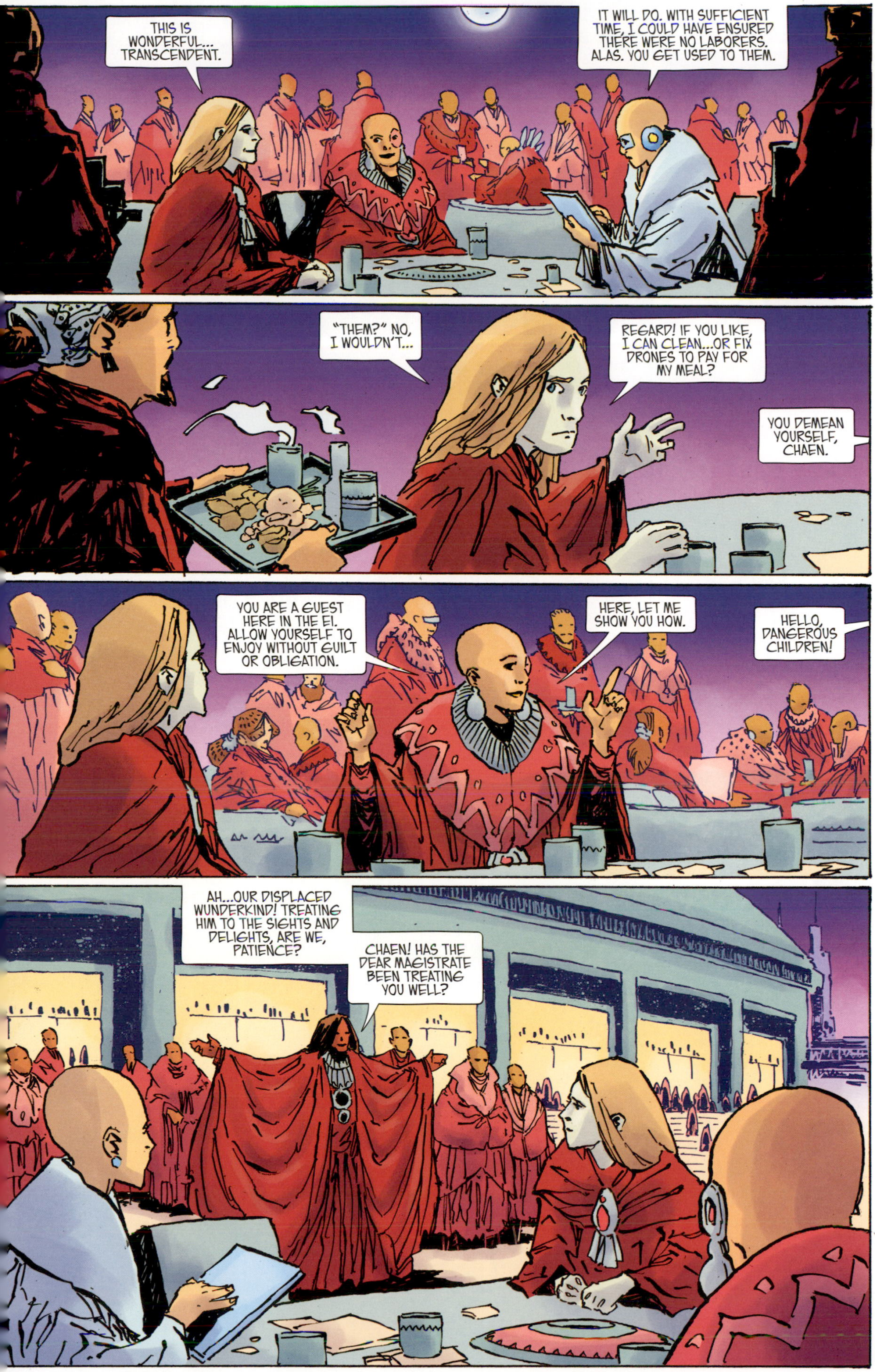
THIS IS WONDERFUL... TRANSCENDENT.
IT WILL DO. WITH SUFFICIENT TIME, I COULD HAVE ENSURED THERE WERE NO LABORERS. ALAS. YOU GET USED TO THEM.
"THEM?" NO, I WOULDN'T...
REGARD! IF YOU LIKE, I CAN CLEAN...OR FIX DRONES TO PAY FOR MY MEAL?
YOU DEMEAN YOURSELF, CHAEN.
YOU ARE A GUEST HERE IN THE EI. ALLOW YOURSELF TO ENJOY WITHOUT GUILT OR OBLIGATION.
HERE, LET ME SHOW YOU HOW.
HELLO, DANGEROUS CHILDREN!
AH...OUR DISPLACED WUNDERKIND! TREATING HIM TO THE SIGHTS AND DELIGHTS, ARE WE, PATIENCE?
CHAEN! HAS THE DEAR MAGISTRATE BEEN TREATING YOU WELL?

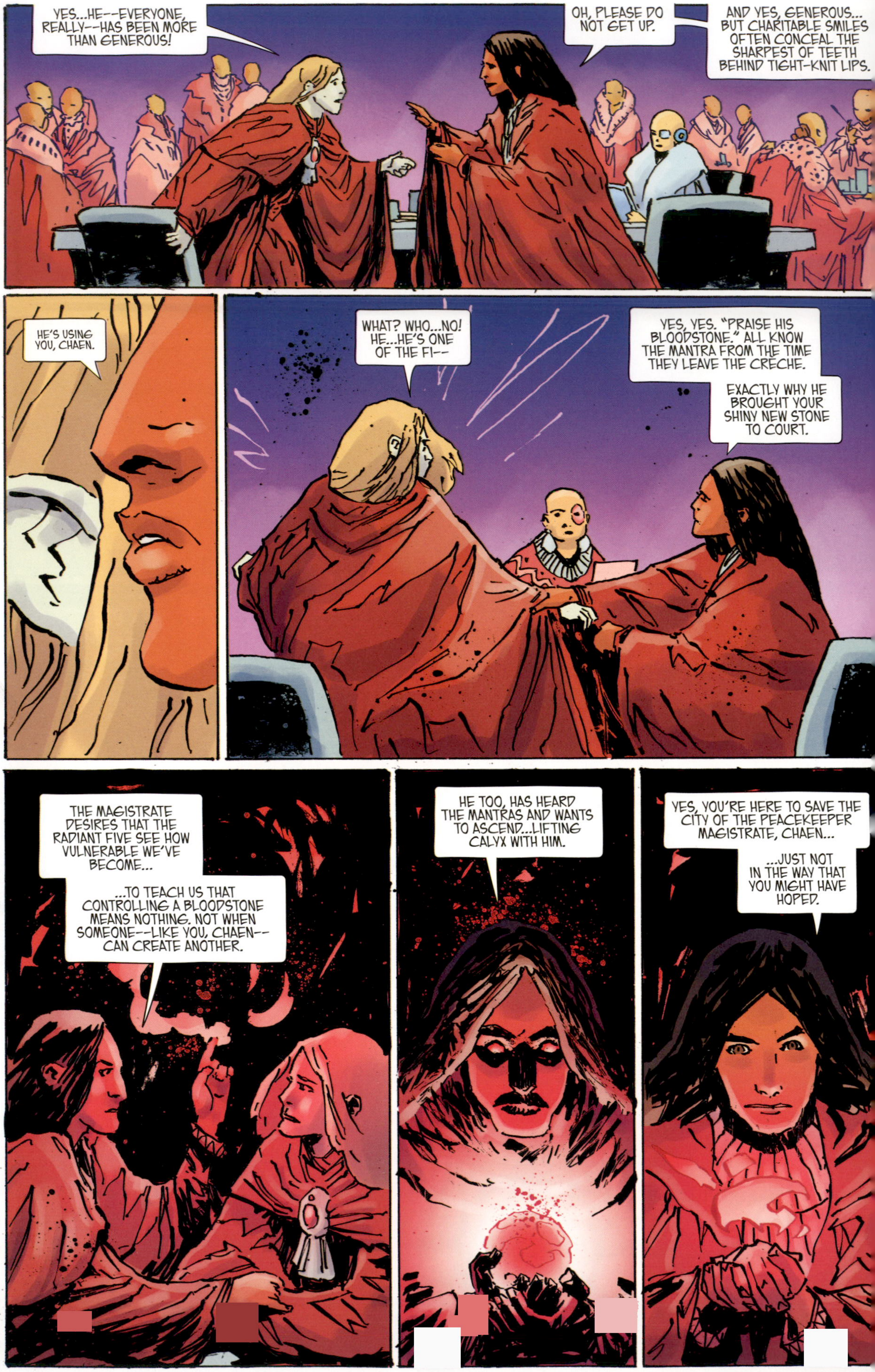
YES...HE--EVERYONE, REALLY--HAS BEEN MORE THAN GENEROUS!
OH, PLEASE DO NOT GET UP.
AND YES, GENEROUS... BUT CHARITABLE SMILES OFTEN CONCEAL THE SHARPEST OF TEETH BEHIND TIGHT-KNIT LIPS.
HE'S USING YOU, CHAEN.
WHAT? WHO...NO! HE...HE'S ONE OF THE FI--
YES, YES. "PRAISE HIS BLOODSTONE." ALL KNOW THE MANTRA FROM THE TIME THEY LEAVE THE CRECHE.
EXACTLY WHY HE BROUGHT YOUR SHINY NEW STONE TO COURT.
THE MAGISTRATE DESIRES THAT THE RADIANT FIVE SEE HOW VULNERABLE WE'VE BECOME...
...TO TEACH US THAT CONTROLLING A BLOODSTONE MEANS NOTHING. NOT WHEN SOMEONE--LIKE YOU, CHAEN--CAN CREATE ANOTHER.
HE TOO, HAS HEARD THE MANTRAS AND WANTS TO ASCEND...LIFTING CALYX WITH HIM.
YES, YOU'RE HERE TO SAVE THE CITY OF THE PEACEKEEPER MAGISTRATE, CHAEN...
...JUST NOT IN THE WAY THAT YOU MIGHT HAVE HOPED.

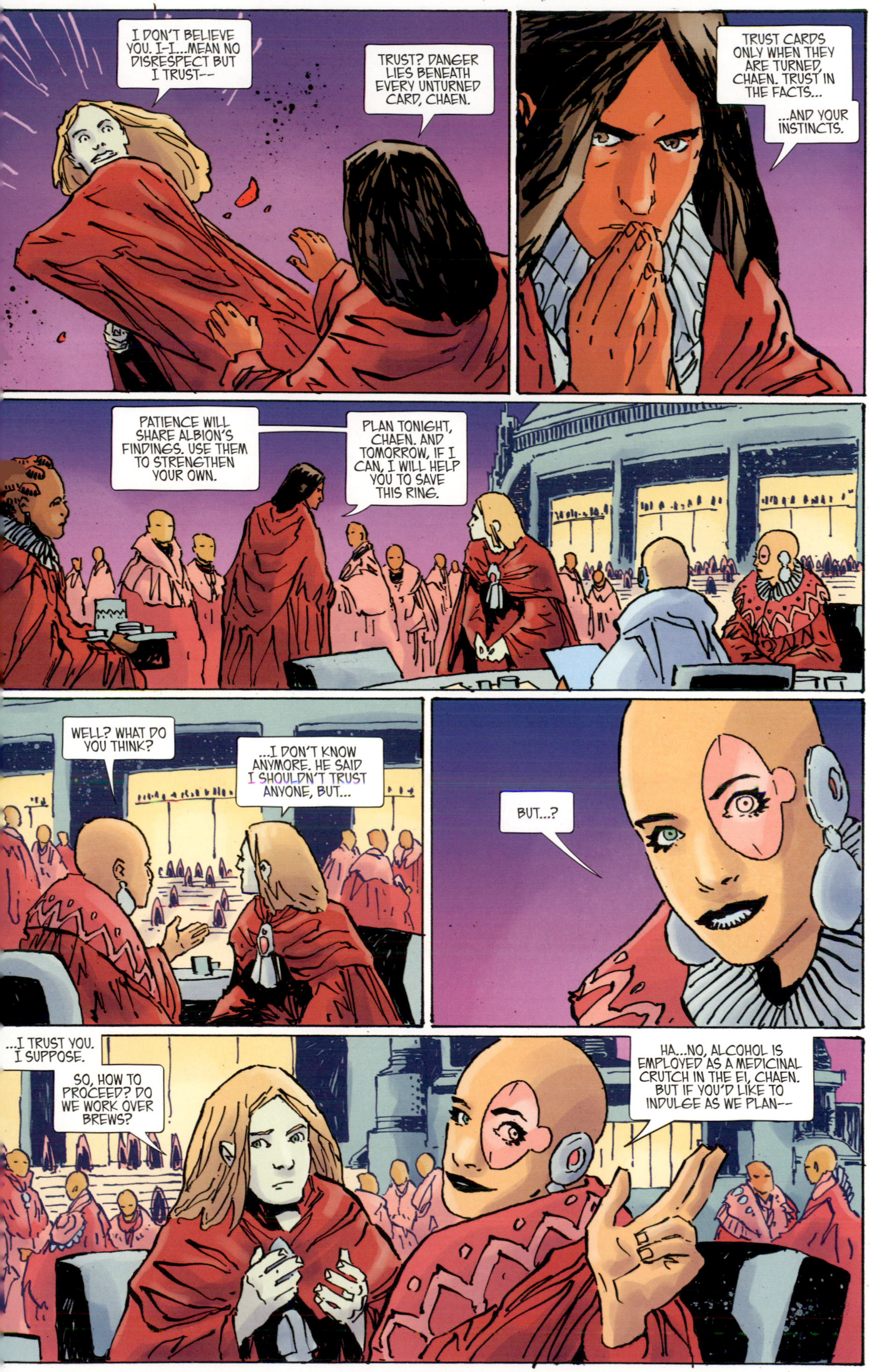
I DON'T BELIEVE YOU. I-I...MEAN NO DISRESPECT BUT I TRUST--
TRUST? DANGER LIES BENEATH EVERY UNTURNED CARD, CHAEN.
TRUST CARDS ONLY WHEN THEY ARE TURNED, CHAEN. TRUST IN THE FACTS...
...AND YOUR INSTINCTS.
PATIENCE WILL SHARE ALBION'S FINDINGS. USE THEM TO STRENGTHEN YOUR OWN.
PLAN TONIGHT, CHAEN. AND TOMORROW, IF I CAN, I WILL HELP YOU TO SAVE THIS RING.
WELL? WHAT DO YOU THINK?
...I DON'T KNOW ANYMORE. HE SAID I SHOULDN'T TRUST ANYONE, BUT...
BUT...?
...I TRUST YOU. I SUPPOSE.
SO, HOW TO PROCEED? DO WE WORK OVER BREWS?
HA...NO, ALCOHOL IS EMPLOYED AS A MEDICINAL CRUTCH IN THE EI, CHAEN. BUT IF YOU'D LIKE TO INDULGE AS WE PLAN--

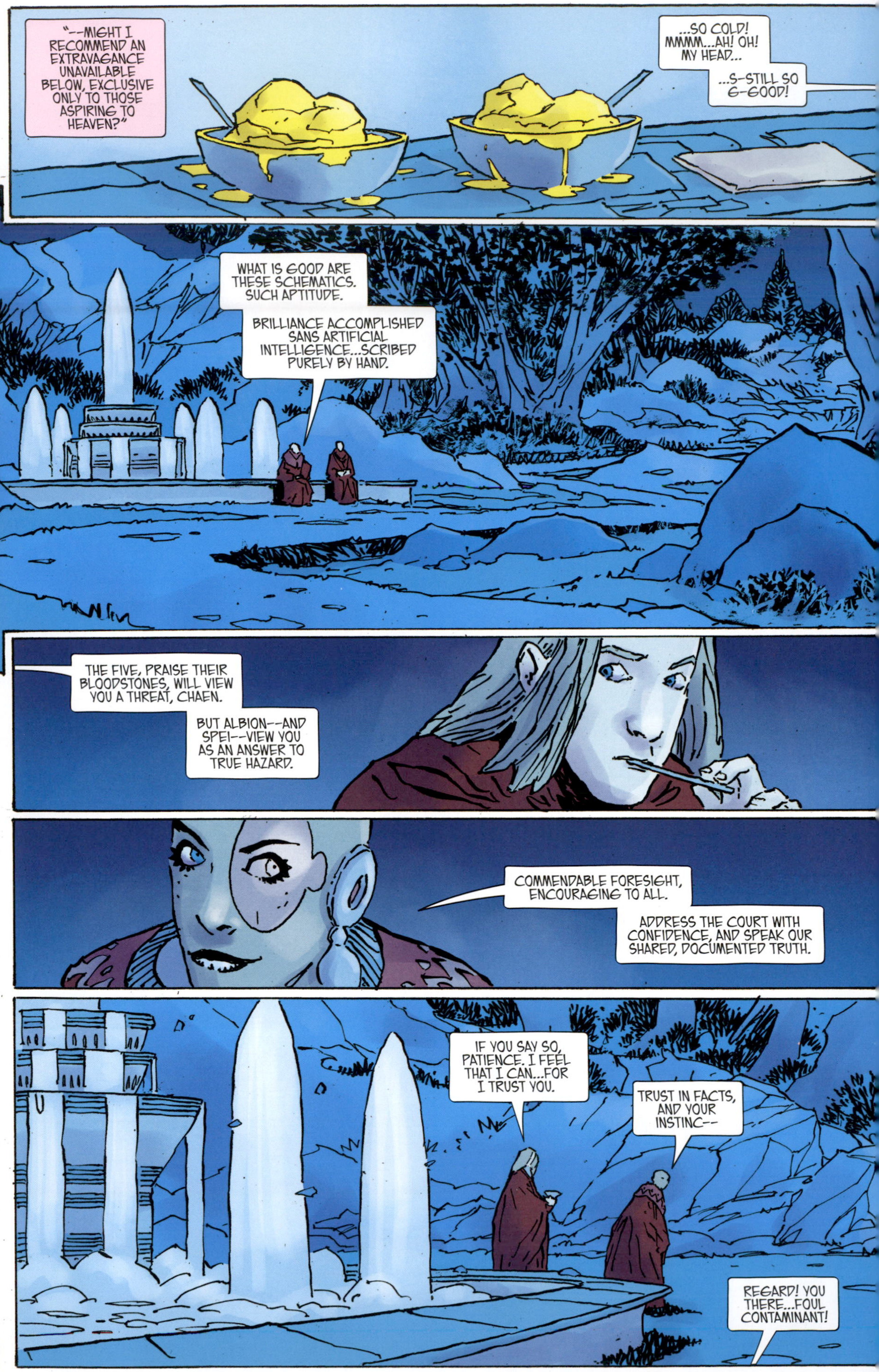
"--MIGHT I RECOMMEND AN EXTRAVAGANCE UNAVAILABLE BELOW, EXCLUSIVE ONLY TO THOSE ASPIRING TO HEAVEN?"
...SO COLD! MMMM...AH! OH! MY HEAD...
...S-STILL SO G-GOOD!
WHAT IS GOOD ARE THESE SCHEMATICS. SUCH APTITUDE.
BRILLIANCE ACCOMPLISHED SANS ARTIFICIAL INTELLIGENCE...SCRIBED PURELY BY HAND.
THE FIVE, PRAISE THEIR BLOODSTONES, WILL VIEW YOU A THREAT, CHAEN.
BUT ALBION--AND SPEI--VIEW YOU AS AN ANSWER TO TRUE HAZARD.
COMMENDABLE FORESIGHT, ENCOURAGING TO ALL.
ADDRESS THE COURT WITH CONFIDENCE, AND SPEAK OUR SHARED, DOCUMENTED TRUTH.
IF YOU SAY SO, PATIENCE. I FEEL THAT I CAN...FOR I TRUST YOU.
TRUST IN FACTS, AND YOUR INSTINC--
REGARD! YOU THERE...FOUL CONTAMINANT!

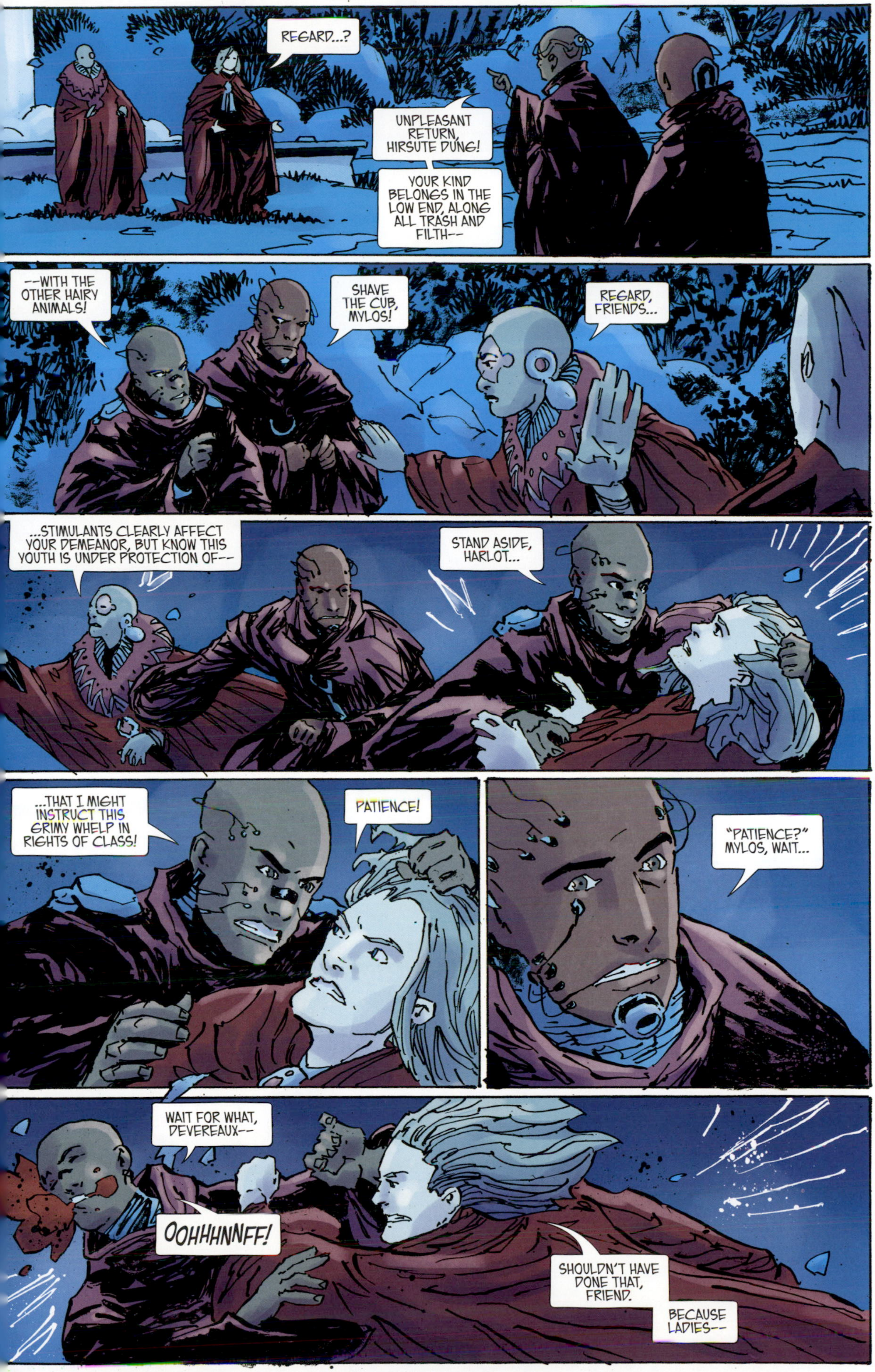
REGARD...?
UNPLEASANT RETURN, HIRSUTE DUNG!
YOUR KIND BELONGS IN THE LOW END, ALONG ALL TRASH AND FILTH--
--WITH THE OTHER HAIRY ANIMALS!
SHAVE THE CUB, MYLOS!
REGARD, FRIENDS...
...STIMULANTS CLEARLY AFFECT YOUR DEMEANOR, BUT KNOW THIS YOUTH IS UNDER PROTECTION OF--
STAND ASIDE, HARLOT...
...THAT I MIGHT INSTRUCT THIS GRIMY WHELP IN RIGHTS OF CLASS!
PATIENCE!
"PATIENCE?" MYLOS, WAIT...
WAIT FOR WHAT, DEVEREAUX--
OOHHHNNFF!
SHOULDN'T HAVE DONE THAT, FRIEND.
BECAUSE LADIES--

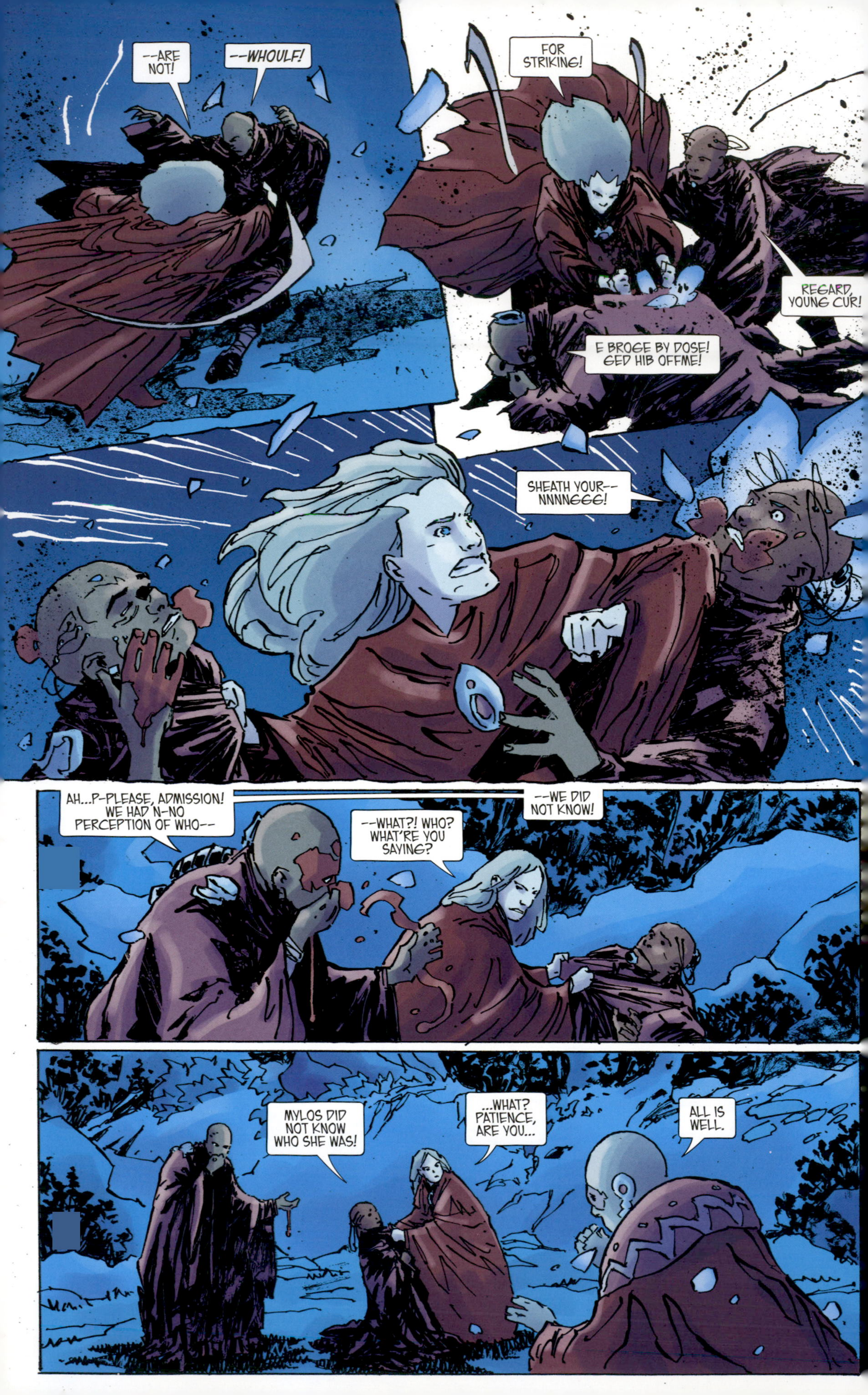
--ARE NOT!
--WHOULF!
FOR STRIKING!
REGARD, YOUNG CUR!
E BROGE BY DOSE! GED HIB OFFME!
SHEATH YOUR-- NNNNGGG!
AH...P-PLEASE, ADMISSION! WE HAD N-NO PERCEPTION OF WHO--
--WE DID NOT KNOW!
--WHAT?! WHO? WHAT'RE YOU SAYING?
MYLOS DID NOT KNOW WHO SHE WAS!
...WHAT? PATIENCE, ARE YOU...
ALL IS WELL.

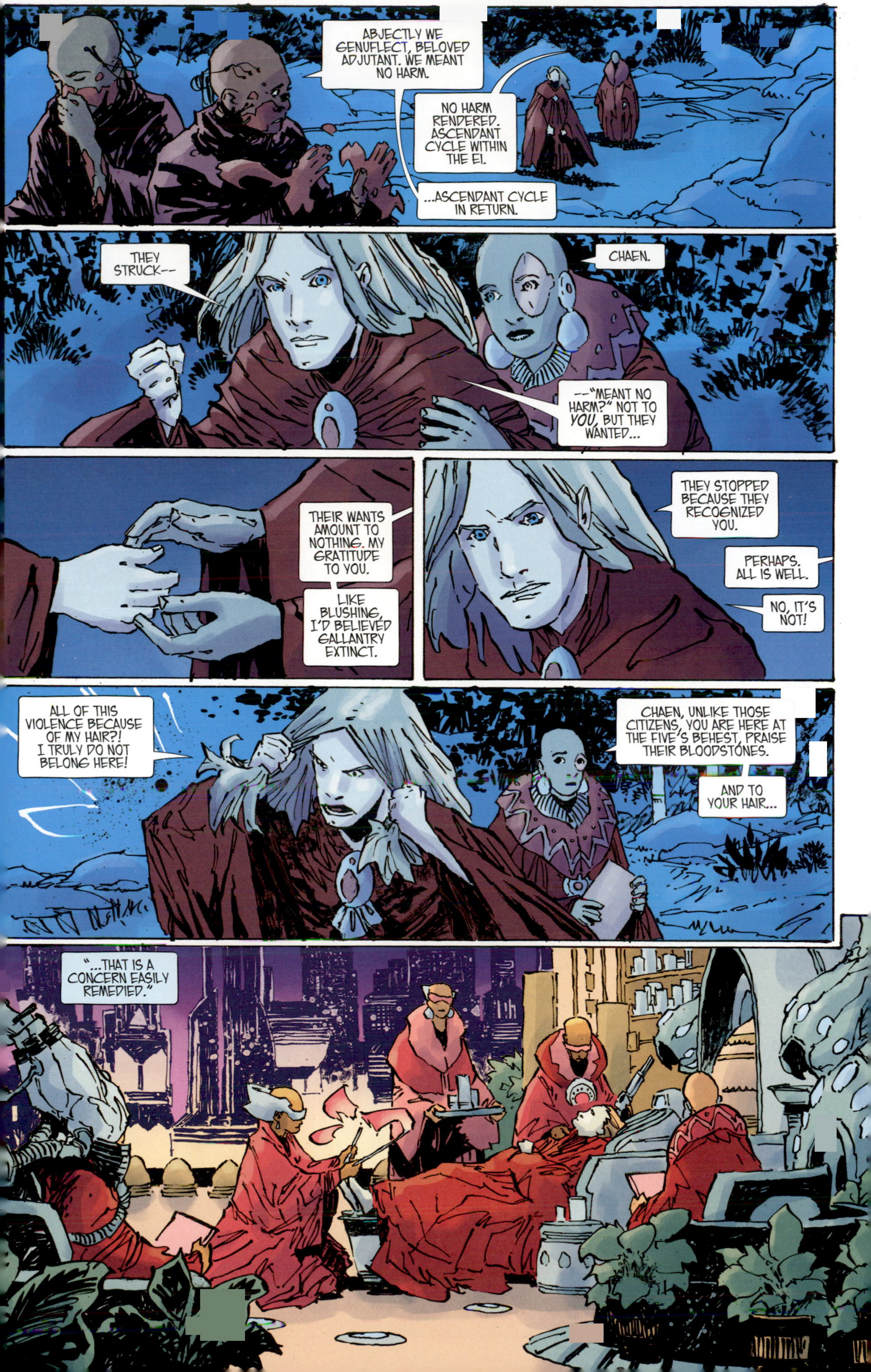
ABJECTLY WE GENUFLECT, BELOVED ADJUTANT. WE MEANT NO HARM.
NO HARM RENDERED. ASCENDANT CYCLE WITHIN THE EI.
...ASCENDANT CYCLE IN RETURN.
THEY STRUCK--
CHAEN.
--"MEANT NO HARM?" NOT TO YOU, BUT THEY WANTED...
THEIR WANTS AMOUNT TO NOTHING. MY GRATITUDE TO YOU.
LIKE BLUSHING, I'D BELIEVED GALLANTRY EXTINCT.
THEY STOPPED BECAUSE THEY RECOGNIZED YOU.
PERHAPS. ALL IS WELL.
NO, IT'S NOT!
ALL OF THIS VIOLENCE BECAUSE OF MY HAIR?! I TRULY DO NOT BELONG HERE!
CHAEN, UNLIKE THOSE CITIZENS, YOU ARE HERE AT THE FIVE'S BEHEST, PRAISE THEIR BLOODSTONES.
AND TO YOUR HAIR...
"...THAT IS A CONCERN EASILY REMEDIED."

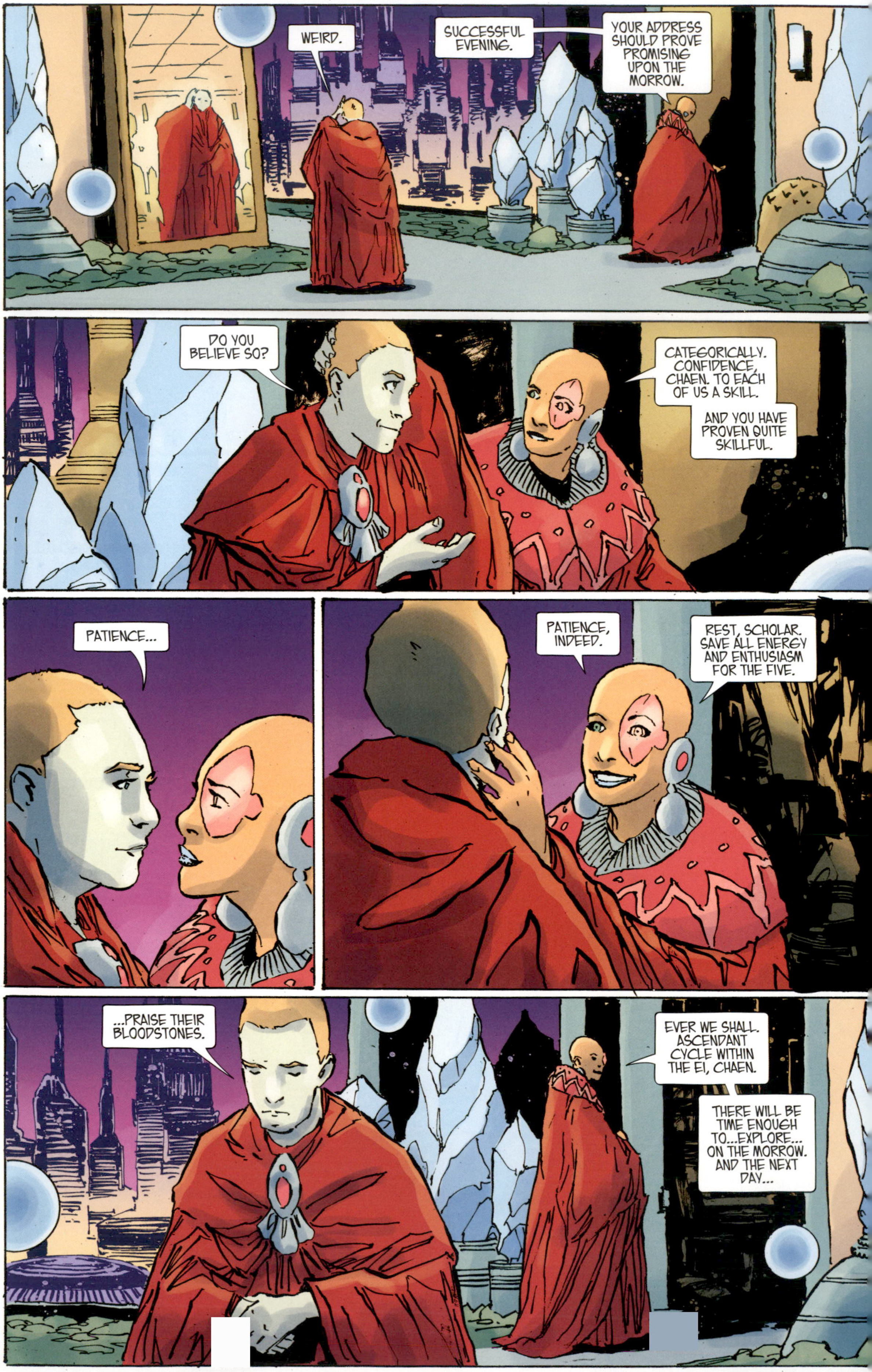
WEIRD.
SUCCESSFUL EVENING.
YOUR ADDRESS SHOULD PROVE PROMISING UPON THE MORROW.
DO YOU BELIEVE SO?
CATEGORICALLY. CONFIDENCE, CHAEN. TO EACH OF US A SKILL.
AND YOU HAVE PROVEN QUITE SKILLFUL.
PATIENCE...
PATIENCE, INDEED.
REST, SCHOLAR. SAVE ALL ENERGY AND ENTHUSIASM FOR THE FIVE.
...PRAISE THEIR BLOODSTONES.
EVER WE SHALL. ASCENDANT CYCLE WITHIN THE EI, CHAEN.
THERE WILL BE TIME ENOUGH TO...EXPLORE... ON THE MORROW. AND THE NEXT DAY...

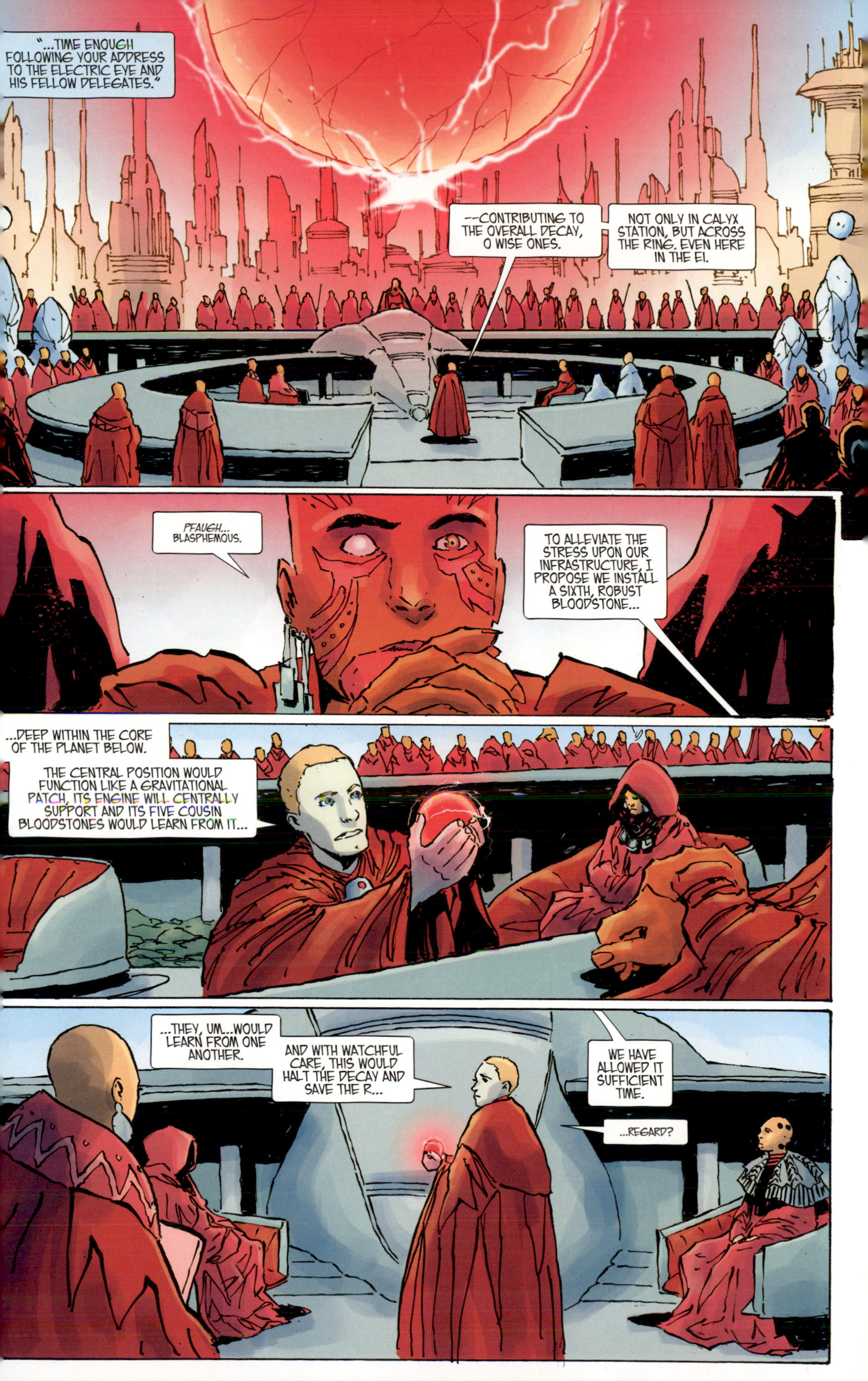
"...TIME ENOUGH FOLLOWING YOUR ADDRESS TO THE ELECTRIC EYE AND HIS FELLOW DELEGATES."
--CONTRIBUTING TO THE OVERALL DECAY, O WISE ONES.
NOT ONLY IN CALYX STATION, BUT ACROSS THE RING. EVEN HERE IN THE EI.
PFAUGH... BLASPHEMOUS.
TO ALLEVIATE THE STRESS UPON OUR INFRASTRUCTURE, I PROPOSE WE INSTALL A SIXTH, ROBUST BLOODSTONE...
...DEEP WITHIN THE CORE OF THE PLANET BELOW.
THE CENTRAL POSITION WOULD FUNCTION LIKE A GRAVITATIONAL PATCH, ITS ENGINE WILL CENTRALLY SUPPORT AND ITS FIVE COUSIN BLOODSTONES WOULD LEARN FROM IT...
...THEY, UM...WOULD LEARN FROM ONE ANOTHER.
AND WITH WATCHFUL CARE, THIS WOULD HALT THE DECAY AND SAVE THE R...
WE HAVE ALLOWED IT SUFFICIENT TIME.
...REGARD?

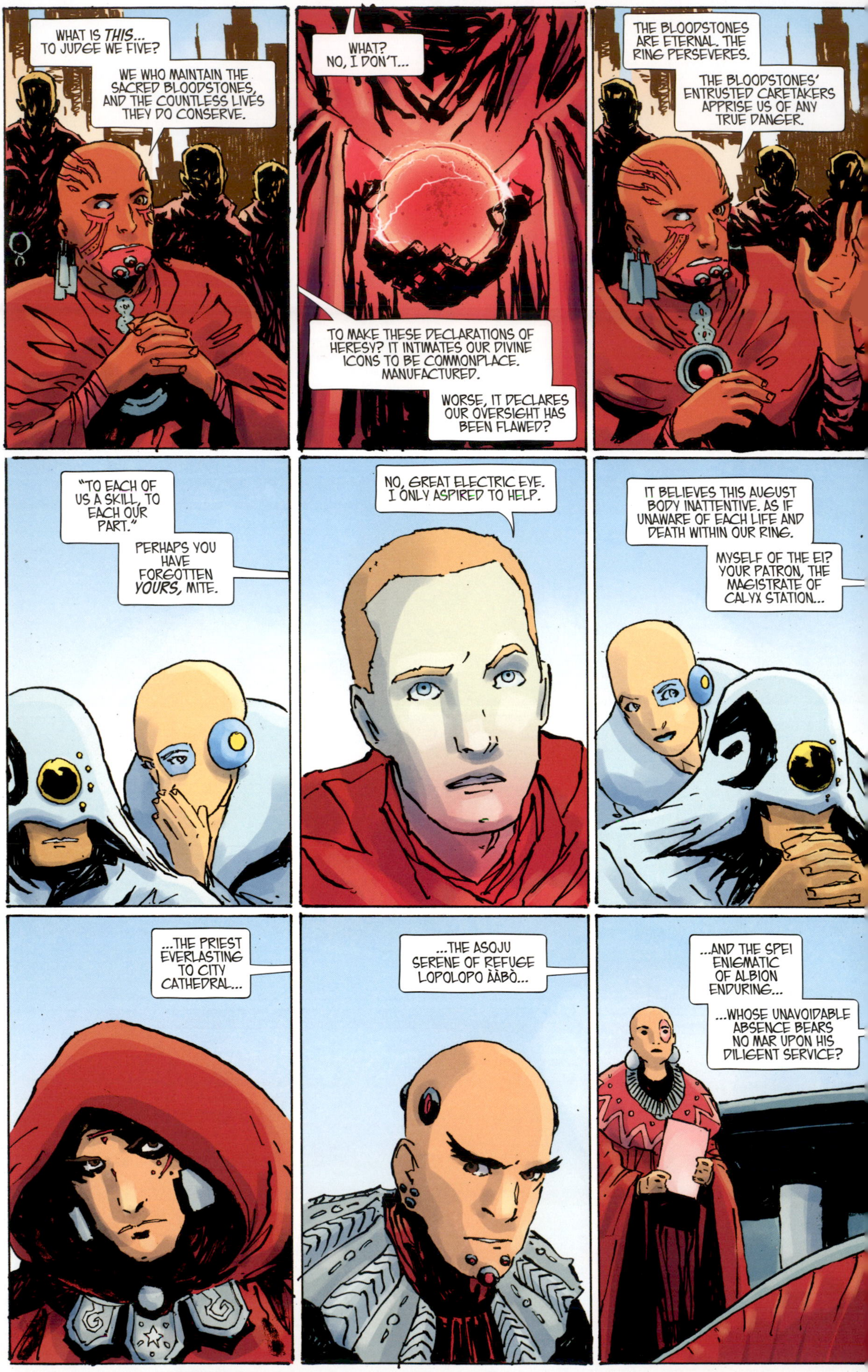
WHAT IS THIS... TO JUDGE WE FIVE?
WE WHO MAINTAIN THE SACRED BLOODSTONES, AND THE COUNTLESS LIVES THEY DO CONSERVE.
WHAT? NO, I DON'T...
TO MAKE THESE DECLARATIONS OF HERESY? IT INTIMATES OUR DIVINE ICONS TO BE COMMONPLACE. MANUFACTURED.
WORSE, IT DECLARES OUR OVERSIGHT HAS BEEN FLAWED?
THE BLOODSTONES ARE ETERNAL. THE RING PERSEVERES.
THE BLOODSTONES' ENTRUSTED CARETAKERS APPRISE US OF ANY TRUE DANGER.
"TO EACH OF US A SKILL, TO EACH OUR PART."
PERHAPS YOU HAVE FORGOTTEN YOURS, MITE.
NO, GREAT ELECTRIC EYE. I ONLY ASPIRED TO HELP.
IT BELIEVES THIS AUGUST BODY INATTENTIVE. AS IF UNAWARE OF EACH LIFE AND DEATH WITHIN OUR RING.
MYSELF OF THE EI? YOUR PATRON, THE MAGISTRATE OF CALYX STATION...
...THE PRIEST EVERLASTING TO CITY CATHEDRAL...
...THE ASOJU SERENE OF REFUGE LOPOLOPO ÀÀBÒ...
...AND THE SPEI ENIGMATIC OF ALBION ENDURING...
...WHOSE UNAVOIDABLE ABSENCE BEARS NO MAR UPON HIS DILIGENT SERVICE?

THIS CONTRIVER DARES BELIEVE OUR EYES BLIND, OUR HEARTS UNAWARE...

...BOTH TO UNAVOIDABLE CATASTROPHE AND ITS TRANSPARENT, OPPORTUNISTIC SACRILEGE?

BUT IT *IS* AVOIDABLE! IF YOU'LL SIMPLY LISTEN--

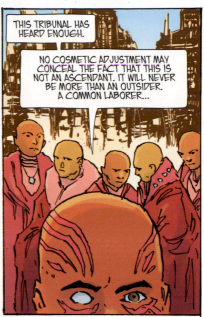

THIS TRIBUNAL HAS HEARD ENOUGH.

NO COSMETIC ADJUSTMENT MAY CONCEAL THE FACT THAT THIS IS NOT AN ASCENDANT. IT WILL NEVER BE MORE THAN AN OUTSIDER. A COMMON LABORER...

...AND A RADICAL.

WHAT...? *NO!* REGARD--

DARE NOT DENY IT.

THIS...ALLEGES OUR NEGLECT FOR THIS RING AS IT APPROACHES TOUTING A PROFANE APPARATUS...

...HOPING TO POSITION A...SCARLET ATROCITY... AS IF IT MIGHT REPLACE THE THROBBING HEARTS OF OUR RING.

ACCURATELY SPOKEN, DELEGATE EYE.

THE GAMIN WOULD HAVE US RATIFY HIM SAVIOR.

IT MOCKS OUR *BELIEFS*, DELEGATE MAGISTRATE!

IS CALYX NOT ASCENDANT? OR HAS IT BRED A NEST OF INSURGENTS, WHOSE FILTH HIDES BENEATH ANGELIC FACADE?

NO! I'M NOT A TRAITOR.

THESE ARE ALBION'S FINDINGS, TOO! SPEI GAVE THEM TO ME! THEY CONCUR--

DO THEY?

APPROACH AND PRODUCE YOUR EVIDENCE.

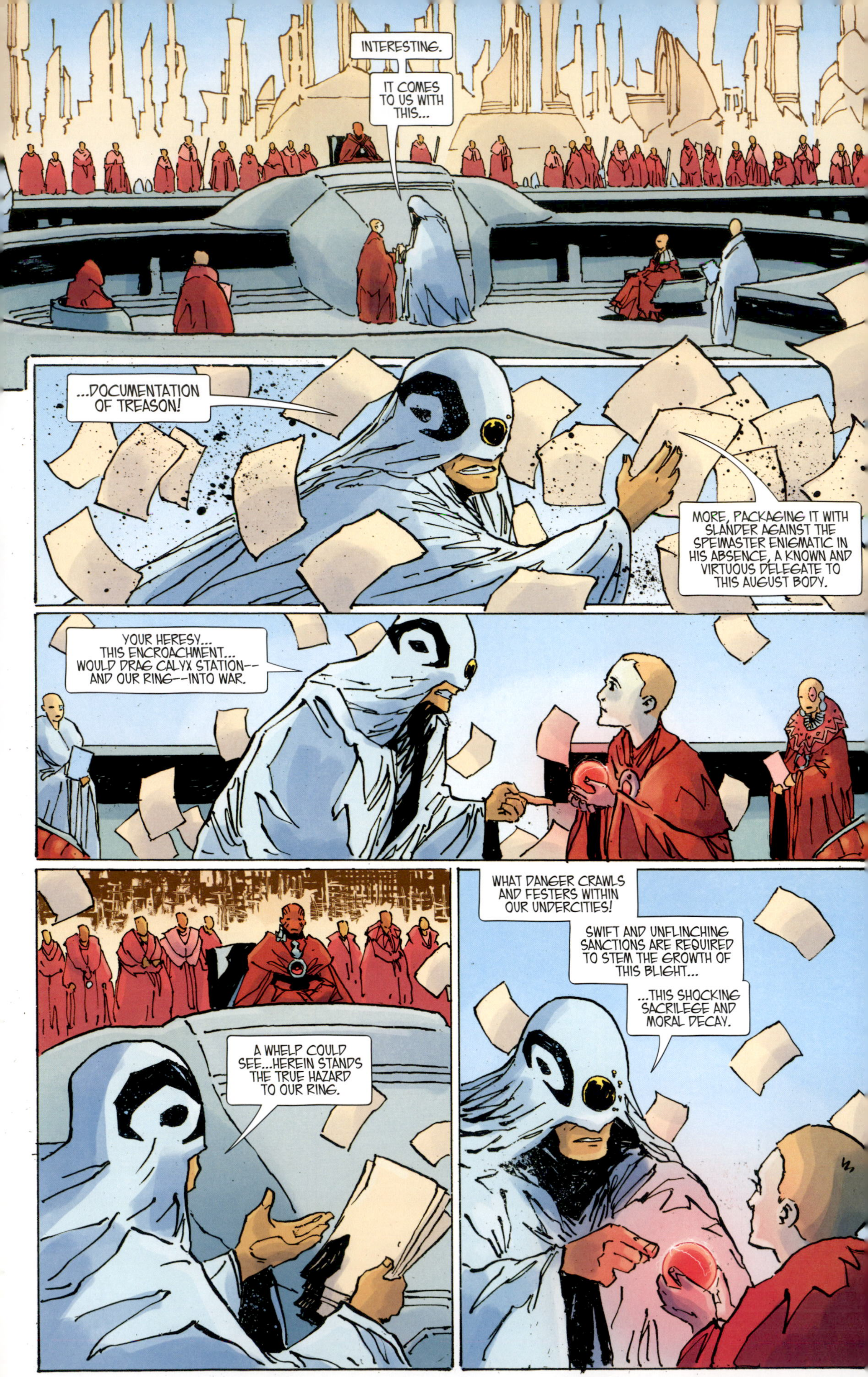
INTERESTING.
IT COMES TO US WITH THIS...
...DOCUMENTATION OF TREASON!
MORE, PACKAGING IT WITH SLANDER AGAINST THE SPEIMASTER ENIGMATIC IN HIS ABSENCE, A KNOWN AND VIRTUOUS DELEGATE TO THIS AUGUST BODY.
YOUR HERESY... THIS ENCROACHMENT... WOULD DRAG CALYX STATION-- AND OUR RING--INTO WAR.
A WHELP COULD SEE...HEREIN STANDS THE TRUE HAZARD TO OUR RING.
WHAT DANGER CRAWLS AND FESTERS WITHIN OUR UNDERCITIES!
SWIFT AND UNFLINCHING SANCTIONS ARE REQUIRED TO STEM THE GROWTH OF THIS BLIGHT...
...THIS SHOCKING SACRILEGE AND MORAL DECAY.

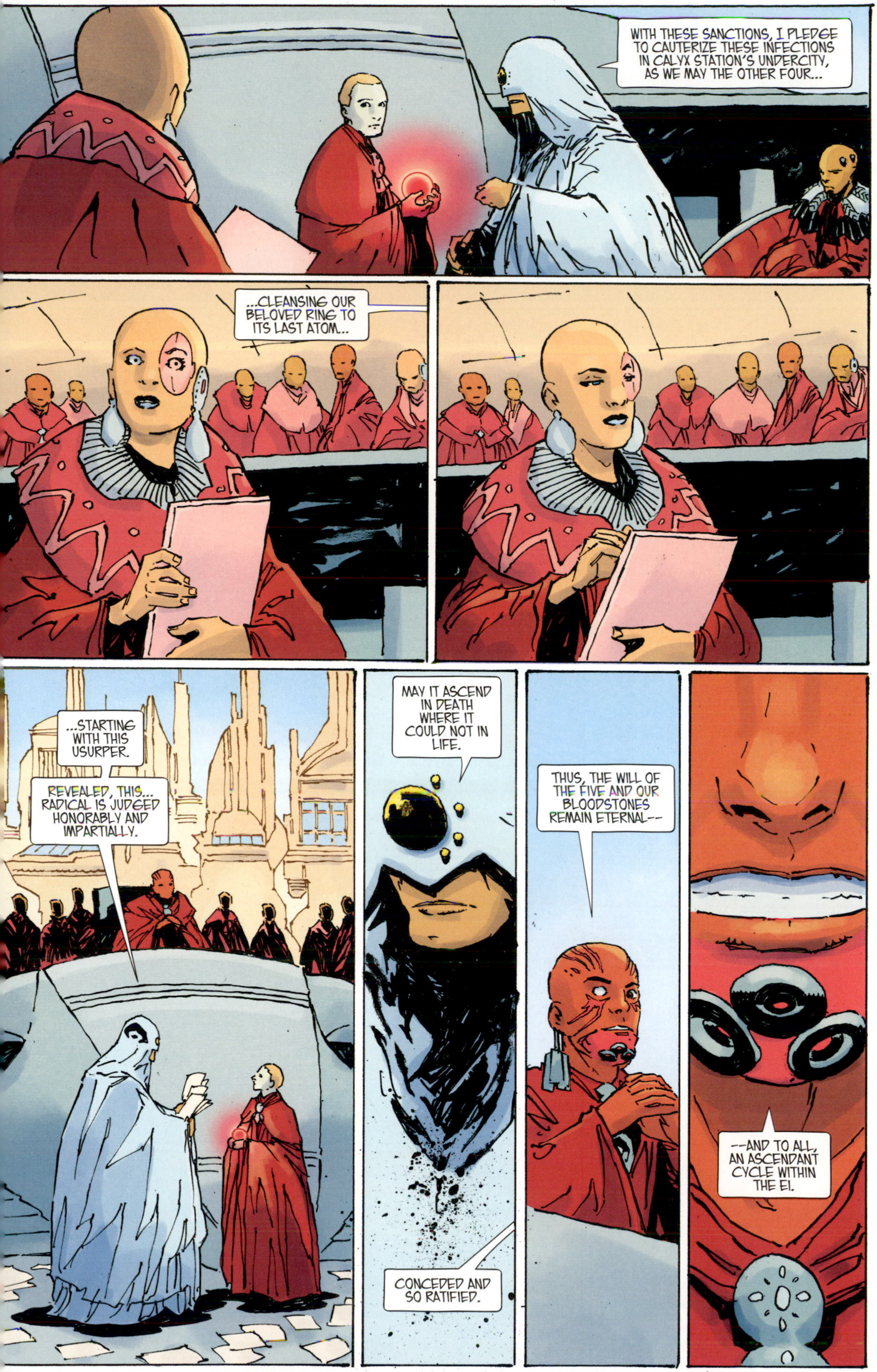
WITH THESE SANCTIONS, I PLEDGE TO CAUTERIZE THESE INFECTIONS IN CALYX STATION'S UNDERCITY, AS WE MAY THE OTHER FOUR...
...CLEANSING OUR BELOVED RING TO ITS LAST ATOM...
...STARTING WITH THIS USURPER.
REVEALED, THIS... RADICAL IS JUDGED HONORABLY AND IMPARTIALLY.
MAY IT ASCEND IN DEATH WHERE IT COULD NOT IN LIFE.
CONCEDED AND SO RATIFIED.
THUS, THE WILL OF THE FIVE AND OUR BLOODSTONES REMAIN ETERNAL--
--AND TO ALL, AN ASCENDANT CYCLE WITHIN THE EI.

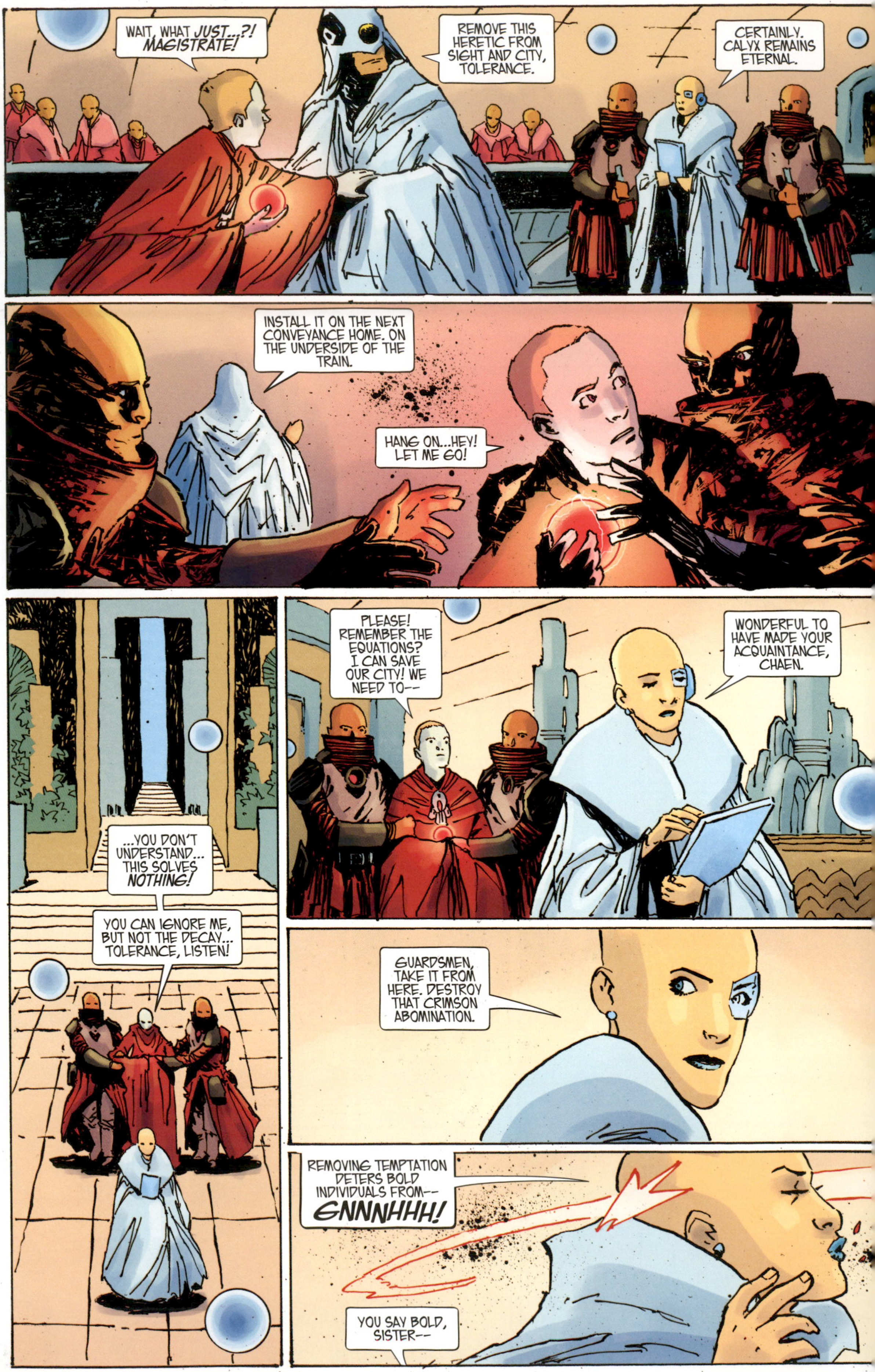
WAIT, WHAT JUST...?! MAGISTRATE!
REMOVE THIS HERETIC FROM SIGHT AND CITY, TOLERANCE.
CERTAINLY. CALYX REMAINS ETERNAL.
INSTALL IT ON THE NEXT CONVEYANCE HOME. ON THE UNDERSIDE OF THE TRAIN.
HANG ON...HEY! LET ME GO!
PLEASE! REMEMBER THE EQUATIONS? I CAN SAVE OUR CITY! WE NEED TO--
WONDERFUL TO HAVE MADE YOUR ACQUAINTANCE, CHAEN.
...YOU DON'T UNDERSTAND... THIS SOLVES NOTHING!
YOU CAN IGNORE ME, BUT NOT THE DECAY... TOLERANCE, LISTEN!
GUARDSMEN, TAKE IT FROM HERE. DESTROY THAT CRIMSON ABOMINATION.
REMOVING TEMPTATION DETERS BOLD INDIVIDUALS FROM-- GNNNHHH!
YOU SAY BOLD, SISTER--

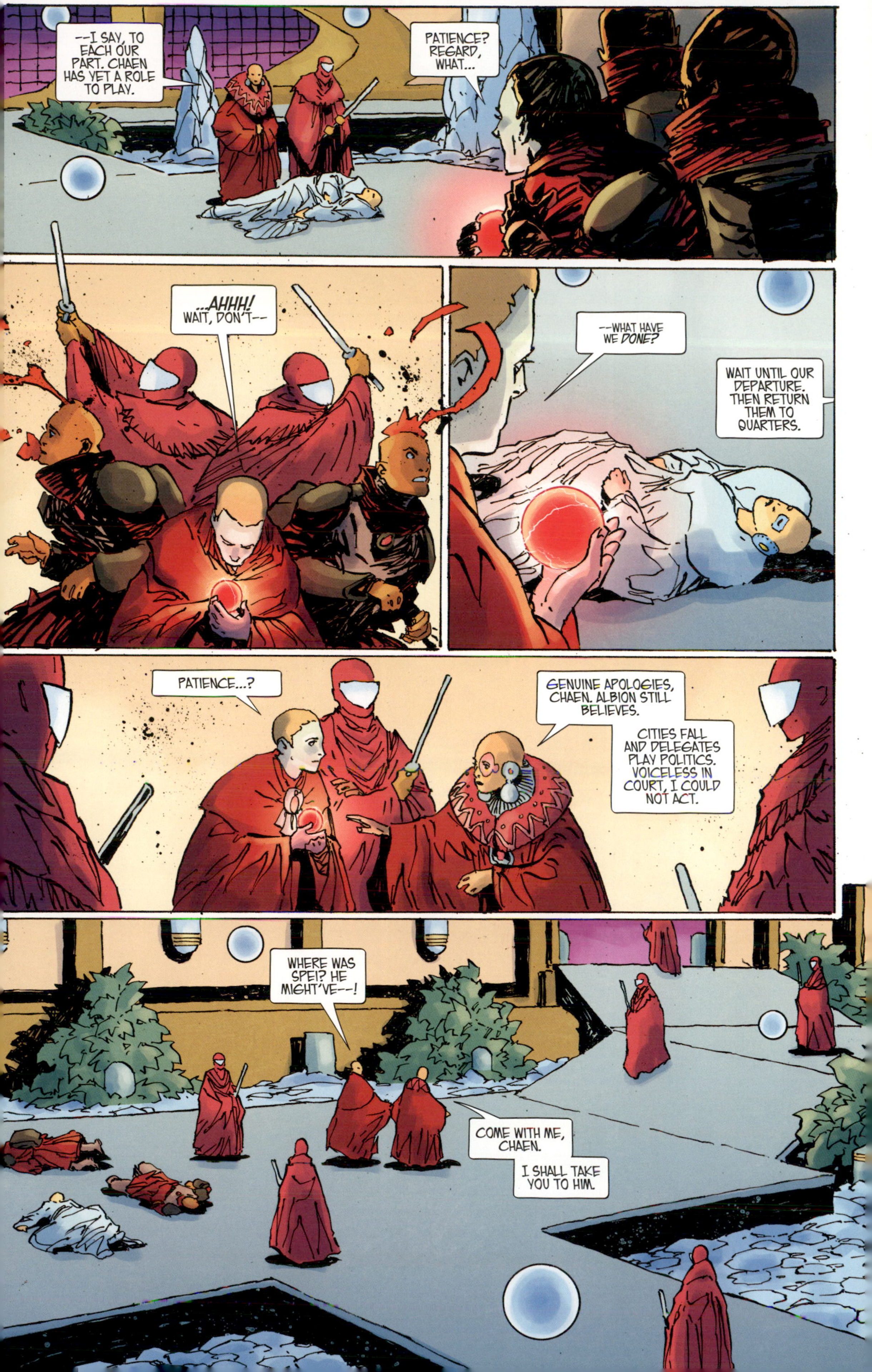
--I SAY, TO EACH OUR PART. CHAEN HAS YET A ROLE TO PLAY.
PATIENCE? REGARD, WHAT...
...AHHH! WAIT, DON'T--
--WHAT HAVE WE DONE?
WAIT UNTIL OUR DEPARTURE. THEN RETURN THEM TO QUARTERS.
PATIENCE...?
GENUINE APOLOGIES, CHAEN. ALBION STILL BELIEVES.
CITIES FALL AND DELEGATES PLAY POLITICS. VOICELESS IN COURT, I COULD NOT ACT.
WHERE WAS SPEI? HE MIGHT'VE--!
COME WITH ME, CHAEN.
I SHALL TAKE YOU TO HIM.

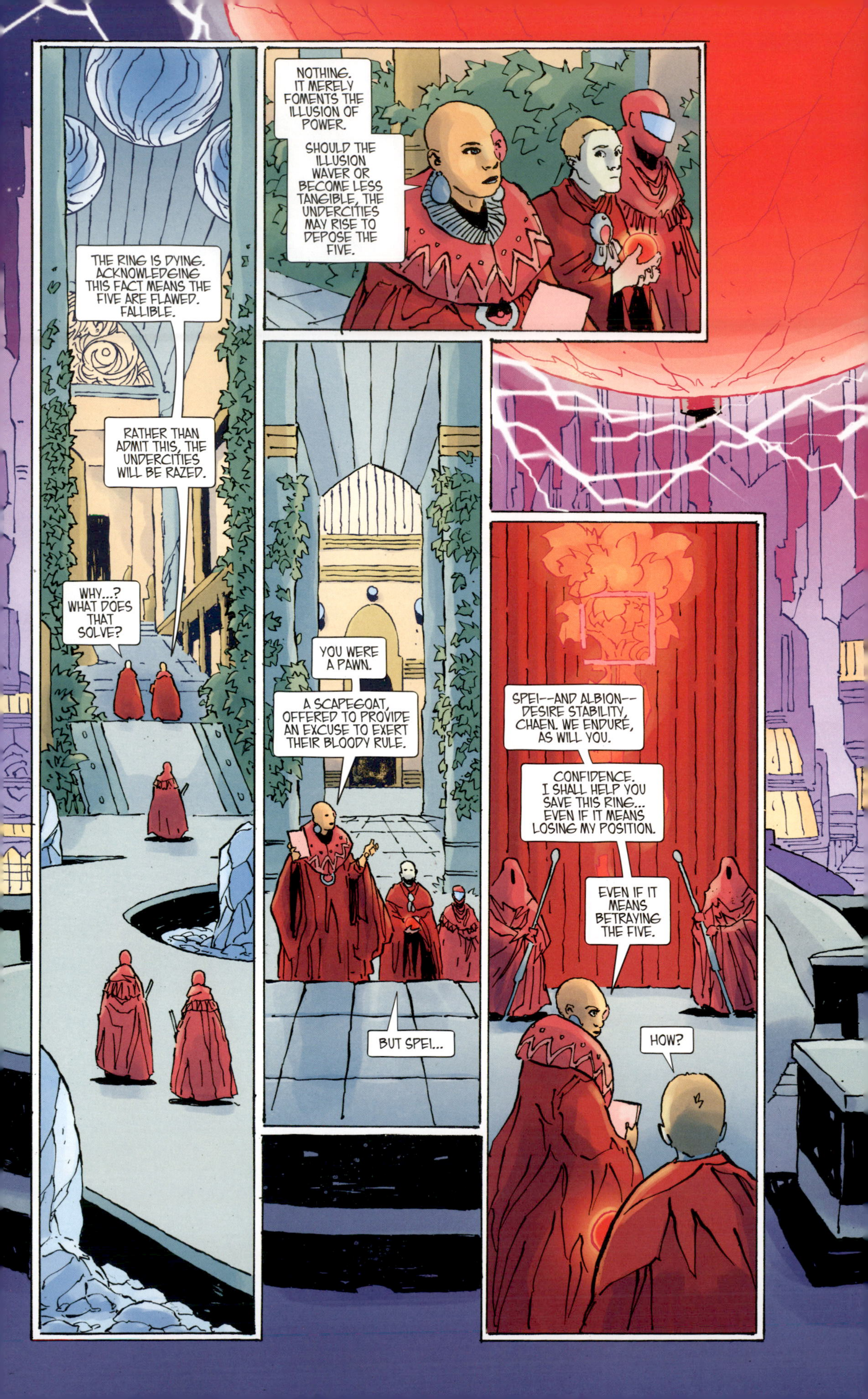
THE RING IS DYING. ACKNOWLEDGING THIS FACT MEANS THE FIVE ARE FLAWED. FALLIBLE.
RATHER THAN ADMIT THIS, THE UNDERCITIES WILL BE RAZED.
WHY...? WHAT DOES THAT SOLVE?
NOTHING. IT MERELY FOMENTS THE ILLUSION OF POWER.
SHOULD THE ILLUSION WAVER OR BECOME LESS TANGIBLE, THE UNDERCITIES MAY RISE TO DEPOSE THE FIVE.
YOU WERE A PAWN.
A SCAPEGOAT, OFFERED TO PROVIDE AN EXCUSE TO EXERT THEIR BLOODY RULE.
BUT SPEI...
SPEI--AND ALBION--DESIRE STABILITY, CHAEN. WE ENDURÉ, AS WILL YOU.
CONFIDENCE. I SHALL HELP YOU SAVE THIS RING... EVEN IF IT MEANS LOSING MY POSITION.
EVEN IF IT MEANS BETRAYING THE FIVE.
HOW?

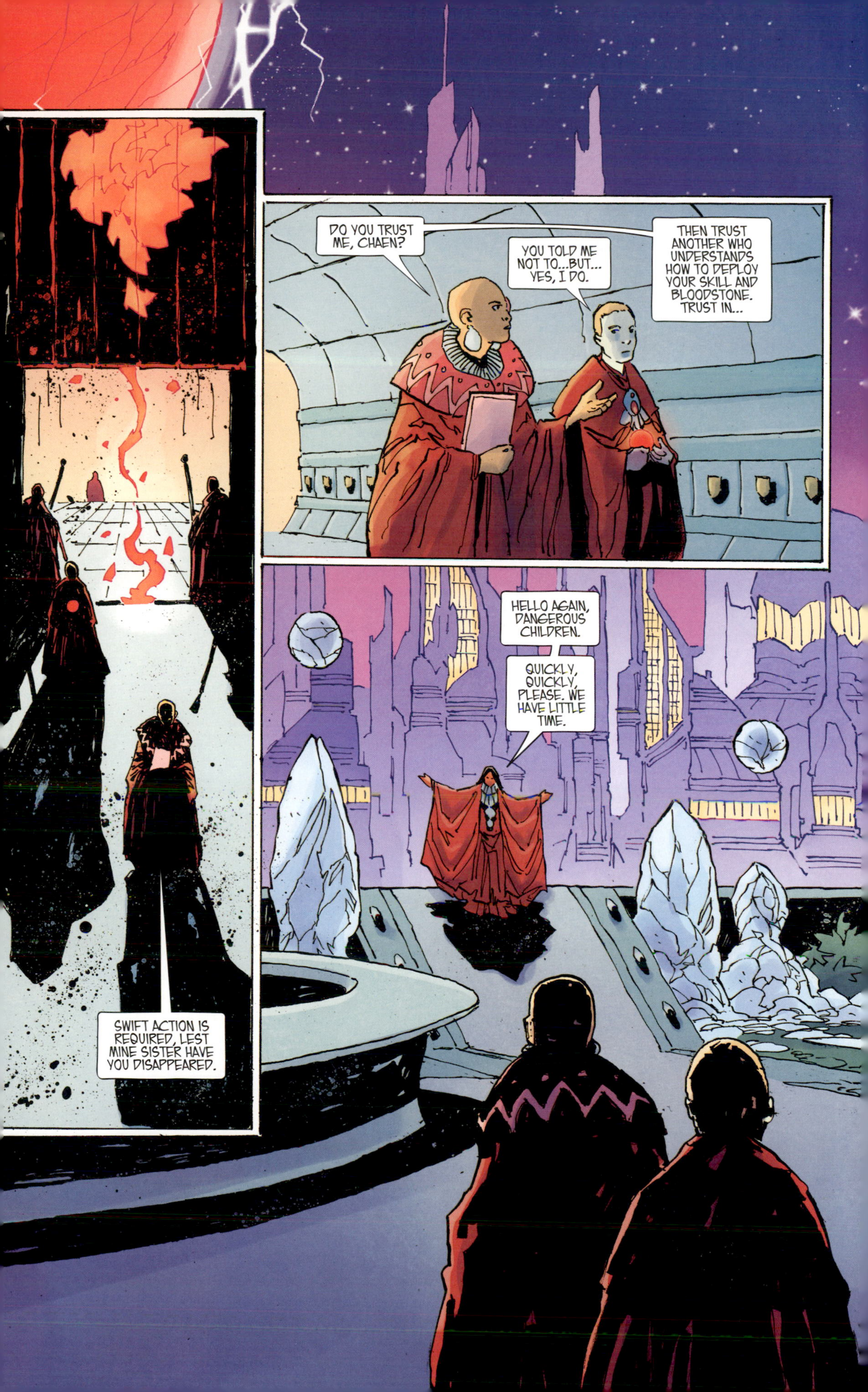
SWIFT ACTION IS REQUIRED, LEST MINE SISTER HAVE YOU DISAPPEARED.
DO YOU TRUST ME, CHAEN?
YOU TOLD ME NOT TO...BUT... YES, I DO.
THEN TRUST ANOTHER WHO UNDERSTANDS HOW TO DEPLOY YOUR SKILL AND BLOODSTONE. TRUST IN...
HELLO AGAIN, DANGEROUS CHILDREN.
QUICKLY, QUICKLY, PLEASE. WE HAVE LITTLE TIME.

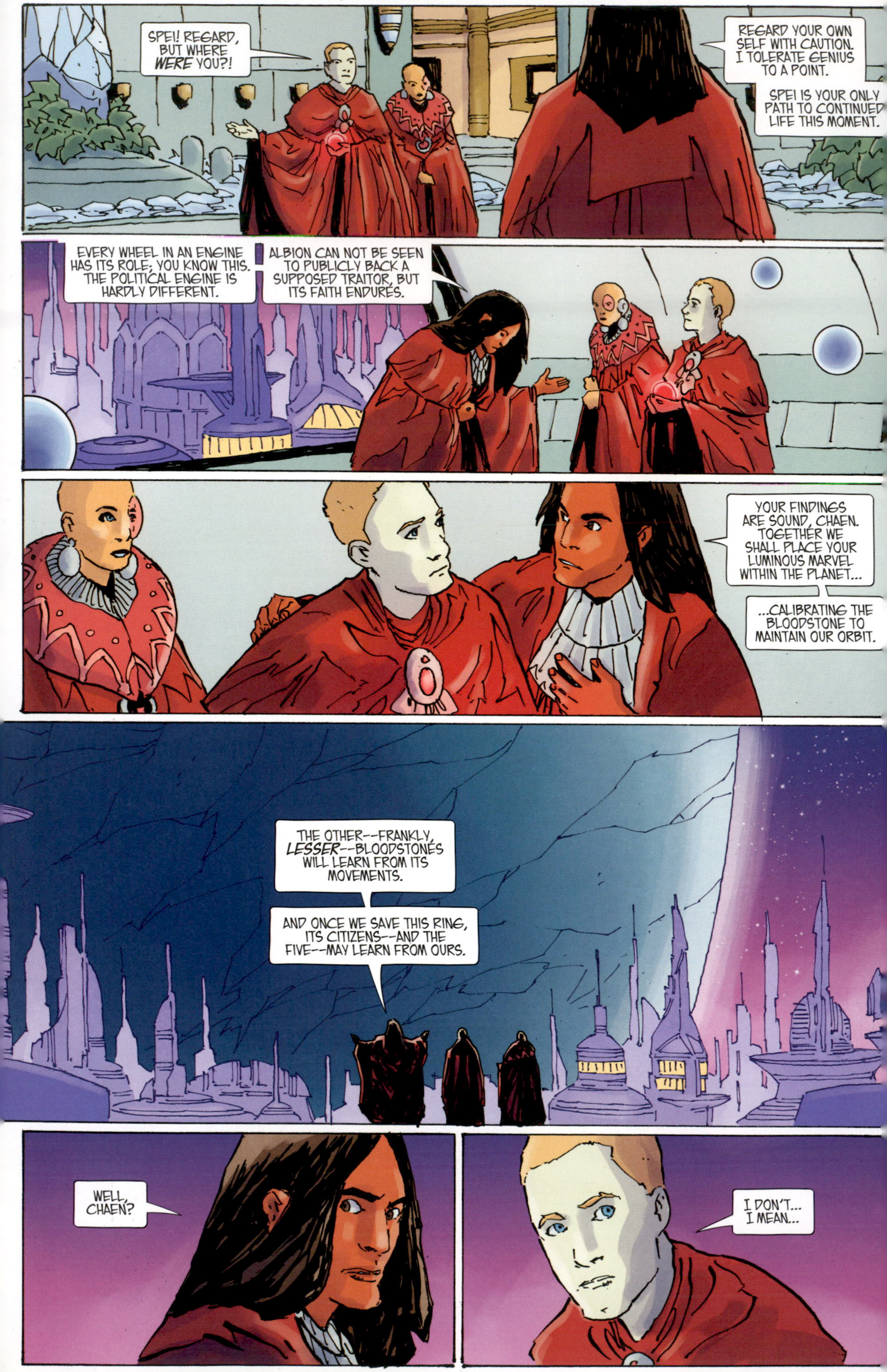
SPEI! REGARD, BUT WHERE *WERE* YOU?!
REGARD YOUR OWN SELF WITH CAUTION. I TOLERATE GENIUS TO A POINT.
SPEI IS YOUR ONLY PATH TO CONTINUED LIFE THIS MOMENT.
EVERY WHEEL IN AN ENGINE HAS ITS ROLE; YOU KNOW THIS. THE POLITICAL ENGINE IS HARDLY DIFFERENT.
ALBION CAN NOT BE SEEN TO PUBLICLY BACK A SUPPOSED TRAITOR, BUT ITS FAITH ENDURES.
YOUR FINDINGS ARE SOUND, CHAEN. TOGETHER WE SHALL PLACE YOUR LUMINOUS MARVEL WITHIN THE PLANET...
...CALIBRATING THE BLOODSTONE TO MAINTAIN OUR ORBIT.
THE OTHER--FRANKLY, *LESSER*--BLOODSTONES WILL LEARN FROM ITS MOVEMENTS.
AND ONCE WE SAVE THIS RING, ITS CITIZENS--AND THE FIVE--MAY LEARN FROM OURS.
WELL, CHAEN?
I DON'T... I MEAN...

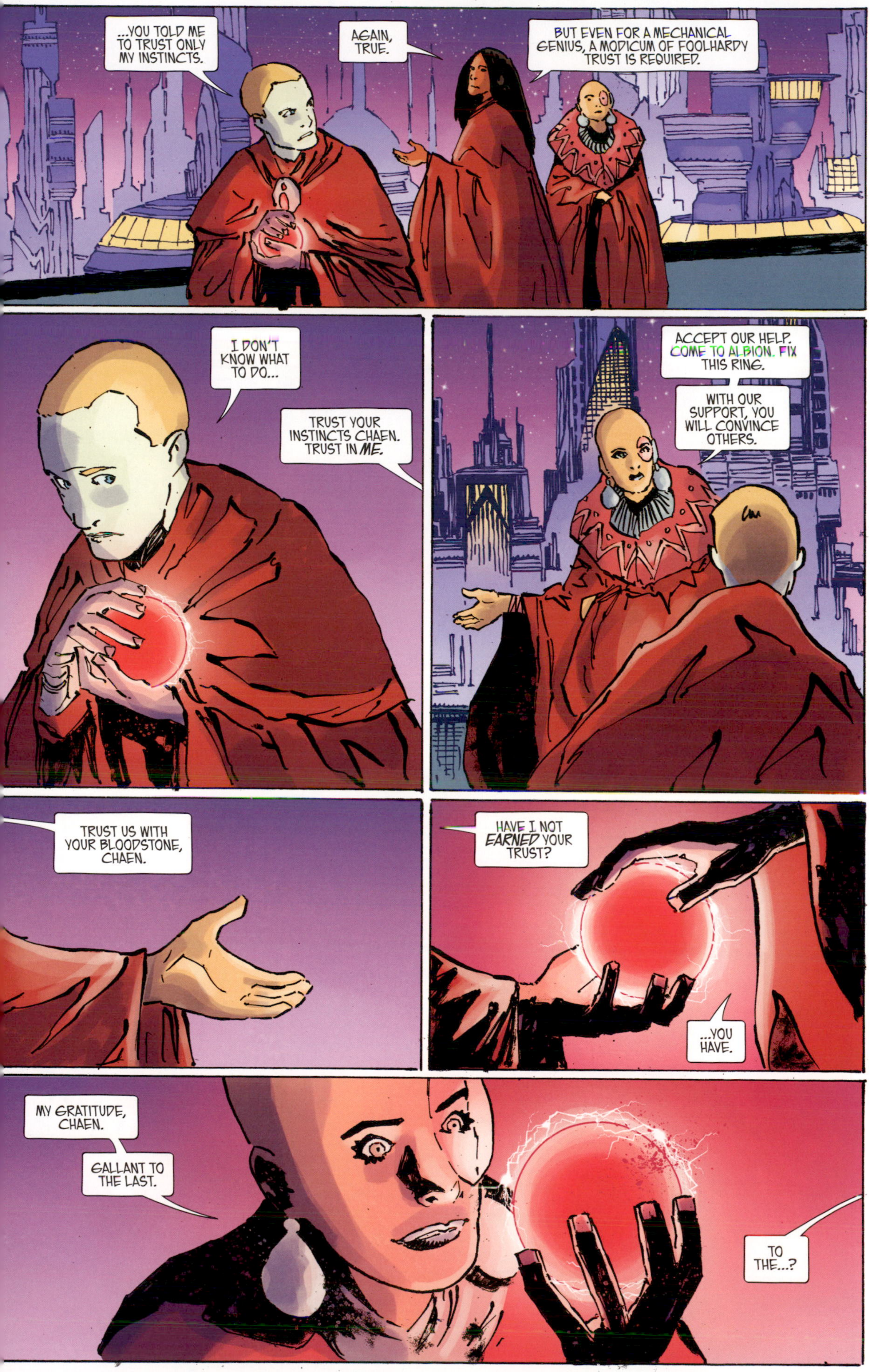
...YOU TOLD ME TO TRUST ONLY MY INSTINCTS.
AGAIN, TRUE.
BUT EVEN FOR A MECHANICAL GENIUS, A MODICUM OF FOOLHARDY TRUST IS REQUIRED.
I DON'T KNOW WHAT TO DO...
TRUST YOUR INSTINCTS CHAEN. TRUST IN ME.
ACCEPT OUR HELP. COME TO ALBION. FIX THIS RING.
WITH OUR SUPPORT, YOU WILL CONVINCE OTHERS.
TRUST US WITH YOUR BLOODSTONE, CHAEN.
HAVE I NOT EARNED YOUR TRUST?
...YOU HAVE.
MY GRATITUDE, CHAEN.
GALLANT TO THE LAST.
TO THE...?

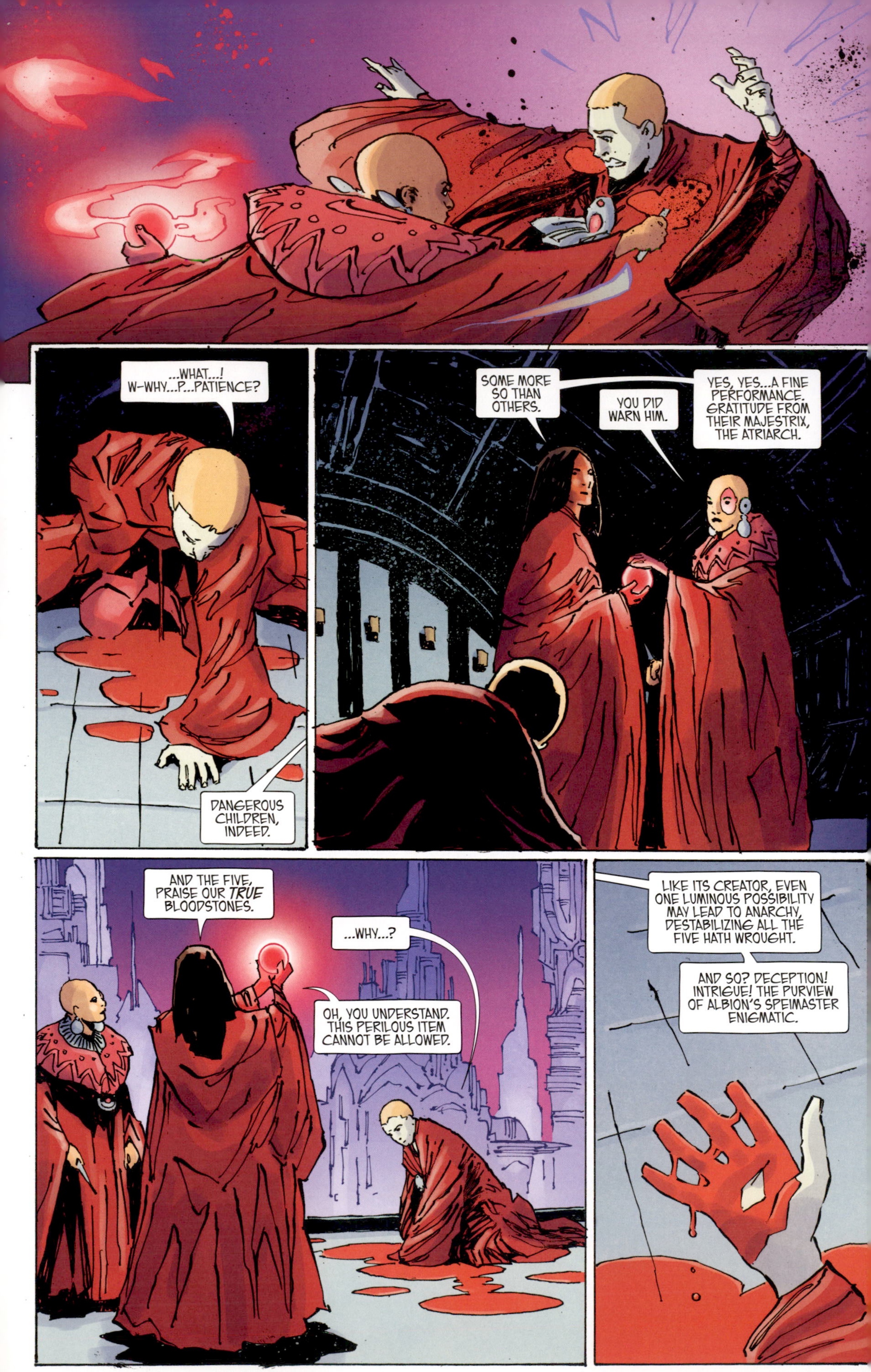

...WHAT...! W-WHY...P...PATIENCE?
DANGEROUS CHILDREN, INDEED.
SOME MORE SO THAN OTHERS.
YOU DID WARN HIM.
YES, YES...A FINE PERFORMANCE. GRATITUDE FROM THEIR MAJESTRIX, THE ATRIARCH.
AND THE FIVE, PRAISE OUR TRUE BLOODSTONES.
...WHY...?
OH, YOU UNDERSTAND. THIS PERILOUS ITEM CANNOT BE ALLOWED.
LIKE ITS CREATOR, EVEN ONE LUMINOUS POSSIBILITY MAY LEAD TO ANARCHY, DESTABILIZING ALL THE FIVE HATH WROUGHT.
AND SO? DECEPTION! INTRIGUE! THE PURVIEW OF ALBION'S SPEIMASTER ENIGMATIC.

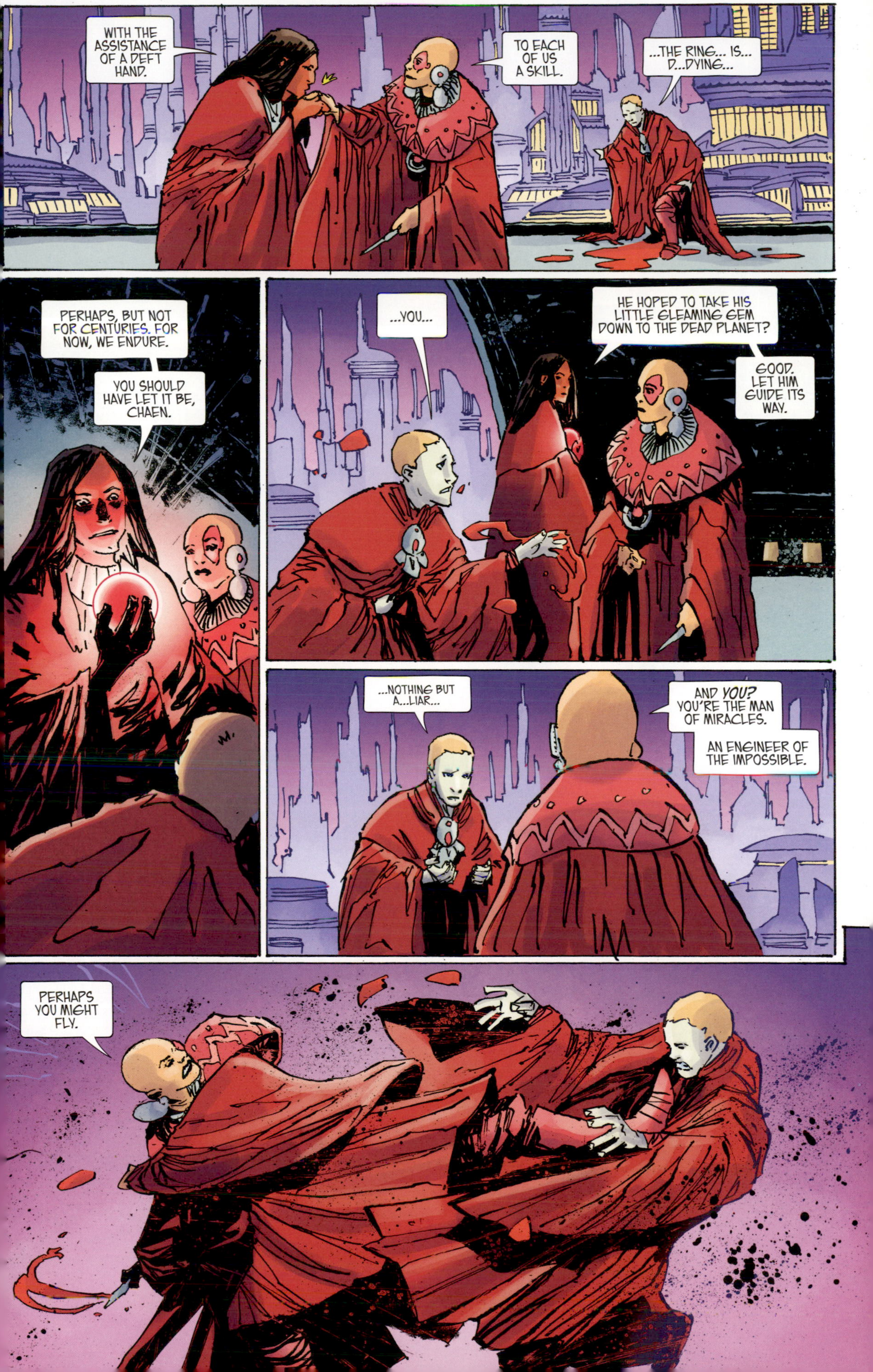

WITH THE ASSISTANCE OF A DEFT HAND.
TO EACH OF US A SKILL.
...THE RING... IS... D...DYING...
PERHAPS, BUT NOT FOR CENTURIES. FOR NOW, WE ENDURE.
YOU SHOULD HAVE LET IT BE, CHAEN.
...YOU...
HE HOPED TO TAKE HIS LITTLE GLEAMING GEM DOWN TO THE DEAD PLANET?
GOOD. LET HIM GUIDE ITS WAY.
...NOTHING BUT A...LIAR...
AND *YOU?* YOU'RE THE MAN OF MIRACLES.
AN ENGINEER OF THE IMPOSSIBLE.
PERHAPS YOU MIGHT FLY.

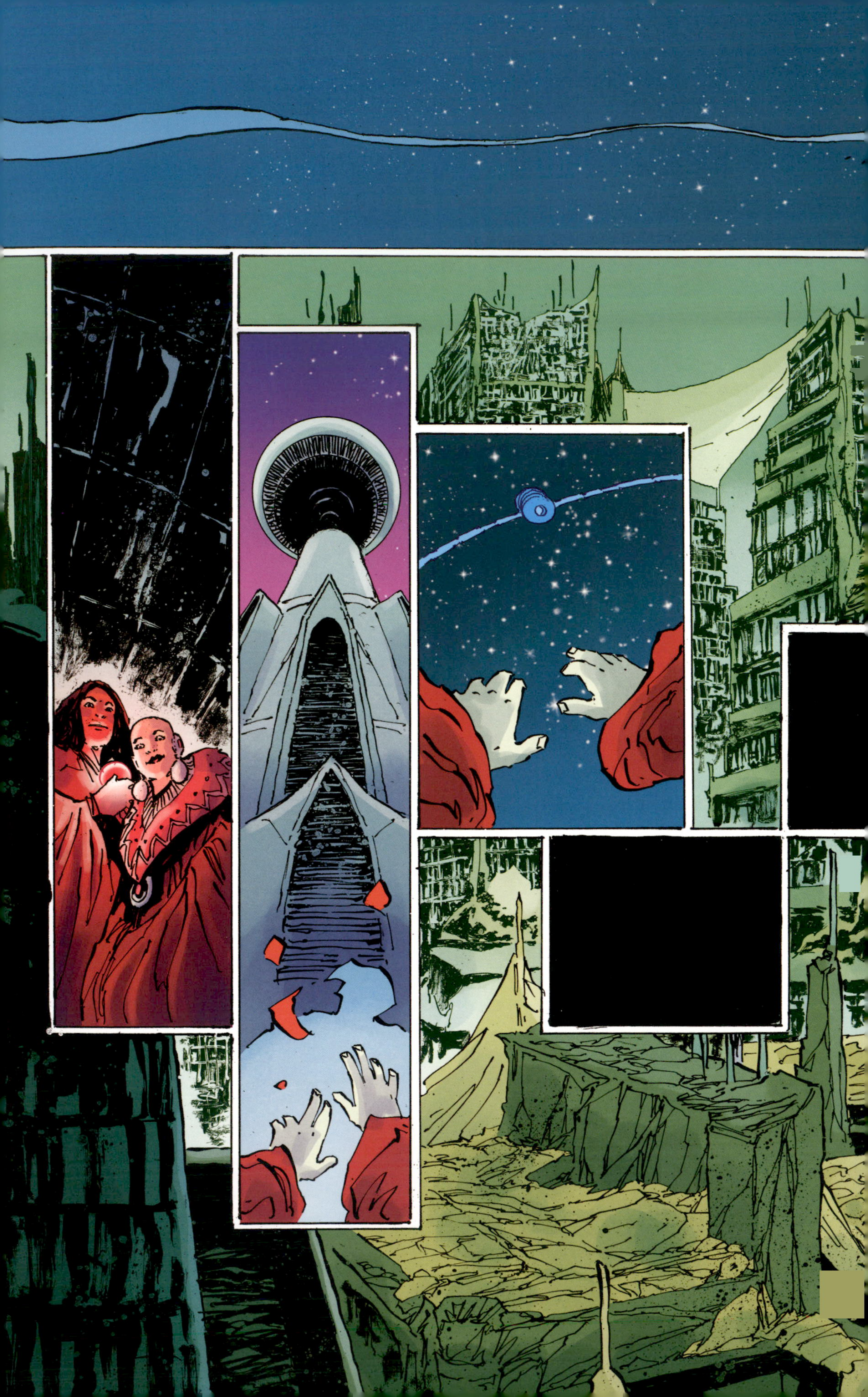

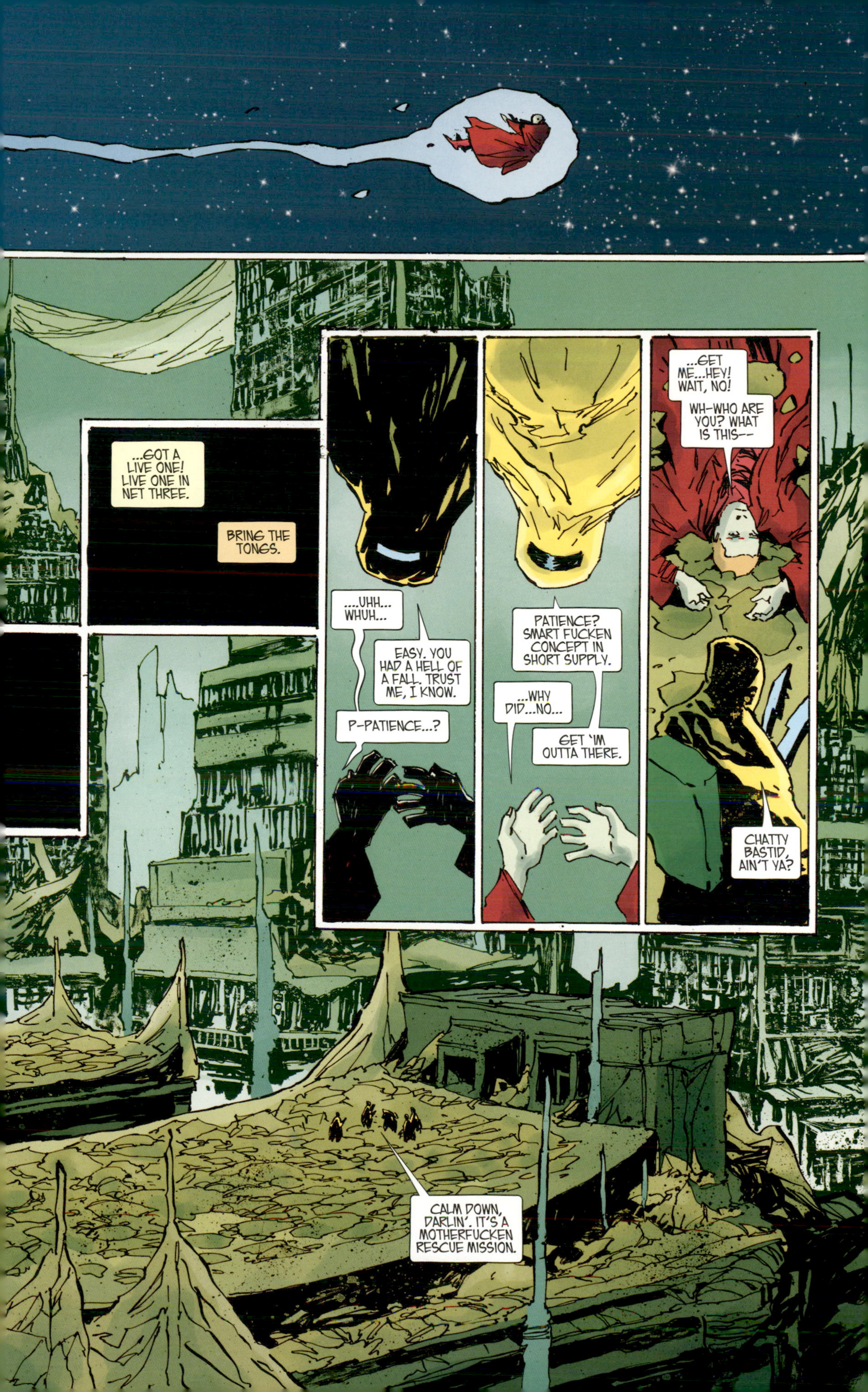

...GOT A LIVE ONE! LIVE ONE IN NET THREE.
BRING THE TONGS.
....UHH... WHUH...
EASY. YOU HAD A HELL OF A FALL. TRUST ME, I KNOW.
P-PATIENCE...?
PATIENCE? SMART FUCKEN CONCEPT IN SHORT SUPPLY.
...WHY DID...NO...
GET 'IM OUTTA THERE.
...GET ME...HEY! WAIT, NO!
WH-WHO ARE YOU? WHAT IS THIS--
CHATTY BASTID, AIN'T YA?
CALM DOWN, DARLIN'. IT'S A MOTHERFUCKEN RESCUE MISSION.

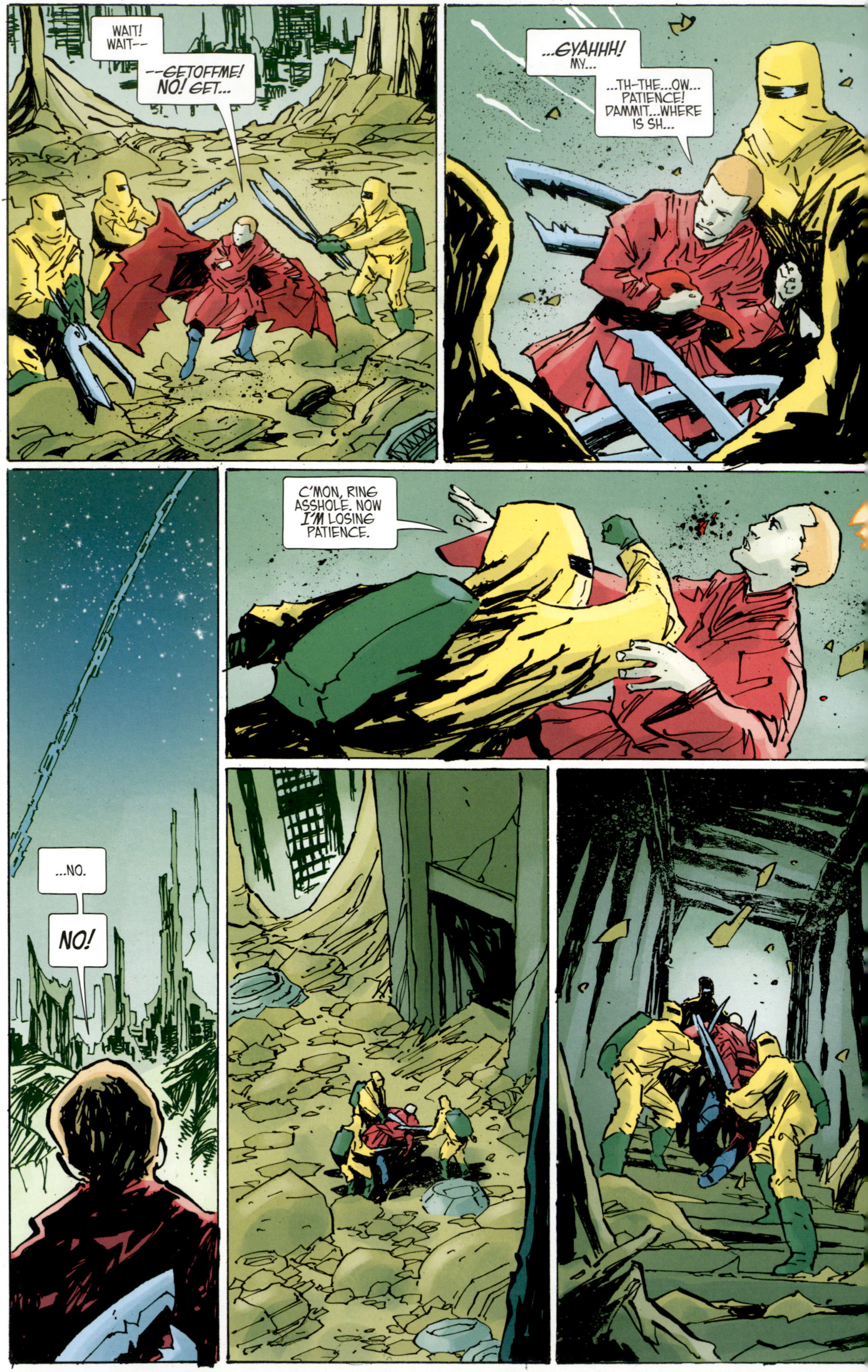

WAIT! WAIT--
--GETOFFME! NO! GET...
...GYAHHH! MY...
...TH-THE...OW... PATIENCE! DAMMIT...WHERE IS SH...
C'MON, RING ASSHOLE. NOW I'M LOSING PATIENCE.
...NO.
NO!

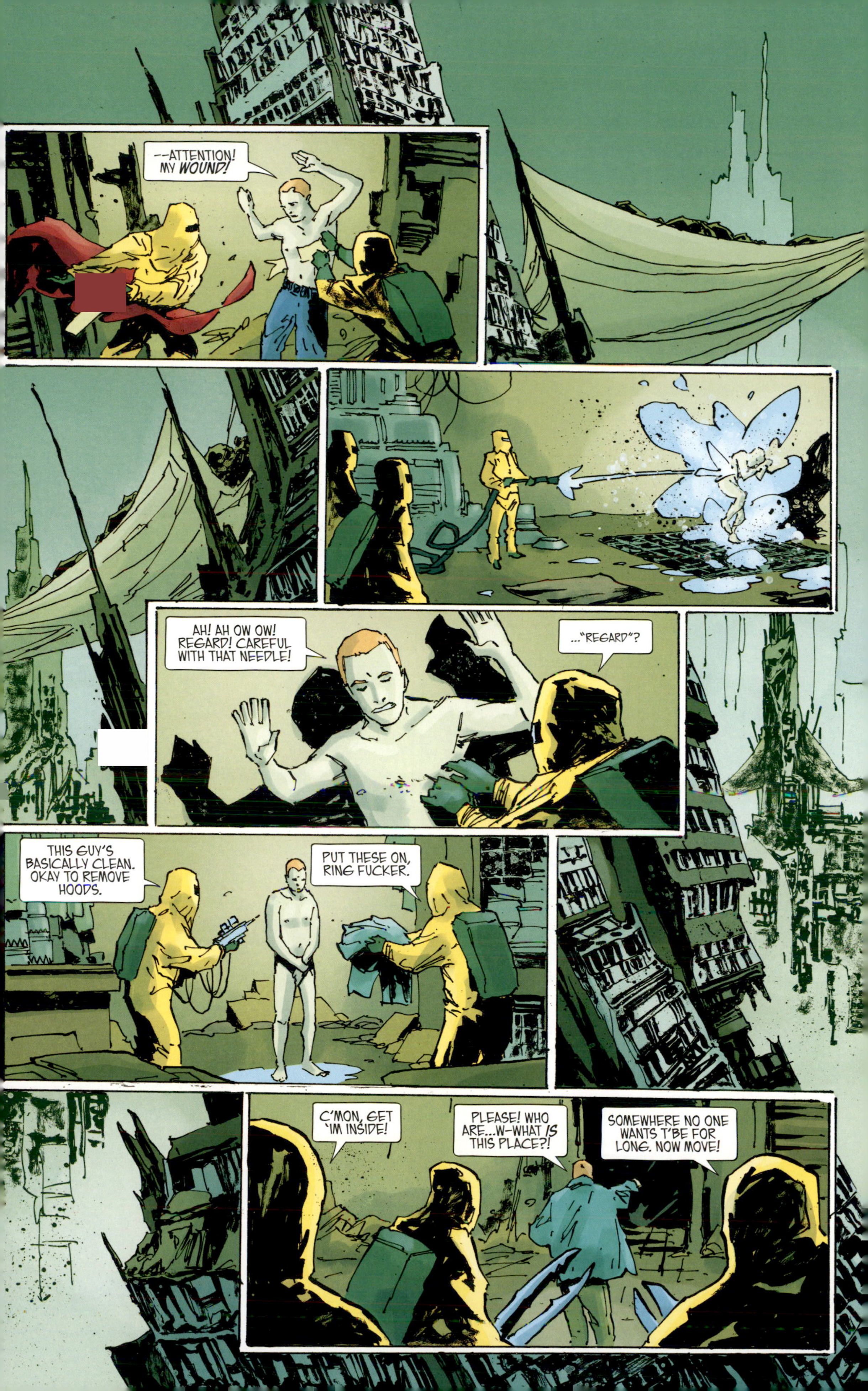
--ATTENTION! MY *WOUND!*
AH! AH OW OW! REGARD! CAREFUL WITH THAT NEEDLE!
..."REGARD"?
THIS GUY'S BASICALLY CLEAN. OKAY TO REMOVE HOODS.
PUT THESE ON, RING FUCKER.
C'MON, GET 'IM INSIDE!
PLEASE! WHO ARE...W-WHAT *IS* THIS PLACE?!
SOMEWHERE NO ONE WANTS T'BE FOR LONG. NOW MOVE!

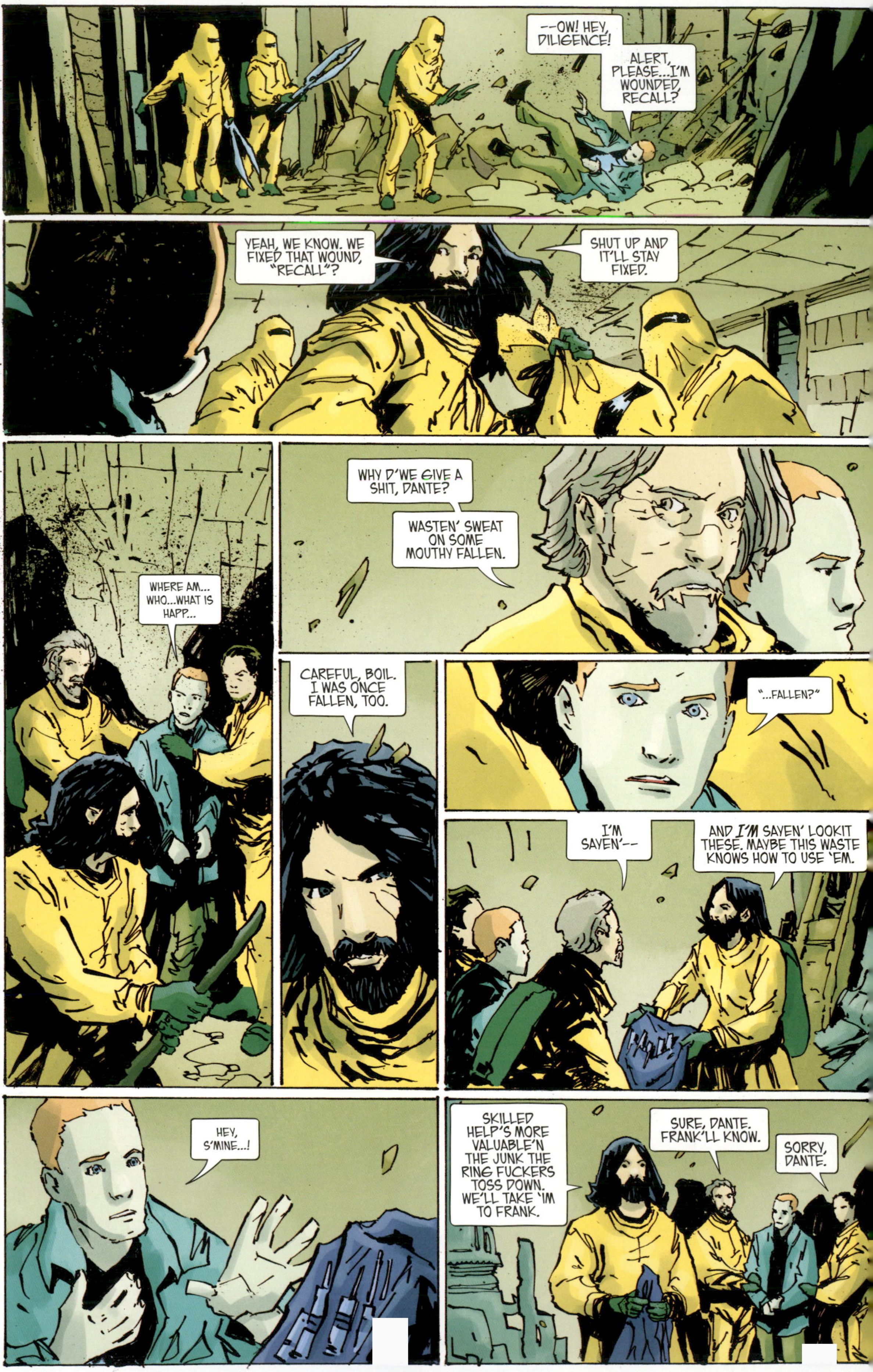
--OW! HEY, DILIGENCE!
ALERT, PLEASE...I'M WOUNDED, RECALL?
YEAH, WE KNOW. WE FIXED THAT WOUND, "RECALL"?
SHUT UP AND IT'LL STAY FIXED.
WHERE AM... WHO...WHAT IS HAPP...
WHY D'WE GIVE A SHIT, DANTE?
WASTEN' SWEAT ON SOME MOUTHY FALLEN.
CAREFUL, BOIL. I WAS ONCE FALLEN, TOO.
"...FALLEN?"
I'M SAYEN'--
AND I'M SAYEN' LOOKIT THESE. MAYBE THIS WASTE KNOWS HOW TO USE 'EM.
HEY, S'MINE...!
SKILLED HELP'S MORE VALUABLE'N THE JUNK THE RING FUCKERS TOSS DOWN. WE'LL TAKE 'IM TO FRANK.
SURE, DANTE. FRANK'LL KNOW.
SORRY, DANTE.

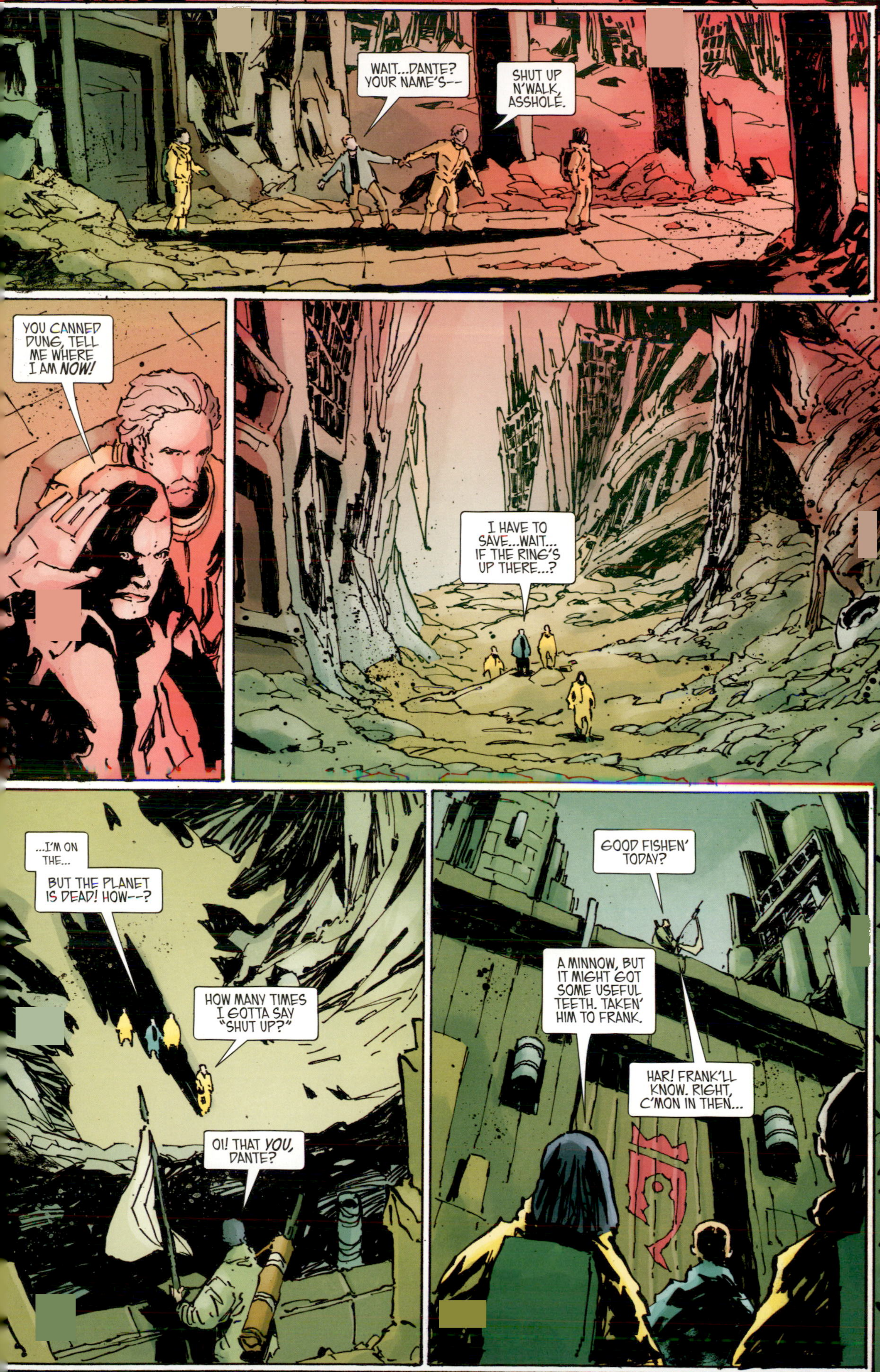
WAIT...DANTE? YOUR NAME'S--
SHUT UP N'WALK, ASSHOLE.
YOU CANNED DUNG, TELL ME WHERE I AM NOW!
I HAVE TO SAVE...WAIT... IF THE RING'S UP THERE...?
...I'M ON THE...
BUT THE PLANET IS DEAD! HOW--?
HOW MANY TIMES I GOTTA SAY "SHUT UP?"
OI! THAT YOU, DANTE?
GOOD FISHEN' TODAY?
A MINNOW, BUT IT MIGHT GOT SOME USEFUL TEETH. TAKEN' HIM TO FRANK.
HAR! FRANK'LL KNOW. RIGHT, C'MON IN THEN...

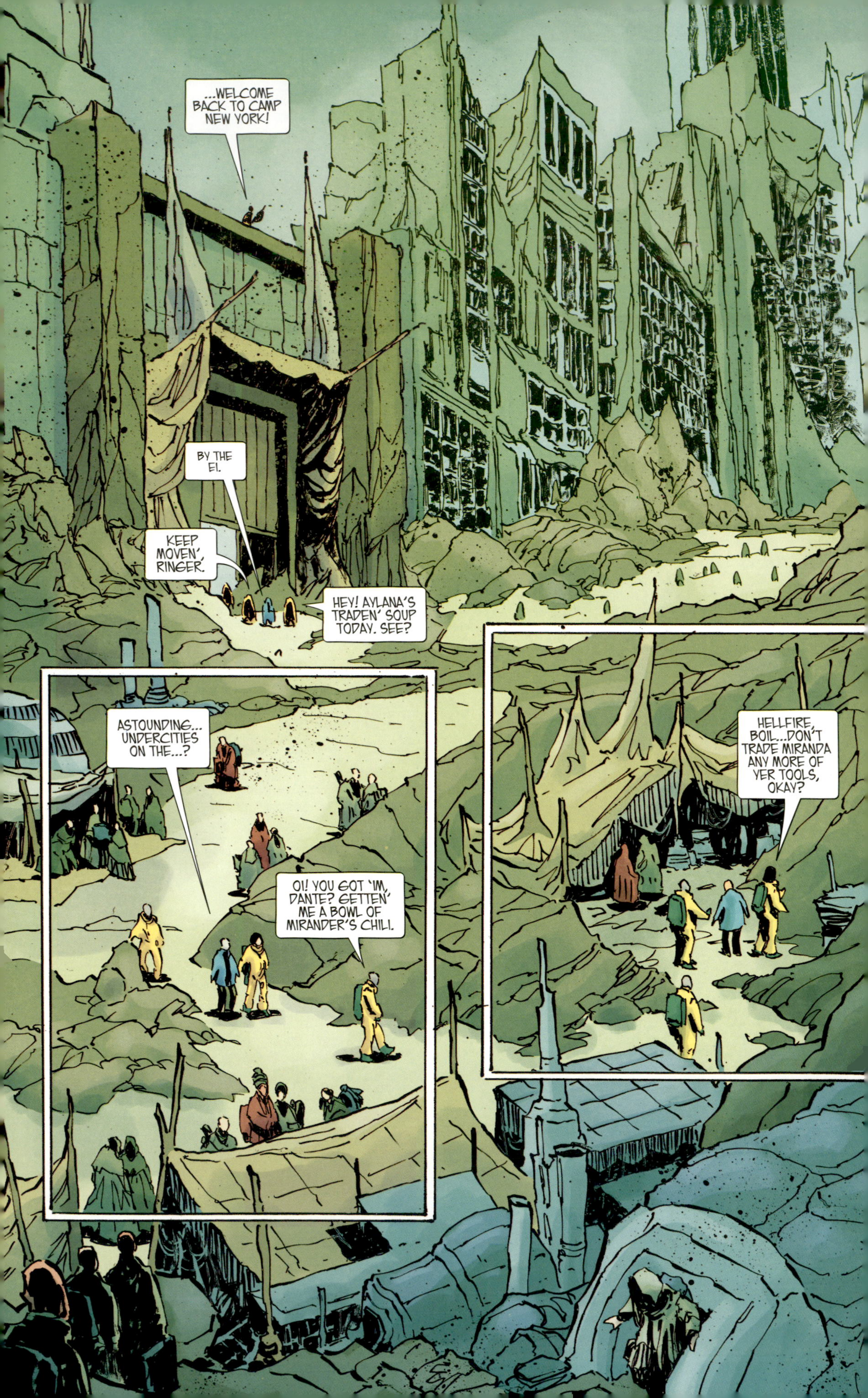
...WELCOME BACK TO CAMP NEW YORK!
BY THE EI.
KEEP MOVEN', RINGER.
HEY! AYLANA'S TRADEN' SOUP TODAY. SEE?
ASTOUNDING... UNDERCITIES ON THE...?
OI! YOU GOT 'IM, DANTE? GETTEN' ME A BOWL OF MIRANDER'S CHILI.
HELLFIRE, BOIL...DON'T TRADE MIRANDA ANY MORE OF YER TOOLS, OKAY?

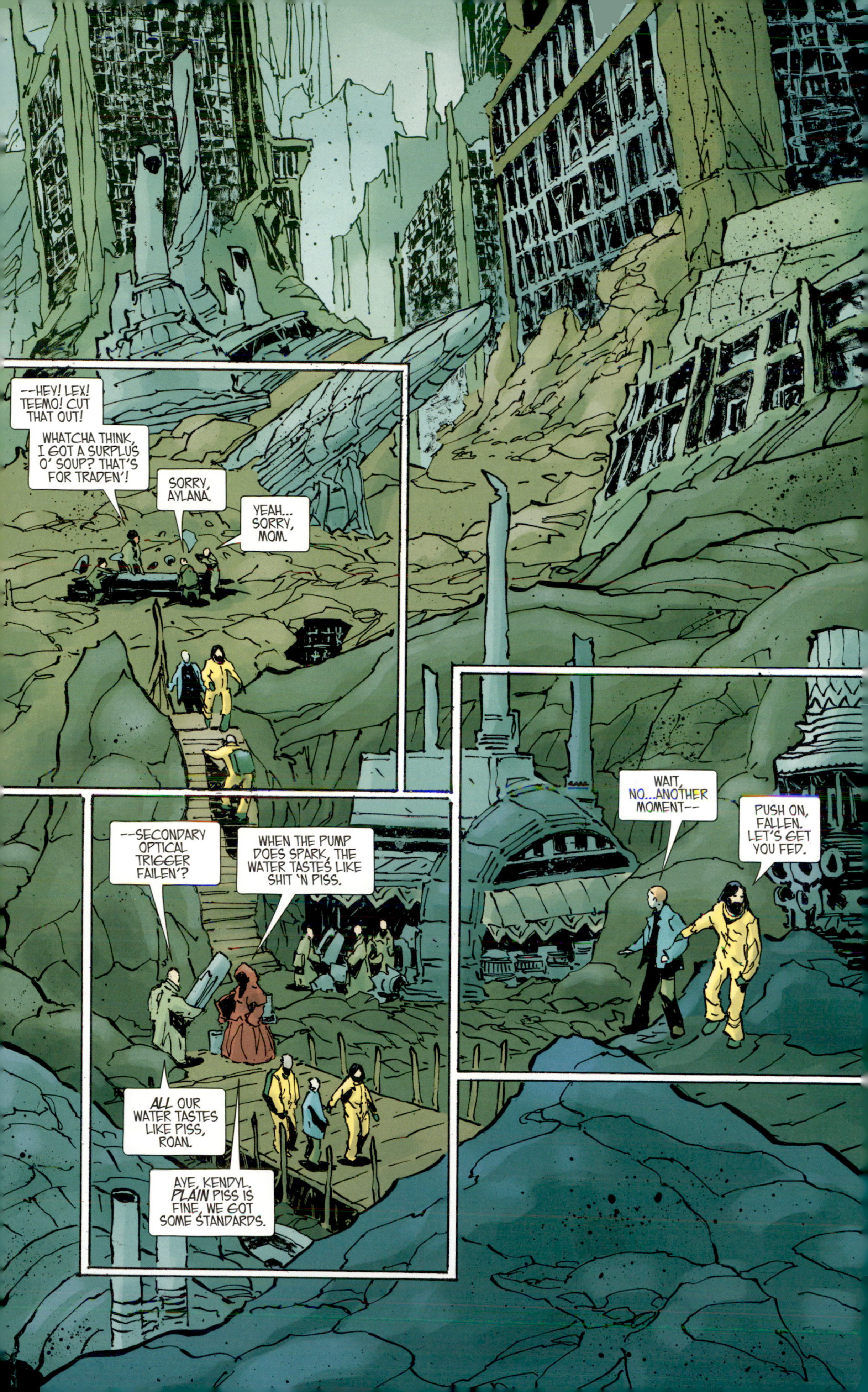
--HEY! LEX! TEEMO! CUT THAT OUT!
WHATCHA THINK, I GOT A SURPLUS O' SOUP? THAT'S FOR TRADEN'!
SORRY, AYLANA.
YEAH... SORRY, MOM.
--SECONDARY OPTICAL TRIGGER FAILEN'?
WHEN THE PUMP DOES SPARK, THE WATER TASTES LIKE SHIT 'N PISS.
ALL OUR WATER TASTES LIKE PISS, ROAN.
AYE, KENDYL. PLAIN PISS IS FINE, WE GOT SOME STANDARDS.
WAIT, NO...ANOTHER MOMENT--
PUSH ON, FALLEN. LET'S GET YOU FED.

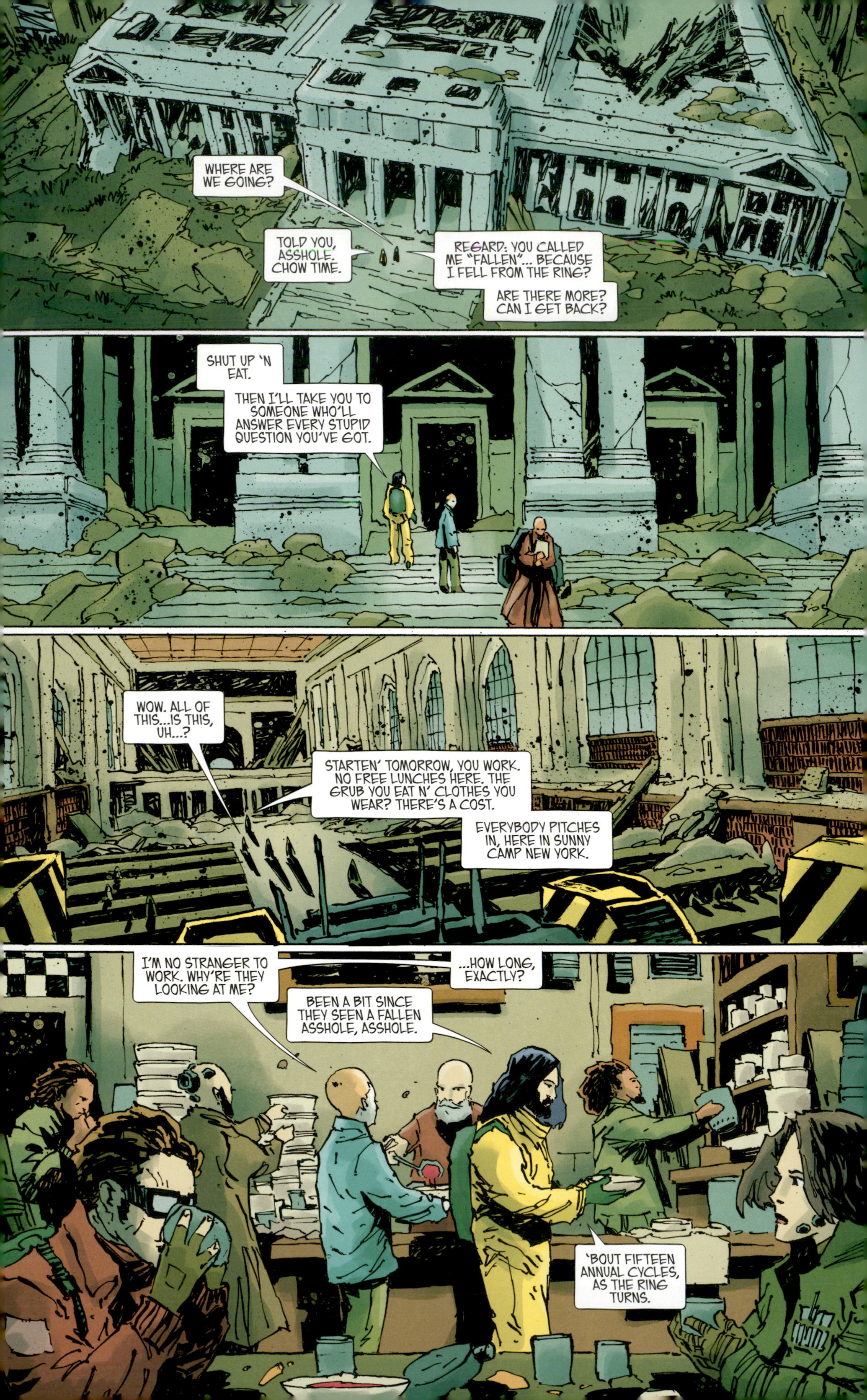
WHERE ARE WE GOING?
TOLD YOU, ASSHOLE. CHOW TIME.
REGARD: YOU CALLED ME "FALLEN"... BECAUSE I FELL FROM THE RING?
ARE THERE MORE? CAN I GET BACK?
SHUT UP 'N EAT.
THEN I'LL TAKE YOU TO SOMEONE WHO'LL ANSWER EVERY STUPID QUESTION YOU'VE GOT.
WOW. ALL OF THIS...IS THIS, UH...?
STARTEN' TOMORROW, YOU WORK. NO FREE LUNCHES HERE. THE GRUB YOU EAT N' CLOTHES YOU WEAR? THERE'S A COST.
EVERYBODY PITCHES IN, HERE IN SUNNY CAMP NEW YORK.
I'M NO STRANGER TO WORK. WHY'RE THEY LOOKING AT ME?
...HOW LONG, EXACTLY?
BEEN A BIT SINCE THEY SEEN A FALLEN ASSHOLE, ASSHOLE.
'BOUT FIFTEEN ANNUAL CYCLES, AS THE RING TURNS.

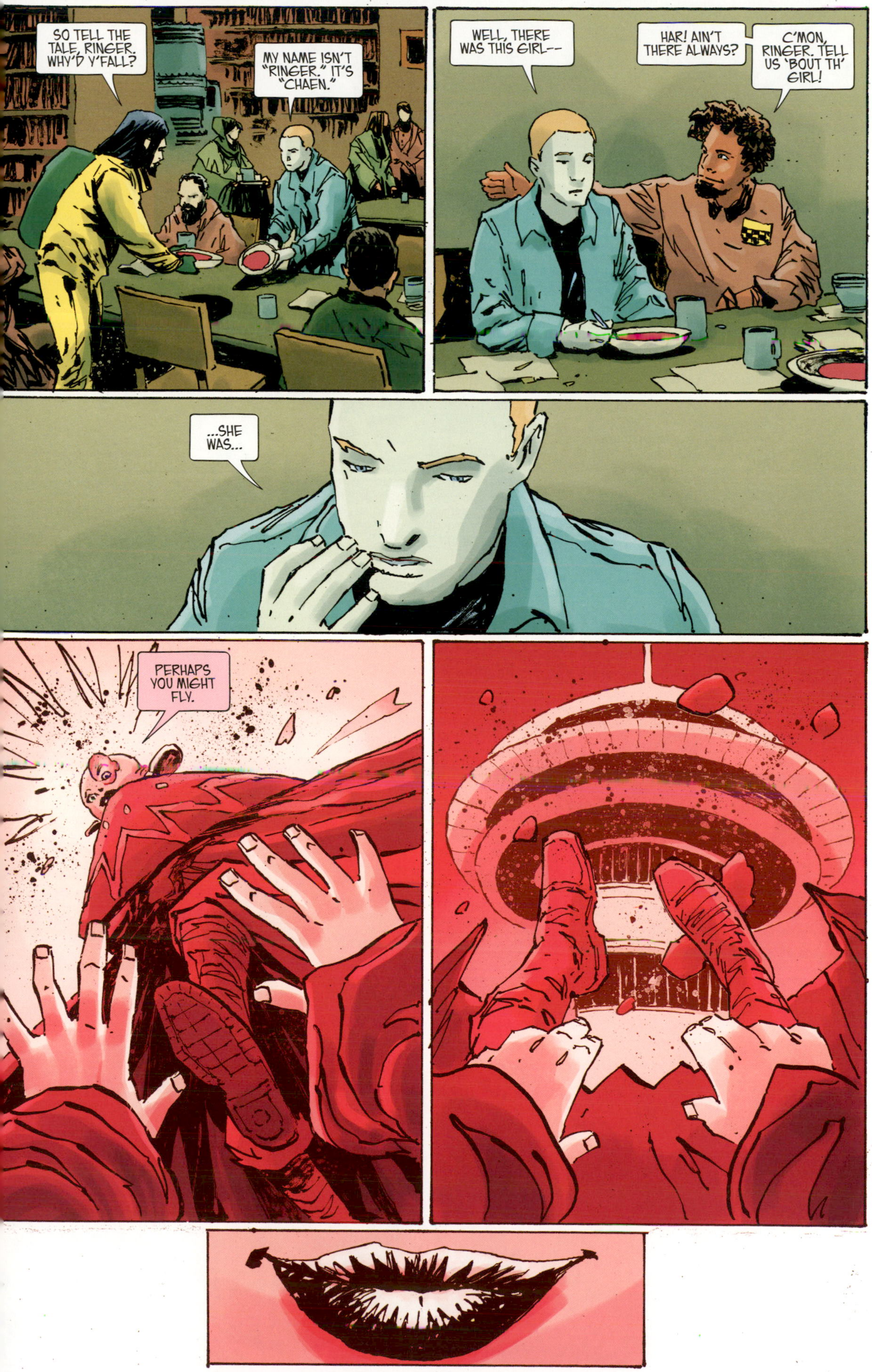
SO TELL THE TALE, RINGER. WHY'D Y'FALL?
MY NAME ISN'T "RINGER." IT'S "CHAEN."
WELL, THERE WAS THIS GIRL--
HAR! AIN'T THERE ALWAYS?
C'MON, RINGER. TELL US 'BOUT TH' GIRL!
...SHE WAS...
PERHAPS YOU MIGHT FLY.

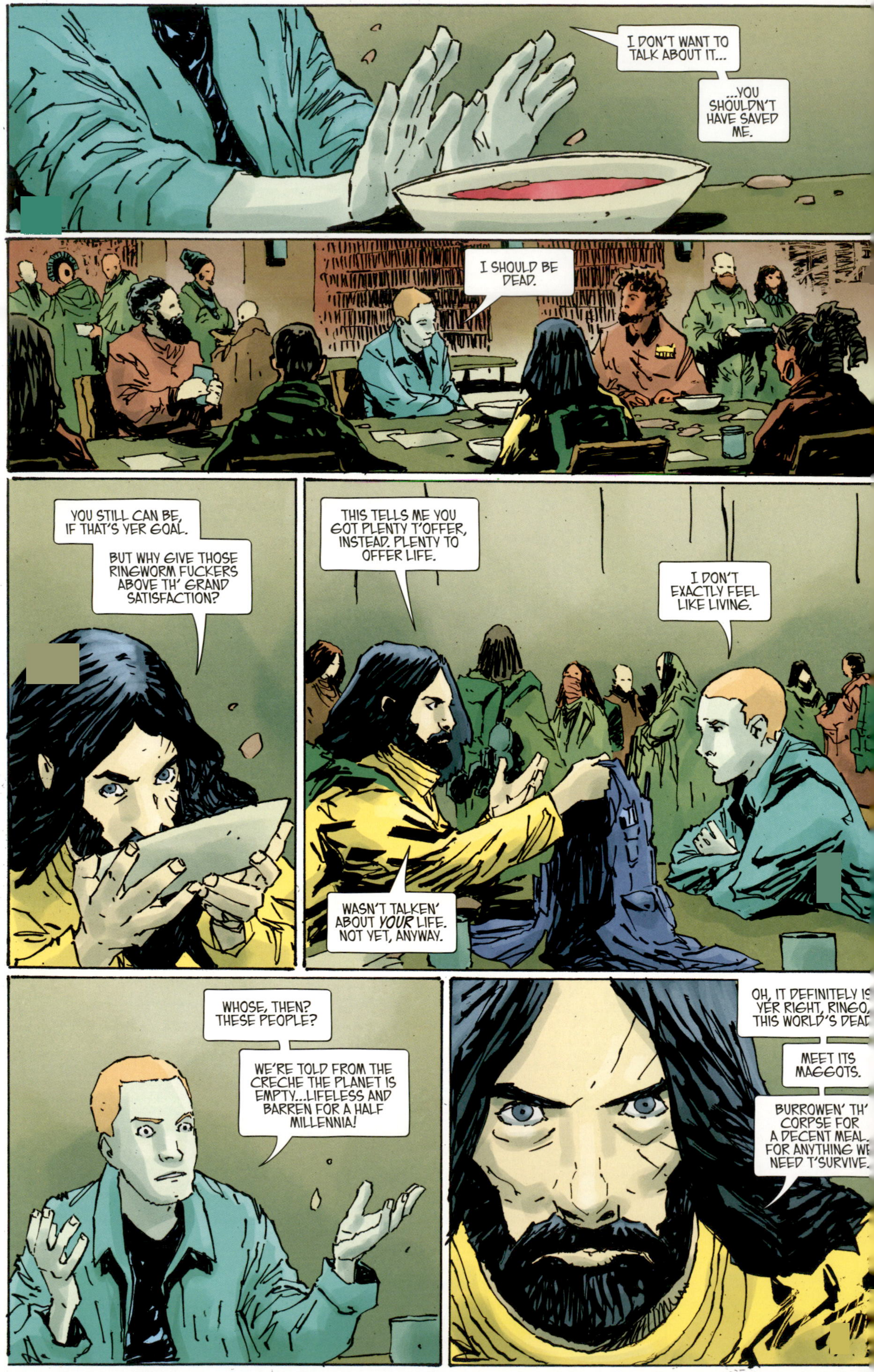
I DON'T WANT TO TALK ABOUT IT...
...YOU SHOULDN'T HAVE SAVED ME.
I SHOULD BE DEAD.
YOU STILL CAN BE, IF THAT'S YER GOAL.
BUT WHY GIVE THOSE RINGWORM FUCKERS ABOVE TH' GRAND SATISFACTION?
THIS TELLS ME YOU GOT PLENTY T'OFFER, INSTEAD. PLENTY TO OFFER LIFE.
I DON'T EXACTLY FEEL LIKE LIVING.
WASN'T TALKEN' ABOUT YOUR LIFE. NOT YET, ANYWAY.
WHOSE, THEN? THESE PEOPLE?
WE'RE TOLD FROM THE CRECHE THE PLANET IS EMPTY...LIFELESS AND BARREN FOR A HALF MILLENNIA!
OH, IT DEFINITELY IS YER RIGHT, RINGO. THIS WORLD'S DEAD
MEET ITS MAGGOTS.
BURROWEN' TH' CORPSE FOR A DECENT MEAL. FOR ANYTHING WE NEED T'SURVIVE.

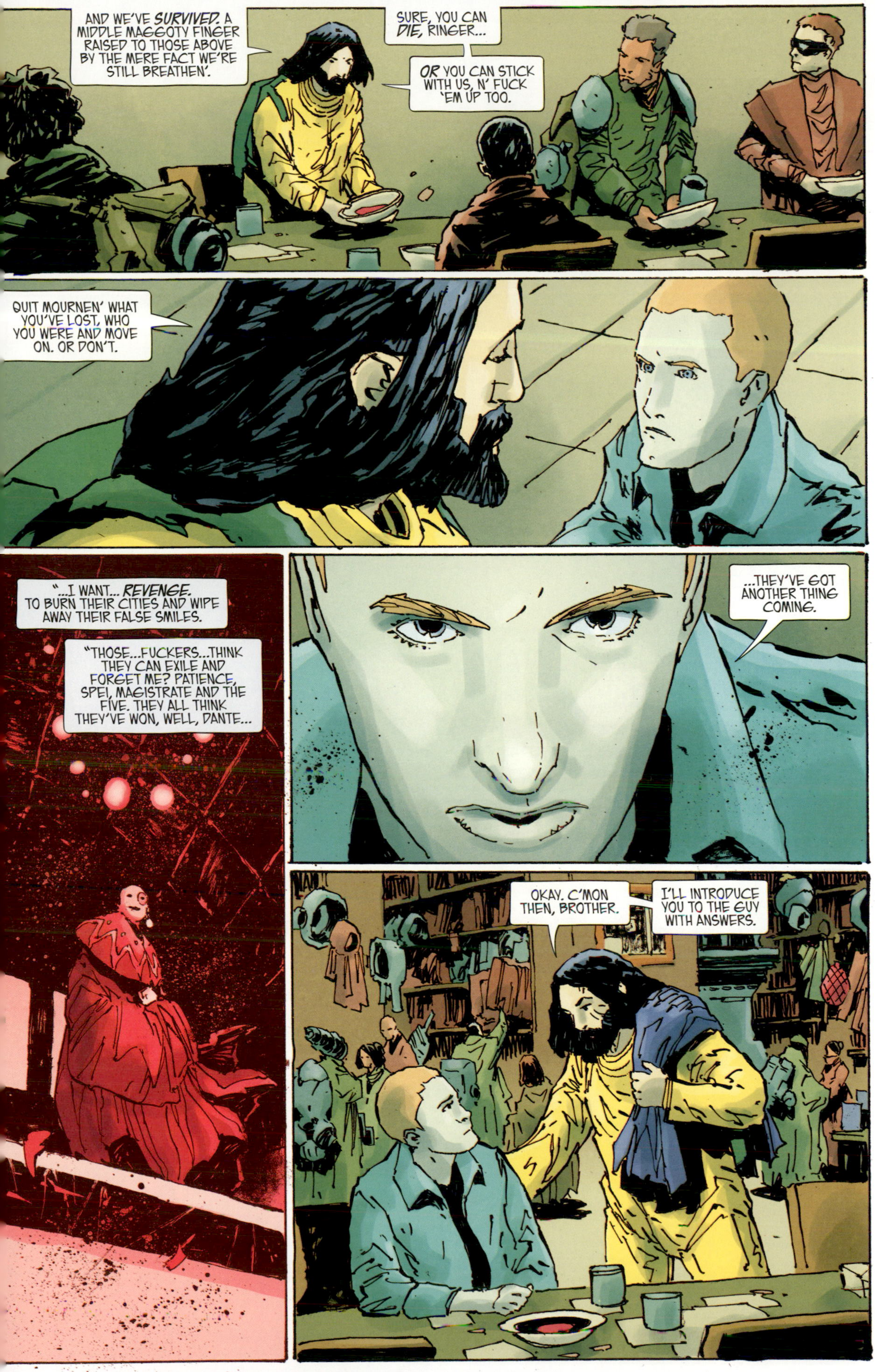
AND WE'VE SURVIVED. A MIDDLE MAGGOTY FINGER RAISED TO THOSE ABOVE BY THE MERE FACT WE'RE STILL BREATHEN'.
SURE, YOU CAN DIE, RINGER...
OR YOU CAN STICK WITH US, N' FUCK 'EM UP TOO.
QUIT MOURNEN' WHAT YOU'VE LOST, WHO YOU WERE AND MOVE ON. OR DON'T.
"...I WANT... REVENGE. TO BURN THEIR CITIES AND WIPE AWAY THEIR FALSE SMILES.
"THOSE...FUCKERS...THINK THEY CAN EXILE AND FORGET ME? PATIENCE, SPEI, MAGISTRATE AND THE FIVE. THEY ALL THINK THEY'VE WON, WELL, DANTE...
...THEY'VE GOT ANOTHER THING COMING.
OKAY. C'MON THEN, BROTHER.
I'LL INTRODUCE YOU TO THE GUY WITH ANSWERS.

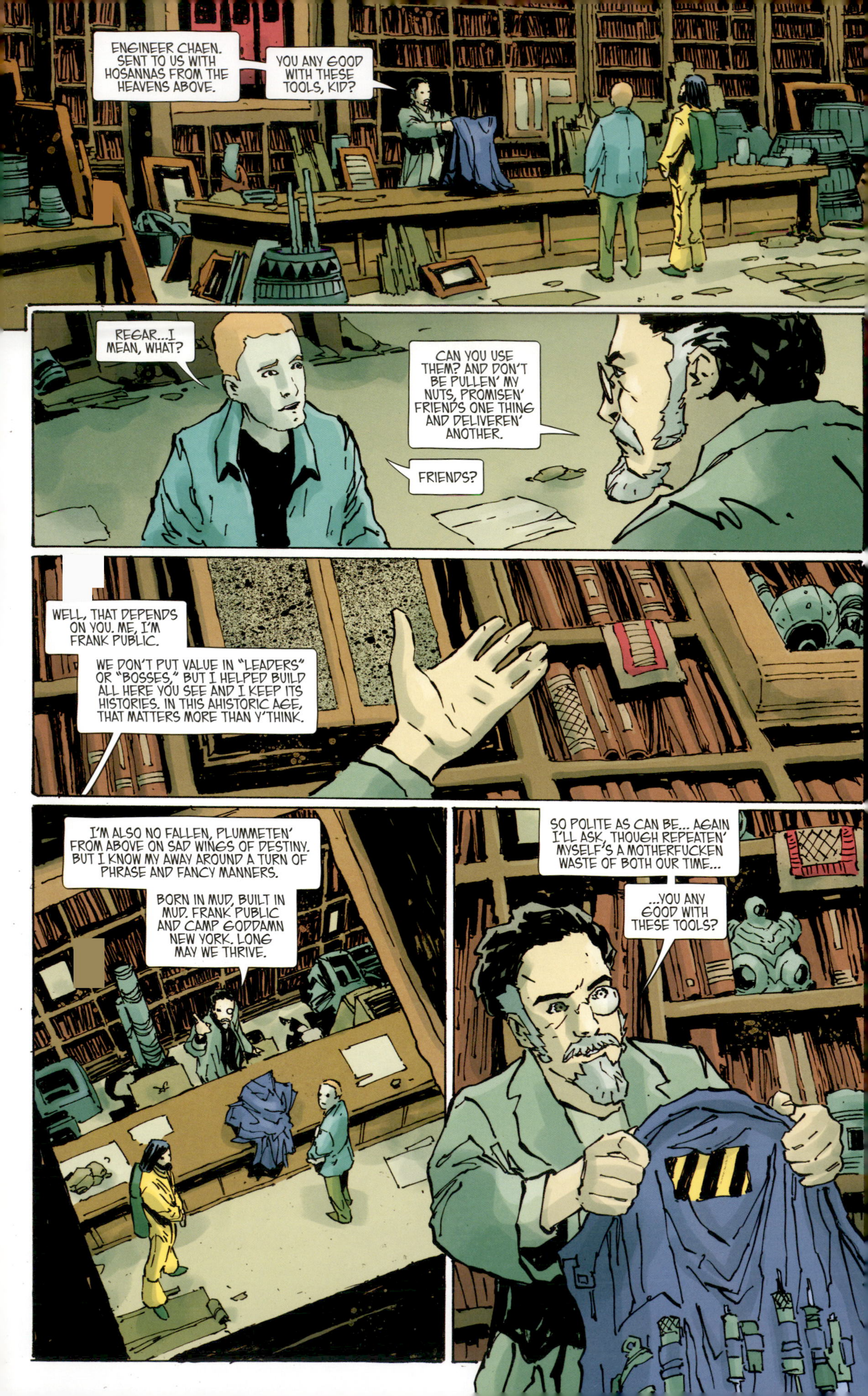
ENGINEER CHAEN. SENT TO US WITH HOSANNAS FROM THE HEAVENS ABOVE.
YOU ANY GOOD WITH THESE TOOLS, KID?
REGAR...I MEAN, WHAT?
CAN YOU USE THEM? AND DON'T BE PULLEN' MY NUTS, PROMISEN' FRIENDS ONE THING AND DELIVEREN' ANOTHER.
FRIENDS?
WELL, THAT DEPENDS ON YOU. ME, I'M FRANK PUBLIC.
WE DON'T PUT VALUE IN "LEADERS" OR "BOSSES," BUT I HELPED BUILD ALL HERE YOU SEE AND I KEEP ITS HISTORIES. IN THIS AHISTORIC AGE, THAT MATTERS MORE THAN Y'THINK.
I'M ALSO NO FALLEN, PLUMMETEN' FROM ABOVE ON SAD WINGS OF DESTINY. BUT I KNOW MY AWAY AROUND A TURN OF PHRASE AND FANCY MANNERS.
BORN IN MUD, BUILT IN MUD. FRANK PUBLIC AND CAMP GODDAMN NEW YORK. LONG MAY WE THRIVE.
SO POLITE AS CAN BE... AGAIN I'LL ASK, THOUGH REPEATEN' MYSELF'S A MOTHERFUCKEN WASTE OF BOTH OUR TIME...
...YOU ANY GOOD WITH THESE TOOLS?

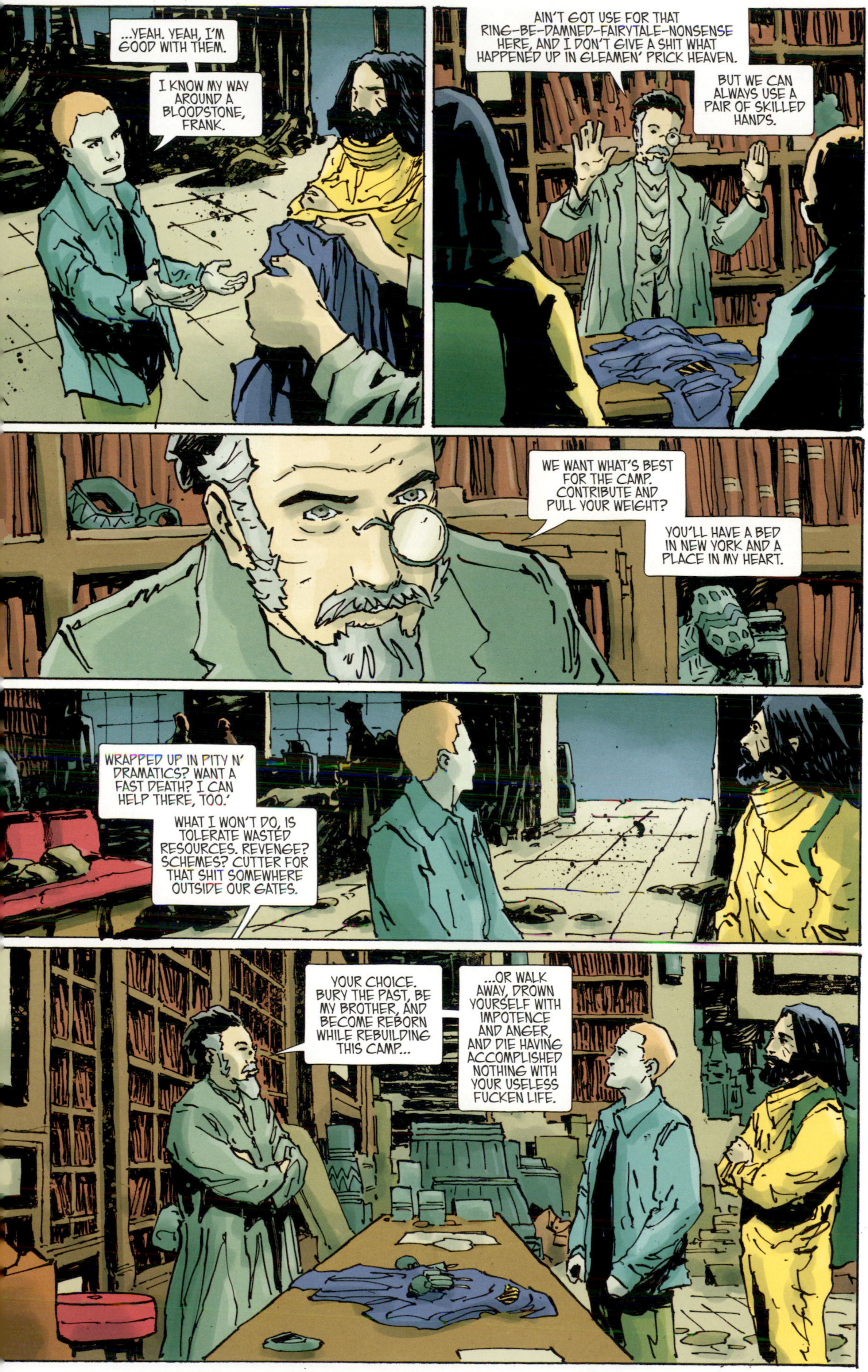
...YEAH. YEAH, I'M GOOD WITH THEM.
I KNOW MY WAY AROUND A BLOODSTONE, FRANK.
AIN'T GOT USE FOR THAT RING-BE-DAMNED-FAIRYTALE-NONSENSE HERE, AND I DON'T GIVE A SHIT WHAT HAPPENED UP IN GLEAMEN' PRICK HEAVEN.
BUT WE CAN ALWAYS USE A PAIR OF SKILLED HANDS.
WE WANT WHAT'S BEST FOR THE CAMP. CONTRIBUTE AND PULL YOUR WEIGHT?
YOU'LL HAVE A BED IN NEW YORK AND A PLACE IN MY HEART.
WRAPPED UP IN PITY N' DRAMATICS? WANT A FAST DEATH? I CAN HELP THERE, TOO.'
WHAT I WON'T DO, IS TOLERATE WASTED RESOURCES. REVENGE? SCHEMES? CUTTER FOR THAT SHIT SOMEWHERE OUTSIDE OUR GATES.
YOUR CHOICE. BURY THE PAST, BE MY BROTHER, AND BECOME REBORN WHILE REBUILDING THIS CAMP...
...OR WALK AWAY, DROWN YOURSELF WITH IMPOTENCE AND ANGER, AND DIE HAVING ACCOMPLISHED NOTHING WITH YOUR USELESS FUCKEN LIFE.

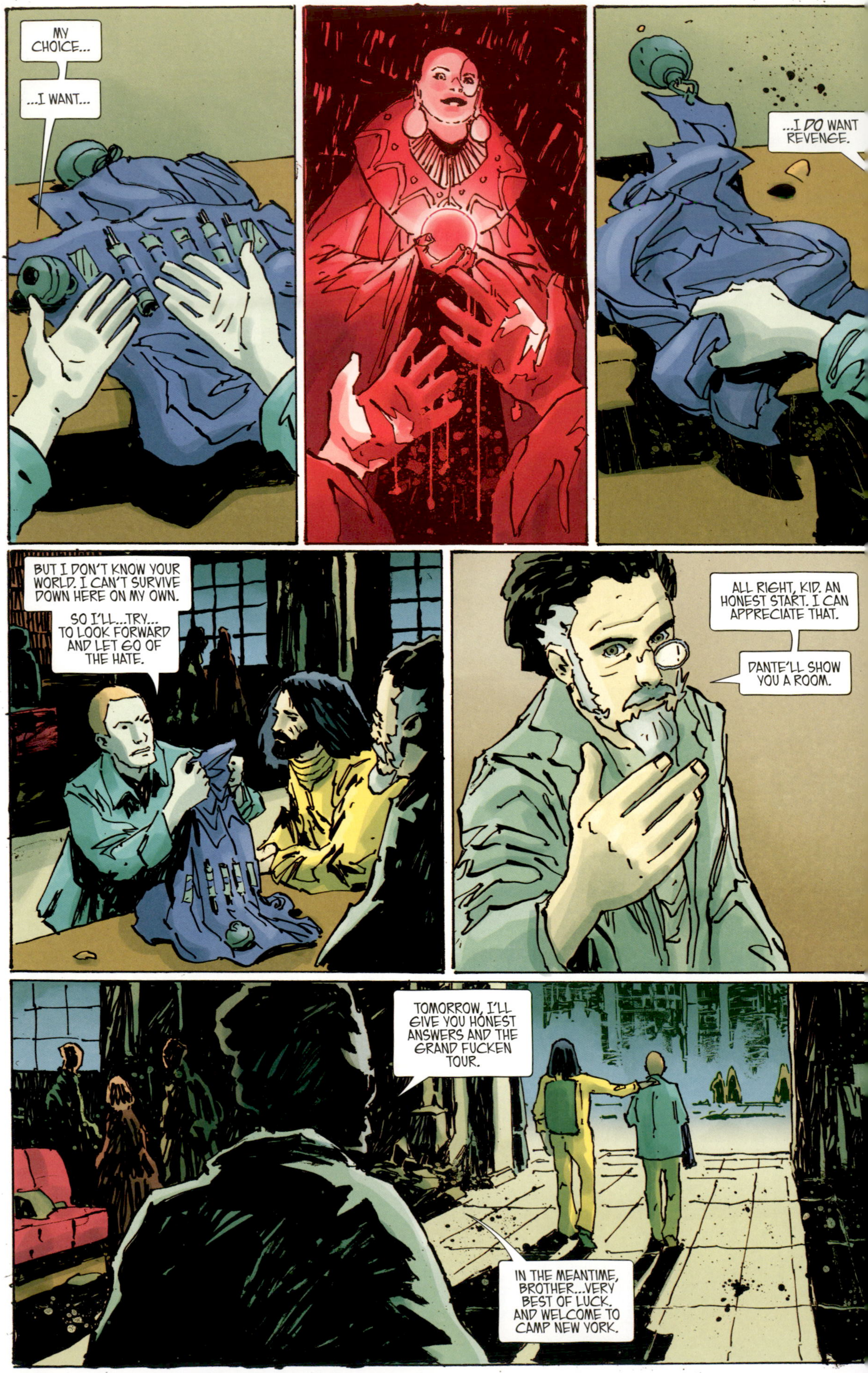
MY CHOICE...
...I WANT...
...I DO WANT REVENGE.
BUT I DON'T KNOW YOUR WORLD. I CAN'T SURVIVE DOWN HERE ON MY OWN.
SO I'LL...TRY... TO LOOK FORWARD AND LET GO OF THE HATE.
ALL RIGHT, KID. AN HONEST START. I CAN APPRECIATE THAT.
DANTE'LL SHOW YOU A ROOM.
TOMORROW, I'LL GIVE YOU HONEST ANSWERS AND THE GRAND FUCKEN TOUR.
IN THE MEANTIME, BROTHER...VERY BEST OF LUCK. AND WELCOME TO CAMP NEW YORK.

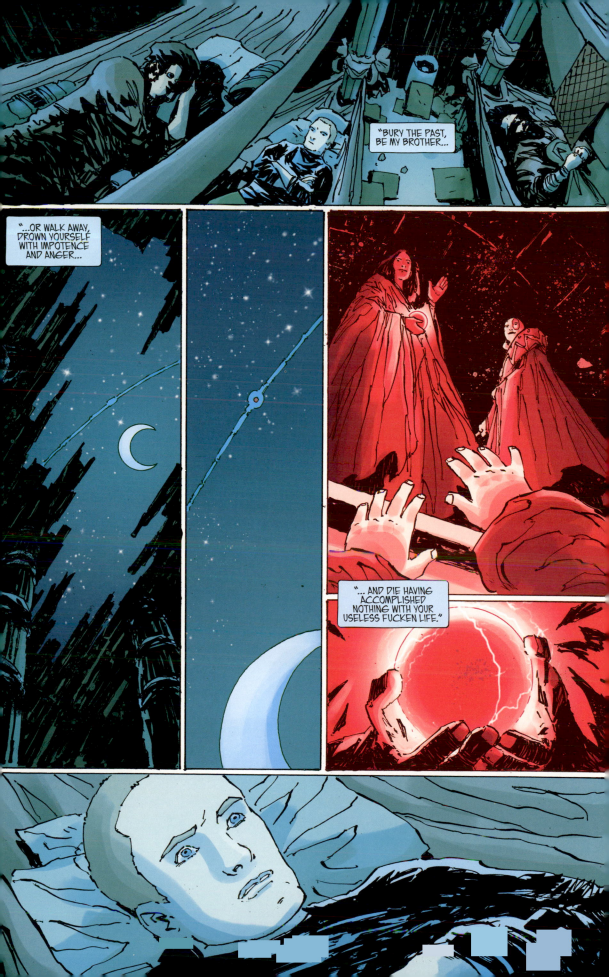

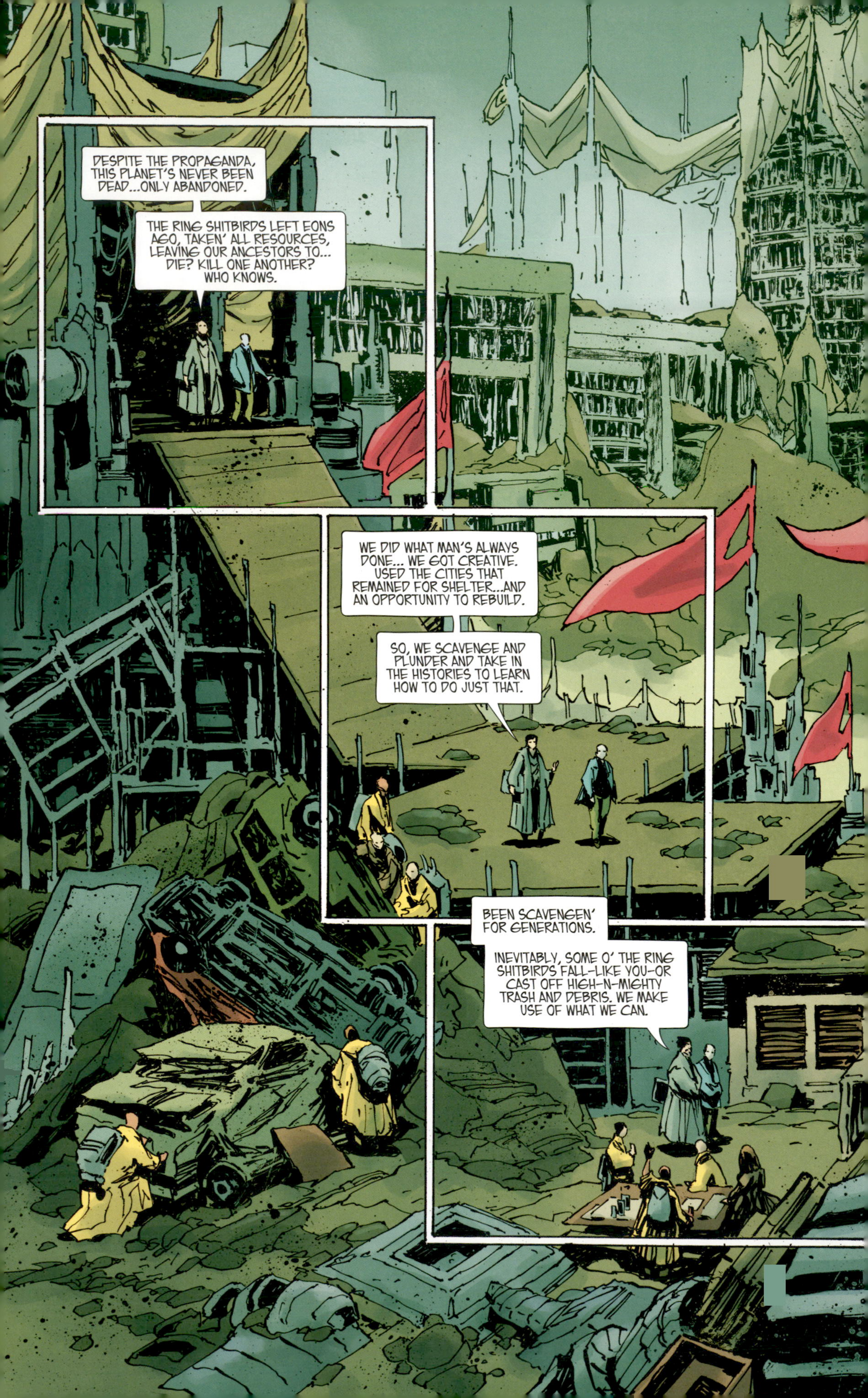
DESPITE THE PROPAGANDA, THIS PLANET'S NEVER BEEN DEAD...ONLY ABANDONED.
THE RING SHITBIRDS LEFT EONS AGO, TAKEN' ALL RESOURCES, LEAVING OUR ANCESTORS TO... DIE? KILL ONE ANOTHER? WHO KNOWS.
WE DID WHAT MAN'S ALWAYS DONE... WE GOT CREATIVE. USED THE CITIES THAT REMAINED FOR SHELTER...AND AN OPPORTUNITY TO REBUILD.
SO, WE SCAVENGE AND PLUNDER AND TAKE IN THE HISTORIES TO LEARN HOW TO DO JUST THAT.
BEEN SCAVENGEN' FOR GENERATIONS.
INEVITABLY, SOME O' THE RING SHITBIRDS FALL-LIKE YOU-OR CAST OFF HIGH-N-MIGHTY TRASH AND DEBRIS. WE MAKE USE OF WHAT WE CAN.

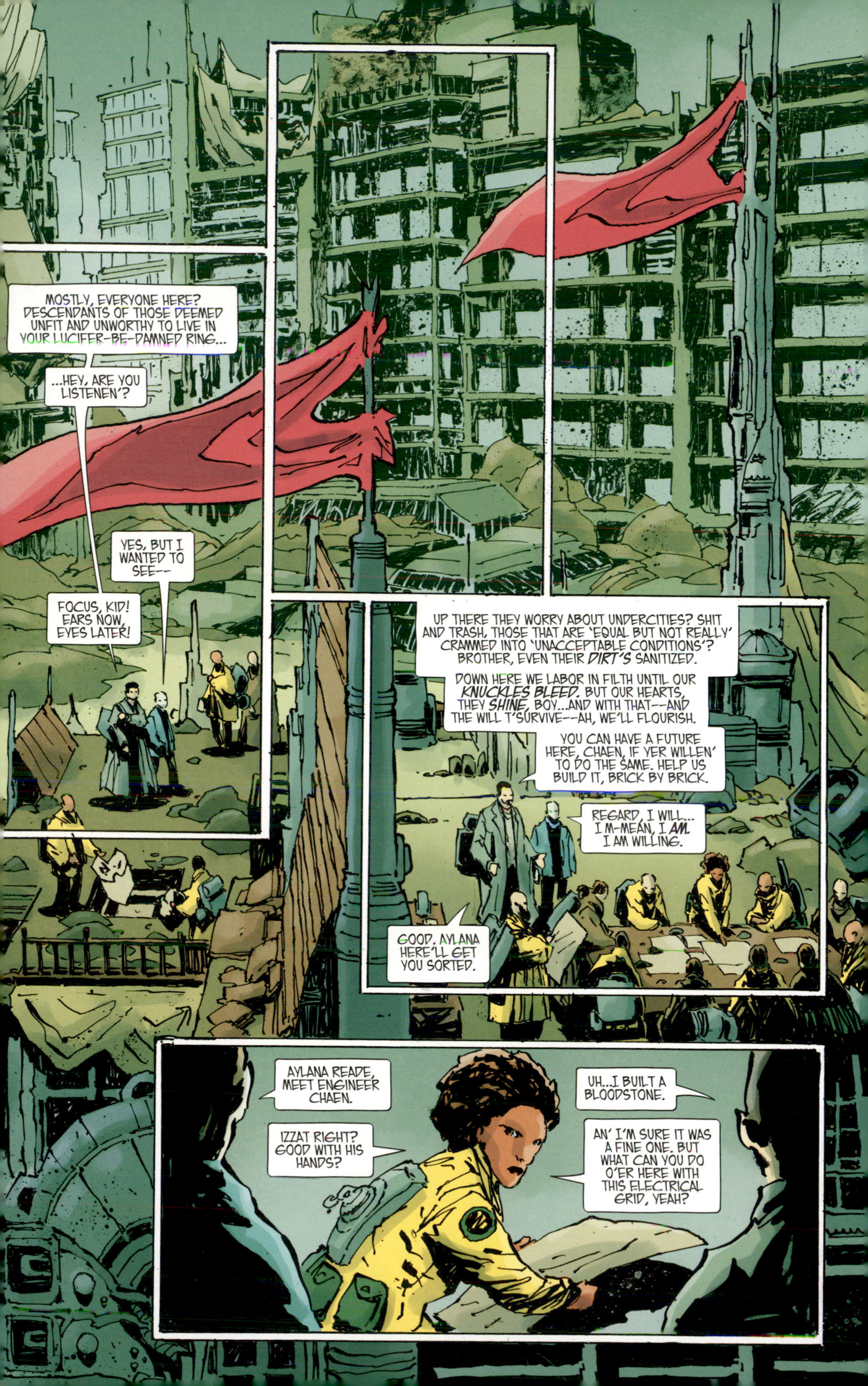
MOSTLY, EVERYONE HERE? DESCENDANTS OF THOSE DEEMED UNFIT AND UNWORTHY TO LIVE IN YOUR LUCIFER-BE-DAMNED RING...
...HEY, ARE YOU LISTENEN'?
YES, BUT I WANTED TO SEE--
FOCUS, KID! EARS NOW, EYES LATER!
UP THERE THEY WORRY ABOUT UNDERCITIES? SHIT AND TRASH, THOSE THAT ARE 'EQUAL BUT NOT REALLY' CRAMMED INTO 'UNACCEPTABLE CONDITIONS'? BROTHER, EVEN THEIR DIRT'S SANITIZED.
DOWN HERE WE LABOR IN FILTH UNTIL OUR KNUCKLES BLEED. BUT OUR HEARTS, THEY SHINE, BOY...AND WITH THAT--AND THE WILL T'SURVIVE--AH, WE'LL FLOURISH.
YOU CAN HAVE A FUTURE HERE, CHAEN, IF YER WILLEN' TO DO THE SAME. HELP US BUILD IT, BRICK BY BRICK.
REGARD, I WILL... I M-MEAN, I AM. I AM WILLING.
GOOD. AYLANA HERE'LL GET YOU SORTED.
AYLANA READE, MEET ENGINEER CHAEN.
UH...I BUILT A BLOODSTONE.
IZZAT RIGHT? GOOD WITH HIS HANDS?
AN' I'M SURE IT WAS A FINE ONE. BUT WHAT CAN YOU DO O'ER HERE WITH THIS ELECTRICAL GRID, YEAH?

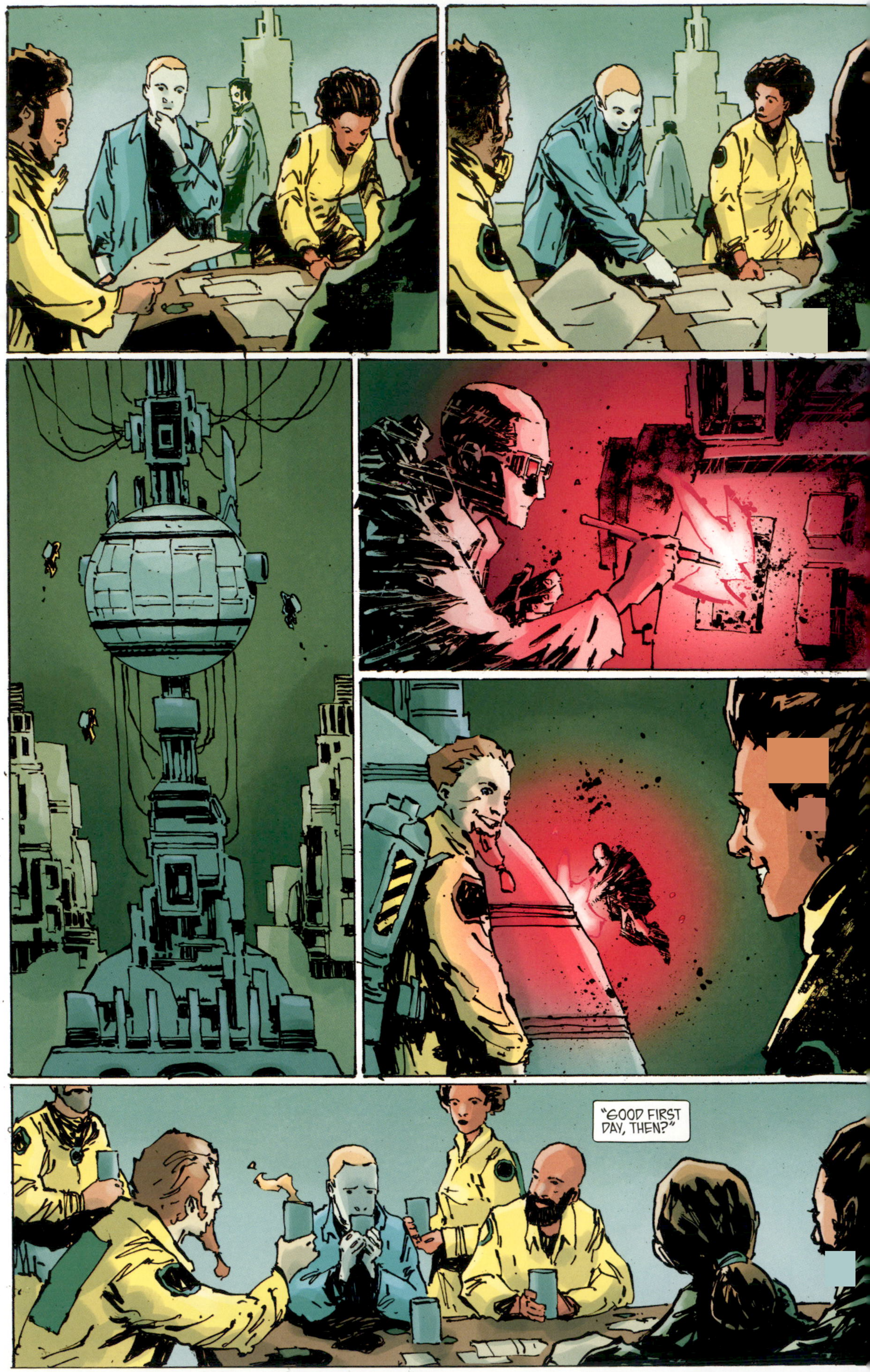
"GOOD FIRST DAY, THEN?"

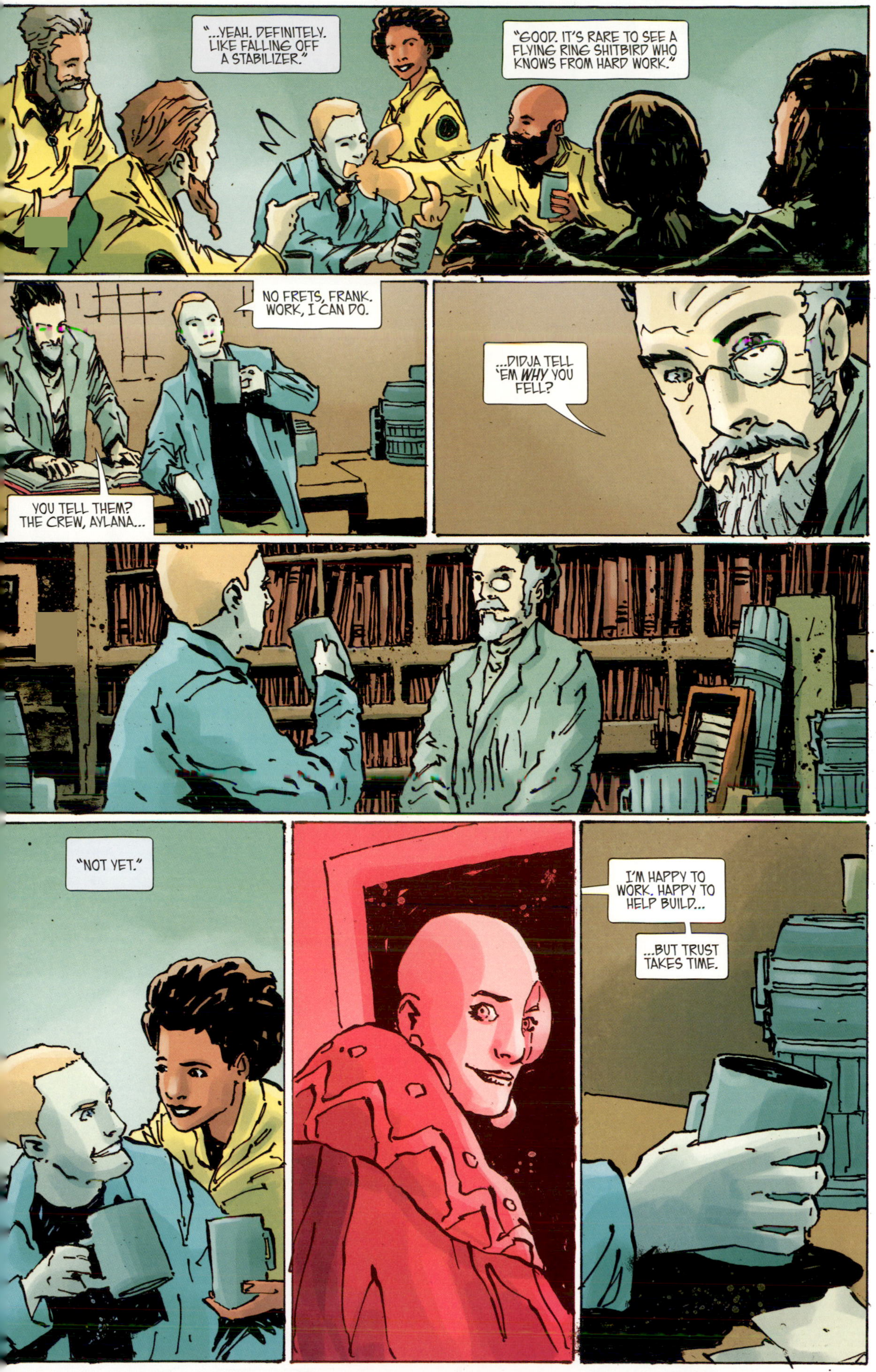
"...YEAH. DEFINITELY. LIKE FALLING OFF A STABILIZER."
"GOOD. IT'S RARE TO SEE A FLYING RING SHITBIRD WHO KNOWS FROM HARD WORK."
YOU TELL THEM? THE CREW, AYLANA...
NO FRETS, FRANK. WORK, I CAN DO.
...DIDJA TELL 'EM *WHY* YOU FELL?
"NOT YET."
I'M HAPPY TO WORK. HAPPY TO HELP BUILD...
...BUT TRUST TAKES TIME.

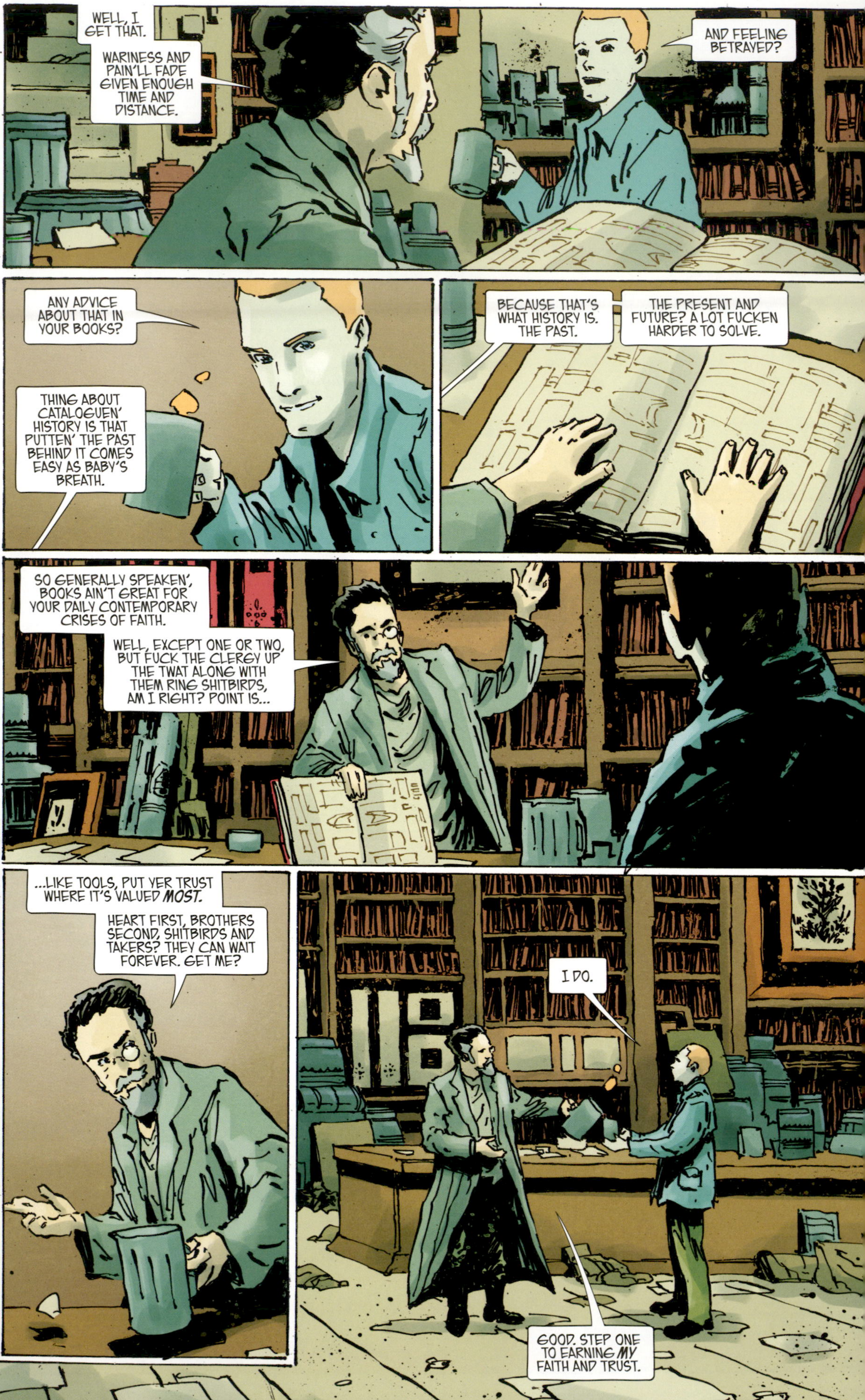
WELL, I GET THAT.
WARINESS AND PAIN'LL FADE GIVEN ENOUGH TIME AND DISTANCE.
AND FEELING BETRAYED?
ANY ADVICE ABOUT THAT IN YOUR BOOKS?
THING ABOUT CATALOGUEN' HISTORY IS THAT PUTTEN' THE PAST BEHIND IT COMES EASY AS BABY'S BREATH.
BECAUSE THAT'S WHAT HISTORY IS. THE PAST.
THE PRESENT AND FUTURE? A LOT FUCKEN HARDER TO SOLVE.
SO GENERALLY SPEAKEN', BOOKS AIN'T GREAT FOR YOUR DAILY CONTEMPORARY CRISES OF FAITH.
WELL, EXCEPT ONE OR TWO, BUT FUCK THE CLERGY UP THE TWAT ALONG WITH THEM RING SHITBIRDS, AM I RIGHT? POINT IS...
...LIKE TOOLS, PUT YER TRUST WHERE IT'S VALUED *MOST.*
HEART FIRST, BROTHERS SECOND. SHITBIRDS AND TAKERS? THEY CAN WAIT FOREVER. GET ME?
I DO.
GOOD. STEP ONE TO EARNING *MY* FAITH AND TRUST.

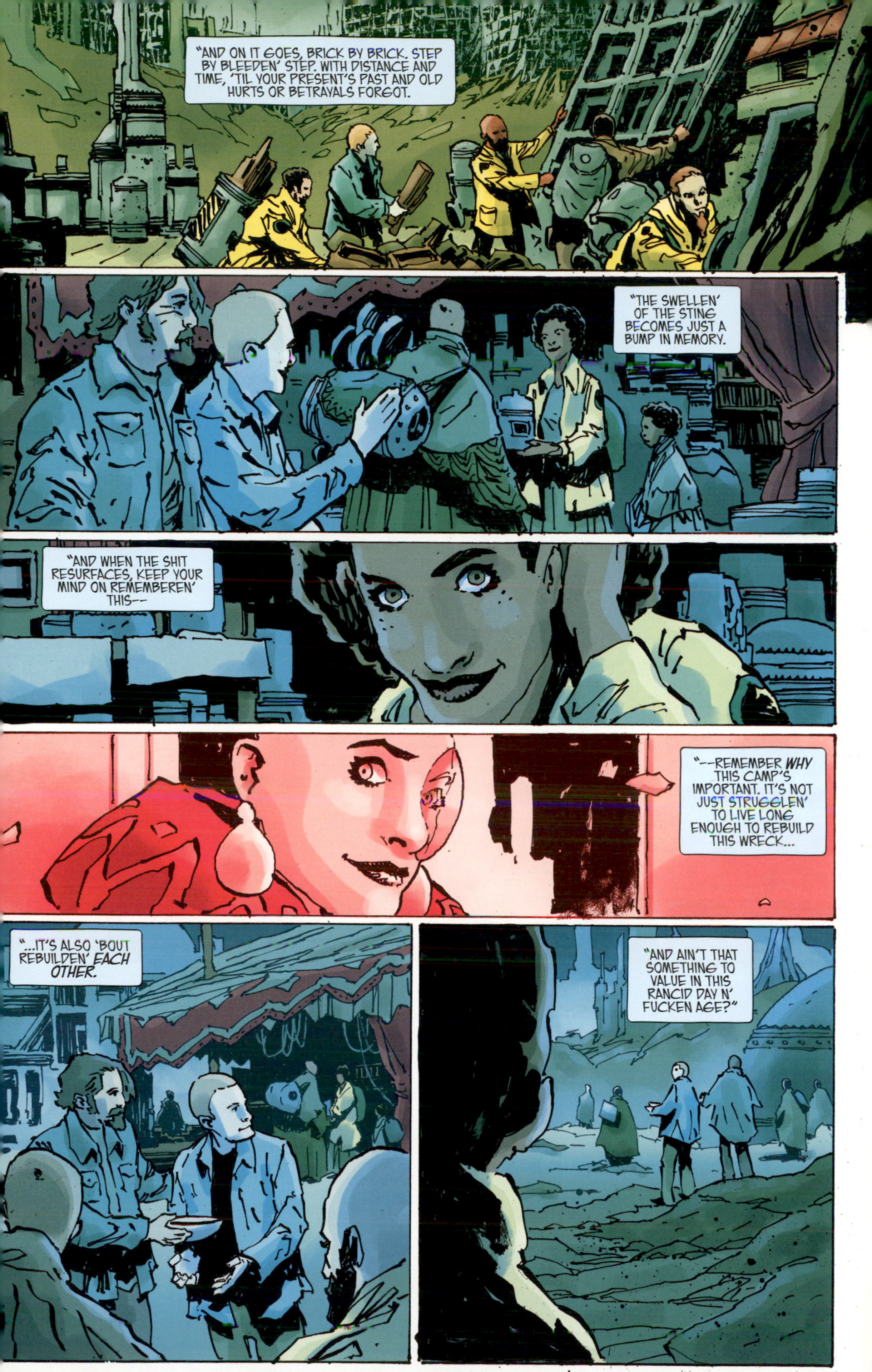
"AND ON IT GOES, BRICK BY BRICK. STEP BY BLEEDEN' STEP. WITH DISTANCE AND TIME, 'TIL YOUR PRESENT'S PAST AND OLD HURTS OR BETRAYALS FORGOT.
"THE SWELLEN' OF THE STING BECOMES JUST A BUMP IN MEMORY.
"AND WHEN THE SHIT RESURFACES, KEEP YOUR MIND ON REMEMBEREN' THIS--
"--REMEMBER *WHY* THIS CAMP'S IMPORTANT. IT'S NOT JUST STRUGGLEN' TO LIVE LONG ENOUGH TO REBUILD THIS WRECK...
"...IT'S ALSO 'BOUT REBUILDEN' *EACH OTHER.*
"AND AIN'T THAT SOMETHING TO VALUE IN THIS RANCID DAY N' FUCKEN AGE?"

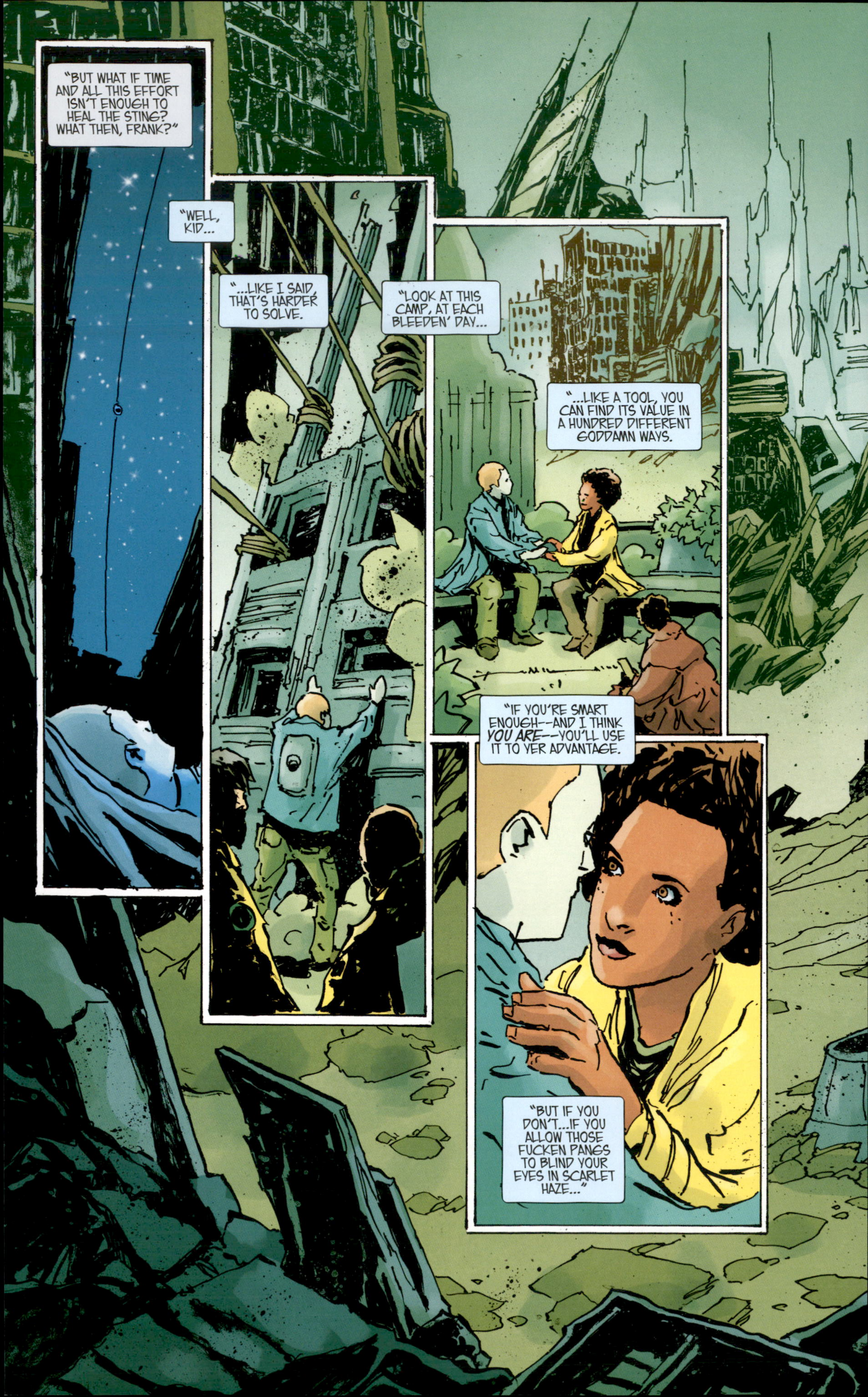
"BUT WHAT IF TIME AND ALL THIS EFFORT ISN'T ENOUGH TO HEAL THE STING? WHAT THEN, FRANK?"
"WELL, KID...
"...LIKE I SAID, THAT'S HARDER TO SOLVE.
"LOOK AT THIS CAMP, AT EACH BLEEDEN' DAY...
"...LIKE A TOOL, YOU CAN FIND ITS VALUE IN A HUNDRED DIFFERENT GODDAMN WAYS.
"IF YOU'RE SMART ENOUGH--AND I THINK YOU ARE--YOU'LL USE IT TO YER ADVANTAGE.
"BUT IF YOU DON'T...IF YOU ALLOW THOSE FUCKEN PANGS TO BLIND YOUR EYES IN SCARLET HAZE..."

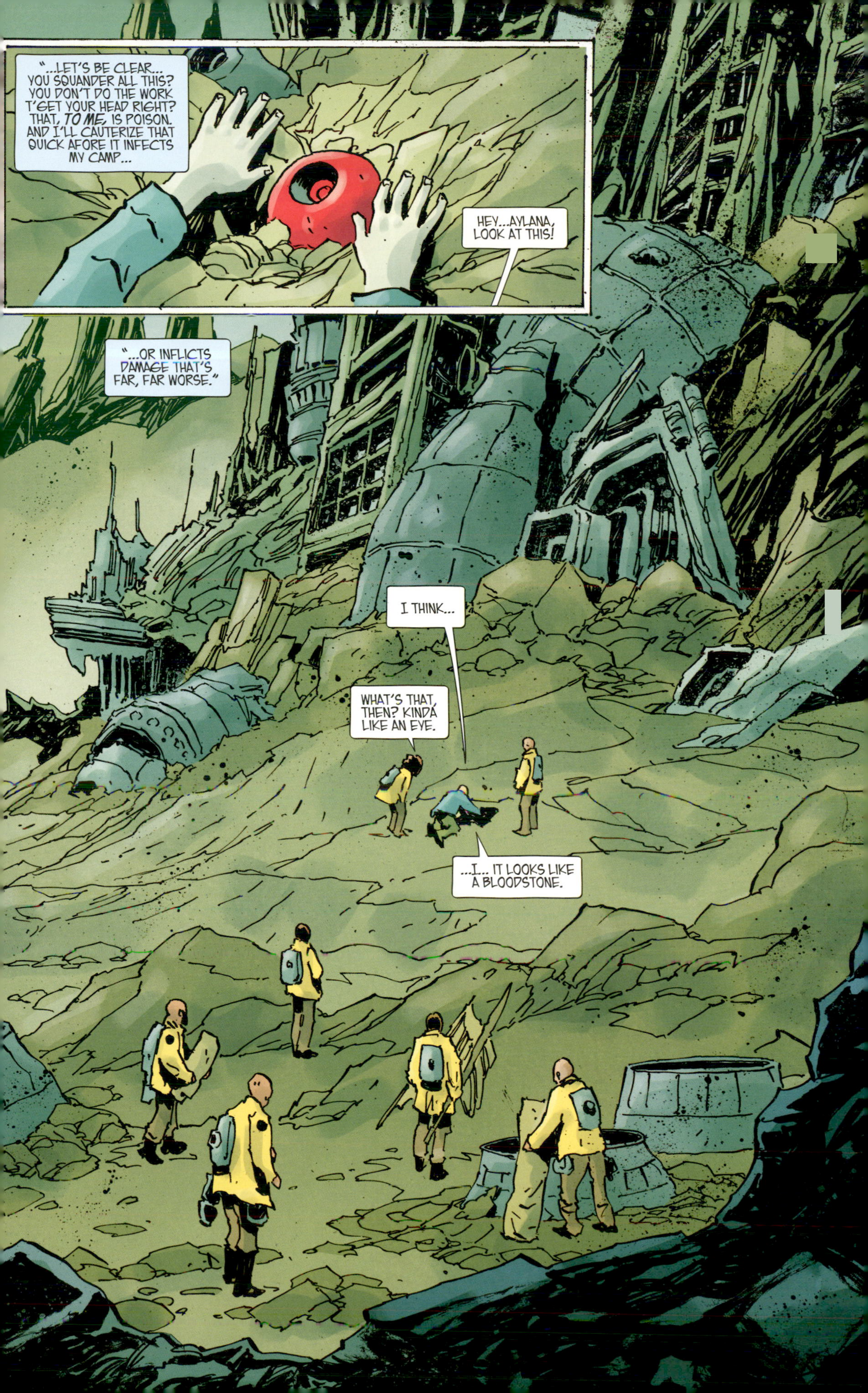
"...LET'S BE CLEAR... YOU SQUANDER ALL THIS? YOU DON'T DO THE WORK T'GET YOUR HEAD RIGHT? THAT, TO ME, IS POISON. AND I'LL CAUTERIZE THAT QUICK AFORE IT INFECTS MY CAMP...
HEY...AYLANA, LOOK AT THIS!
"...OR INFLICTS DAMAGE THAT'S FAR, FAR WORSE."
I THINK...
WHAT'S THAT, THEN? KINDA LIKE AN EYE.
...I... IT LOOKS LIKE A BLOODSTONE.

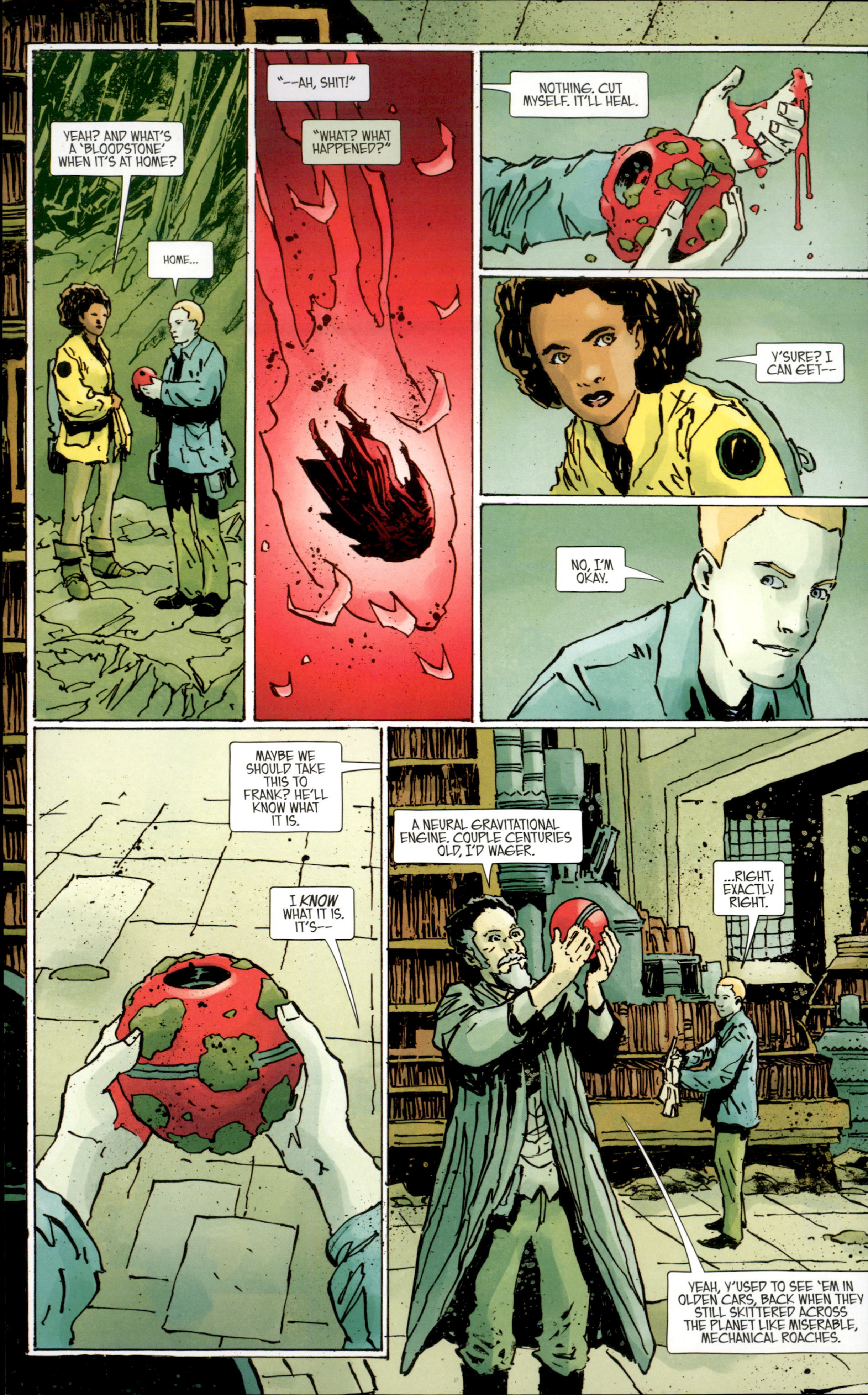
YEAH? AND WHAT'S A 'BLOODSTONE' WHEN IT'S AT HOME?
HOME...
"--AH, SHIT!"
"WHAT? WHAT HAPPENED?"
NOTHING. CUT MYSELF. IT'LL HEAL.
Y'SURE? I CAN GET--
NO, I'M OKAY.
MAYBE WE SHOULD TAKE THIS TO FRANK? HE'LL KNOW WHAT IT IS.
I *KNOW* WHAT IT IS. IT'S--
A NEURAL GRAVITATIONAL ENGINE. COUPLE CENTURIES OLD, I'D WAGER.
...RIGHT. EXACTLY RIGHT.
YEAH, Y'USED TO SEE 'EM IN OLDEN CARS, BACK WHEN THEY STILL SKITTERED ACROSS THE PLANET LIKE MISERABLE, MECHANICAL ROACHES.

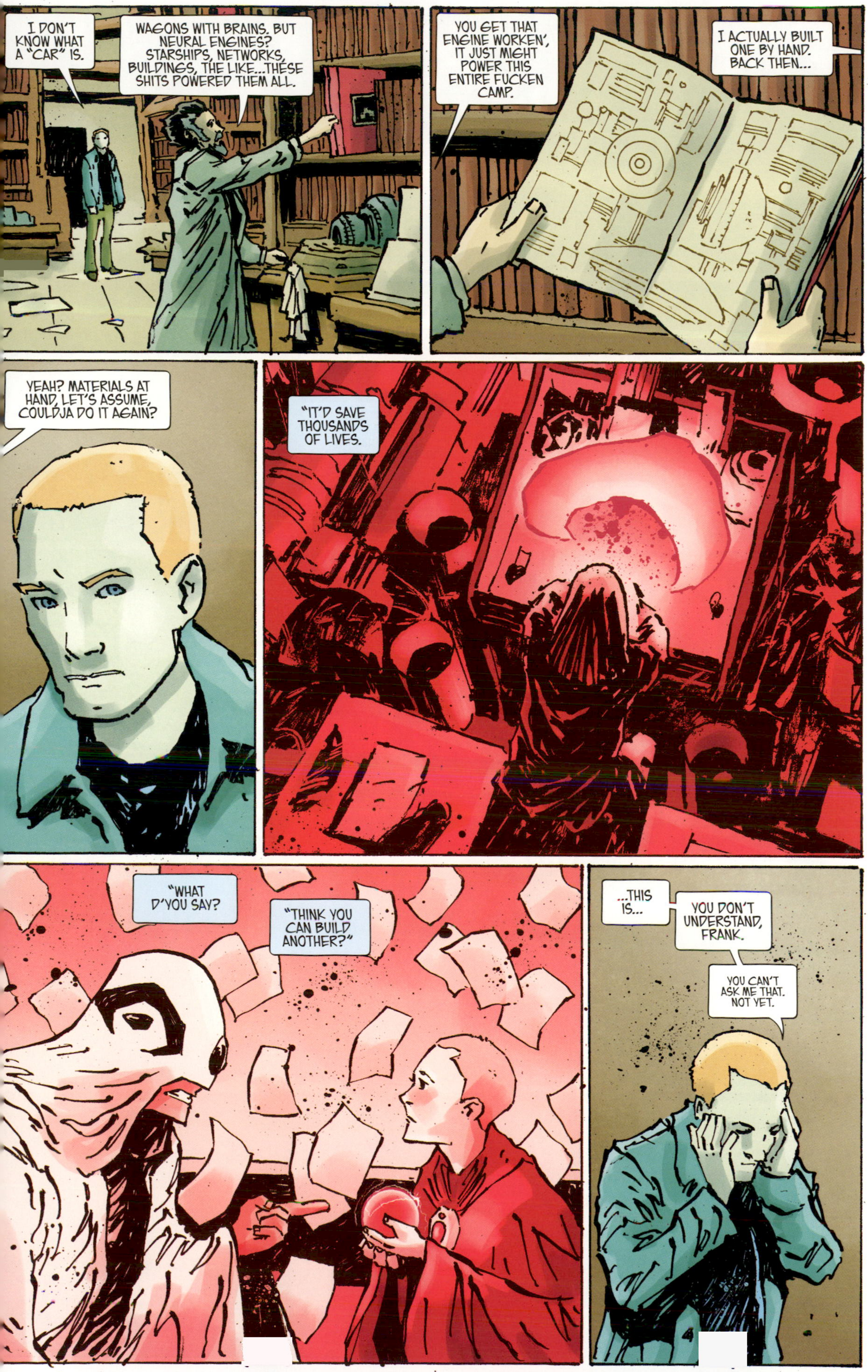
I DON'T KNOW WHAT A "CAR" IS.
WAGONS WITH BRAINS. BUT NEURAL ENGINES? STARSHIPS, NETWORKS, BUILDINGS, THE LIKE...THESE SHITS POWERED THEM ALL.
YOU GET THAT ENGINE WORKEN', IT JUST MIGHT POWER THIS ENTIRE FUCKEN CAMP.
I ACTUALLY BUILT ONE BY HAND. BACK THEN...
YEAH? MATERIALS AT HAND, LET'S ASSUME, COULDJA DO IT AGAIN?
"IT'D SAVE THOUSANDS OF LIVES.
"WHAT D'YOU SAY?
"THINK YOU CAN BUILD ANOTHER?"
...THIS IS...
YOU DON'T UNDERSTAND, FRANK.
YOU CAN'T ASK ME THAT. NOT YET.

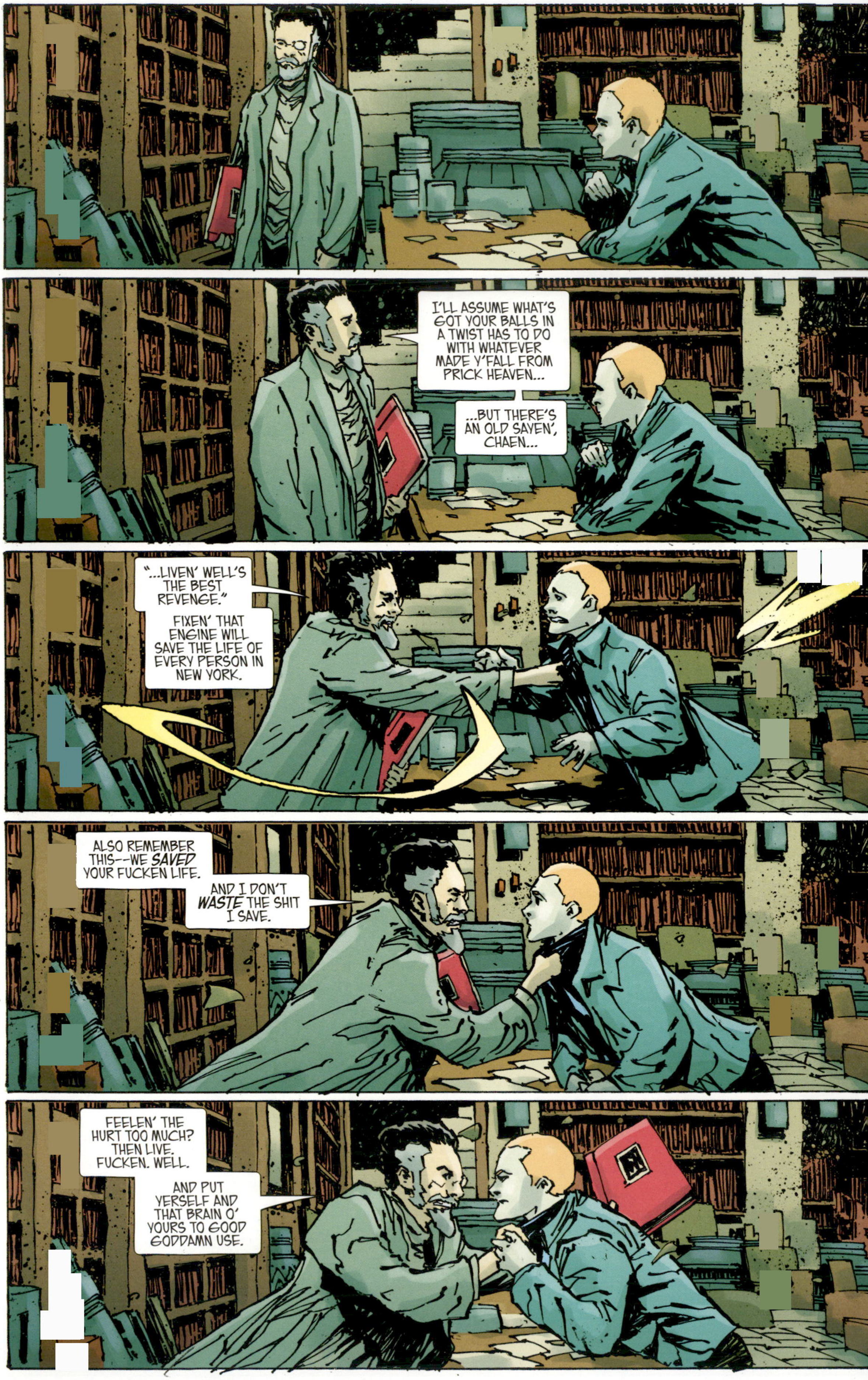
I'LL ASSUME WHAT'S GOT YOUR BALLS IN A TWIST HAS TO DO WITH WHATEVER MADE Y'FALL FROM PRICK HEAVEN...
...BUT THERE'S AN OLD SAYEN', CHAEN...
"...LIVEN' WELL'S THE BEST REVENGE."
FIXEN' THAT ENGINE WILL SAVE THE LIFE OF EVERY PERSON IN NEW YORK.
ALSO REMEMBER THIS--WE *SAVED* YOUR FUCKEN LIFE.
AND I DON'T *WASTE* THE SHIT I SAVE.
FEELEN' THE HURT TOO MUCH? THEN LIVE. FUCKEN. WELL.
AND PUT YERSELF AND THAT BRAIN O' YOURS TO GOOD GODDAMN USE.

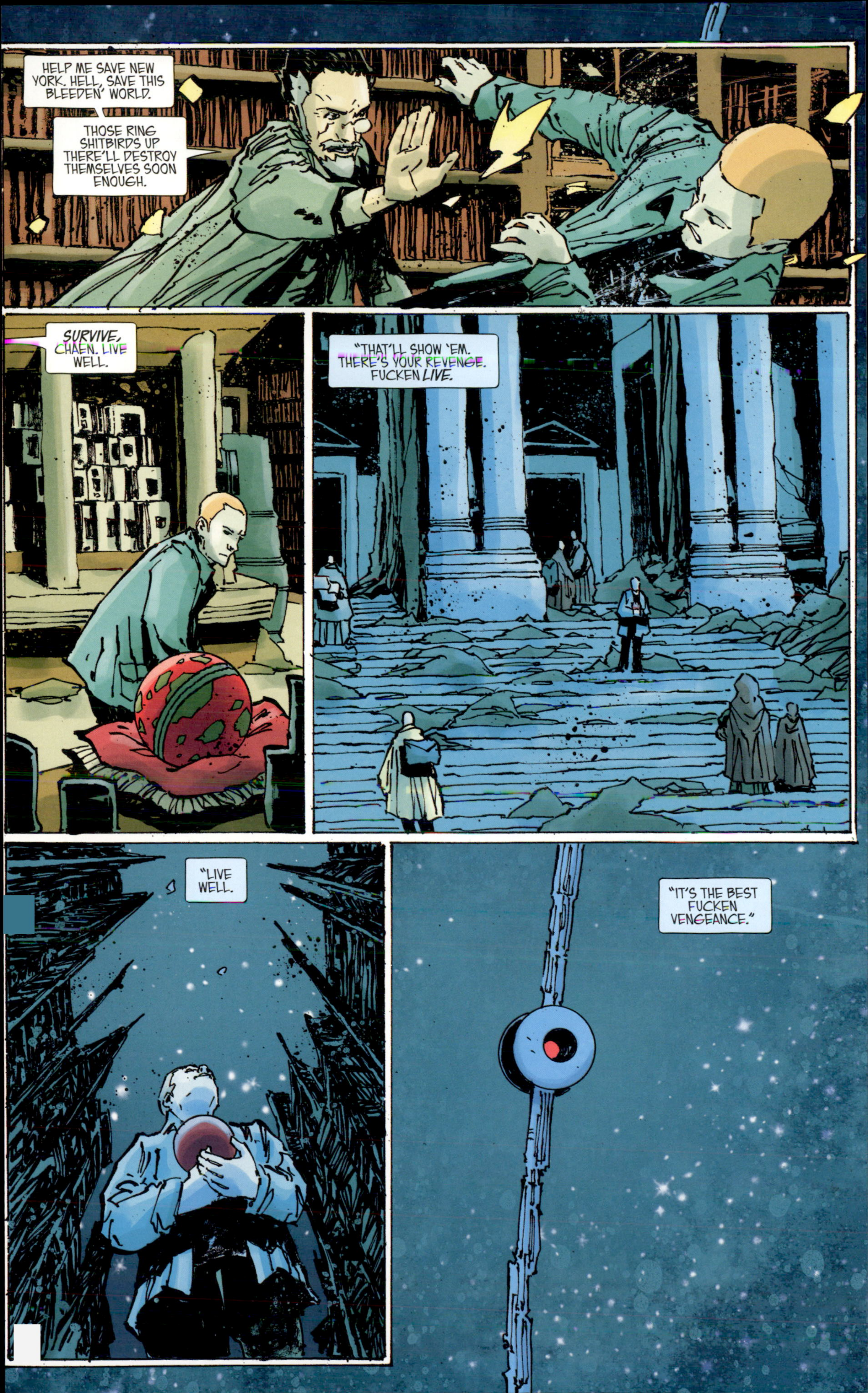
HELP ME SAVE NEW YORK. HELL, SAVE THIS BLEEDEN' WORLD.
THOSE RING SHITBIRDS UP THERE'LL DESTROY THEMSELVES SOON ENOUGH.
SURVIVE, CHAEN. LIVE WELL.
"THAT'LL SHOW 'EM. THERE'S YOUR REVENGE. FUCKEN LIVE.
"LIVE WELL.
"IT'S THE BEST FUCKEN VENGEANCE."

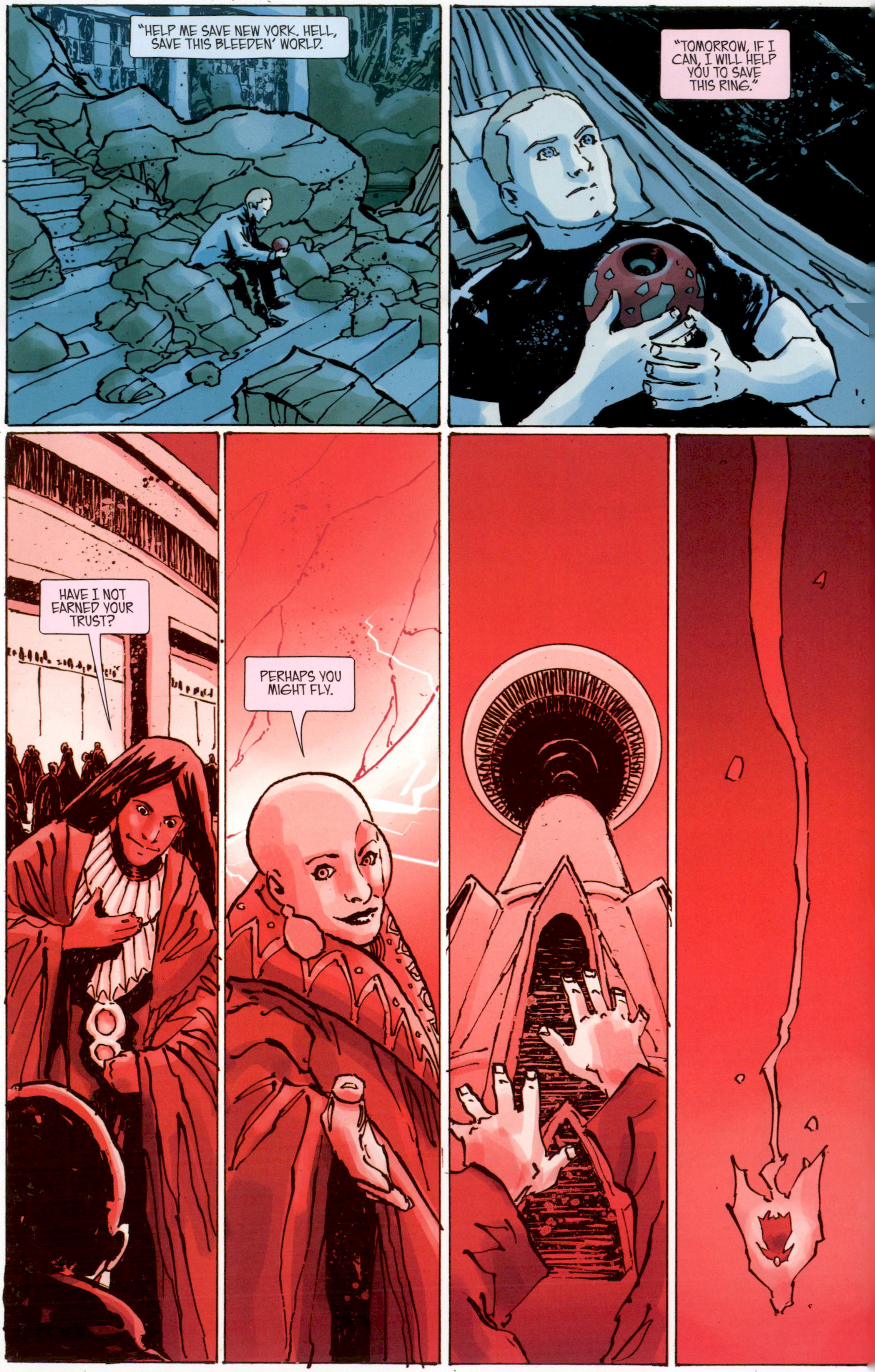
"HELP ME SAVE NEW YORK. HELL, SAVE THIS BLEEDEN' WORLD.
"TOMORROW, IF I CAN, I WILL HELP YOU TO SAVE THIS RING."
HAVE I NOT EARNED YOUR TRUST?
PERHAPS YOU MIGHT FLY.

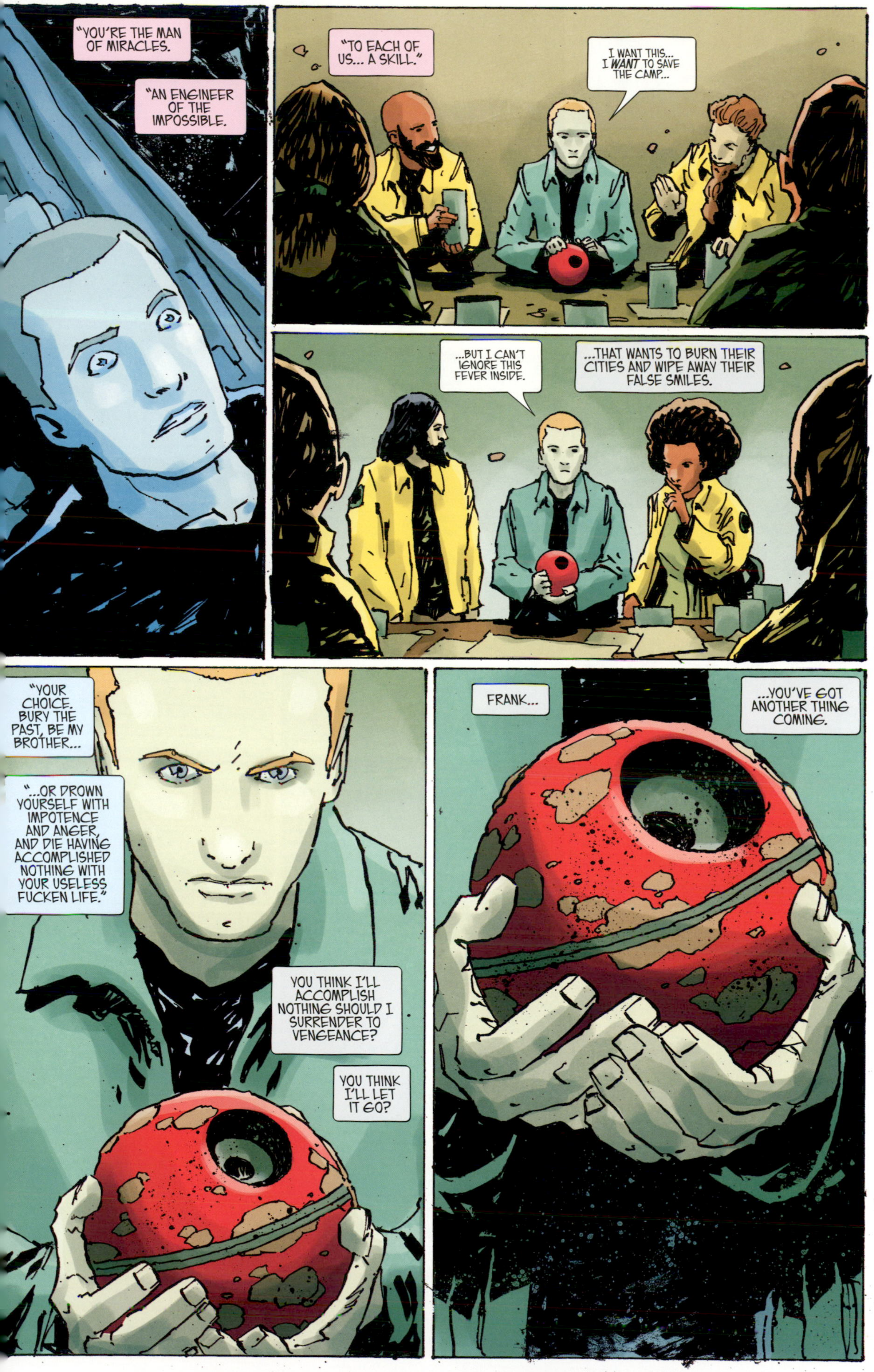
"YOU'RE THE MAN OF MIRACLES.
"AN ENGINEER OF THE IMPOSSIBLE.
"TO EACH OF US... A SKILL."
I WANT THIS... I WANT TO SAVE THE CAMP...
...BUT I CAN'T IGNORE THIS FEVER INSIDE.
...THAT WANTS TO BURN THEIR CITIES AND WIPE AWAY THEIR FALSE SMILES.
"YOUR CHOICE. BURY THE PAST, BE MY BROTHER...
"...OR DROWN YOURSELF WITH IMPOTENCE AND ANGER, AND DIE HAVING ACCOMPLISHED NOTHING WITH YOUR USELESS FUCKEN LIFE."
YOU THINK I'LL ACCOMPLISH NOTHING SHOULD I SURRENDER TO VENGEANCE?
YOU THINK I'LL LET IT GO?
FRANK...
...YOU'VE GOT ANOTHER THING COMING.

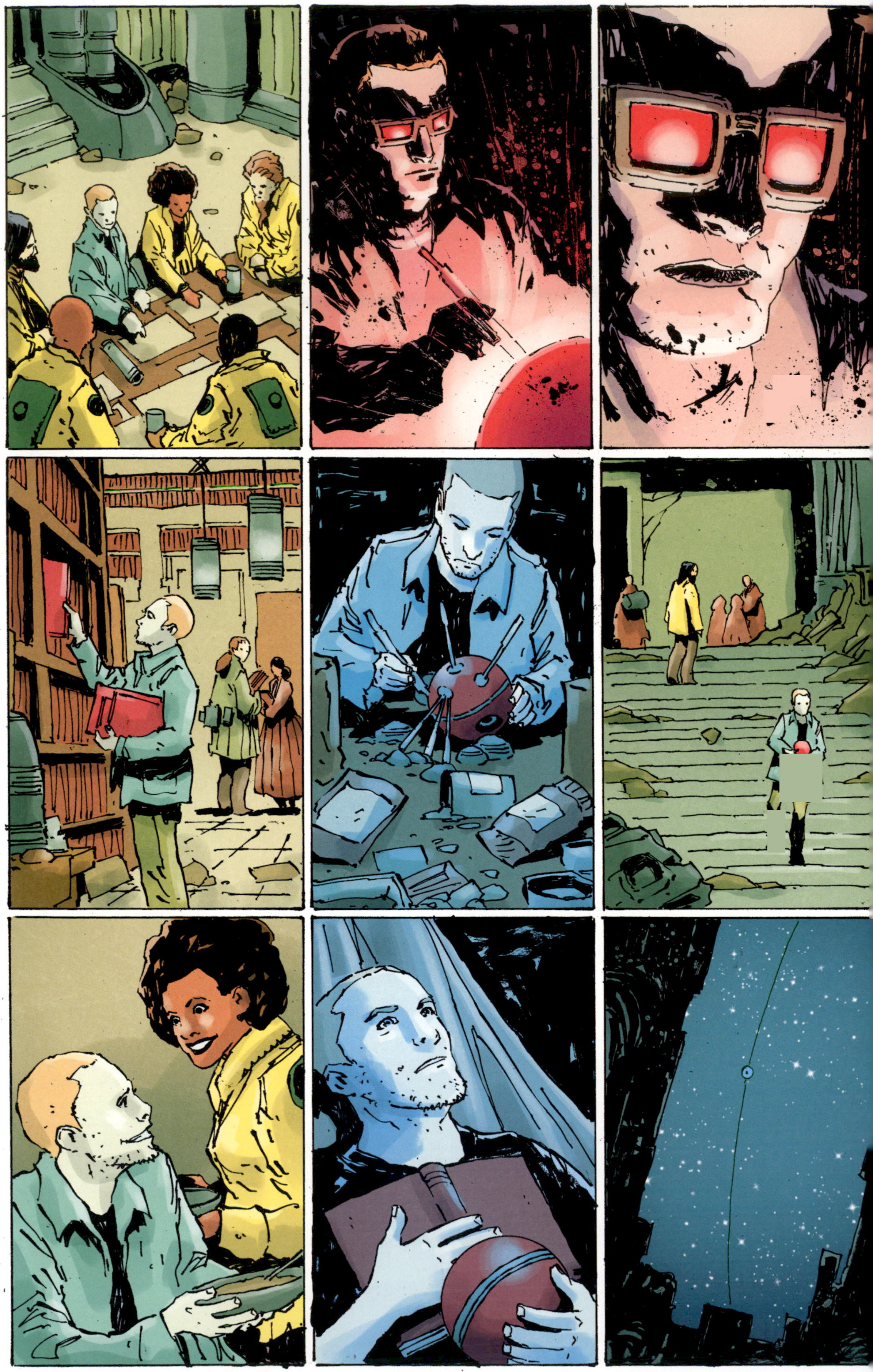

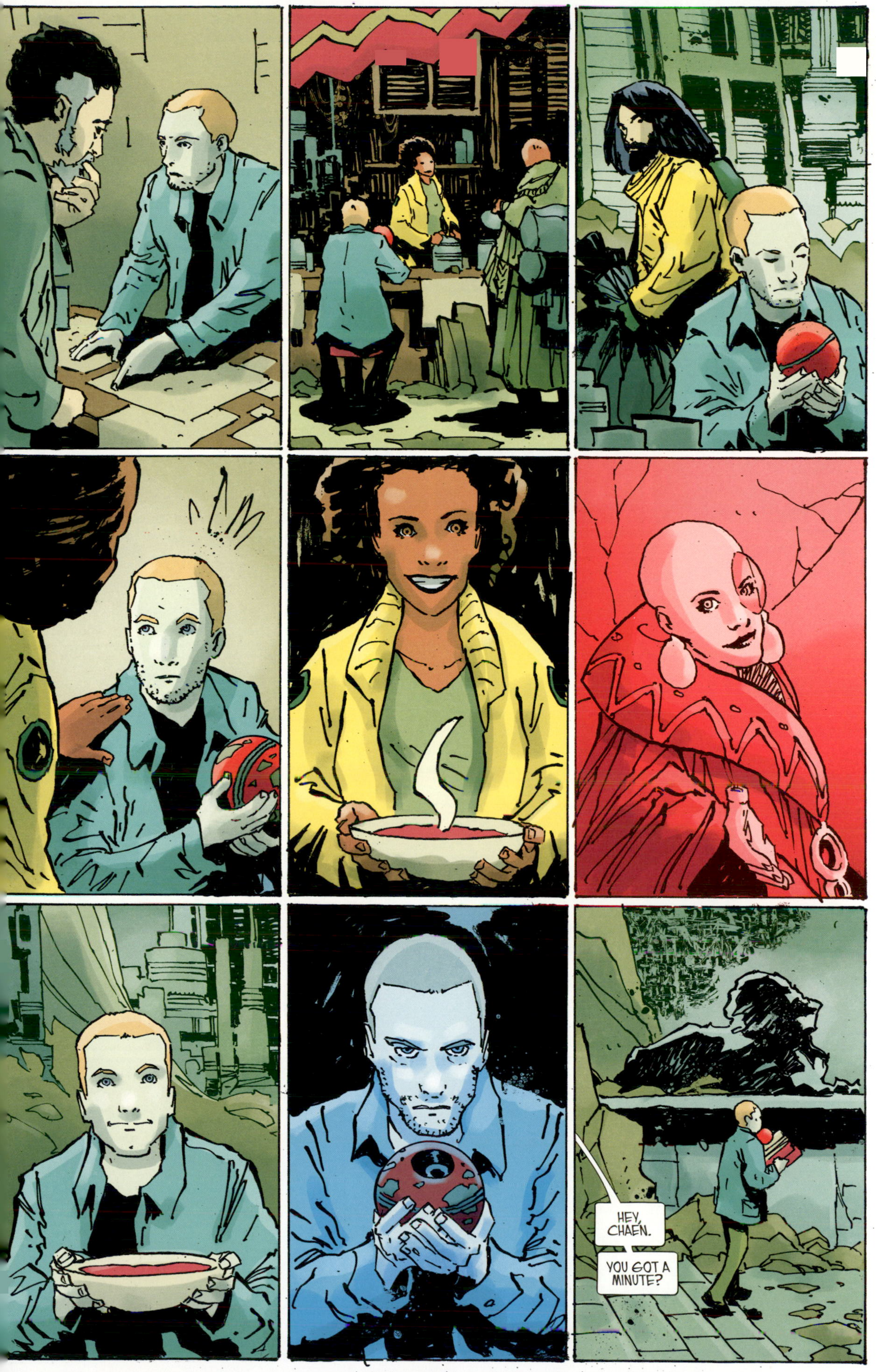
HEY, CHAEN.
YOU GOT A MINUTE?

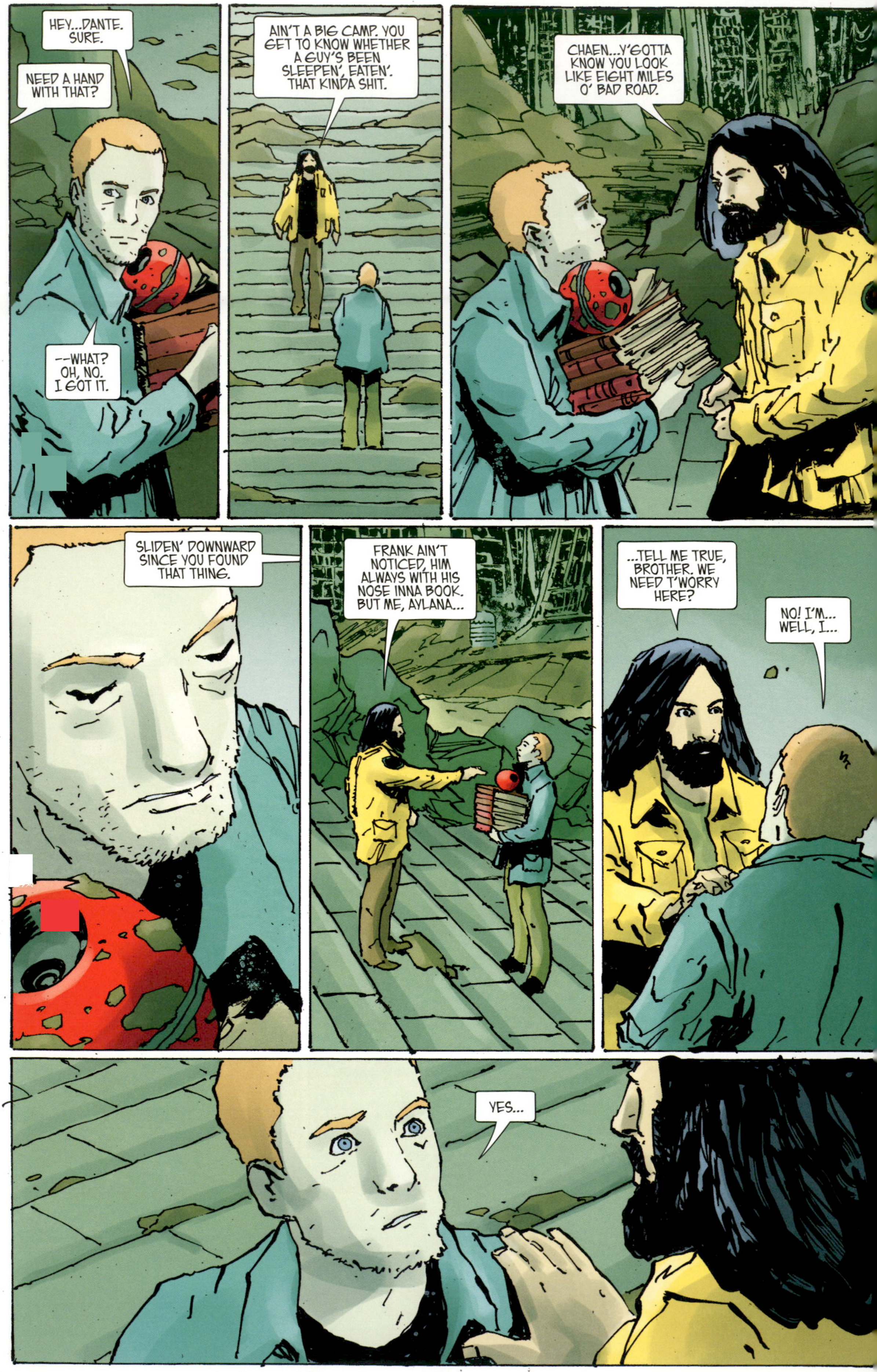
HEY...DANTE. SURE.
NEED A HAND WITH THAT?
--WHAT? OH, NO. I GOT IT.
AIN'T A BIG CAMP. YOU GET TO KNOW WHETHER A GUY'S BEEN SLEEPEN', EATEN'. THAT KINDA SHIT.
CHAEN...Y'GOTTA KNOW YOU LOOK LIKE EIGHT MILES O' BAD ROAD.
SLIDEN' DOWNWARD SINCE YOU FOUND THAT THING.
FRANK AIN'T NOTICED, HIM ALWAYS WITH HIS NOSE INNA BOOK. BUT ME, AYLANA...
...TELL ME TRUE, BROTHER. WE NEED T'WORRY HERE?
NO! I'M... WELL, I...
YES...

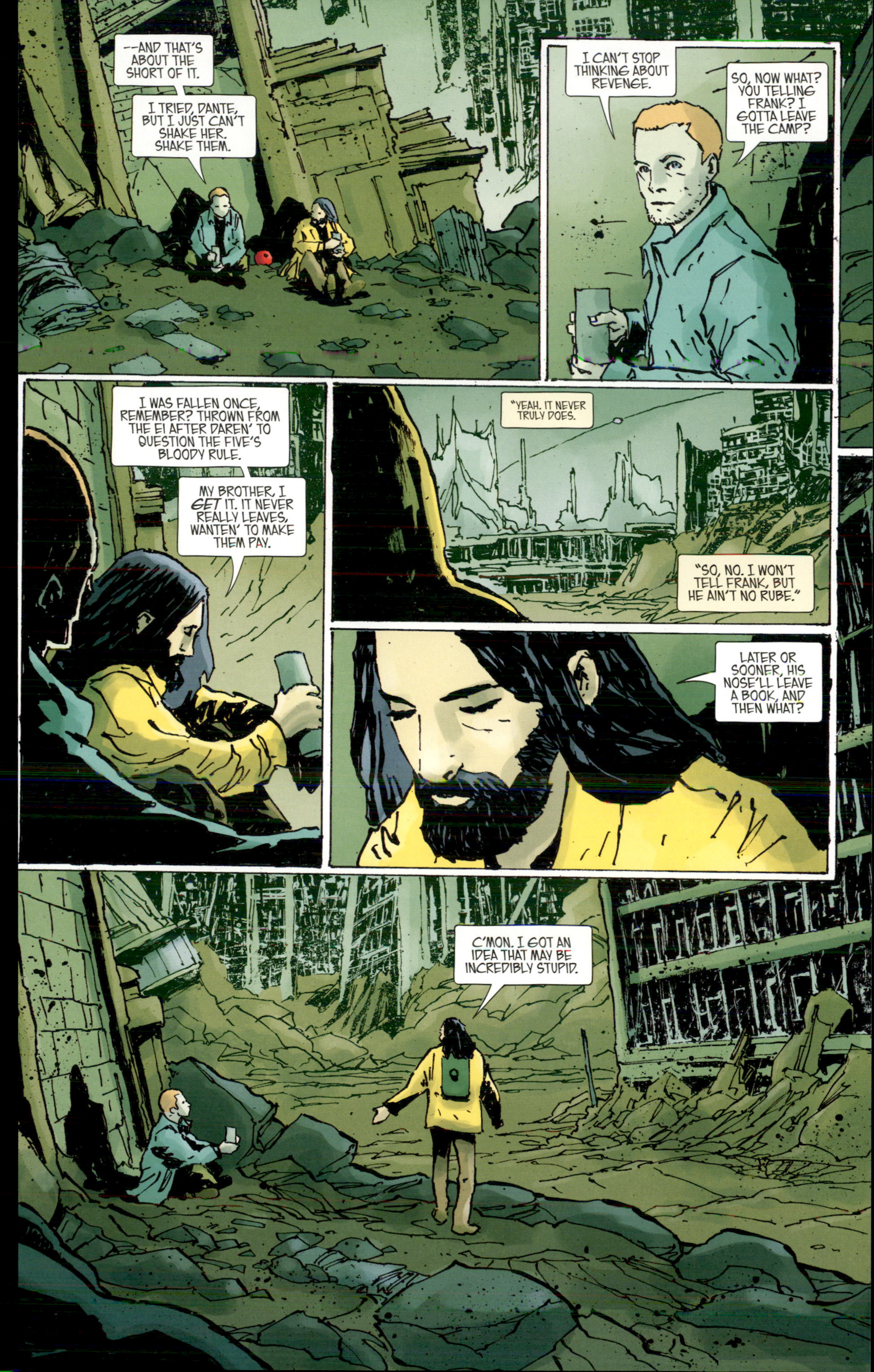
--AND THAT'S ABOUT THE SHORT OF IT.
I TRIED, DANTE, BUT I JUST CAN'T SHAKE HER. SHAKE THEM.
I CAN'T STOP THINKING ABOUT REVENGE.
SO, NOW WHAT? YOU TELLING FRANK? I GOTTA LEAVE THE CAMP?
I WAS FALLEN ONCE, REMEMBER? THROWN FROM THE EI AFTER DAREN' TO QUESTION THE FIVE'S BLOODY RULE.
MY BROTHER, I GET IT. IT NEVER REALLY LEAVES, WANTEN' TO MAKE THEM PAY.
"YEAH. IT NEVER TRULY DOES.
"SO, NO. I WON'T TELL FRANK, BUT HE AIN'T NO RUBE."
LATER OR SOONER, HIS NOSE'LL LEAVE A BOOK, AND THEN WHAT?
C'MON. I GOT AN IDEA THAT MAY BE INCREDIBLY STUPID.

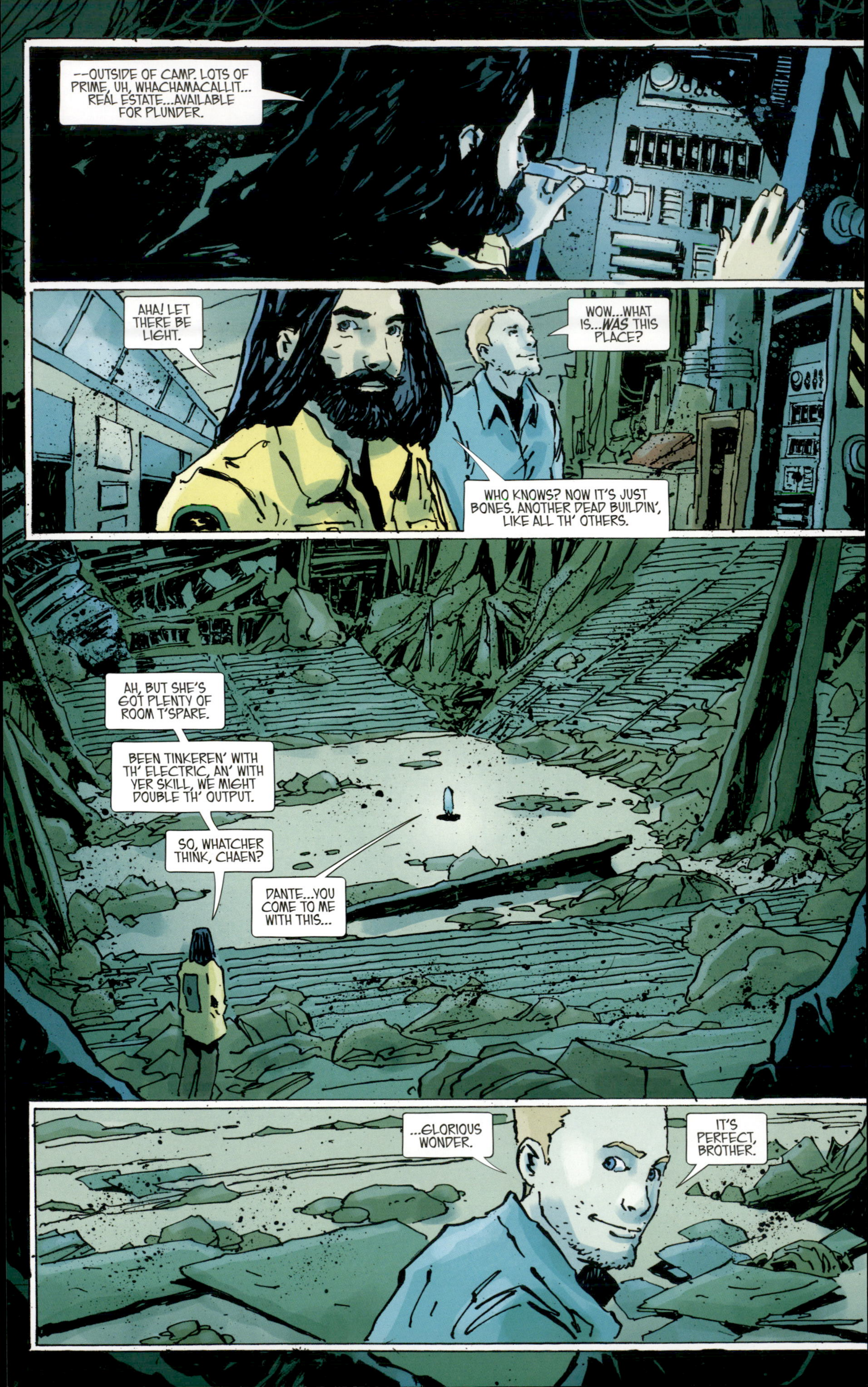
--OUTSIDE OF CAMP. LOTS OF PRIME, UH, WHACHAMACALLIT... REAL ESTATE...AVAILABLE FOR PLUNDER.
AHA! LET THERE BE LIGHT.
WOW...WHAT IS...WAS THIS PLACE?
WHO KNOWS? NOW IT'S JUST BONES. ANOTHER DEAD BUILDIN', LIKE ALL TH' OTHERS.
AH, BUT SHE'S GOT PLENTY OF ROOM T'SPARE.
BEEN TINKEREN' WITH TH' ELECTRIC, AN' WITH YER SKILL, WE MIGHT DOUBLE TH' OUTPUT.
SO, WHATCHER THINK, CHAEN?
DANTE...YOU COME TO ME WITH THIS...
...GLORIOUS WONDER.
IT'S PERFECT, BROTHER.

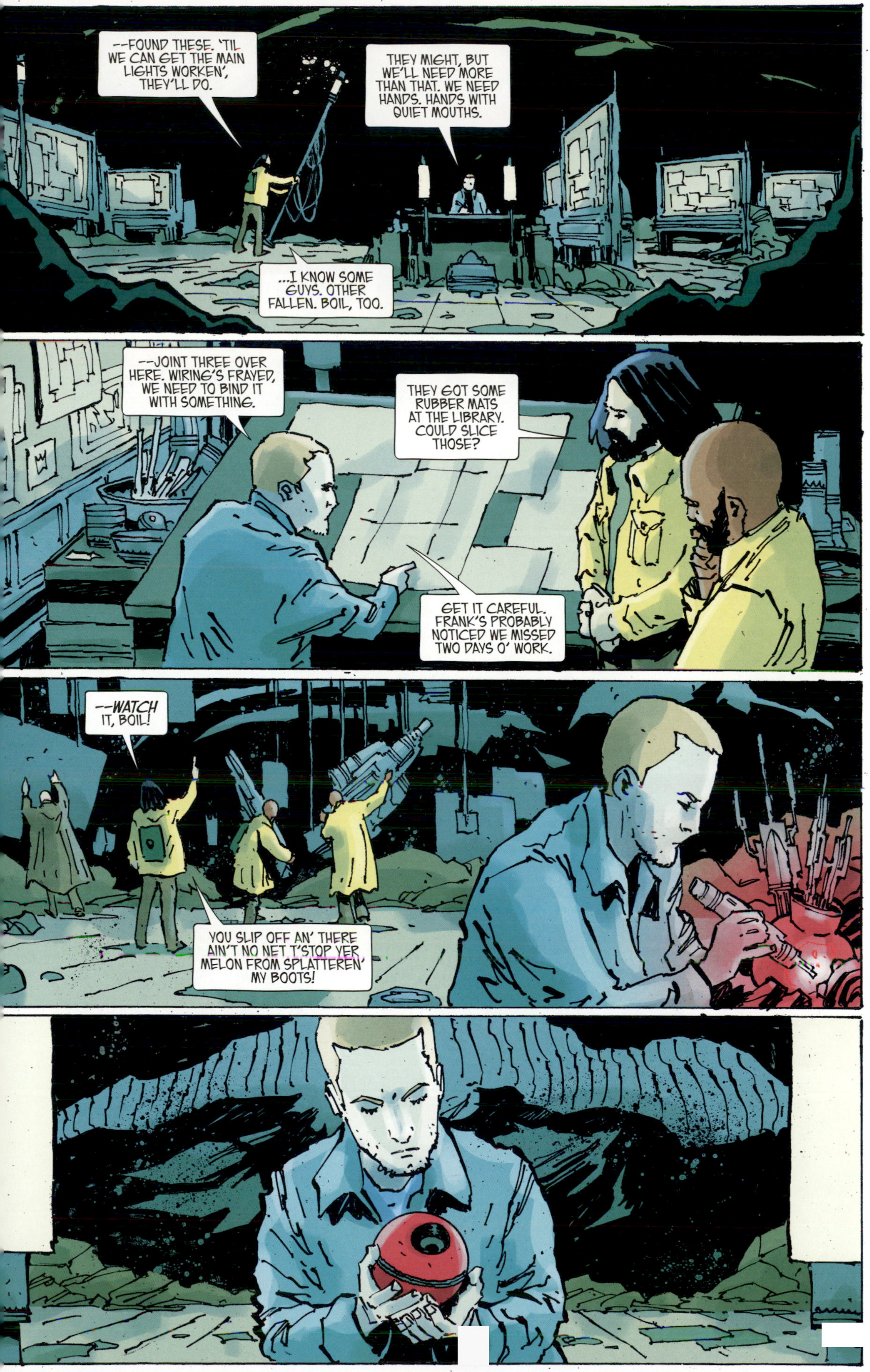
--FOUND THESE. 'TIL WE CAN GET THE MAIN LIGHTS WORKEN', THEY'LL DO.
THEY MIGHT, BUT WE'LL NEED MORE THAN THAT. WE NEED HANDS. HANDS WITH QUIET MOUTHS.
...I KNOW SOME GUYS. OTHER FALLEN. BOIL, TOO.
--JOINT THREE OVER HERE. WIRING'S FRAYED, WE NEED TO BIND IT WITH SOMETHING.
THEY GOT SOME RUBBER MATS AT THE LIBRARY. COULD SLICE THOSE?
GET IT CAREFUL. FRANK'S PROBABLY NOTICED WE MISSED TWO DAYS O' WORK.
--WATCH IT, BOIL!
YOU SLIP OFF AN' THERE AIN'T NO NET T'STOP YER MELON FROM SPLATTEREN' MY BOOTS!

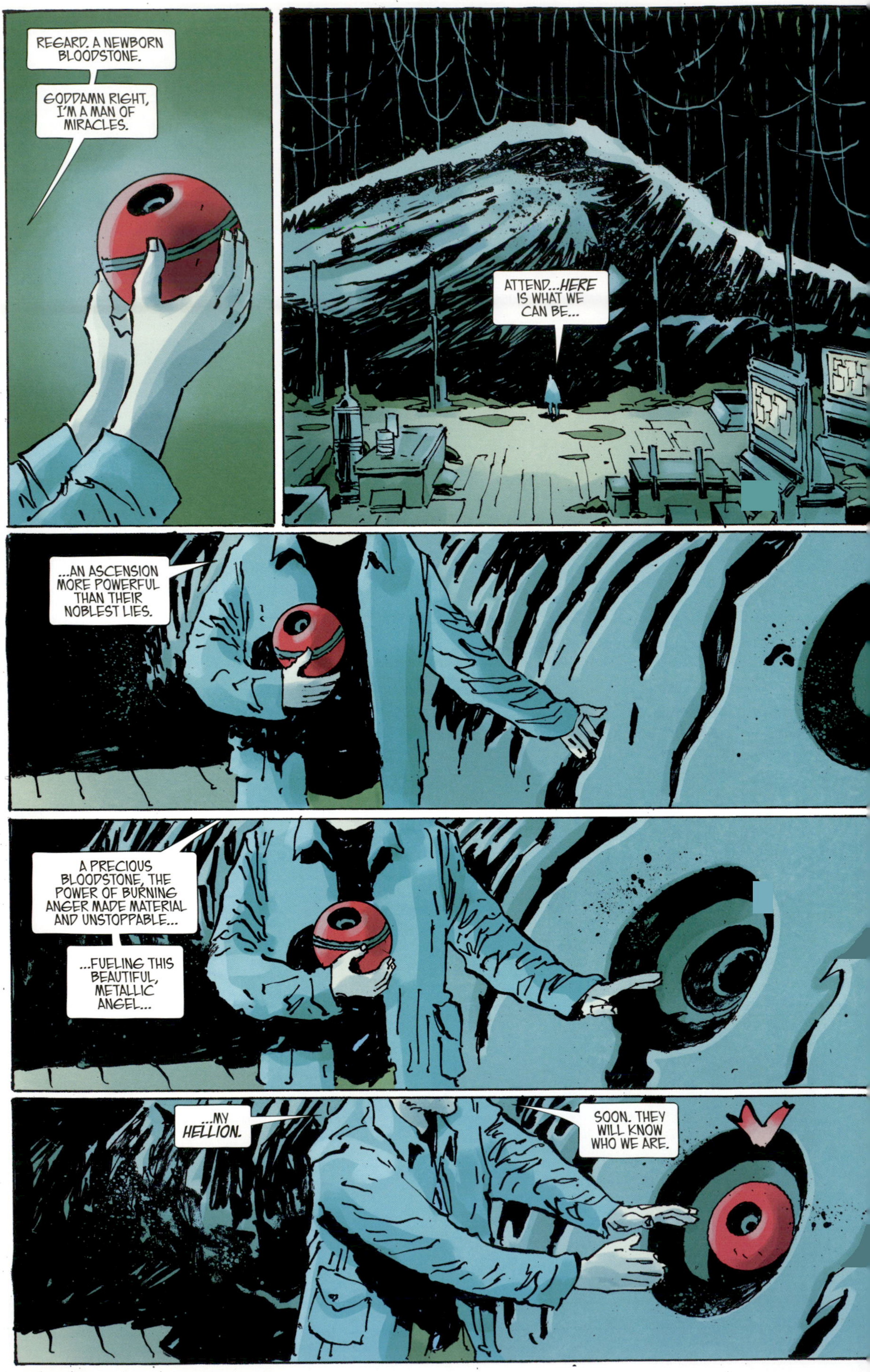
REGARD. A NEWBORN BLOODSTONE.
GODDAMN RIGHT, I'M A MAN OF MIRACLES.
ATTEND...HERE IS WHAT WE CAN BE...
...AN ASCENSION MORE POWERFUL THAN THEIR NOBLEST LIES.
A PRECIOUS BLOODSTONE, THE POWER OF BURNING ANGER MADE MATERIAL AND UNSTOPPABLE...
...FUELING THIS BEAUTIFUL, METALLIC ANGEL...
...MY HELLION.
SOON. THEY WILL KNOW WHO WE ARE.

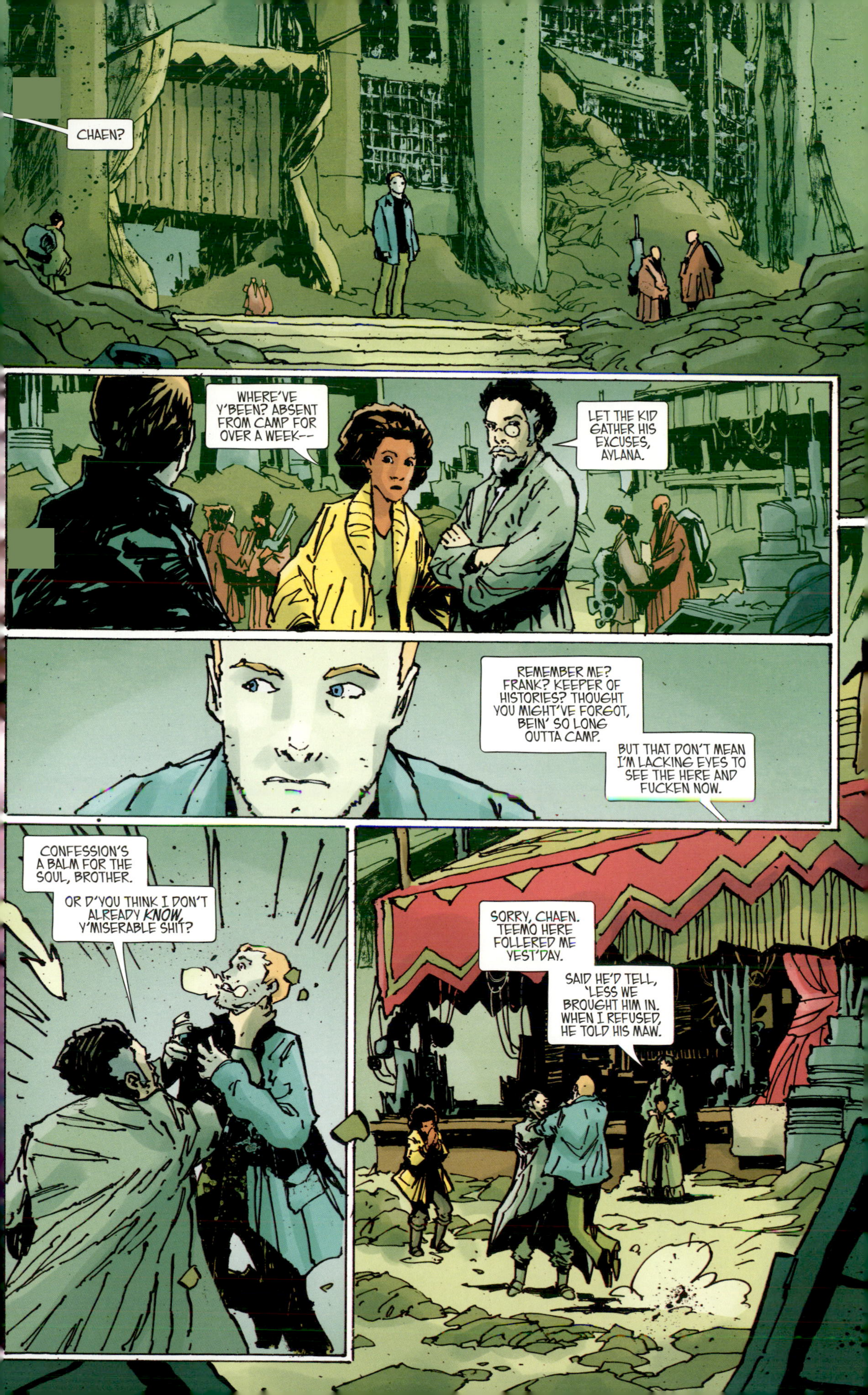
CHAEN?
WHERE'VE Y'BEEN? ABSENT FROM CAMP FOR OVER A WEEK--
LET THE KID GATHER HIS EXCUSES, AYLANA.
REMEMBER ME? FRANK? KEEPER OF HISTORIES? THOUGHT YOU MIGHT'VE FORGOT, BEIN' SO LONG OUTTA CAMP.
BUT THAT DON'T MEAN I'M LACKING EYES TO SEE THE HERE AND FUCKEN NOW.
CONFESSION'S A BALM FOR THE SOUL, BROTHER.
OR D'YOU THINK I DON'T ALREADY KNOW, Y'MISERABLE SHIT?
SORRY, CHAEN. TEEMO HERE FOLLERED ME YEST'DAY.
SAID HE'D TELL, 'LESS WE BROUGHT HIM IN. WHEN I REFUSED, HE TOLD HIS MAW.

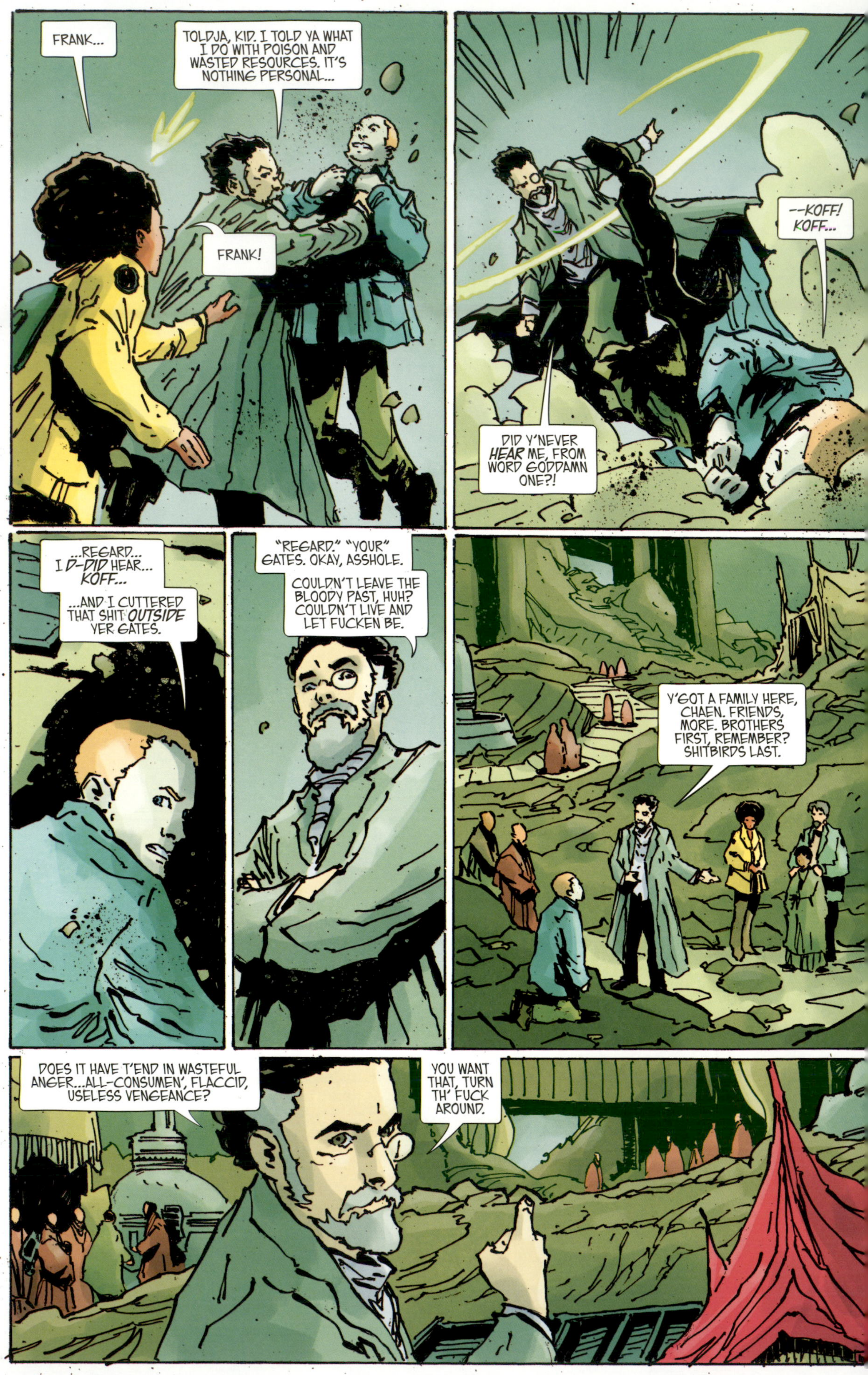
FRANK...
TOLDJA, KID. I TOLD YA WHAT I DO WITH POISON AND WASTED RESOURCES. IT'S NOTHING PERSONAL...
FRANK!
--KOFF! KOFF...
DID Y'NEVER HEAR ME, FROM WORD GODDAMN ONE?!
...REGARD... I D-DID HEAR... KOFF...
...AND I CUTTERED THAT SHIT OUTSIDE YER GATES.
"REGARD." "YOUR" GATES. OKAY, ASSHOLE.
COULDN'T LEAVE THE BLOODY PAST, HUH? COULDN'T LIVE AND LET FUCKEN BE.
Y'GOT A FAMILY HERE, CHAEN. FRIENDS, MORE. BROTHERS FIRST, REMEMBER? SHITBIRDS LAST.
DOES IT HAVE T'END IN WASTEFUL ANGER...ALL-CONSUMEN', FLACCID, USELESS VENGEANCE?
YOU WANT THAT, TURN TH' FUCK AROUND.

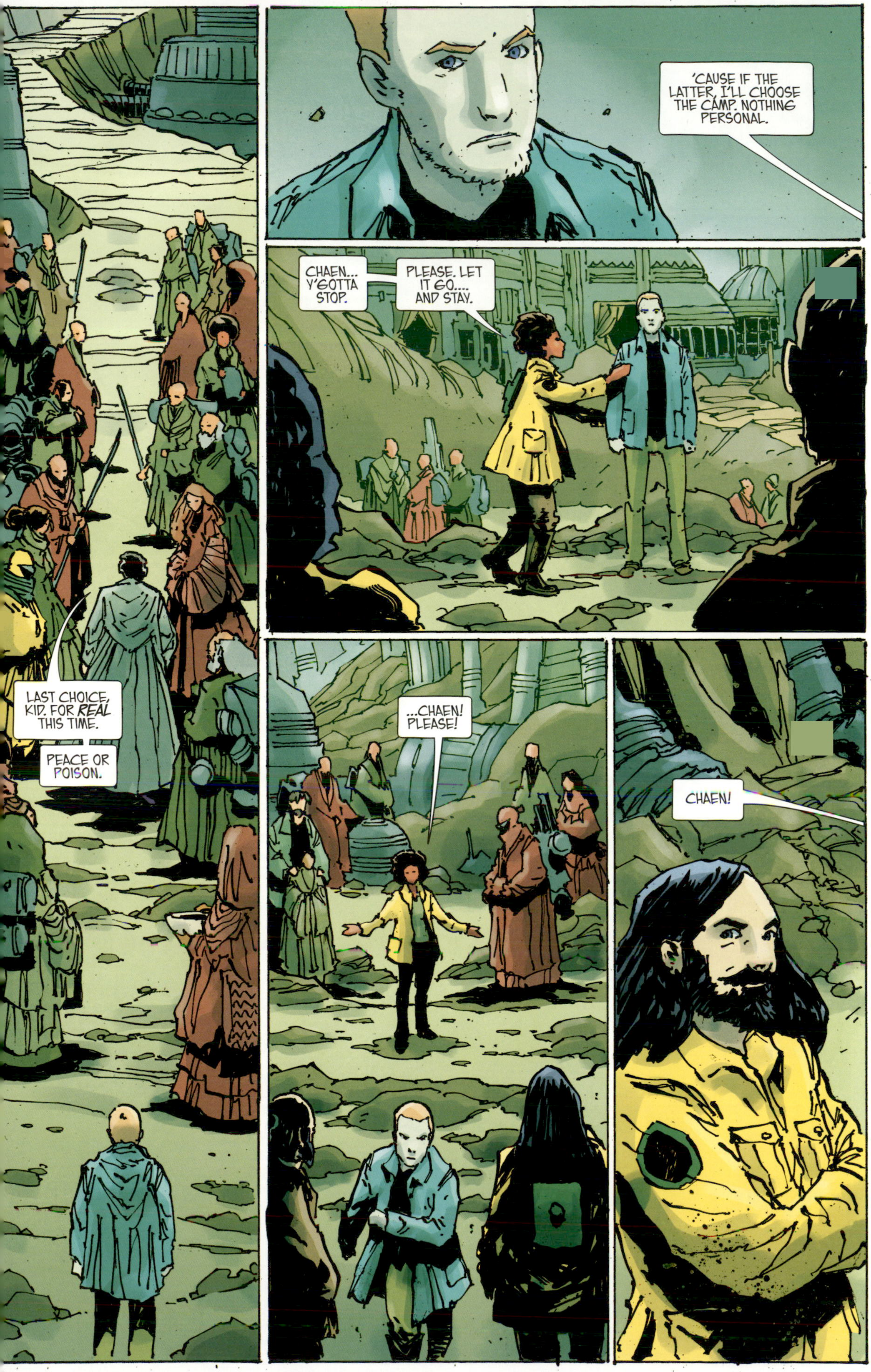
LAST CHOICE, KID. FOR *REAL* THIS TIME.
PEACE OR POISON.
'CAUSE IF THE LATTER, I'LL CHOOSE THE CAMP. NOTHING PERSONAL.
CHAEN... Y'GOTTA STOP.
PLEASE. LET IT GO.... AND STAY.
...CHAEN! PLEASE!
CHAEN!

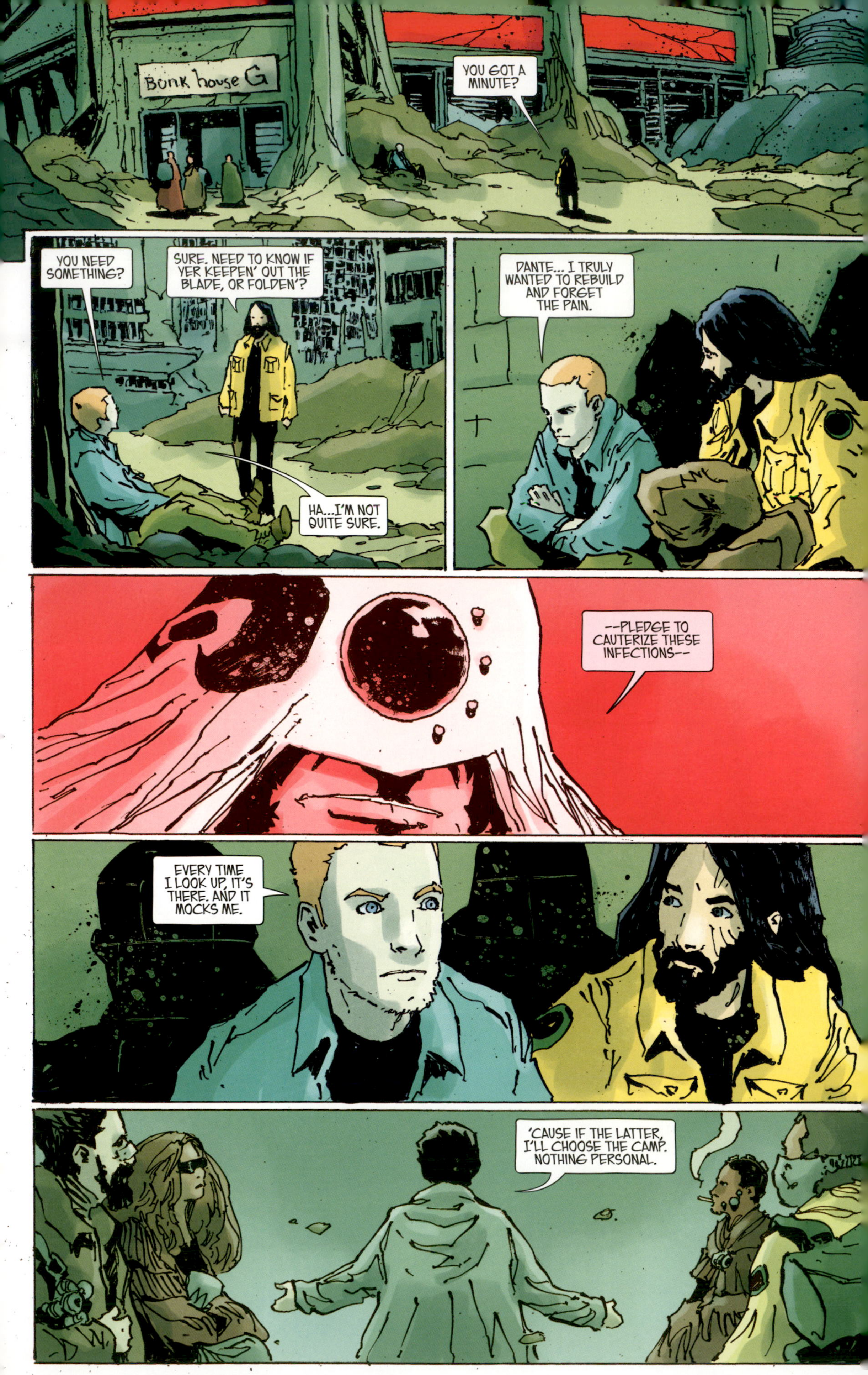
Bunk house G
YOU GOT A MINUTE?
YOU NEED SOMETHING?
SURE. NEED TO KNOW IF YER KEEPEN' OUT THE BLADE, OR FOLDEN'?
HA...I'M NOT QUITE SURE.
DANTE... I TRULY WANTED TO REBUILD AND FORGET THE PAIN.
--PLEDGE TO CAUTERIZE THESE INFECTIONS--
EVERY TIME I LOOK UP, IT'S THERE. AND IT MOCKS ME.
'CAUSE IF THE LATTER, I'LL CHOOSE THE CAMP. NOTHING PERSONAL.

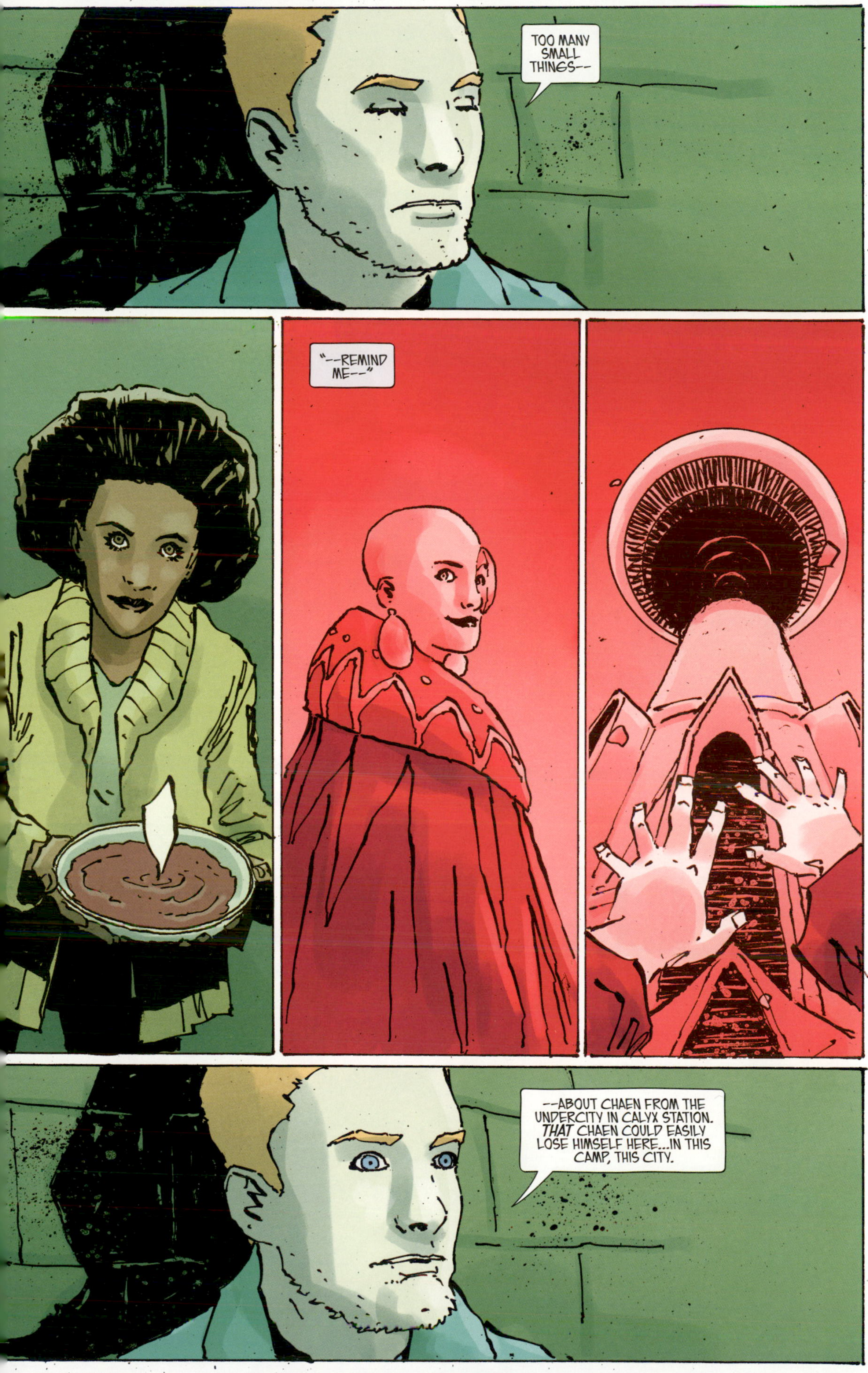
TOO MANY SMALL THINGS--
"--REMIND ME--"
--ABOUT CHAEN FROM THE UNDERCITY IN CALYX STATION. *THAT* CHAEN COULD EASILY LOSE HIMSELF HERE...IN THIS CAMP, THIS CITY.

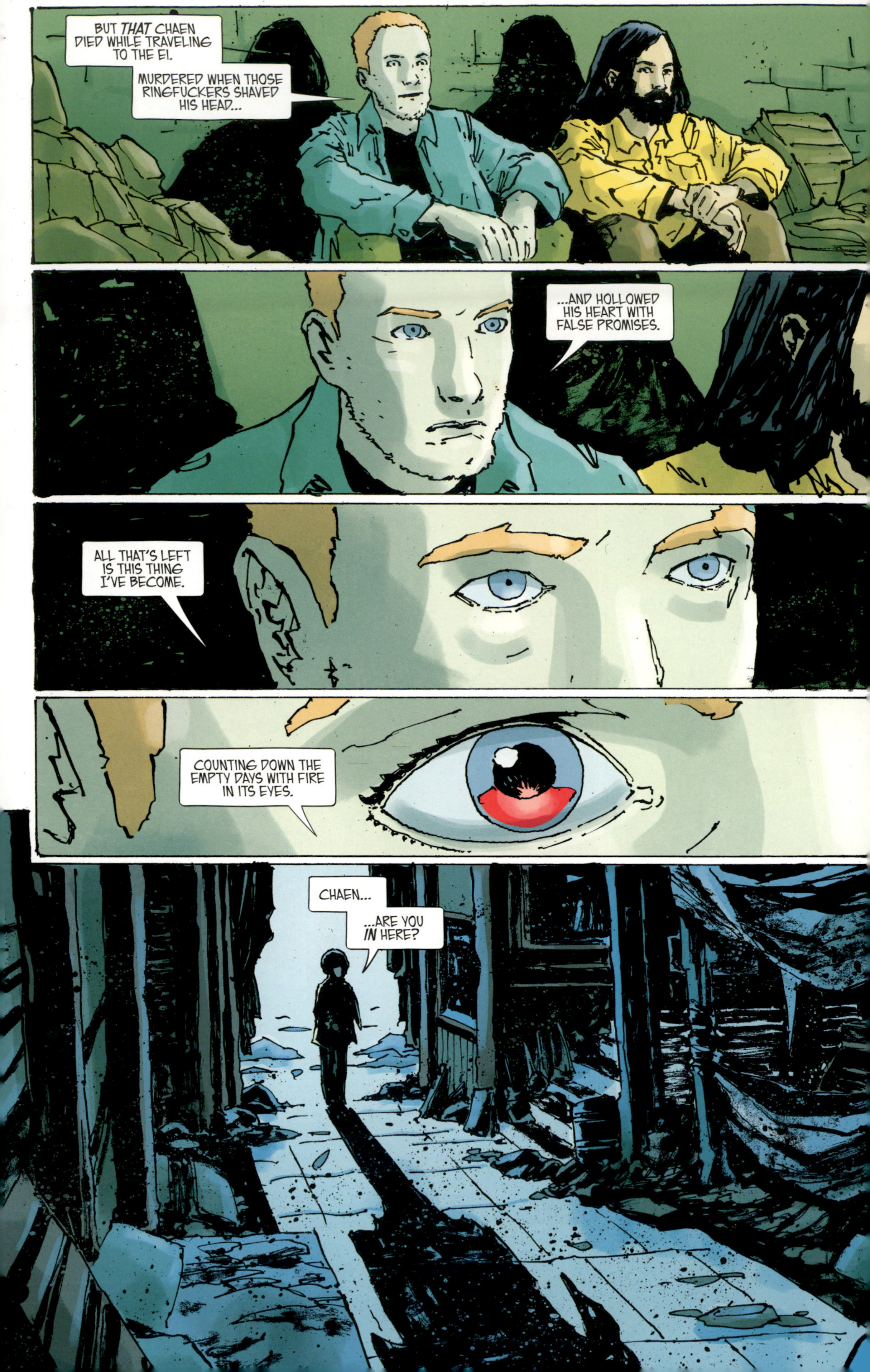
BUT THAT CHAEN DIED WHILE TRAVELING TO THE EI.
MURDERED WHEN THOSE RINGFUCKERS SHAVED HIS HEAD...
...AND HOLLOWED HIS HEART WITH FALSE PROMISES.
ALL THAT'S LEFT IS THIS THING I'VE BECOME.
COUNTING DOWN THE EMPTY DAYS WITH FIRE IN ITS EYES.
CHAEN...
...ARE YOU IN HERE?

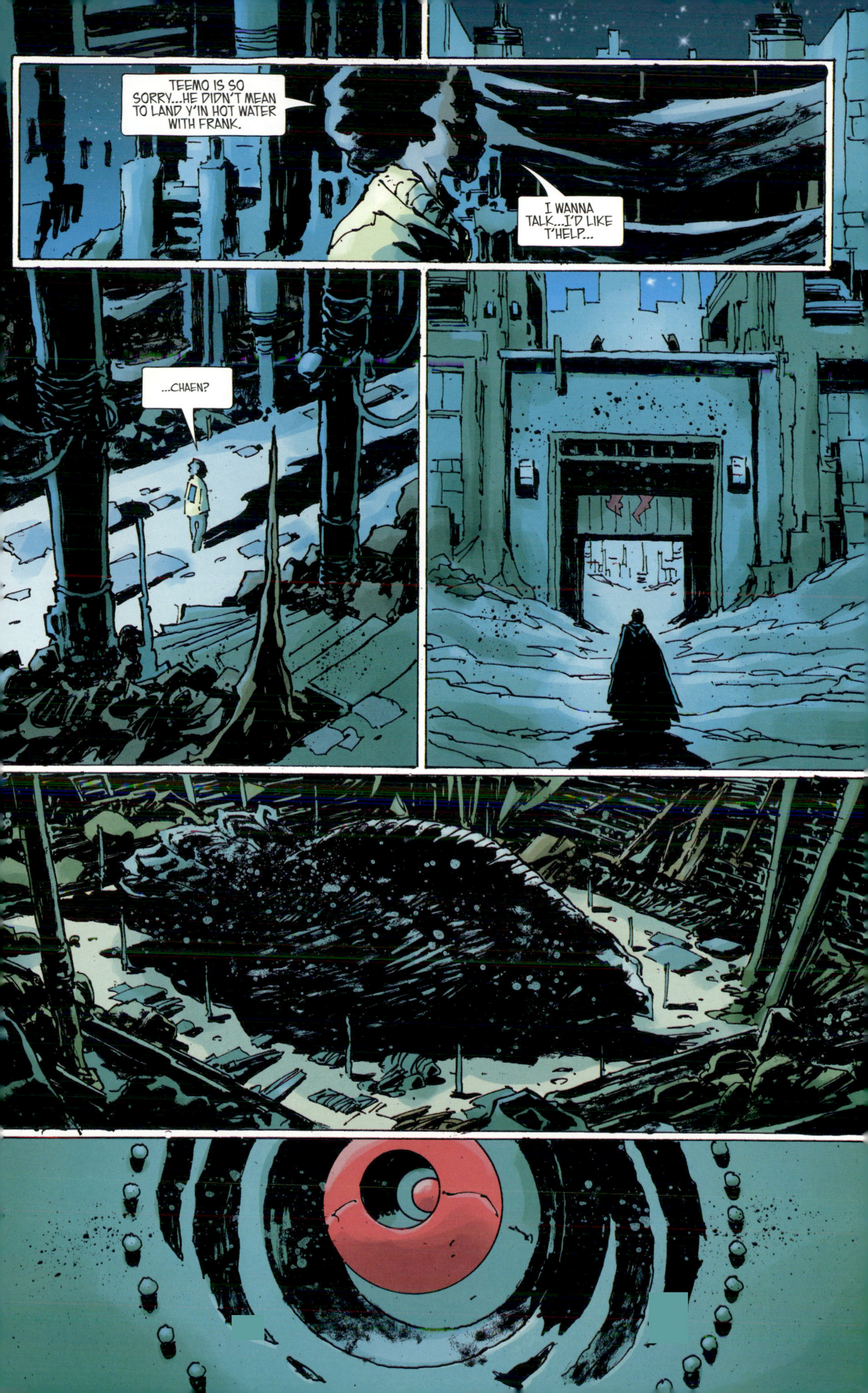

TEEMO IS SO SORRY...HE DIDN'T MEAN TO LAND Y'IN HOT WATER WITH FRANK.
I WANNA TALK...I'D LIKE T'HELP...
...CHAEN?

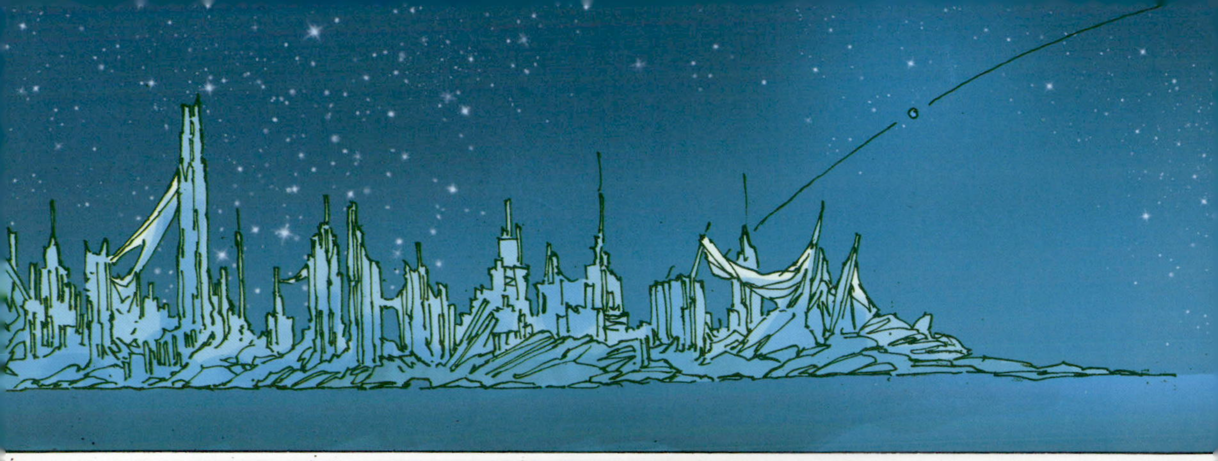

Three Weeks Later

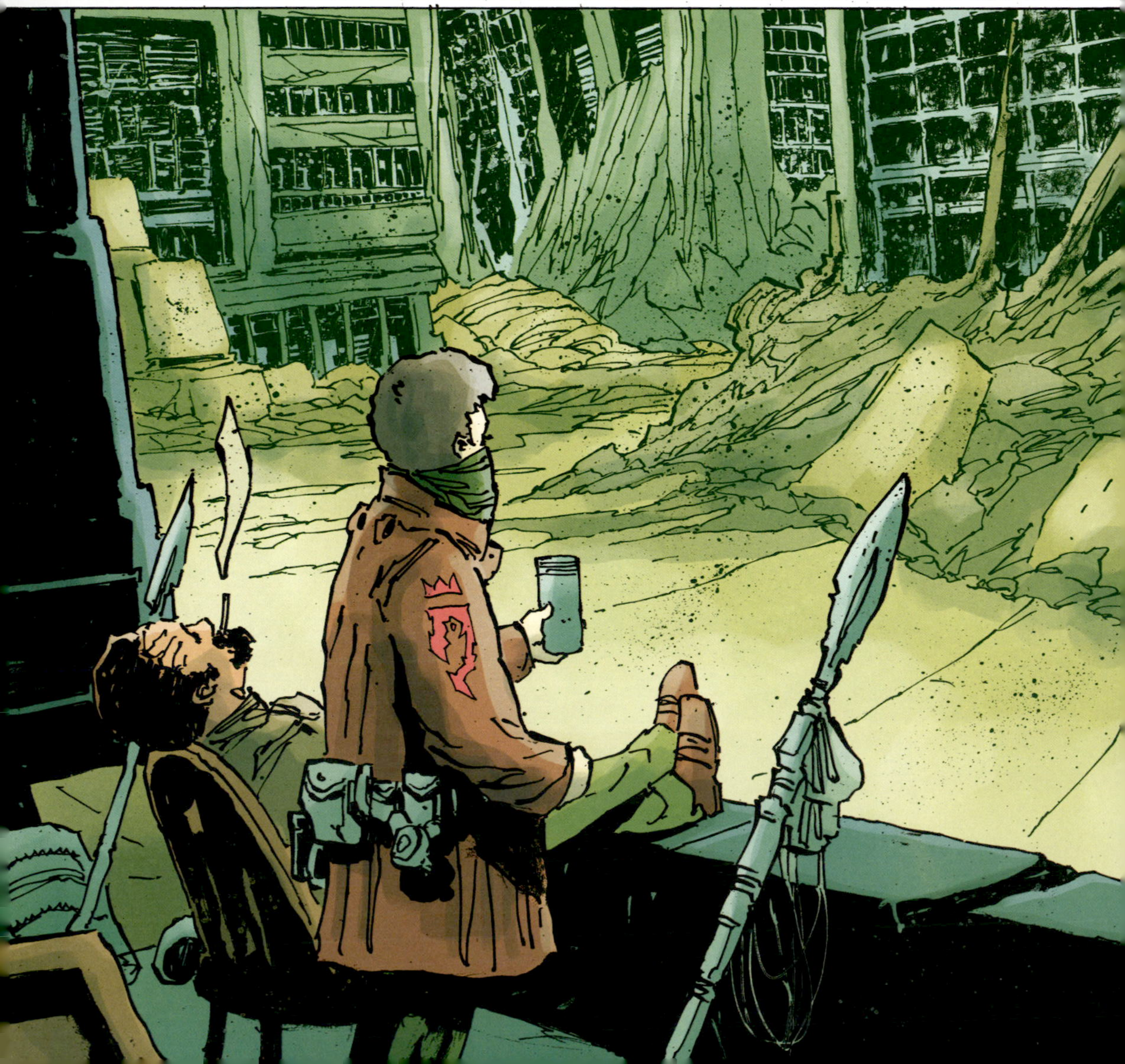

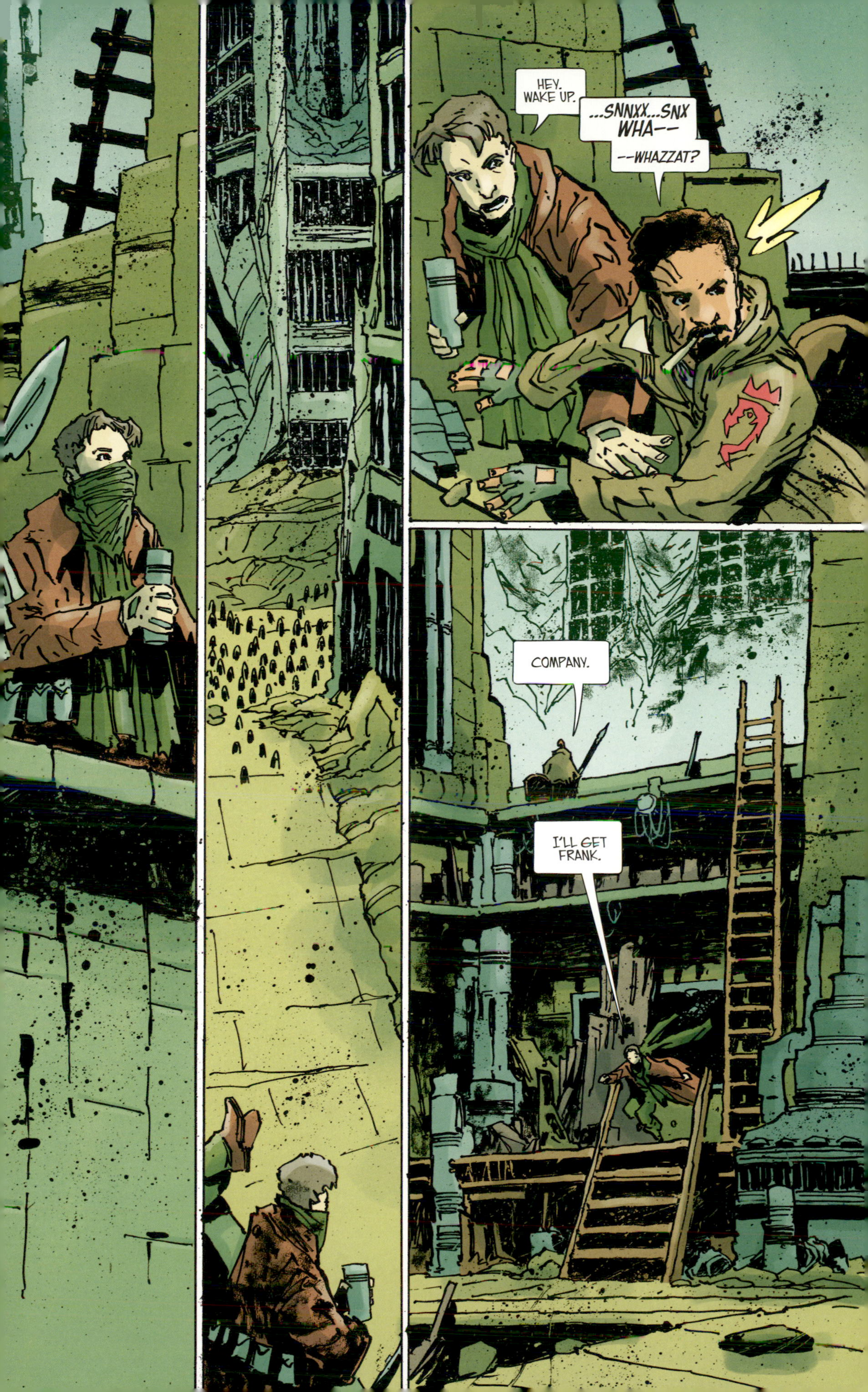
HEY. WAKE UP.
...SNNXX...SNX WHA--
--WHAZZAT?
COMPANY.
I'LL GET FRANK.

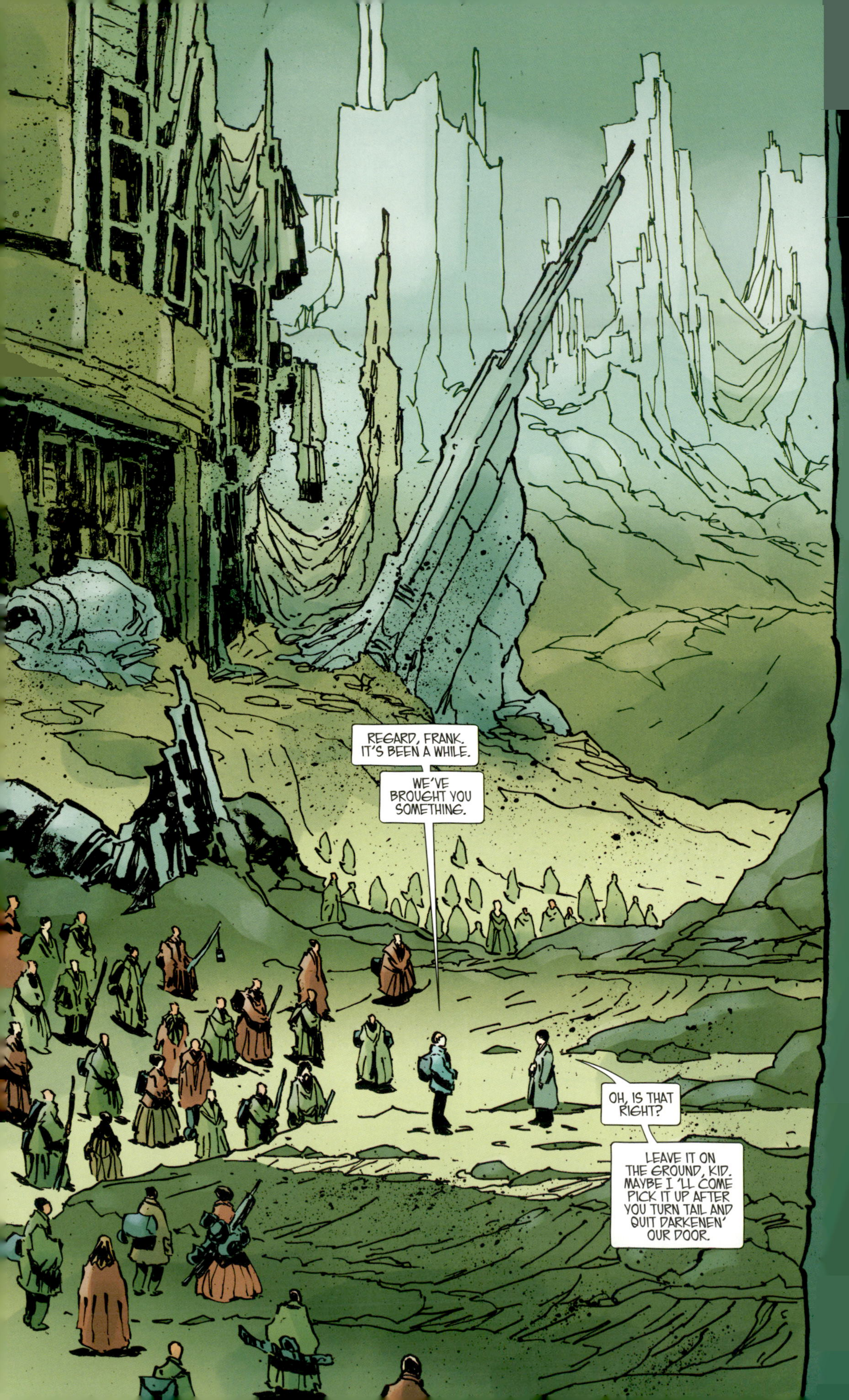
REGARD, FRANK. IT'S BEEN A WHILE.
WE'VE BROUGHT YOU SOMETHING.
OH, IS THAT RIGHT?
LEAVE IT ON THE GROUND, KID. MAYBE I 'LL COME PICK IT UP AFTER YOU TURN TAIL AND QUIT DARKENEN' OUR DOOR.

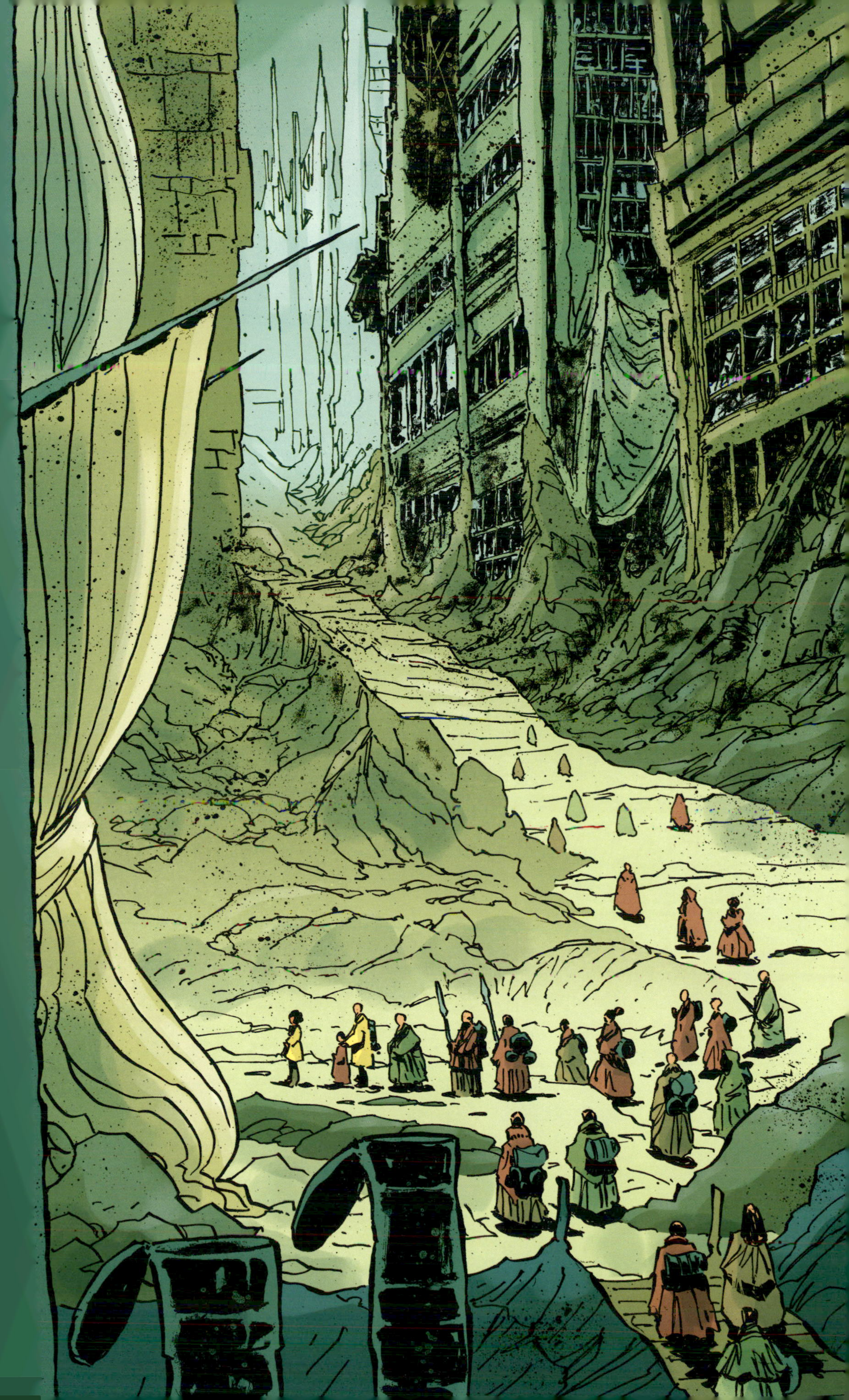

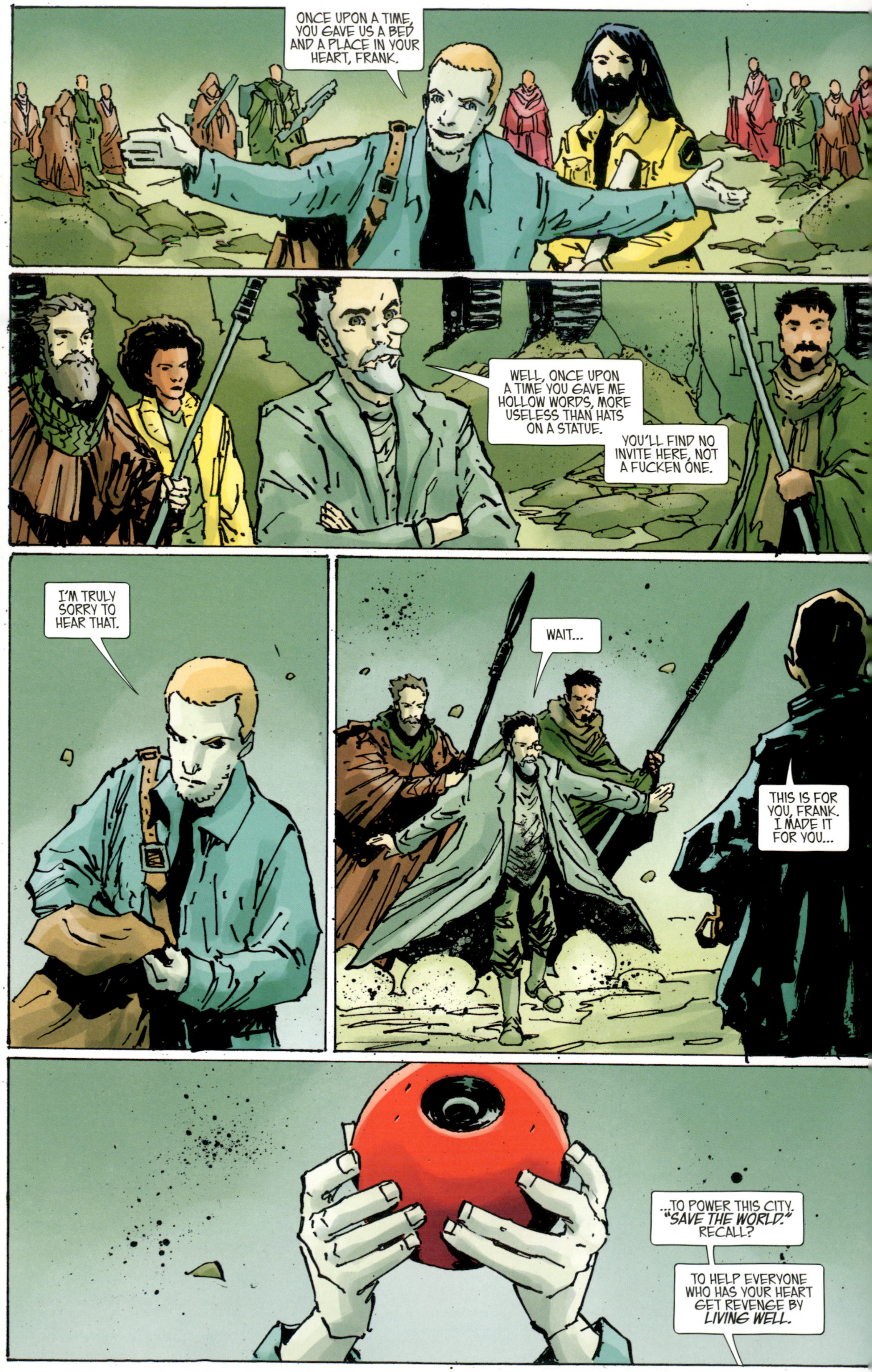
ONCE UPON A TIME, YOU GAVE US A BED AND A PLACE IN YOUR HEART, FRANK.
WELL, ONCE UPON A TIME YOU GAVE ME HOLLOW WORDS, MORE USELESS THAN HATS ON A STATUE.
YOU'LL FIND NO INVITE HERE, NOT A FUCKEN ONE.
I'M TRULY SORRY TO HEAR THAT.
WAIT...
THIS IS FOR YOU, FRANK. I MADE IT FOR YOU...
...TO POWER THIS CITY. "SAVE THE WORLD." RECALL?
TO HELP EVERYONE WHO HAS YOUR HEART GET REVENGE BY LIVING WELL.

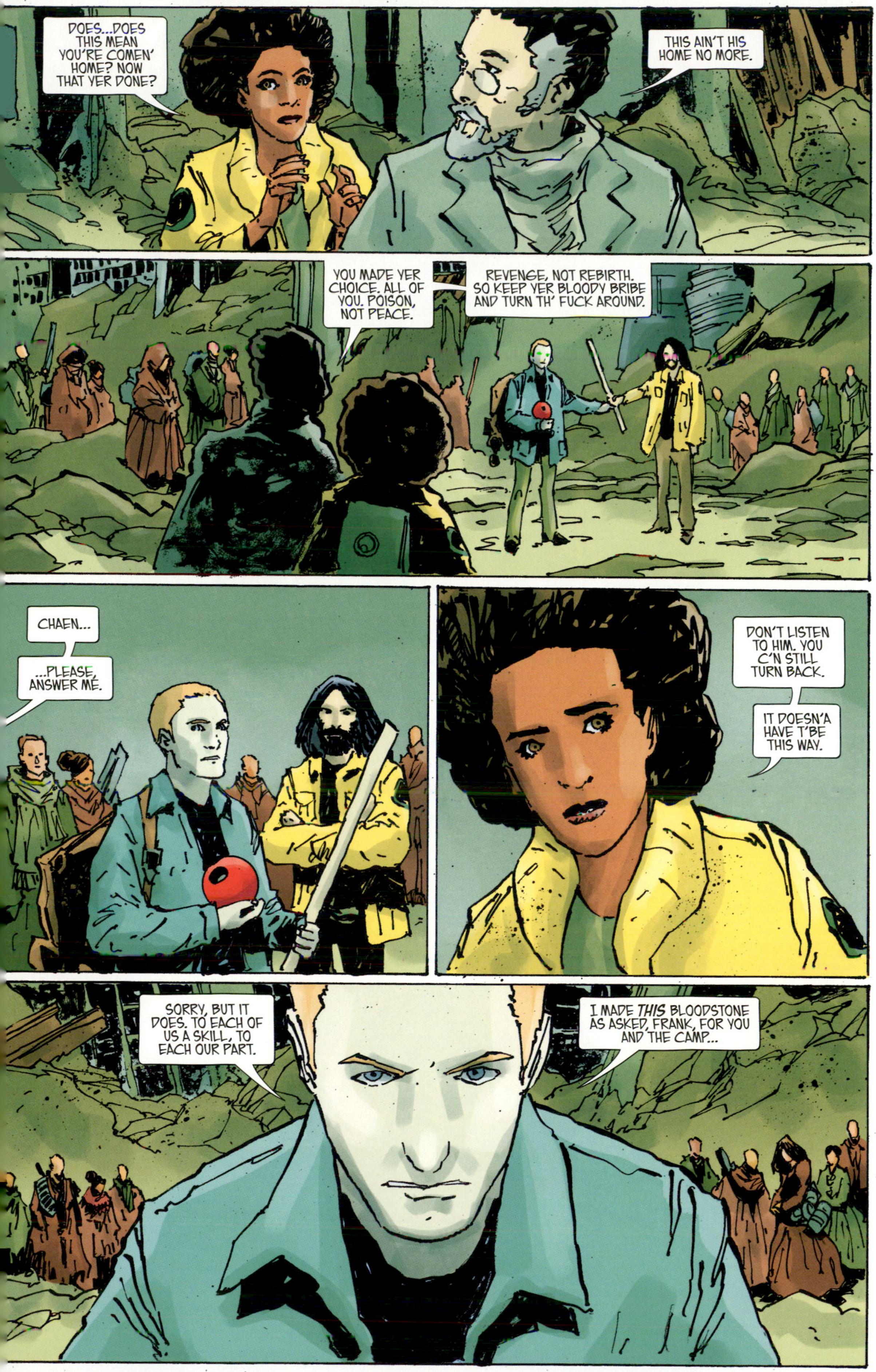
DOES...DOES THIS MEAN YOU'RE COMEN' HOME? NOW THAT YER DONE?
THIS AIN'T HIS HOME NO MORE.
YOU MADE YER CHOICE. ALL OF YOU. POISON, NOT PEACE.
REVENGE, NOT REBIRTH. SO KEEP YER BLOODY BRIBE AND TURN TH' FUCK AROUND.
CHAEN...
...PLEASE, ANSWER ME.
DON'T LISTEN TO HIM. YOU C'N STILL TURN BACK.
IT DOESN'A HAVE T'BE THIS WAY.
SORRY, BUT IT DOES. TO EACH OF US A SKILL, TO EACH OUR PART.
I MADE THIS BLOODSTONE AS ASKED, FRANK, FOR YOU AND THE CAMP...

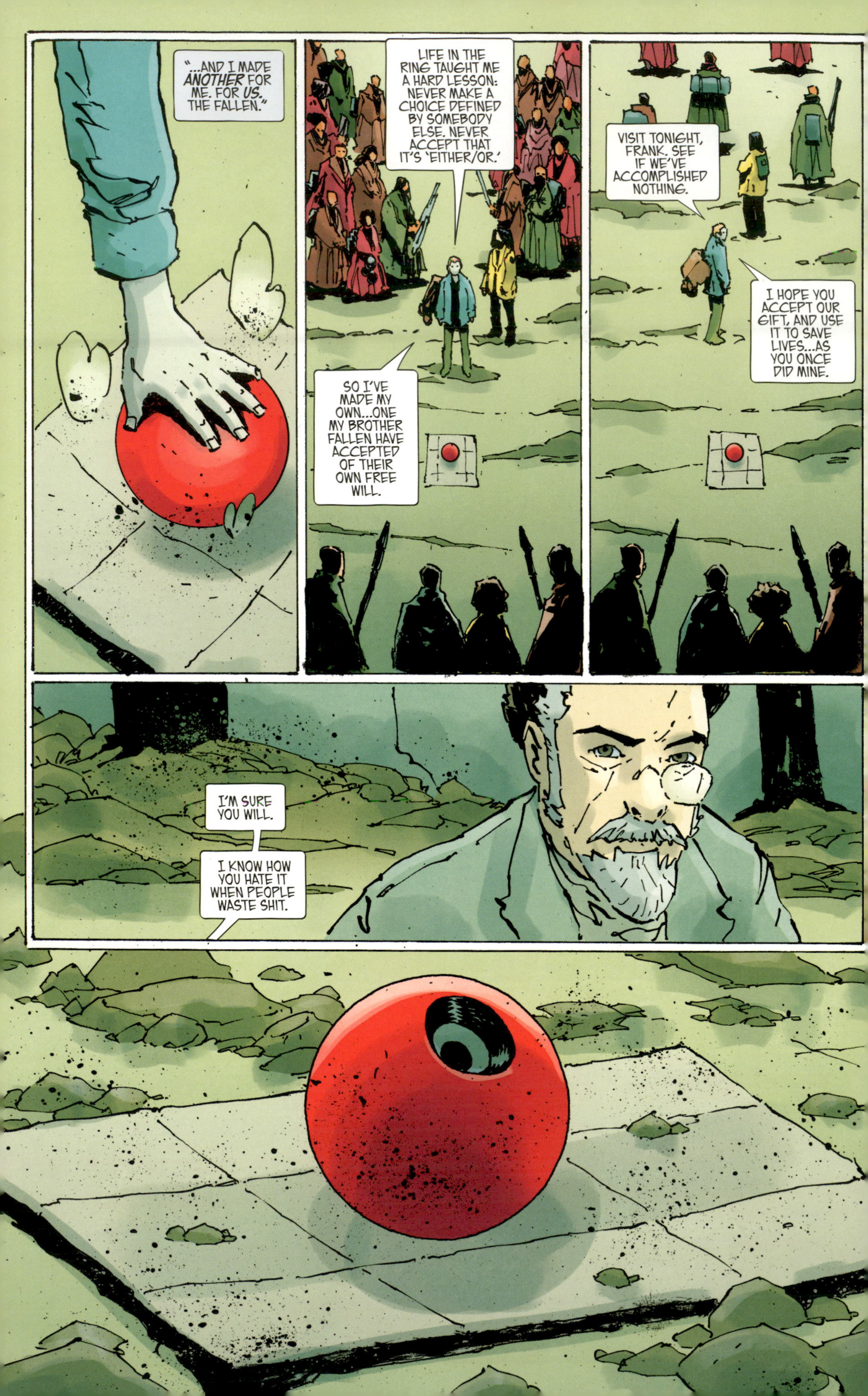
"...AND I MADE ANOTHER FOR ME. FOR US. THE FALLEN."
LIFE IN THE RING TAUGHT ME A HARD LESSON: NEVER MAKE A CHOICE DEFINED BY SOMEBODY ELSE. NEVER ACCEPT THAT IT'S 'EITHER/OR.'
SO I'VE MADE MY OWN...ONE MY BROTHER FALLEN HAVE ACCEPTED OF THEIR OWN FREE WILL.
VISIT TONIGHT, FRANK. SEE IF WE'VE ACCOMPLISHED NOTHING.
I HOPE YOU ACCEPT OUR GIFT, AND USE IT TO SAVE LIVES...AS YOU ONCE DID MINE.
I'M SURE YOU WILL.
I KNOW HOW YOU HATE IT WHEN PEOPLE WASTE SHIT.

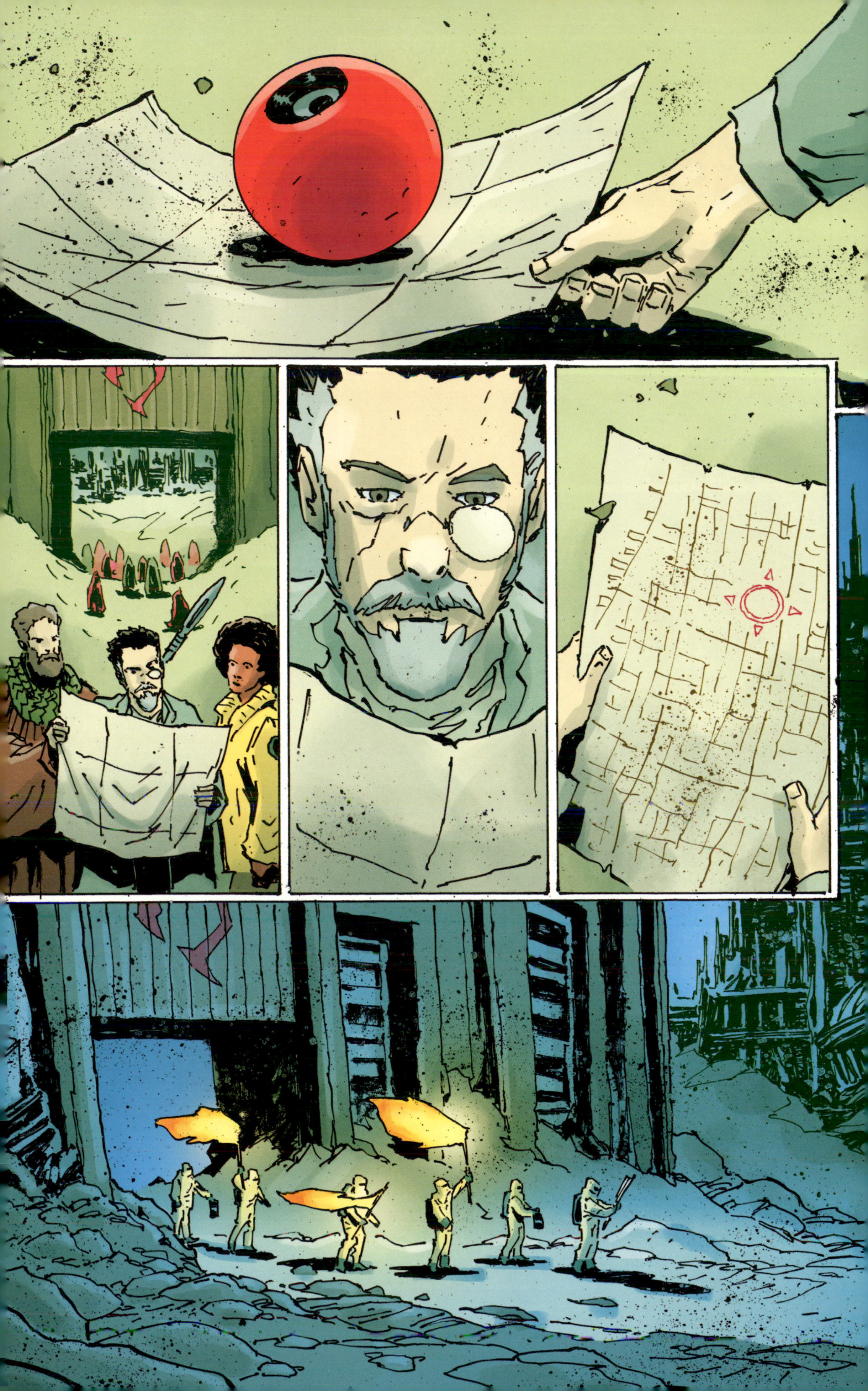

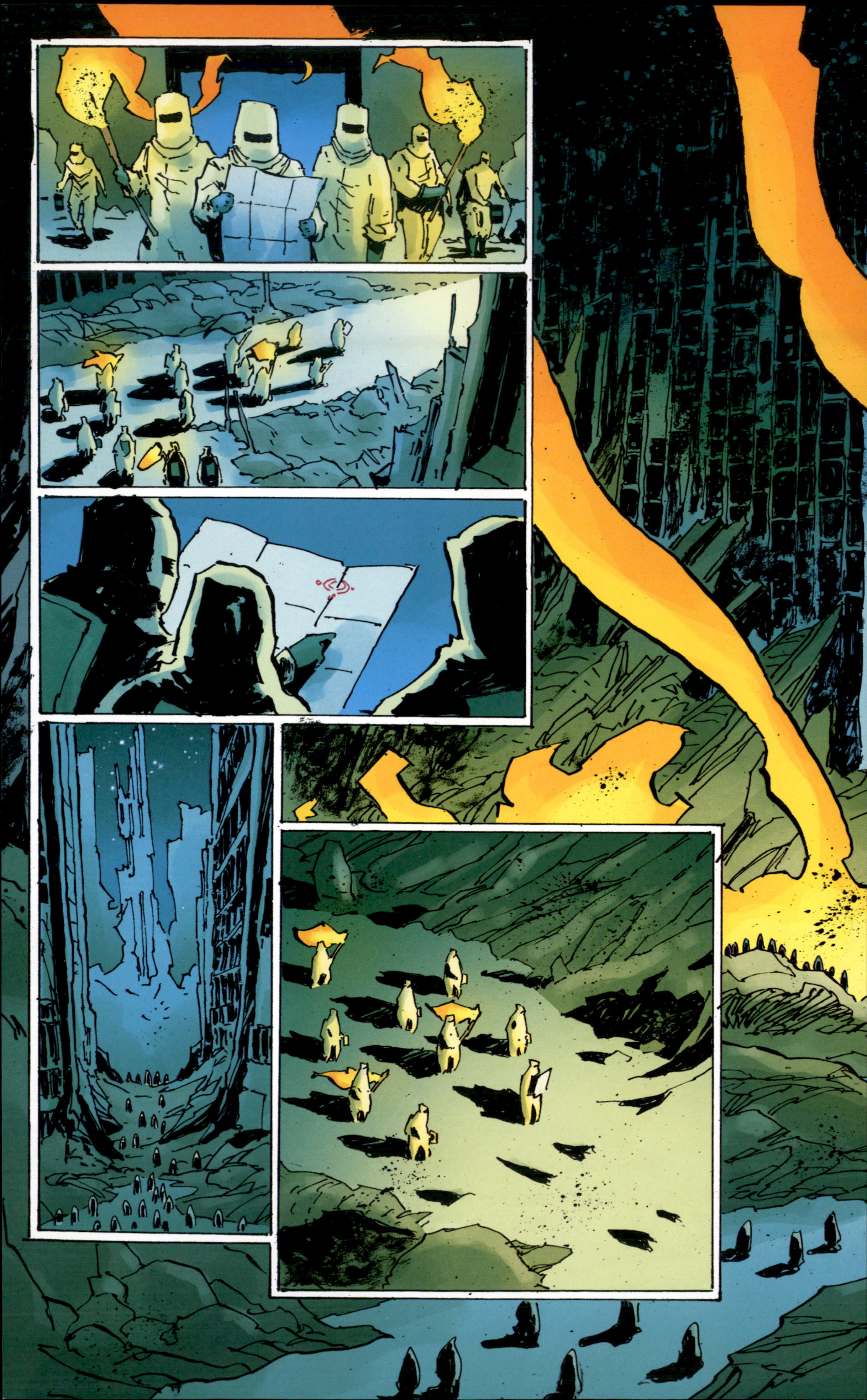

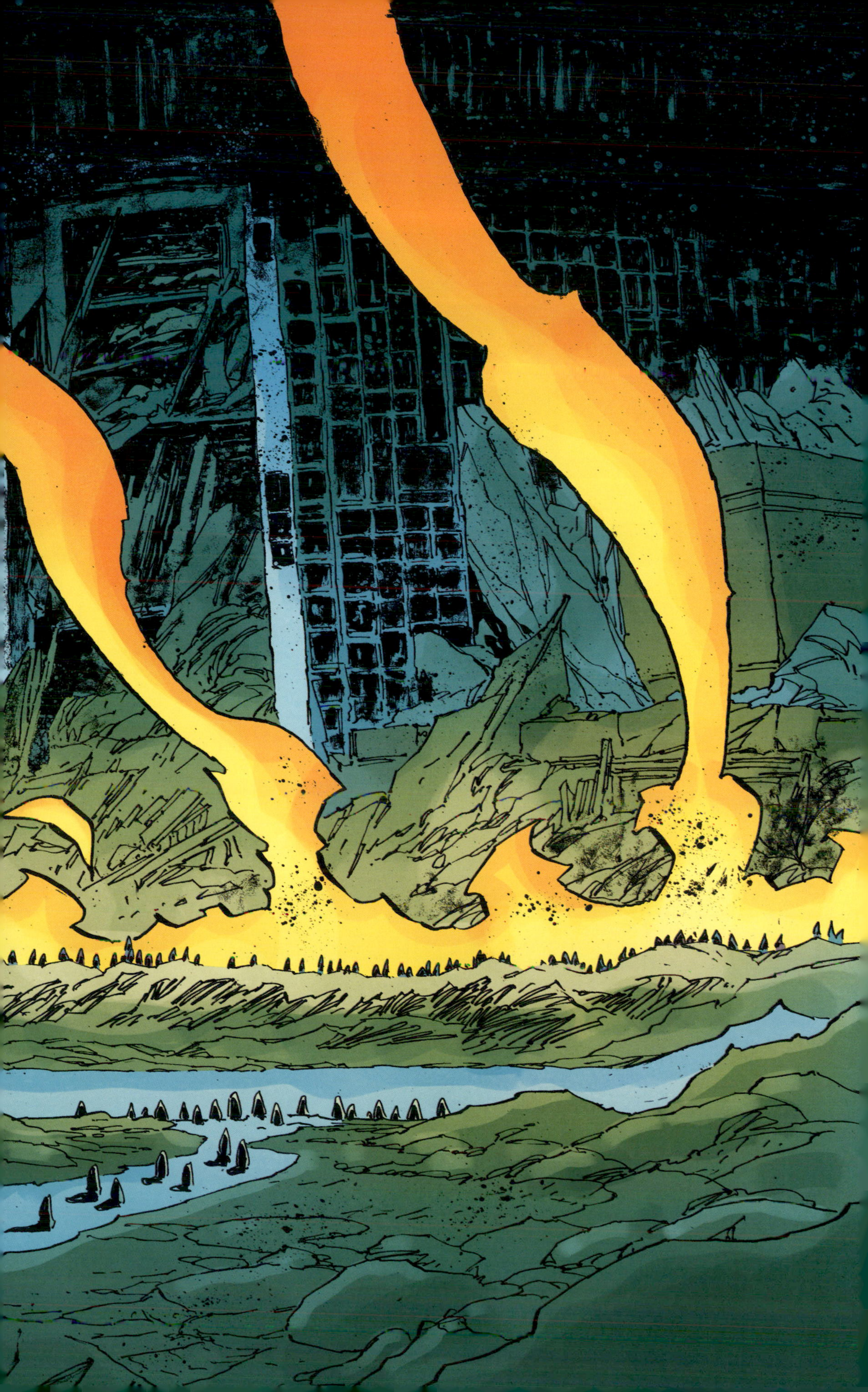

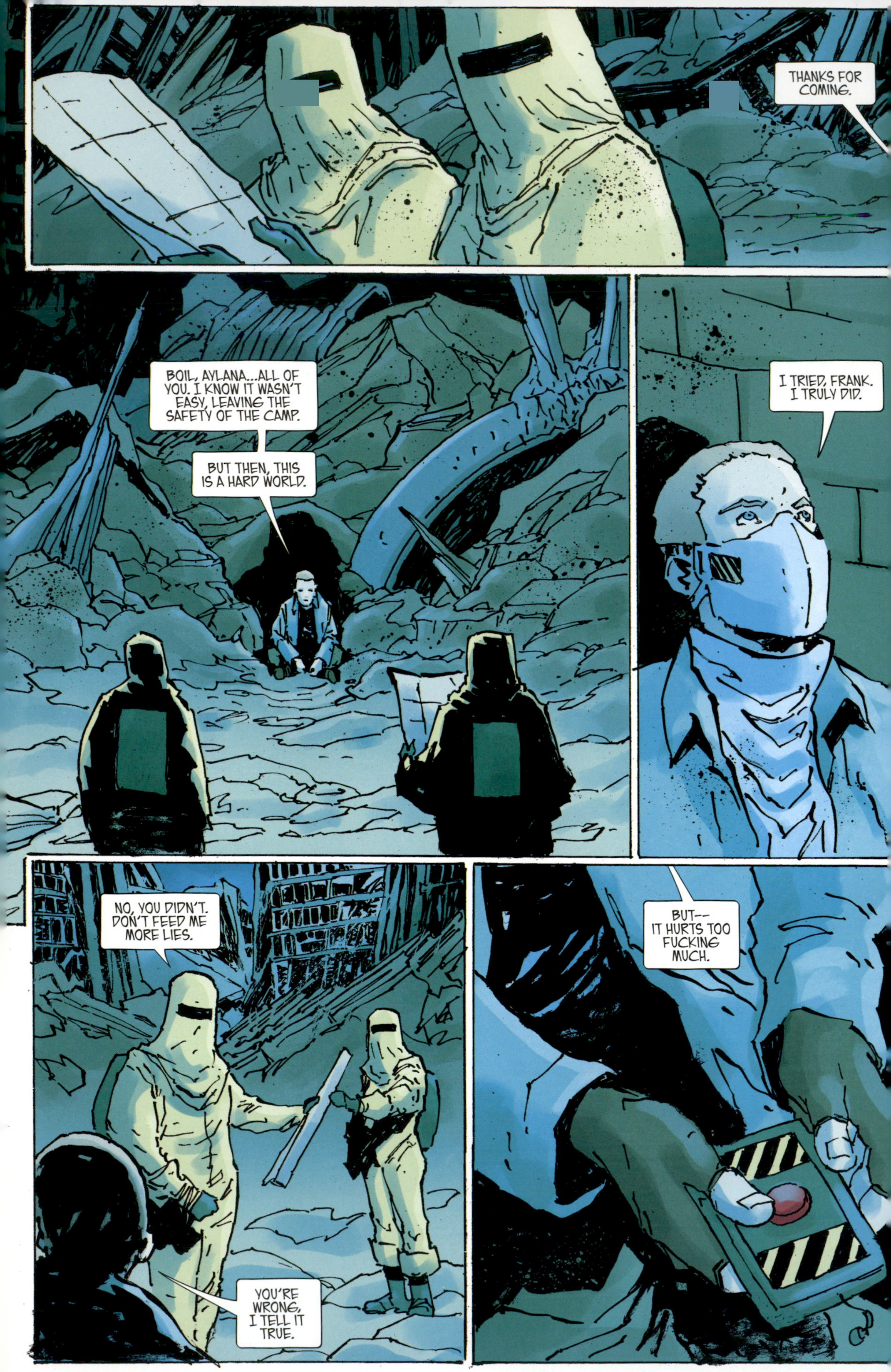
THANKS FOR COMING.
BOIL, AYLANA...ALL OF YOU. I KNOW IT WASN'T EASY, LEAVING THE SAFETY OF THE CAMP.
BUT THEN, THIS IS A HARD WORLD.
I TRIED, FRANK. I TRULY DID.
NO, YOU DIDN'T. DON'T FEED ME MORE LIES.
YOU'RE WRONG, I TELL IT TRUE.
BUT-- IT HURTS TOO FUCKING MUCH.

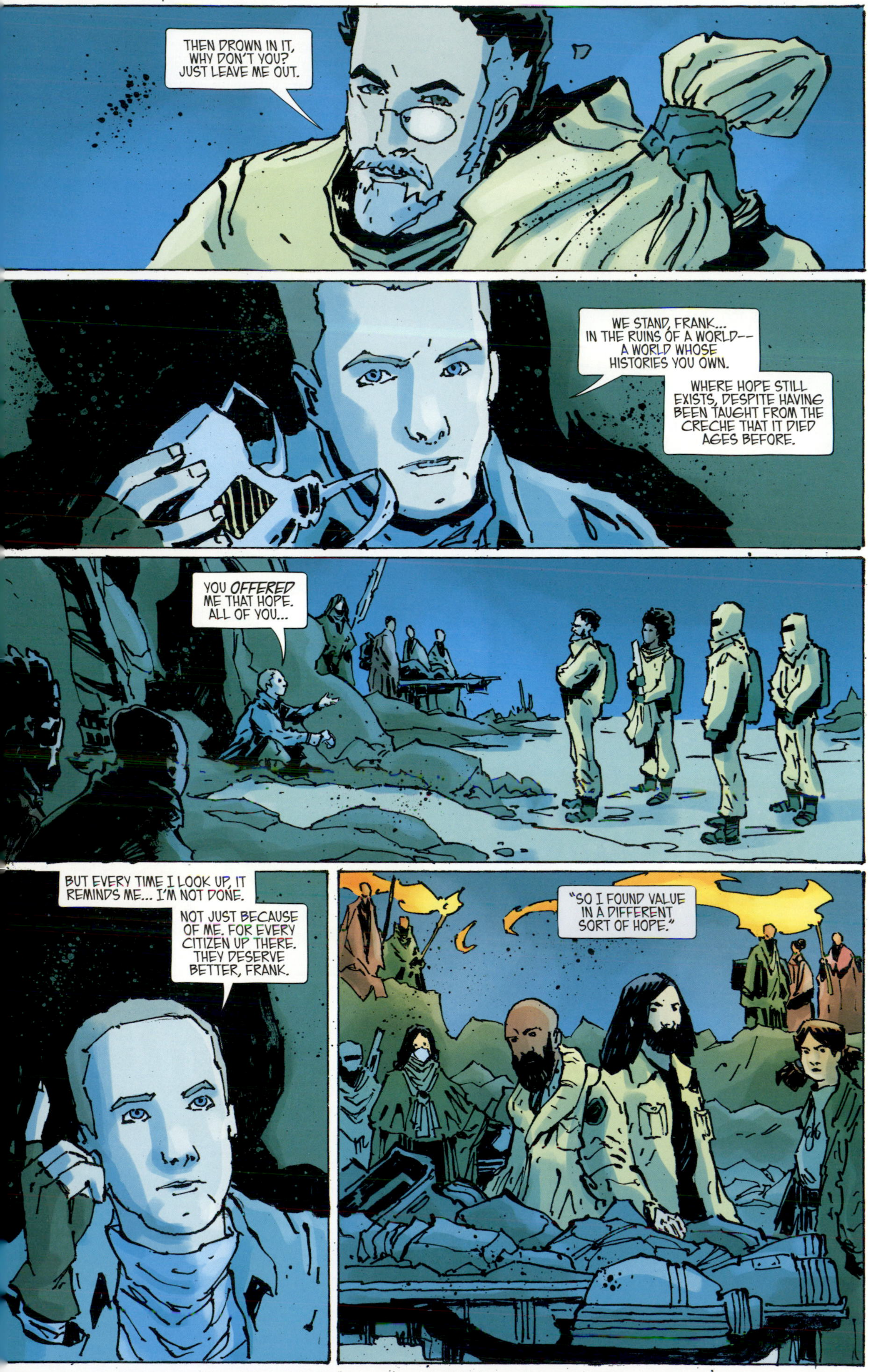
THEN DROWN IN IT, WHY DON'T YOU? JUST LEAVE ME OUT.
WE STAND, FRANK... IN THE RUINS OF A WORLD-- A WORLD WHOSE HISTORIES YOU OWN.
WHERE HOPE STILL EXISTS, DESPITE HAVING BEEN TAUGHT FROM THE CRECHE THAT IT DIED AGES BEFORE.
YOU *OFFERED* ME THAT HOPE. ALL OF YOU...
BUT EVERY TIME I LOOK UP, IT REMINDS ME... I'M NOT DONE.
NOT JUST BECAUSE OF ME. FOR EVERY CITIZEN UP THERE. THEY DESERVE BETTER, FRANK.
"SO I FOUND VALUE IN A DIFFERENT SORT OF HOPE."

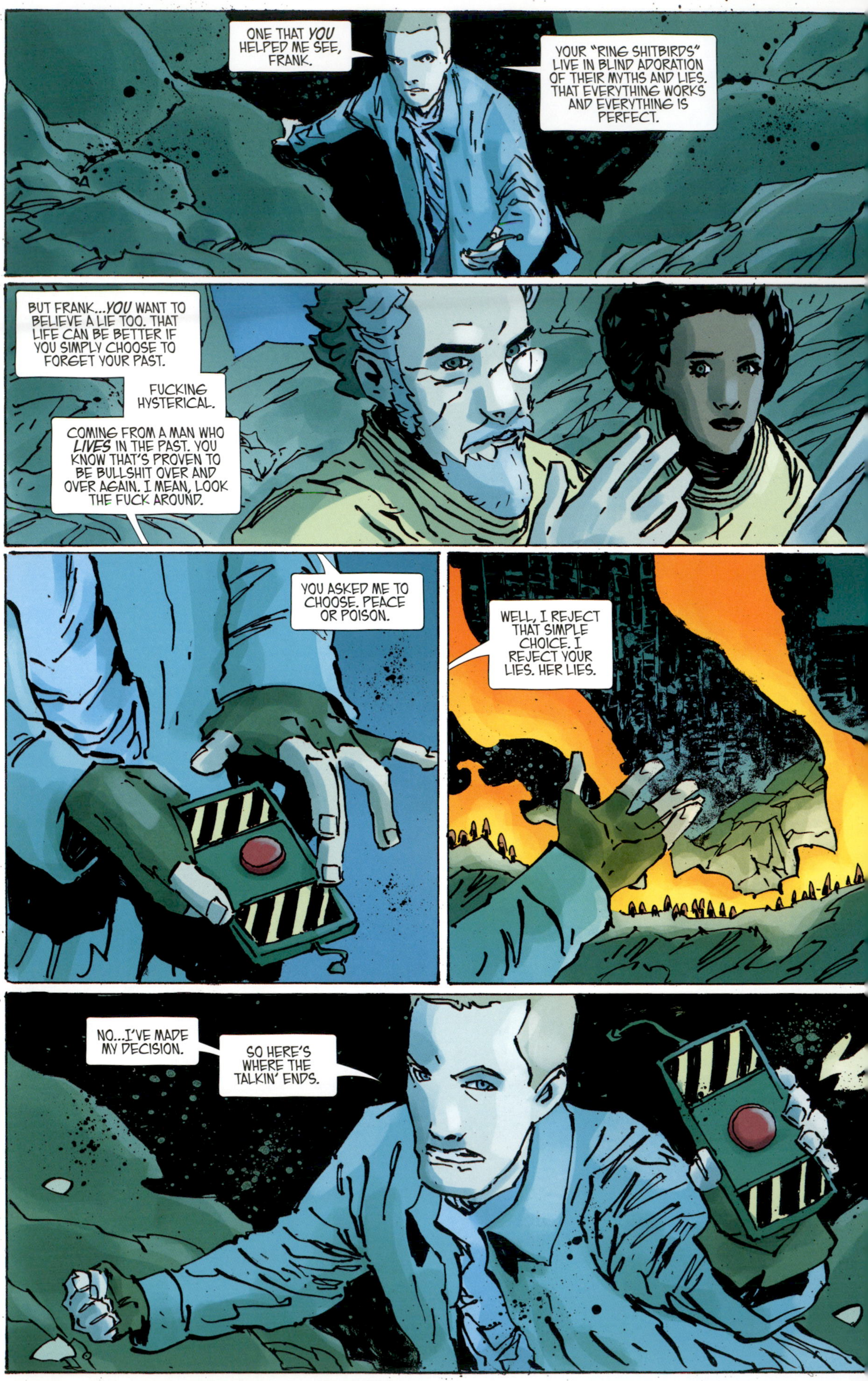
ONE THAT *YOU* HELPED ME SEE, FRANK.
YOUR "RING SHITBIRDS" LIVE IN BLIND ADORATION OF THEIR MYTHS AND LIES. THAT EVERYTHING WORKS AND EVERYTHING IS PERFECT.
BUT FRANK...*YOU* WANT TO BELIEVE A LIE TOO. THAT LIFE CAN BE BETTER IF YOU SIMPLY CHOOSE TO FORGET YOUR PAST.
FUCKING HYSTERICAL.
COMING FROM A MAN WHO *LIVES* IN THE PAST. YOU KNOW THAT'S PROVEN TO BE BULLSHIT OVER AND OVER AGAIN. I MEAN, LOOK THE FUCK AROUND.
YOU ASKED ME TO CHOOSE. PEACE OR POISON.
WELL, I REJECT THAT SIMPLE CHOICE. I REJECT YOUR LIES. HER LIES.
NO...I'VE MADE MY DECISION.
SO HERE'S WHERE THE TALKIN' ENDS.

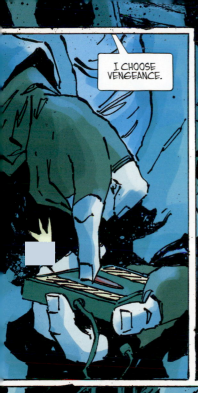

I CHOOSE VENGEANCE.

THEY PREACHED ASCENSION, WELL...

THIS IS WHO WE ARE, PEOPLE. WHO I AM...

"...SCREAMING FOR VENGEANCE."

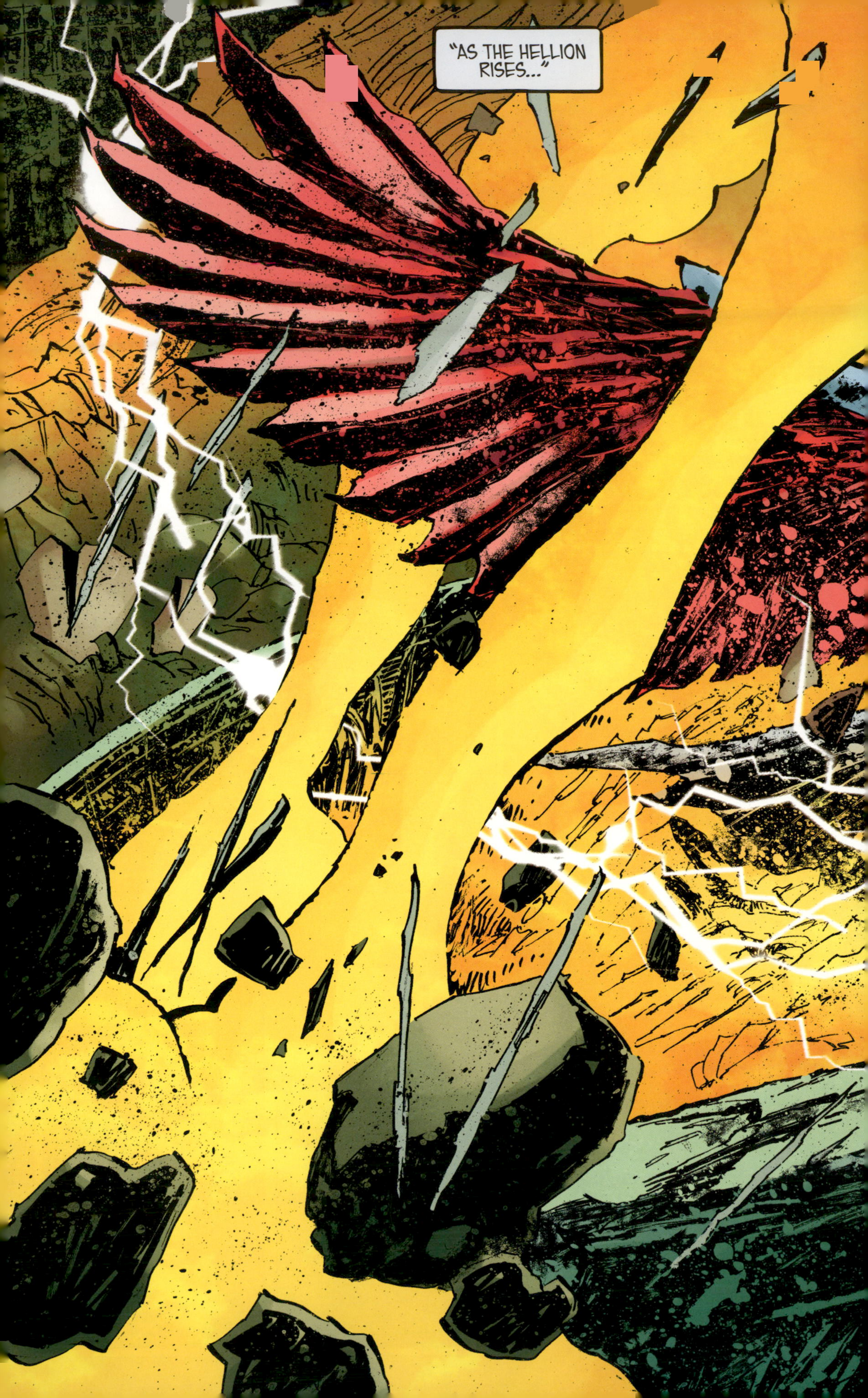
"AS THE HELLION RISES..."

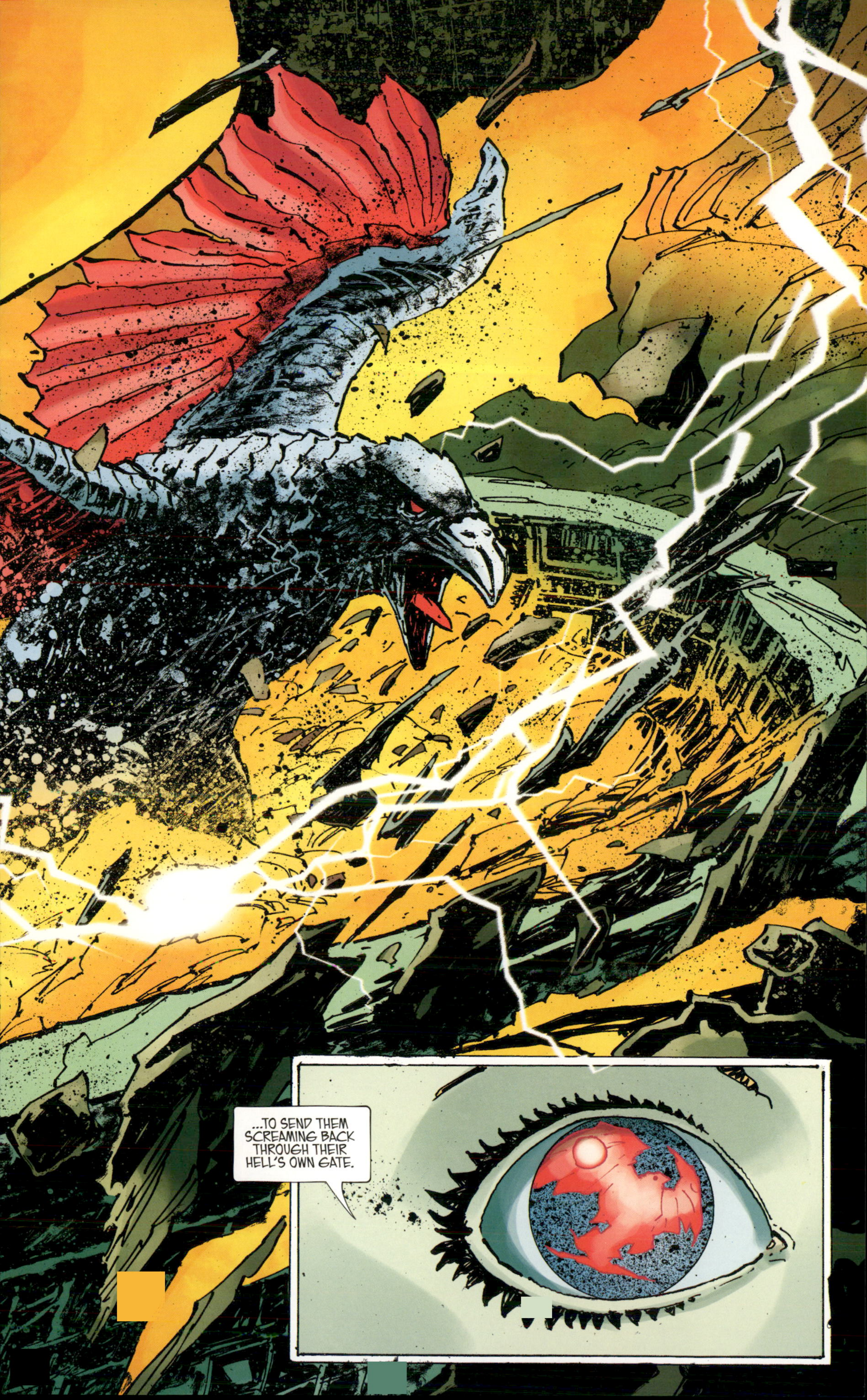
...TO SEND THEM SCREAMING BACK THROUGH THEIR HELL'S OWN GATE.

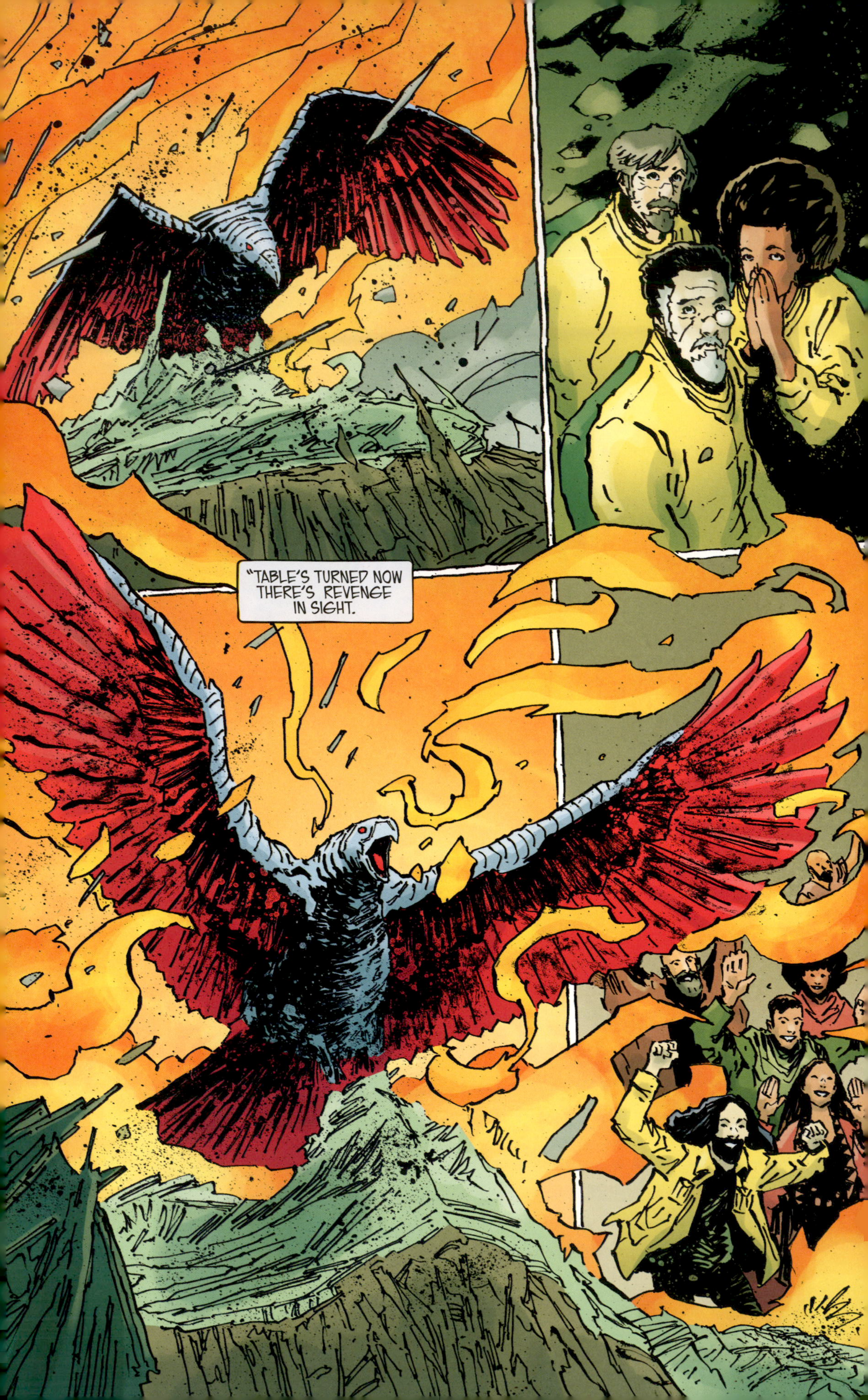
"TABLE'S TURNED NOW
THERE'S REVENGE
IN SIGHT.

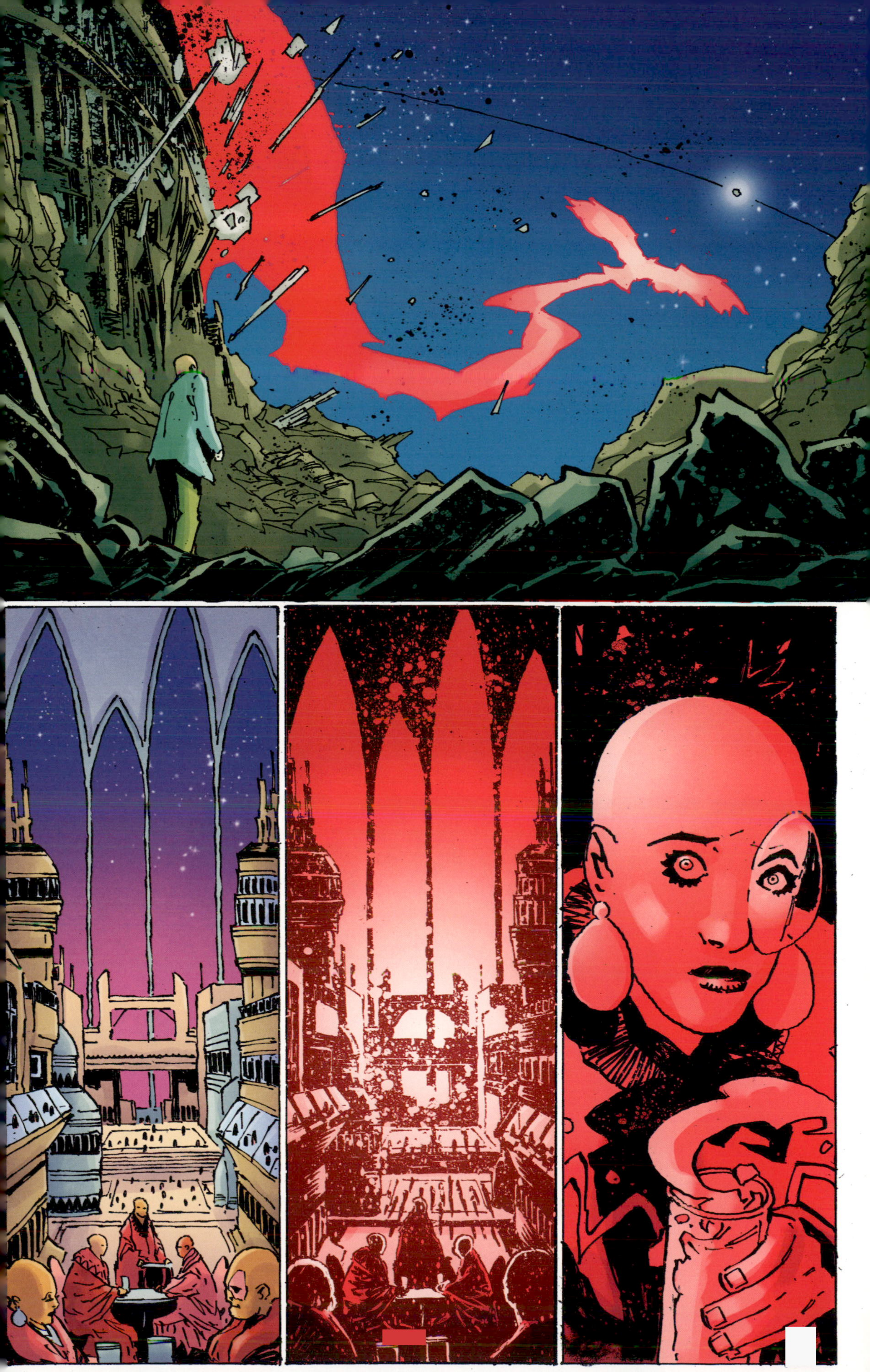

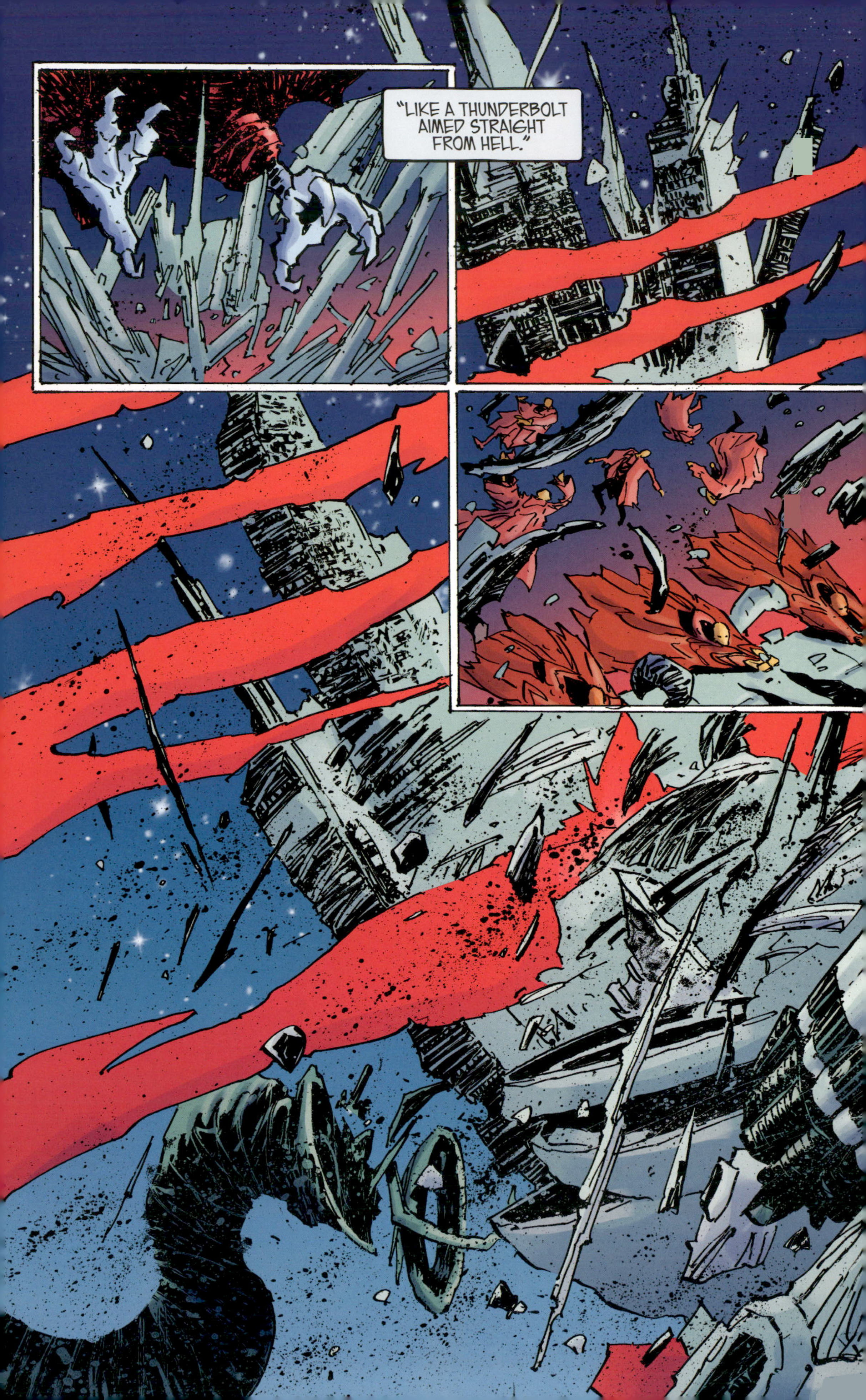
"LIKE A THUNDERBOLT AIMED STRAIGHT FROM HELL."

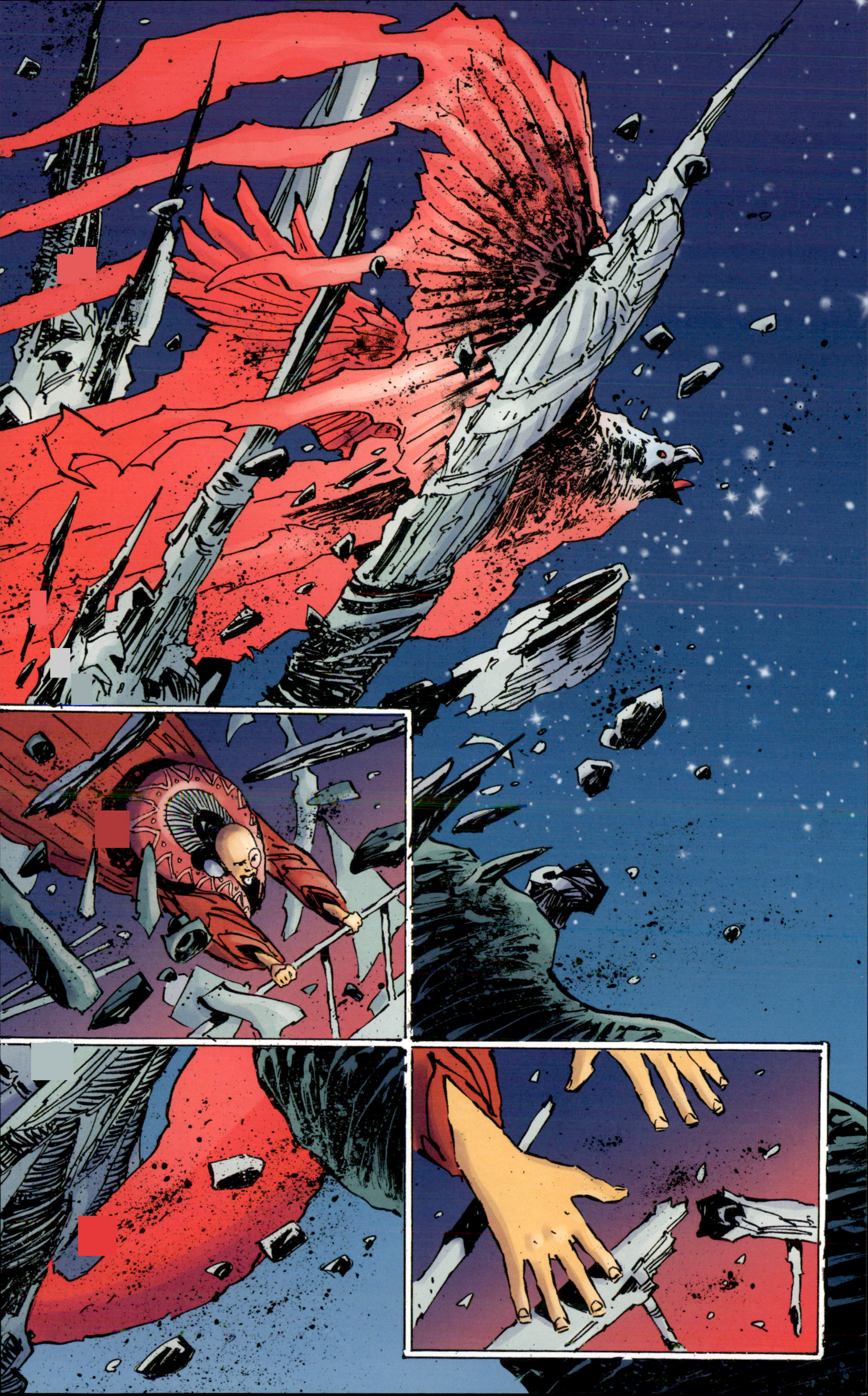

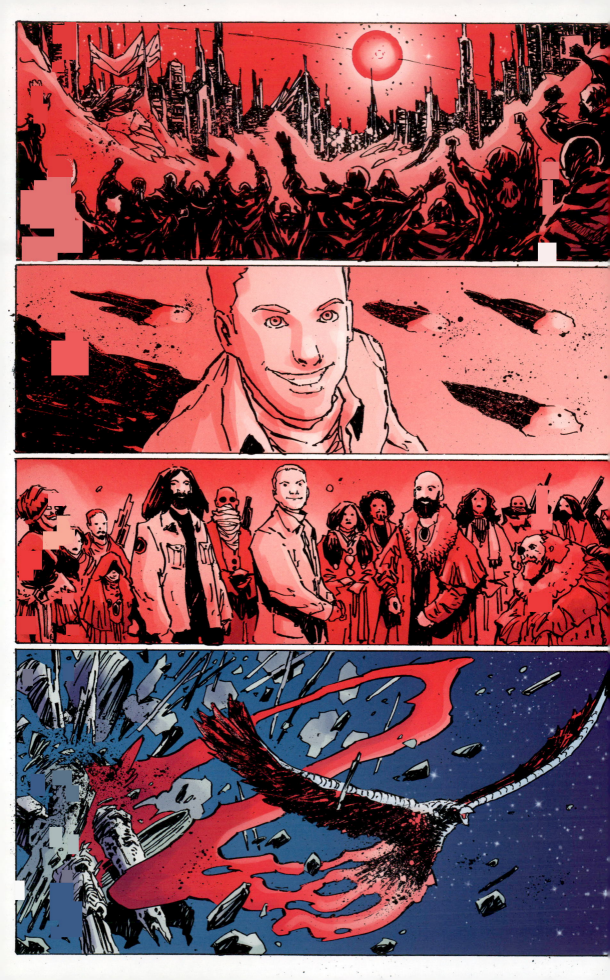

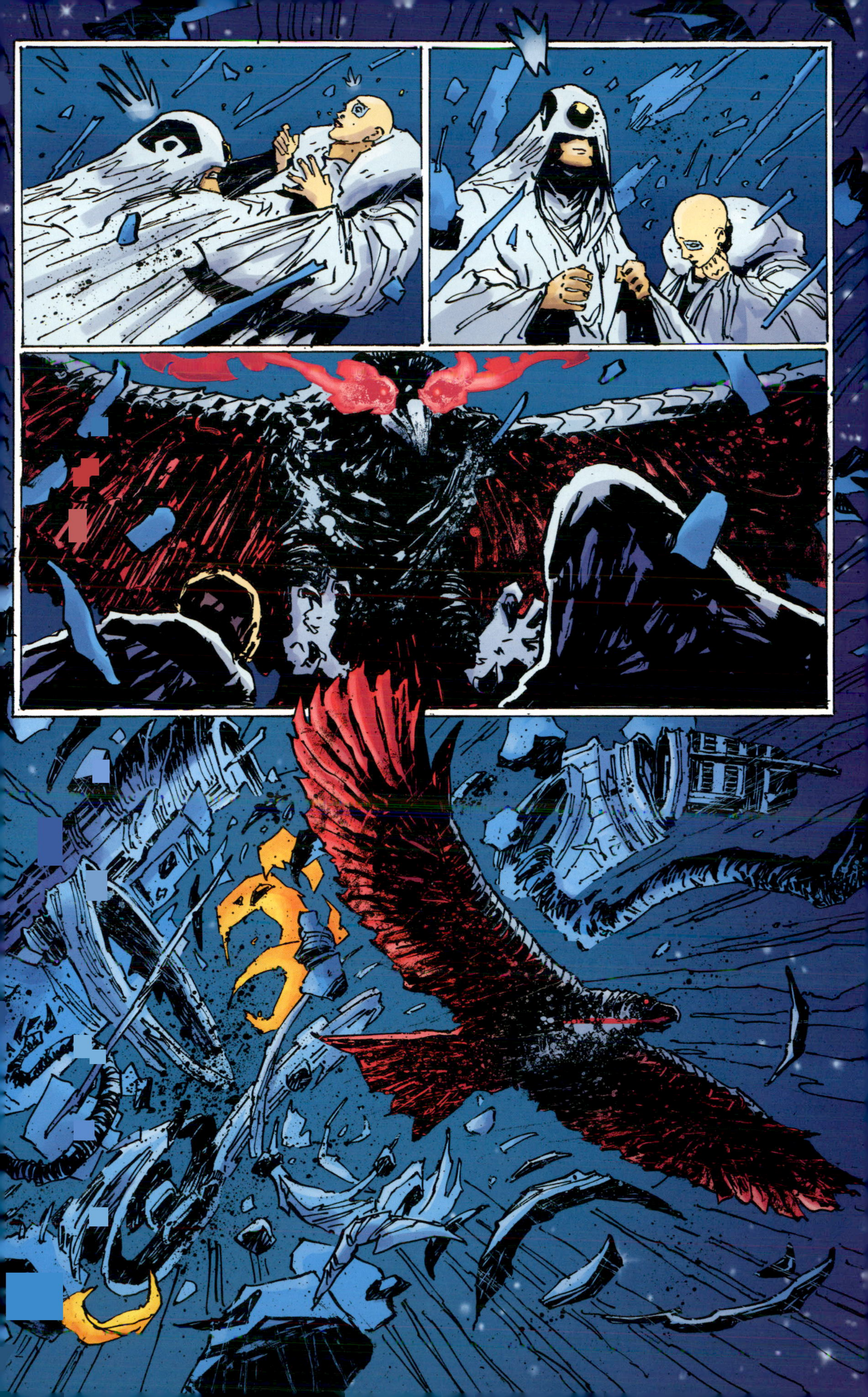

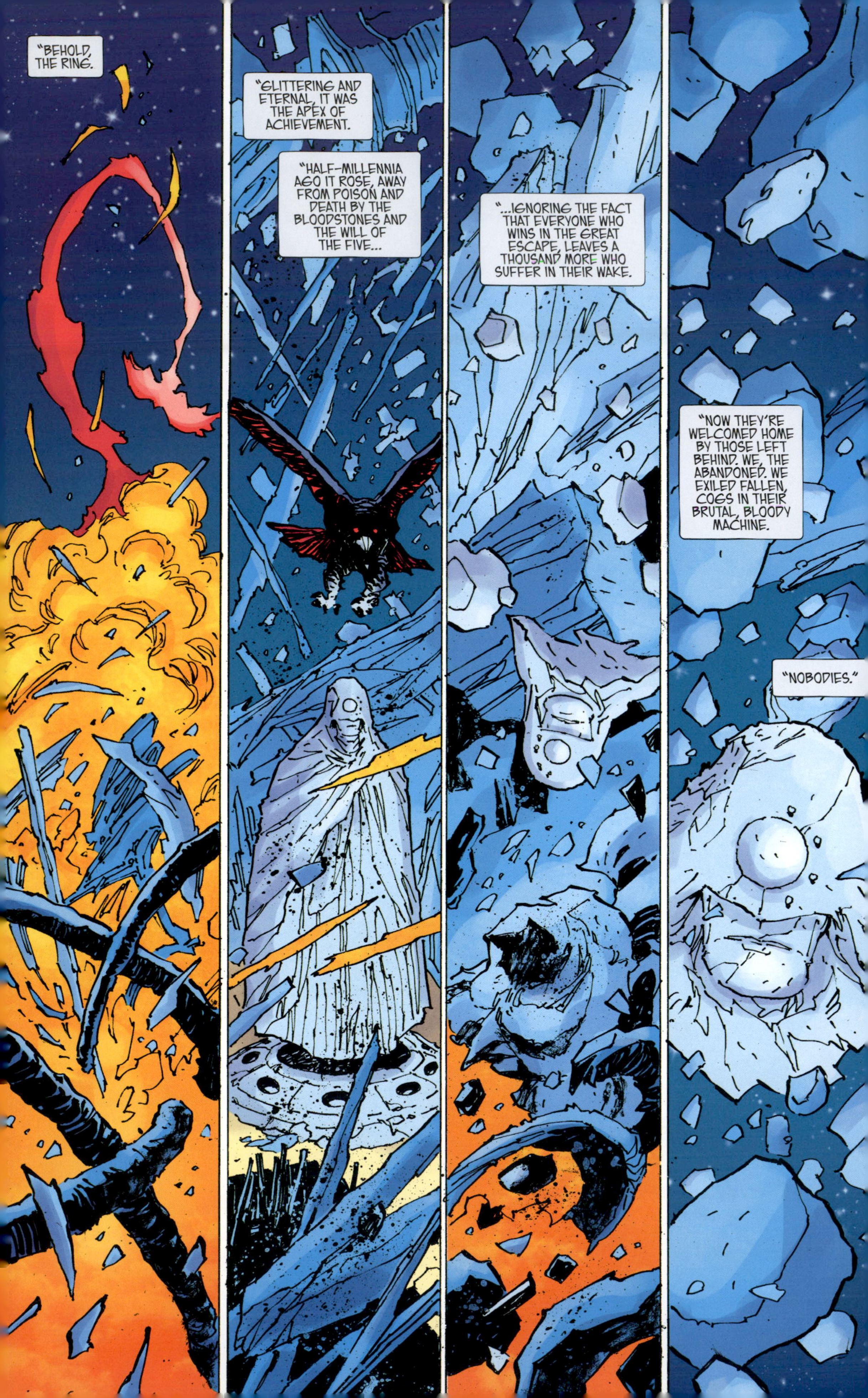
"BEHOLD, THE RING.
"GLITTERING AND ETERNAL, IT WAS THE APEX OF ACHIEVEMENT.
"HALF-MILLENNIA AGO IT ROSE, AWAY FROM POISON AND DEATH BY THE BLOODSTONES AND THE WILL OF THE FIVE...
"...IGNORING THE FACT THAT EVERYONE WHO WINS IN THE GREAT ESCAPE, LEAVES A THOUSAND MORE WHO SUFFER IN THEIR WAKE.
"NOW THEY'RE WELCOMED HOME BY THOSE LEFT BEHIND. WE, THE ABANDONED. WE EXILED FALLEN, COGS IN THEIR BRUTAL, BLOODY MACHINE.
"NOBODIES."

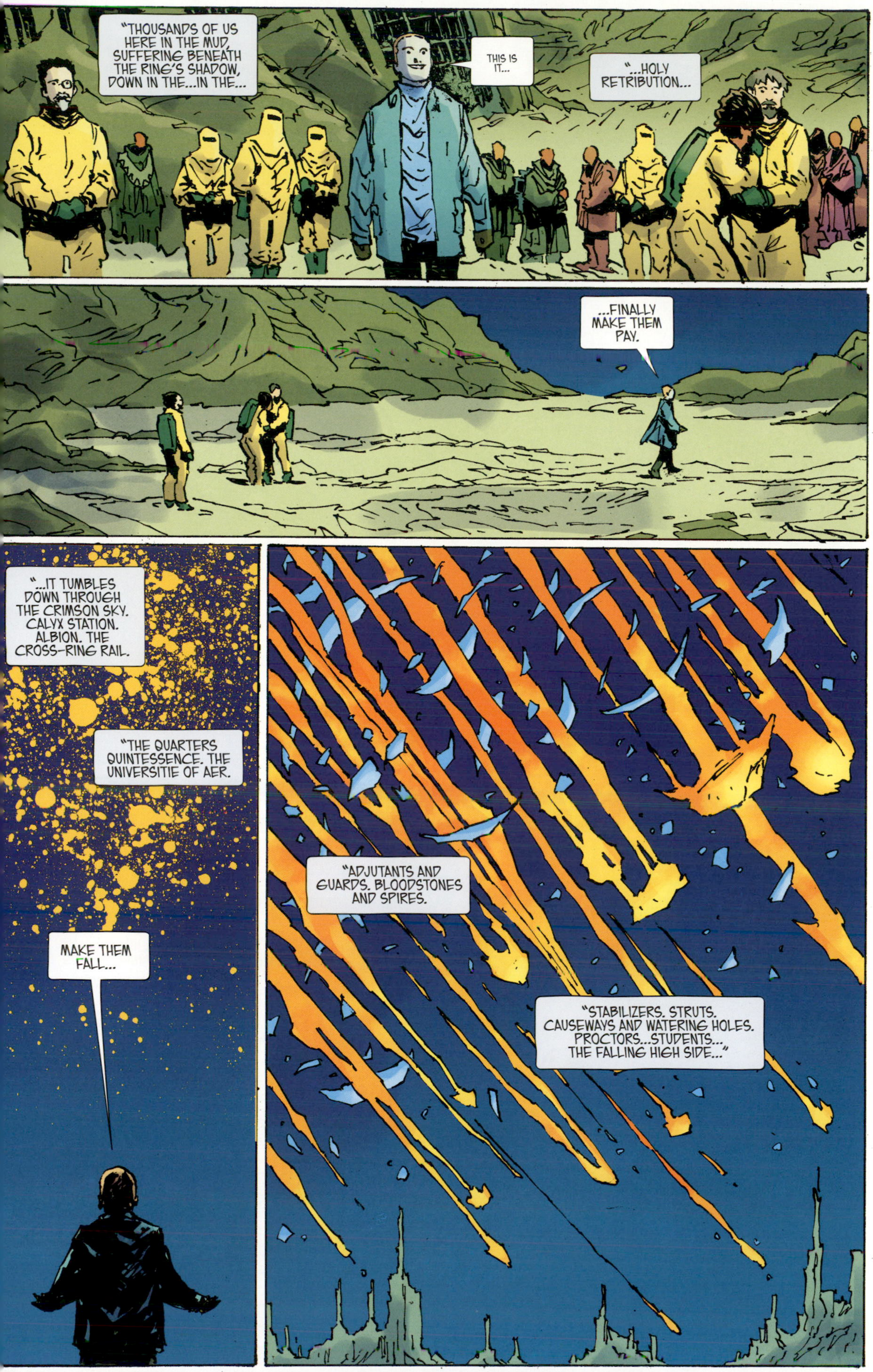
"THOUSANDS OF US HERE IN THE MUD, SUFFERING BENEATH THE RING'S SHADOW, DOWN IN THE...IN THE...
THIS IS IT...
"...HOLY RETRIBUTION...
...FINALLY MAKE THEM PAY.
"...IT TUMBLES DOWN THROUGH THE CRIMSON SKY. CALYX STATION. ALBION. THE CROSS-RING RAIL.
"THE QUARTERS QUINTESSENCE. THE UNIVERSITIE OF AER.
MAKE THEM FALL...
"ADJUTANTS AND GUARDS. BLOODSTONES AND SPIRES.
"STABILIZERS. STRUTS. CAUSEWAYS AND WATERING HOLES. PROCTORS...STUDENTS... THE FALLING HIGH SIDE..."

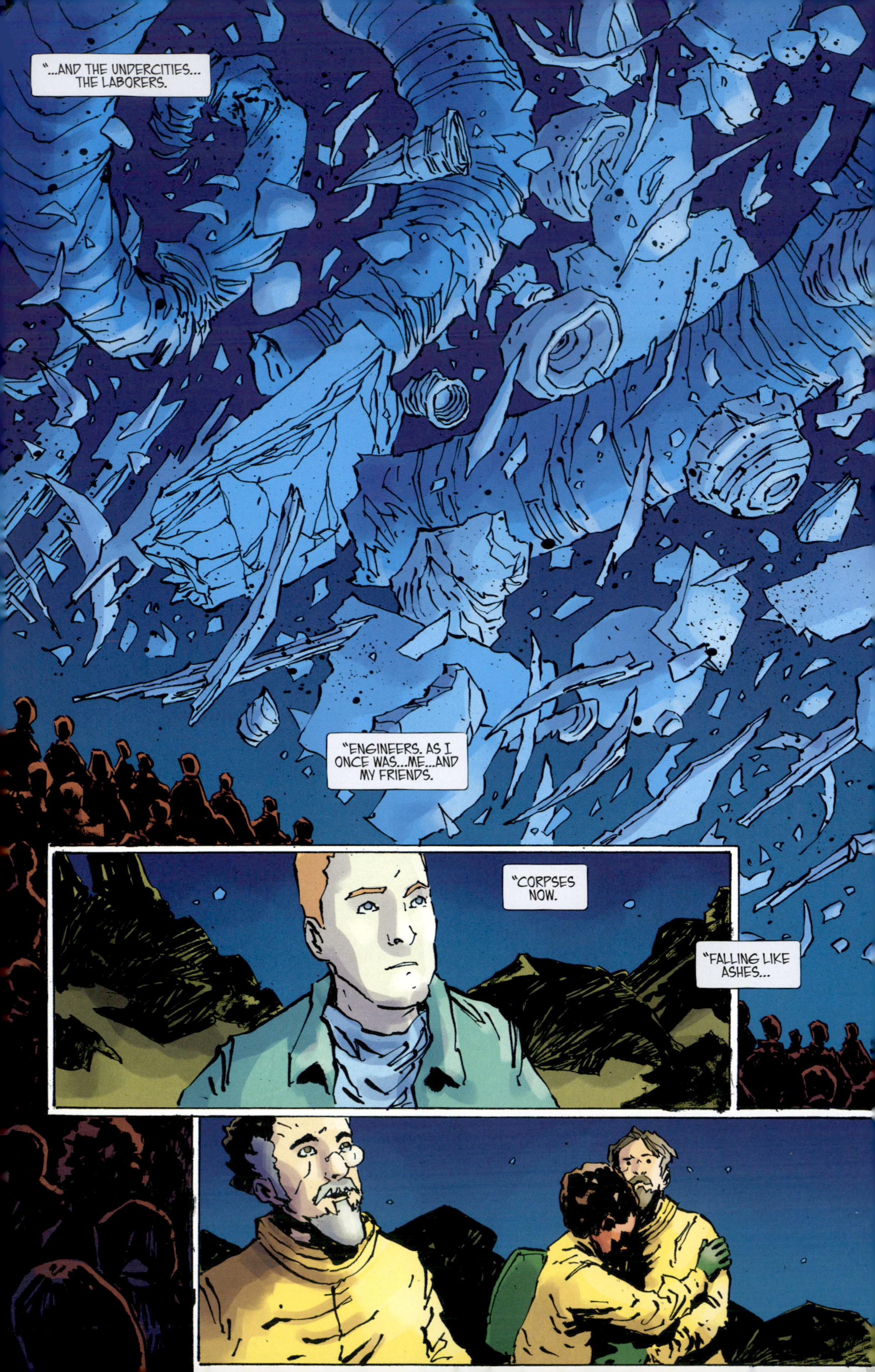
"...AND THE UNDERCITIES... THE LABORERS.
"ENGINEERS. AS I ONCE WAS...ME...AND MY FRIENDS.
"CORPSES NOW.
"FALLING LIKE ASHES...

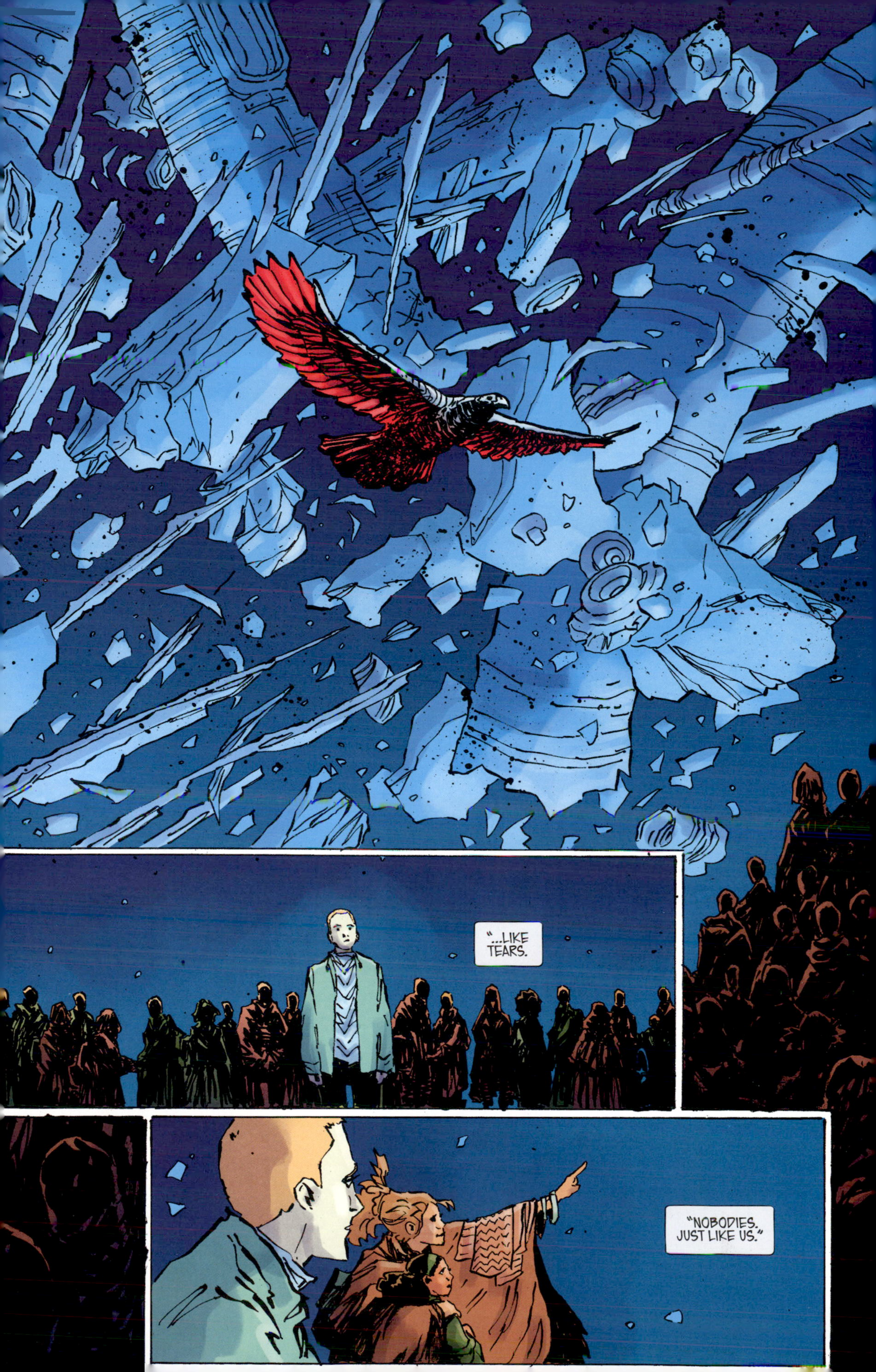
"...LIKE TEARS.
"NOBODIES. JUST LIKE US."

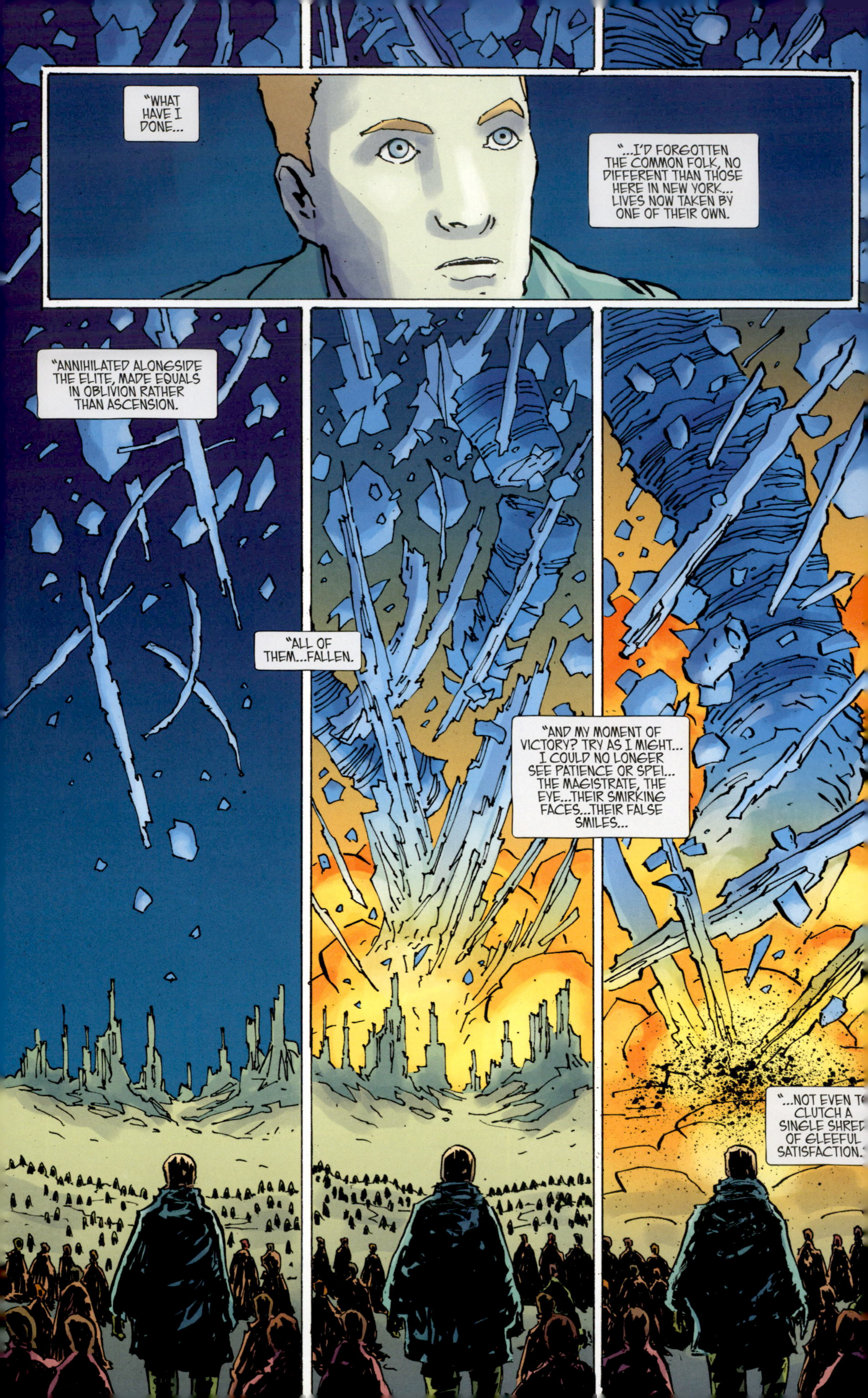

"WHAT HAVE I DONE...
"...I'D FORGOTTEN THE COMMON FOLK, NO DIFFERENT THAN THOSE HERE IN NEW YORK... LIVES NOW TAKEN BY ONE OF THEIR OWN.
"ANNIHILATED ALONGSIDE THE ELITE, MADE EQUALS IN OBLIVION RATHER THAN ASCENSION.
"ALL OF THEM...FALLEN.
"AND MY MOMENT OF VICTORY? TRY AS I MIGHT... I COULD NO LONGER SEE PATIENCE OR SPEI... THE MAGISTRATE, THE EYE...THEIR SMIRKING FACES...THEIR FALSE SMILES...
"...NOT EVEN T
CLUTCH A
SINGLE SHRE
OF GLEEFUL
SATISFACTION.

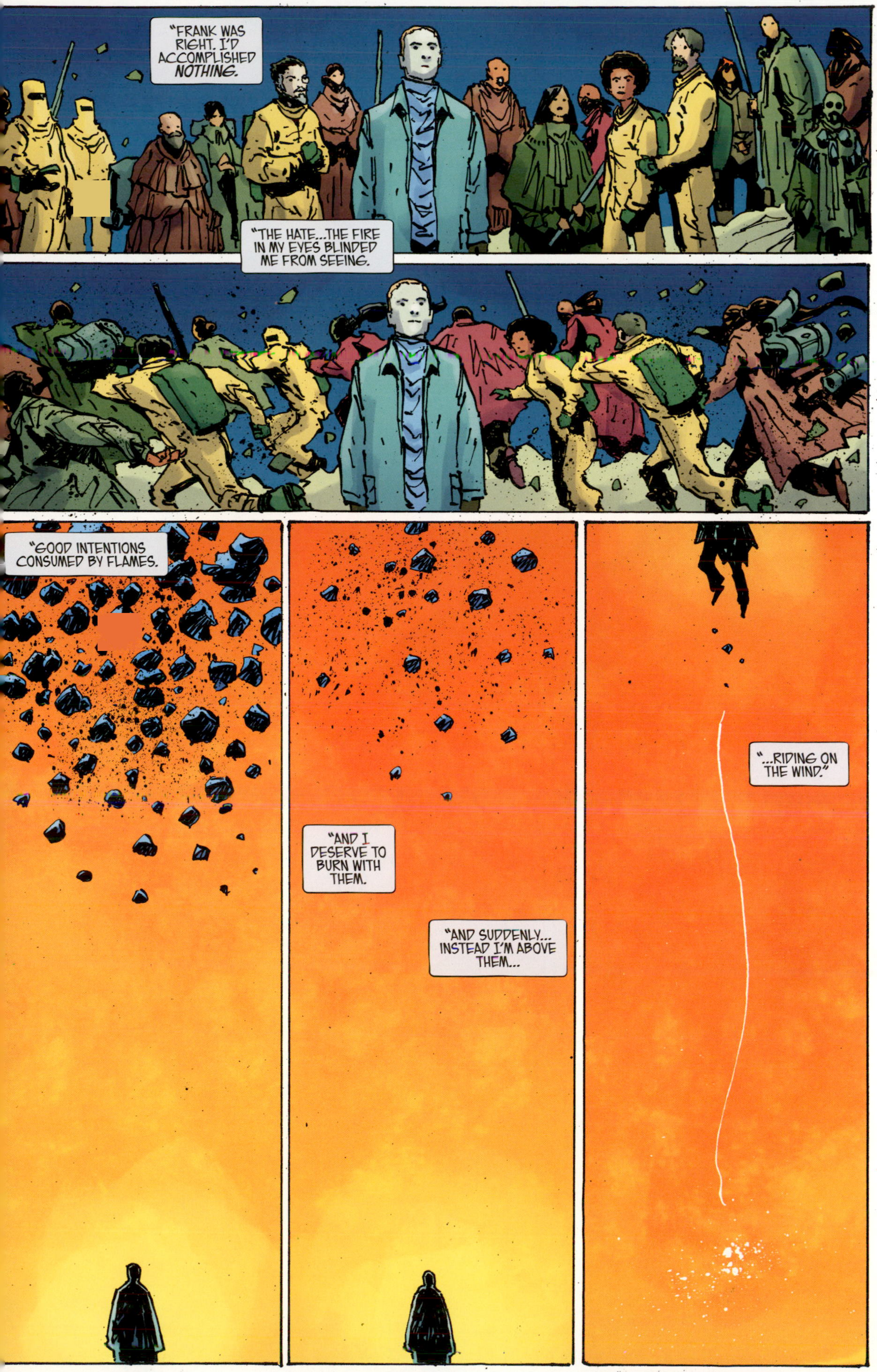
"FRANK WAS RIGHT. I'D ACCOMPLISHED NOTHING.
"THE HATE...THE FIRE IN MY EYES BLINDED ME FROM SEEING.
"GOOD INTENTIONS CONSUMED BY FLAMES.
"AND I DESERVE TO BURN WITH THEM.
"AND SUDDENLY... INSTEAD I'M ABOVE THEM...
"...RIDING ON THE WIND."

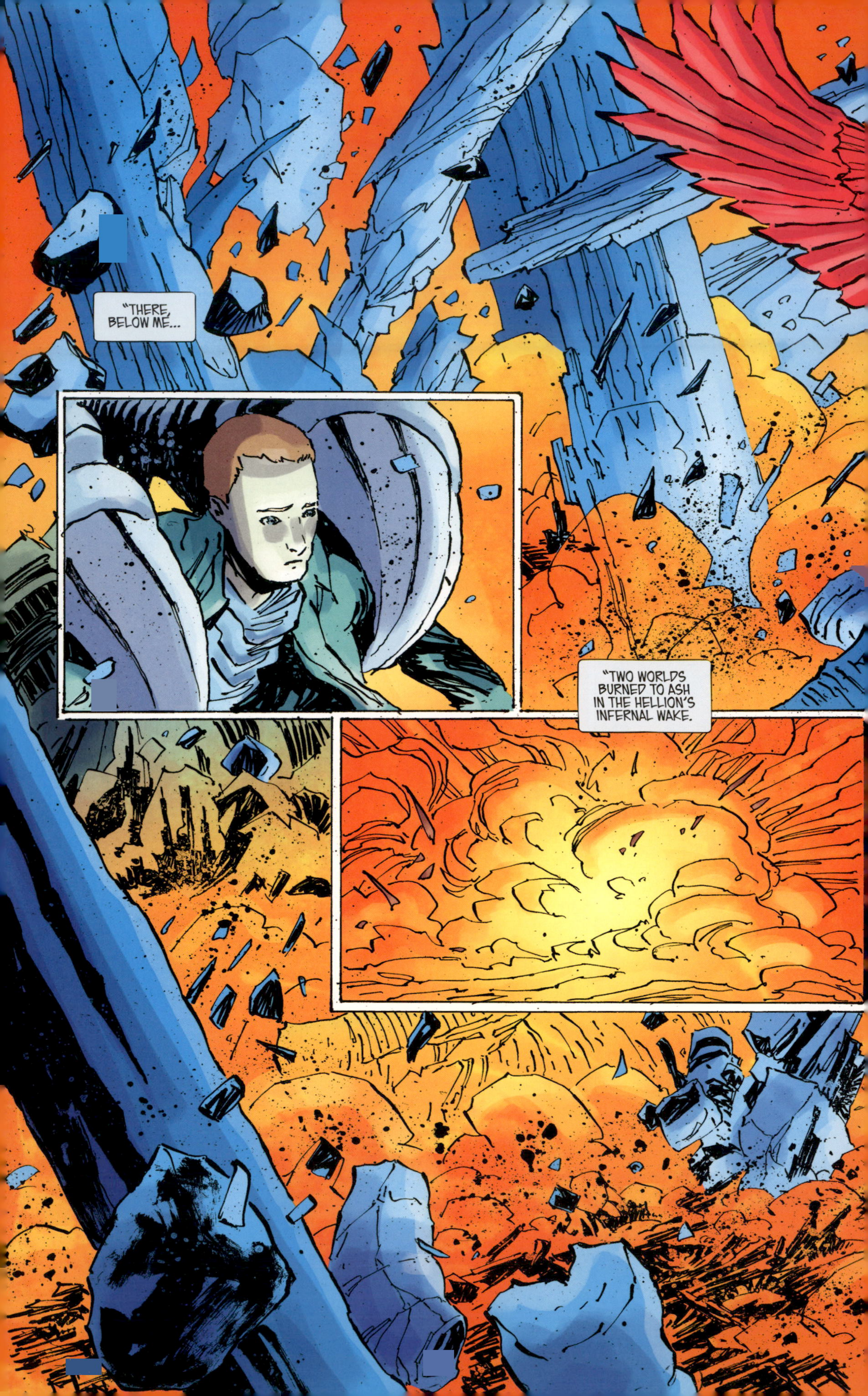
"THERE, BELOW ME...
"TWO WORLDS BURNED TO ASH IN THE HELLION'S INFERNAL WAKE.

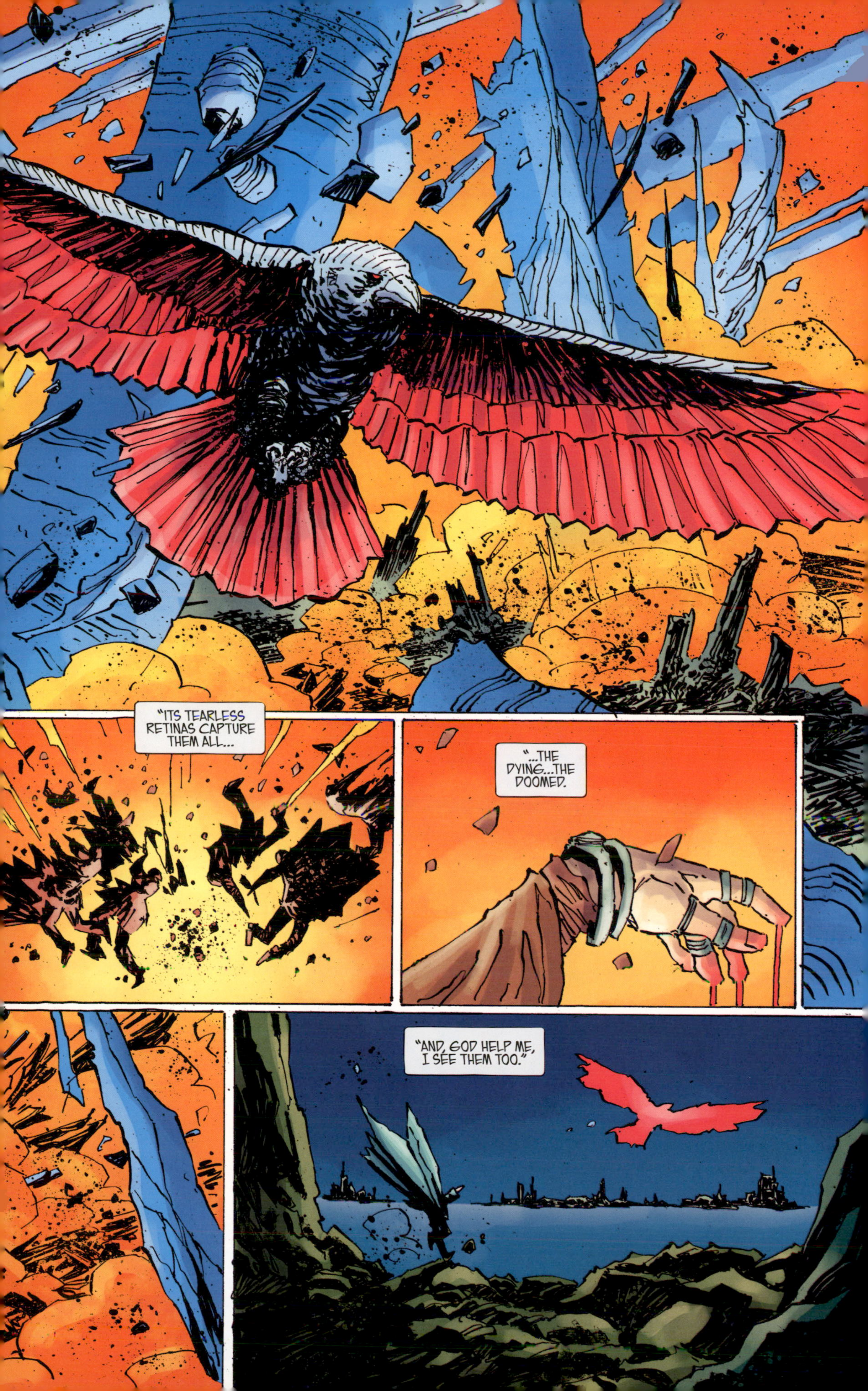
"ITS TEARLESS RETINAS CAPTURE THEM ALL...
"...THE DYING...THE DOOMED.
"AND, GOD HELP ME, I SEE THEM TOO."

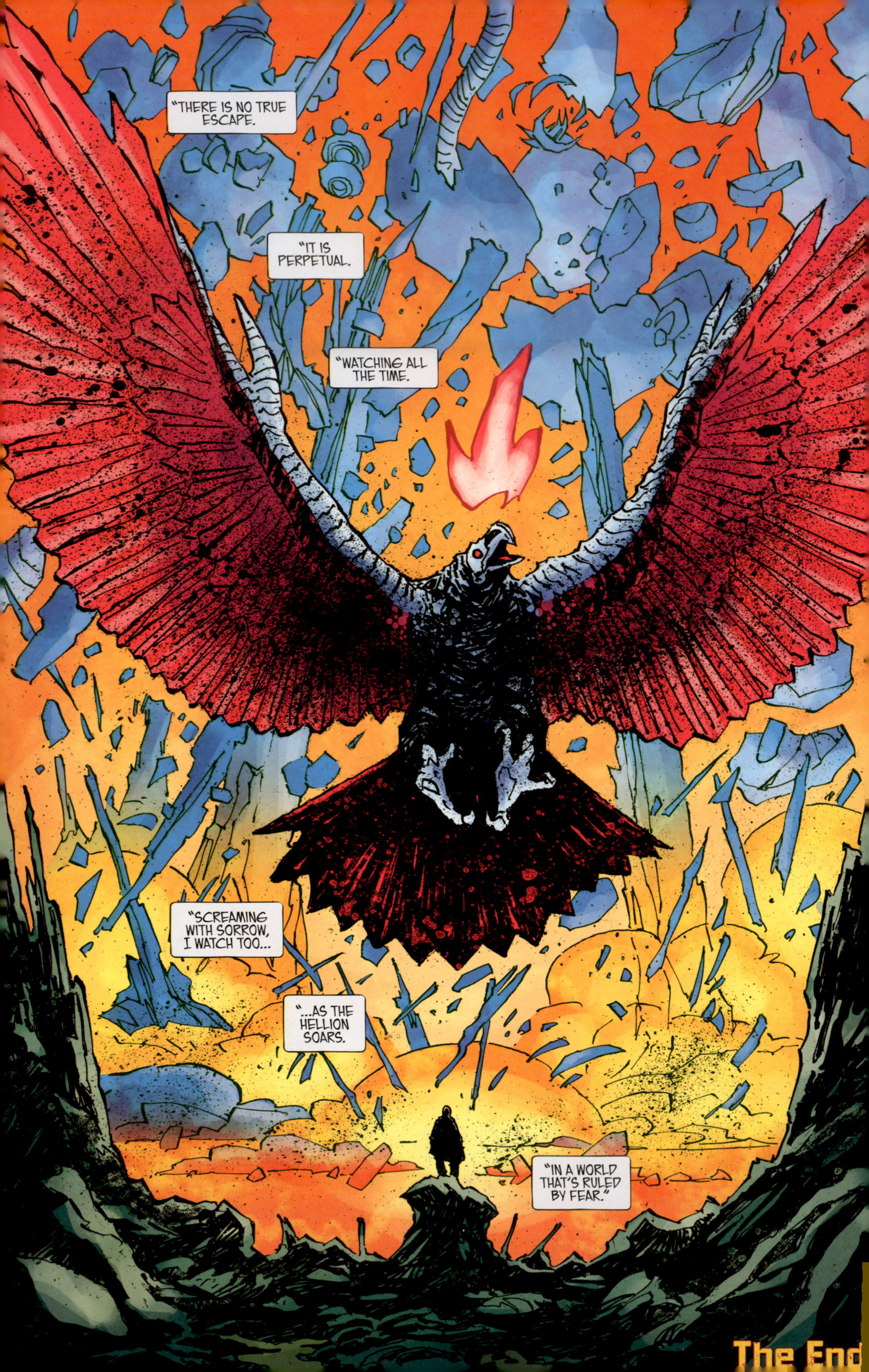
"THERE IS NO TRUE ESCAPE.
"IT IS PERPETUAL.
"WATCHING ALL THE TIME.
"SCREAMING WITH SORROW, I WATCH TOO...
"...AS THE HELLION SOARS.
"IN A WORLD THAT'S RULED BY FEAR."
The End

GALLERY

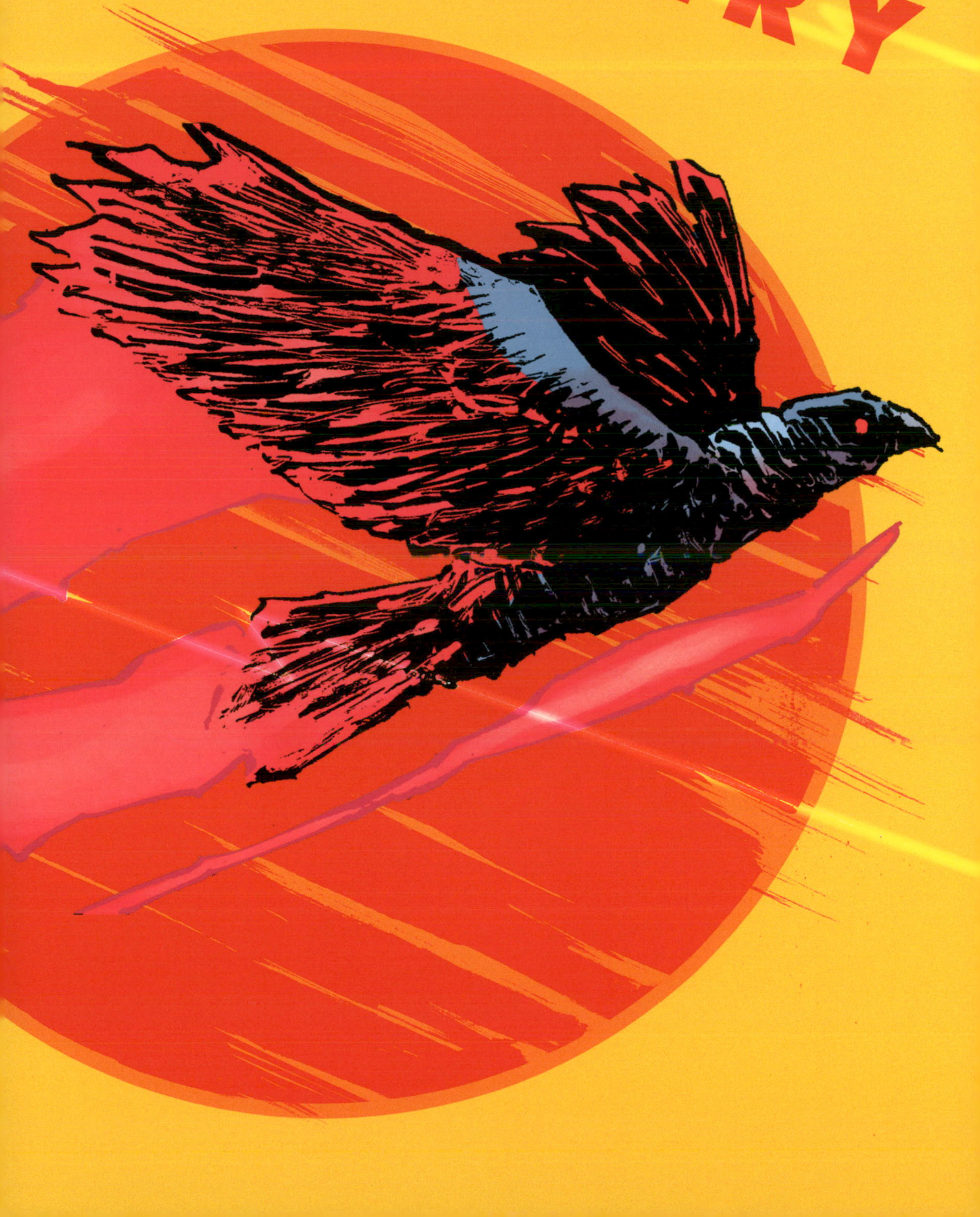

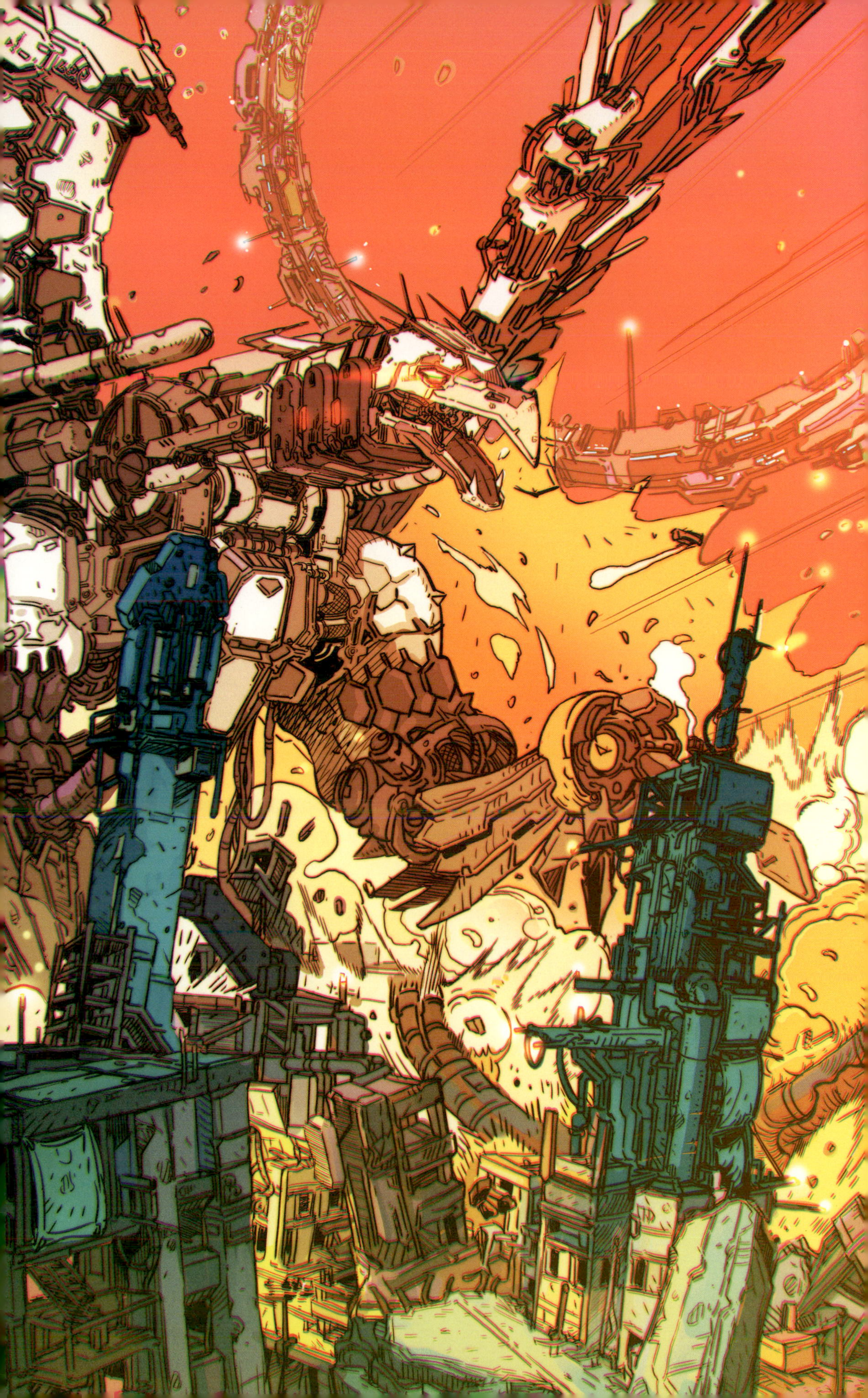

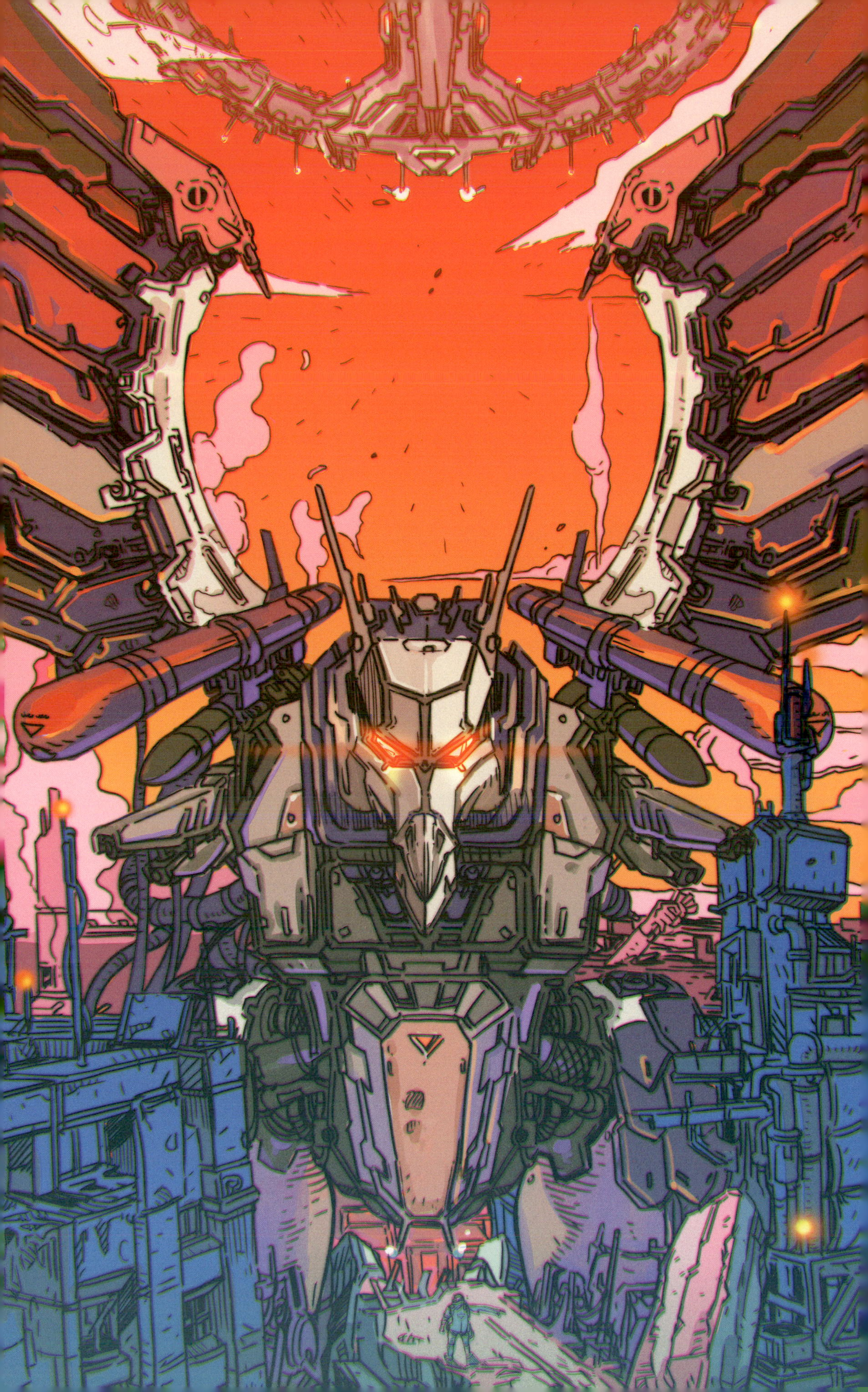

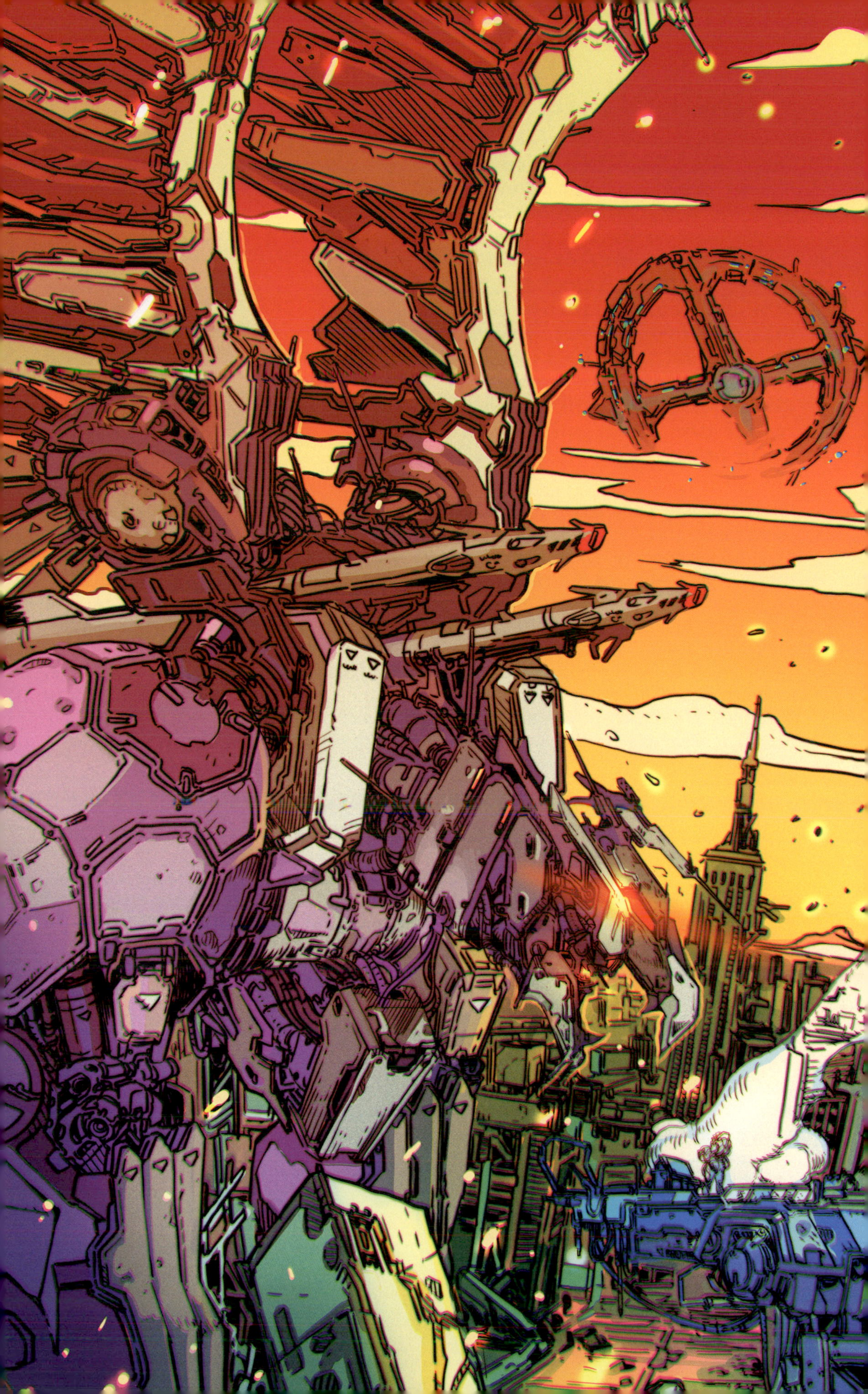

BEHIND THE HELLION

There was a time when the cover of a vinyl record was seen as art, and with the cover for Screaming for Vengeance, artist Doug Johnson created album art that retains all of its power and impact 40 years after its release, remaining one of the most instantly recognizable covers of all time. Doug was kind enough to sit down with editor Rantz Hoseley to talk about his career and the creation of this iconic image.

Rantz Hoseley: I appreciate you making the time for this. Let's start with a little bit of background. First off, when did you decide to pursue a career in art and design?

Doug Johnson: Oh I think very, very, very early. I just drew all the time. I grew up in Canada, so I drew hockey players. I went to a technical high school—a [school for] plumbing, auto mechanics, welding, and art, so it all made sense. I worked for a while, and then went to the art college in Toronto. [I] received scholarships on graduation, then went to Europe and painted for awhile. I came back to Toronto and my paintings did not, so… I became an illustrator. After a few years I realized I couldn't do what I wanted to do up in Canada and that there were more opportunities down in the States. So, [I] came down and did okay.

Rantz: How old were you when you made the transition of moving to the States?

Doug: I was 28.

Rantz: Did you immediately illustrate poster art and design albums when you arrived in the states?

Doug: You know when you're starting out you do anything. My agent at that time represented a lot of fashion artists so I did fashion art. And then I kept pressing and pressing because I wanted to do more illustrations. Eventually I dropped him and went to someone else. This is really the mists of time, a long time ago. I did everything from teen magazine ads, then *Time* covers and finally album covers. Bo Diddley, Ike and Tina Turner, Stevie Wonder. I did a lot of sports illustration. It was a real mix.

The Judas Priest cover came along and the art director of Columbia called me and said, "It's right up your alley." Well… I had never done anything like that. Ever. I came in and he gave me a bunch of their previous albums and I said, "Well, when do you need the sketch?" And he said tomorrow. That was pretty much the way you worked. It was fun because I had not really done anything like that before. I just enjoyed it. The most information he gave me was that he said the guys (in the band) wanted something like an eagle, and I was like, "Wow… *That's* a lot of information." [Laughs]

So, I did the sketch and the band was in Florida at the time, so he'd sent it off to Florida and then called me and said, "They want to use it." I said great! Then he said, "The sketch, they really love it. They want to use the sketch." I said, "They can't use the sketch, it's just a *sketch*." The way I did the sketches… unlike today with computers where you see everything clearly… I would make things as blobby and undefined as possible in order to have greater range when I finished.

I said, okay I promise I'll send the sketch back if you don't like the *finish*, but I was pretty sure they'd be happy with the final art. I had a lot of fun, but it was really the first of that kind of thing I had ever done.

Rantz: Well, it's interesting for me because looking at the *Screaming for Vengeance* cover and the stuff that you had previously done, for instance for Bo Diddley, Ike and Tina Turner… you can see growth and the refinement of the style. There's this sense of abstraction to the form and how you are using airbrush in a way that was very different than what other artists were doing. The style was very distinctive and instantly recognizable. I'd love to talk a little about how that style evolved and who were your influences. I know, given that era of illustration, there were very predefined categories... 'You're going to be this kind of illustrator, or you're going to be that kind of illustrator,' and your stuff felt very, very different from that.

Doug: Yeah, well of course you kill yourself trying to be different. It came about that I'd initially been influenced by Francis Bacon, a British painter. He had a show at the Tate that I had gone to see, and I had never seen anything like it. I saw the power of the broad impasto brush strokes on flat backgrounds and realized that what made the brushwork so powerful was the contrast, the flat... almost mechanical aspects.

But, I really couldn't sell anyone on that [approach]. They'd be like... 'What is *that*? Finger painting? My child finger paints!'

Also, there was a certain amount... not a lot... of airbrush. I thought the airbrush would solve the very mechanical aspect and I could paint on top of it, and that's really how that came about. There were [fewer] people airbrushing at that time. Charlie White, who was from California, and I shared a studio in New York and he was *committed* to airbrush. There was a lot of real growth with airbrush artists as time went by. They would do books on airbrush and they'd include me and... I wasn't really an 'airbrush artist' any more than I was a 'pencil artist,' or a 'number four brush artist' or whatever. I was *me*.

Rantz: It's interesting because when I went to art school, you were one of the artists that I know inspired a number of artists to pick up the airbrush. The preconception was that airbrush was... we'll call it 'van art'... some gauzy fantasy scene on the side of a van or some sunset that really lacked a sense of physicality and power. So, the way you used airbrush was a revelation, like, 'Oh you can also use this tool in *this* way.' I think that's one of the reason that *Screaming for Vengeance* hit with such an impact because it was so

unlike anything we had seen on album covers, much less on a metal album cover.

Doug: I appreciate that. And as you have said, I realized it was a tool. However, it was a temperamental, *miserable* tool. [Laughs]

I remember Charlie and I discovering that they actually made *left-handed* airbrushes and we're like, 'Wow, *that* would solve a lot of problems. We could actually see what we're airbrushing!' It was a tool for me. Later, I would meet airbrush artists and they were a little like dentists. They would explain to me the white cotton gloves they'd use to me and I was [using] elbows and knees and footprints. I remember Charlie would characterize my use of the airbrush as putting my feet on the board and leaning back. I was not a delicate airbrush person.

Rantz: That's pretty amazing, because the gradients and the edging on that painting are just immaculate, and to hear that the process was that physical and almost irreverent is one of those things that makes your jaw drop with an 'Oh my *God*.'

Doug: [Laughs] I was careful by that time. And I really enjoyed doing the cover. But the sad thing is, you didn't get to keep things like sketches. You didn't get to keep things like original artwork. Years and years later, I was one of a very small group, which had seen the effectiveness of unions on Broadway and we formed a guild where we asked for our artwork back. In those days they'd just keep everything, and you never knew where it would end up. On their walls? I remember one magazine would auction off original art at Christmas to the staff.

Rantz: The comic industry was that way at that time as well. You knew work for hire meant you didn't own the original art.

Doug: My first experience with that was when I was starting and I had done something for *Seventeen Magazine* and I was very proud of it, and I got the original back. It was in a show and I had to frame it. And then I got a note from their attorney saying that I had better get it back to them otherwise I'd be open to a lawsuit. I think they paid like $300 for the original. And they were threatening a great deal more and I said, "Well I didn't sign anything, and I didn't know you guys got to keep it." And he was like, "Well you cashed the check, and if you looked on the back of the check there was the release form." [Laughs] It was absolutely the realization, as you would know in the comic industry, that you are the least important element.

Rantz: The most vital and the least important. I remember stories of friends of mine who were working for Marvel in the '80s, about Jack Kirby fighting to get his original pages back and at the same time they were using pages from the Morgue to prop up uneven desks. And it was just this 'Oh my lord,' this moment of disconnect on value there.

Doug: I remember meeting Stan Lee. He was very personable. Meeting him at the Society of Illustrators at some function and he seemed like such a nice guy. Then all the stories just came to me... he was like Walt Disney, sort of a tyrant, treated his artists pretty badly.

Rantz: It's the classic example of the difference of an era. Getting original art back is now more of a standard, as opposed to rare exceptions, but the fight had to happen to change the mindset.

Now after *Screaming for Vengeance* was such a success on every level, you went on to paint the next two albums as well. I know from a fan's standpoint it was thrilling, like there was a continuity going forward. From a music standpoint there was this sense with *Screaming for Vengeance* that the band was evolving. It was a different guitar sound, a more aggressive focus, and, as we've discussed in developing the graphic novel, there's an almost operatic sense to the song structure. And we saw that carried through with those two albums. The great thing about you doing the album covers for *Defenders of the Faith* and for *Turbo* was

that there was this sense of expansion... a new era of Judas Priest. So I wanted to talk a little bit about how those two albums came about as well.

Doug: As I say, at the time, art directors of record companies... this is RCA and Columbia... they had everything coming through their system so if it was their kind of music, then they were interested. If it wasn't, they weren't. If you were lucky... and I always felt lucky, because they didn't like metal... they handed it off to me. In other words, they let me solve it. And with Columbia they were happy to say, "Well, the band said they want to deal directly with you." and I said, "Great!" [Laughs]

They are such great guys. In this business, you don't know what you're going to encounter and their agent, Bill Curbishley, and a young English woman named Ann Weldon handled the U.S. bands, and I met with her. She was great and I ask if the guys kind of were like how they appear to be on stage? She said if they were, that way they'd be dead in a couple of weeks. [Laughs]

No, she said they're very nice young men, and we got together, and they were terrific. I basically knew Glenn Tipton and Kenny (K.K. Downing), and Rob. I knew the three of them pretty well and they are the guys I really worked with. Rob was very quiet. We would meet often at my loft at the time, which had no heat in the middle of winter. Really liked them. We got along, liked each other, and I began to see... like they understood their audience *perfectly*. They were professionals. They had been working and touring for 10 years before *Vengeance*, so that was a big breakthrough for them. That was kind of the basis, of... I guess... their loyalty. They were like, this worked and they were not going to mess with it, so came back to me.

Rantz: So with *Defenders*, you were talking about how the label said they wanted an eagle like on *Screaming for Vengeance* as the starting point. How much of the idea for the Metallion (The metallic beast on the cover of *Defenders*) was from the band and the starting point with you?

Doug: I think they had an idea of air and earth and water. They were going to do a kind of theme throughout the albums—I have no idea what happened to water. I think actually we played a lot with a sub-mariner monster, and then they decided they wanted earth. That became a kind of tank thing. We did a lot of back and forth and then came up with that. And then they turned that into a stage for the tour.

Rantz: I saw that tour, and it was a mind boggling thing to see. As a teenager who loves this band... to see this giant metallic cat with paws that come up and the motor-cycle comes out.

Doug: Rob rode down one of the paws. Like with anything else, it was hard to put together Rob, who was very, very quiet, with this screaming guy. I remember they were playing the Meadowlands in New Jersey. They said come backstage after the show. So I had all these tags, and I had taken friends with me, walked up, and spoke to a cop and I asked him, "Where is a good place to be?" and he said, "Well, don't go down there because they have blow torches." [Laughs]

I was not familiar with the heavy metal audience, which ranged in age from 12 to 14 and then leapt to 40 and above. It was a different crowd. Then I tried to get back-stage and ran into the roadies and I had all the proper passes, but after awhile I just said I'll just see them later. But the guys in the band called out and said, "We had our moms and dads here. We wanted you to meet them!" You'd think these things didn't really fit together, but they did.

They had a wonderful rapport with their audience, and I don't want to say con-trol, but they *worked* with them. It was great to see. They really had tremendous respect for the fans, all the way through. It was like, well we're not sure if the fans would like this. They were great guys. Then they were doing a double album

that went on and on and it never happen-ed because they got involved in that Florida lawsuit. That was a brutal thing. There was a documentary I saw which was just sickening, what it did to their career. I think they were the second big-gest tour group anywhere and that just put an end to that and to radioplay, it was just awful. And that turned out to be completely specious.

Rantz: It's hard for people who didn't live through that really to understand the impact of how big of a deal something like that, and the whole PMRC hearings, were at the Senate. As a music fan and someone involved in the music industry, you genuinely felt there was a threat not only to your livelihood, but your ability to be creative. It was a terrifying feeling.

Doug: Yeah, it was like the Kefauver hear-ings for comics

Rantz: Yes exactly.

Doug: What's her name, Tipper Gore?

Rantz: Tipper Gore, yeah.

Doug: There was a concerted effort to put an end to music that frightened her, and I don't know what the ultimate goal was.

Rantz: Control. Most of these things come down to one of two things: control or money. It was the whole thing with the Kefauver hearings with comics. You want to run for the senate, okay here's your platform: *I'm going to save the children*. The most bulletproof thing you can do, no matter how abhorrent your policies are, is to say you're doing it for the children because how is someone going to argue with that? Like, 'Oh, you're saving the children? Okay, I can't really say you're a horrible person because you're saving the children.'

Doug: Power in politics is everything.

Rantz: What have you been up to since doing the Judas Priest album covers?

Doug: How long ago was that? About 30 years?

Rantz: We are at 40 years from *Screaming for Vengeance*.

Doug: Well I've aged. [Laughs] Well, I had been involved a little bit with off, off, off Broadway shows. You know, doing artwork. We had done a show and I got connected again with the same group of guys... they kind of made me part of the group. I suspect they just didn't know any other artists. But as it was, I went from being the poster artist to being one of the partners, and we started producing. Then we had to become commercial instead of not-for-profit, which I think characterizes most of Broadway. Bit by bit we went from being the 'kids on the block,' to being successful producers. We did a lot of shows in 30 years or whatever it was. Then we hooked up, strangely enough, with Bill Curbishley when we did *Tommy* on Broadway, because Bill Curbishley represented two groups: Judas Priest and The Who.

Rantz: Well there you go.

Doug: And it was fun.

Rantz: One thing I get reminded of on a daily basis is that the world is small...

Doug: Yeah, absolutely. I had tried to get the rights to *Tommy* at a certain point. Pete Townshend wasn't interested in doing a show. They had done the movie and done double albums with various good artists, but he wasn't interested in doing another show interpretation. It came around that I got to work with them. Pete was the same kind of guy. The people who are successful in rock 'n roll tend to be the kind of people who will be successful in pretty much anything they put their mind to. They're very bright. And they are creative artists.

I did one thing with The Rolling Stones and had to meet Mick Jagger late at night, and it was the year that Lennon had been shot, and they said, "Oh just stand by the doorway," and I was like, "I'm *not* going to stand by the doorway." Anyways, I remember at the time it was the same situation. I had a sketch I was going to be working on all night and he asked how long do you have on this, and I said tonight and he said, 'Well that's pretty typical." We just got along. They're businessmen, they're artists, and they're performers. It's like confusing a performer with their personality. I didn't meet any whose company I didn't enjoy.

Rantz: I definitely feel that the ones that last, it's like you said, there is a mindset and a professionalism that allows for endurance on that because you can't be living an insane life and have any sustainability. The thing that I don't think most people get is that rock 'n roll is a lot of work, and a lot of work on different fronts. Your intellect has to be aggressive in it, constantly thinking 'how do I solve this problem? How does this fit into what I'm trying to do as an artist?' And those that have that longevity are the ones that can navigate that year after year after year.

Doug: Yeah they're successful artists. Business and art and ambition and determination to make their own mark... As I say, I've always enjoyed their company.

Rantz: Are you doing any art now, or are you officially retired?

Doug: I actually did an awful lot of Broadway stuff. I would have meetings all day long and come home and work all night long on the artwork. And I think I burned out to be quite honest. And people say, 'how can artists not keep making art?' Art is the solution given for a lot of stressed out people, so what is the solution as a stressed-out artist? We can become shoe salesmen or whatever.

Rantz: That or spare-time plumbers.

Doug: Yeah, so I haven't done anything really and people say, 'Well don't you do things for yourself?' And it's like no. I still have nightmares about deadlines. That's why I'm not doing any artwork. So, we run our ranch in Wyoming, ride... move cattle. And I play tennis when I'm not injured from one or the other.

Rantz: I can relate to that. My training is in art, and it definitely changes your mindset and your relationship with it when taking it from something you loved into a responsibility.

Doug: I used to encounter it with students who would be under pressure to come up with their portfolios. They were art school seniors and I would talk to them about a box they were putting themselves into. I'd say, 'You have one year left of school, make every mistake you can, because you won't be allowed to after this.'

Rantz: Exactly

Doug: You'll be paying rent, you'll be buying food, having children, you know. Enjoy school, fill out your portfolio, but enjoy yourself because you won't have that kind of freedom. Or rarely.

Rantz: I know that, for multiple generations of artists at this point, you've been a massive inspiration for a lot of people. A platonic ideal to chase after. What is your advice to someone foolish enough to pursue this crazy art and rock 'n roll career thing?

Doug: I honestly don't know. Life has changed with computers. We kind of crossed paths: as computers came in, I was leaving. I'd say the biggest change, maybe sliding back, is when I was doing album covers, they were posters, which went up on a record store wall.

Rantz: Yeah at huge scale.

Doug: And now it comes through the air. You stream the album you want. That's like doing matchbook covers. I have no idea what people think about it now. I really don't know. I would probably put more emphasis on type, creating the idea of standing out when you're dealing with a format that small. It's really, really, really difficult.

Rantz: You have to kind of figure out what within the state of play is the niche that you can define yourself in.

Doug: Yeah. With albums, I'd go down to the record stores and walk around and look and be like, 'What is it missing? What would jump here?' I used to do the same with Broadway because we had certain billboards that were kind of ours and I would wander Times Square and say, 'What are we missing here?'

Rantz: I think that's a really great way to look at solving the problem too, because you have a lot of people who I think make the mistake of chasing the trends, instead of asking what isn't there and what needs to be there. What ghost is needing to be summoned?

Doug: Exactly, you have it. You're right—that is a mistake to try to fit in, because that's no way to lead. No way to be creative in anything. And oddly enough, the art director at Columbia made the right call to bring in a complete novice, who had no knowledge of metal. So I just ran with it and added a fresh eye.

Rantz: ...and in the process created one of the most iconic images in metal of all time.

Doug: It's unusual for me, but I'm still very happy with it. ∎